PRAISE FOR LORELEI BLACKTOP COWBOY

T0249339

"Takes readers on a satisfying ride.... While James is known for erotic interludes, she never forgets to bolster the story with plenty of emotional power."   —*Publishers Weekly*

"No one writes contemporary erotic romance better than Lorelei James. Her sexy cowboys are to die for!"
                                    —*New York Times* bestselling author Maya Banks

"Lorelei James knows how to write one hot, sexy cowboy."
                                    —*New York Times* bestselling author Jaci Burton

"The down-and-dirty, rough-and-tumble Blacktop Cowboys kept me up long past my bedtime. Scorchingly hot, wickedly naughty."
                                    —Lacey Alexander, author of *Give In to Me*

"Combining the erotic and family, love and romance with doubt and vulnerabilities, and throwing in some plain old fun always make her reads favorites of mine every time."   —The Good, the Bad, and the Unread

"Hang on to your cowboy hats because this book is scorching hot!"
                                    —Romance Junkies

"Lorelei James knows how to write fun, sexy, and hot stories."
                                    —Joyfully Reviewed

continued ...

"Sexy and highly erotic."   —TwoLips Reviews

"Incredibly hot."   —The Romance Studio

"[A] wild, sexy ride."   —*RT Book Reviews*

Wrapped
and
Strapped

A BLACKTOP COWBOYS® NOVEL

LORELEI JAMES

A SIGNET ECLIPSE BOOK

SIGNET ECLIPSE
Published by New American Library,
an imprint of Penguin Random House LLC
375 Hudson Street, New York, New York 10014

This book is an original publication of New American Library.

First Printing, November 2015

Copyright © LJLA, LLC, 2015
Penguin Random House supports copyright. Copyright fuels creativity, encourages diverse voices, promotes free speech, and creates a vibrant culture. Thank you for buying an authorized edition of this book and for complying with copyright laws by not reproducing, scanning, or distributing any part of it in any form without permission. You are supporting writers and allowing Penguin Random House to continue to publish books for every reader.

Signet Eclipse and the Signet Eclipse colophon are trademarks of
Penguin Random House LLC.

For more information about Penguin Random House, visit penguinrandomhouse.com.

LIBRARY OF CONGRESS CATALOGING-IN-PUBLICATION DATA:

Wrapped and strapped: a blacktop cowboys novel/Lorelei James.
p. cm.
ISBN 978-0-451-47378-3
I. Title.
PS3610.A4475W72 2015
813'.6—dc23   2015019610

Printed in the United States of America
10 9 8 7 6 5 4 3

Penguin
Random
House

Wrapped and Strapped

Prologue

She resisted the urge to leave at the crack of dawn the morning after.

Not because she wanted to give him a chance to explain the harsh words he'd spit at her as he'd hastily thrown on his clothes after leaving her bed. No, she'd stuck around, refusing to allow him the satisfaction of believing he'd chased her off.

Even when he had.

She always traveled light. So it hadn't taken long to pack her belongings. She hugged her sister and said good-bye to the friends she'd made these past four months.

Gravel crunched beneath her tires as she headed for the main road to leave the Split Rock Ranch and Resort. She hit the brakes when she saw him sitting alone on the top of the corral outside the barn.

She exited the car and rested her forearms on the roof, watching him. Only a few hundred feet separated them, but it may as well have been a few hundred miles.

She waited for some kind of acknowledgment. A tip of his cowboy hat perhaps. Or a two-fingered salute from the brim of his hat. A dip of his chin.

But she got nothing.

At all.

He remained so still he could've been a bronze statue. Hard. Weathered. Immovable. In the beginning she'd attributed all those characteristics and nothing more to him. But then she'd unearthed the real man beneath the stoic demeanor. She'd experienced his heat and passion. Especially last night.

And then she'd experienced his coldness and disdain.

The beginning she'd envisioned for them turned out to be the end.

So she drove away, ready to put him—and Wyoming—in her rearview mirror.

Chapter One

Three years later . . .

$\mathscr{H}$arlow Pratt panicked when she saw her sister Tierney's name on her caller ID. She answered with, "*Please* tell me you didn't go into labor a month early."

"No, that's not why I'm calling." Tierney paused. "You know Dad is here visiting. He had a heart attack."

"What? When?"

"This morning. We got him to the hospital in Rawlins right away and they opted to have him flown to the cardiac unit at Denver General."

"Is he all right?"

"He's having emergency heart bypass surgery now."

In shock, Harlow lowered herself into the closest chair. "How do you know what's going on?"

"There's a nurse who's keeping me updated because I can't travel this late in my pregnancy—"

"Don't feel guilty, T." Harlow grabbed a pen and a notepad from the night-stand. "Give me the nurse's name and extension number."

Tierney rattled off more info than necessary, but that was her way.

"Got it. Now stop pacing and put your feet up. I imagine Renner is fit to be tied." Tierney's husband's behavior defined tyrannical since Tierney had been prescribed bed rest for the last month of her pregnancy. Sometimes she needed a reminder that she had to limit her activity.

"You have no idea," Tierney whispered. "He made Hugh drive Dad and meet the ambulance halfway to town because he refused to leave me alone with Isabelle. He worried the stress would put me into labor the second he wasn't around."

"It's a valid concern." Harlow ignored the way her stomach jumped at the mere mention of the man's name.

"Where are you?"

"Still in LA." By the heavy pause, she knew what her sister was about to ask.

"Someone needs to be with Dad, Harlow. I hate to ask you to drop everything and fly to Denver—"

"But it can't be helped." Her snarky side pointed out that her father wouldn't think she was doing "real" work anyway. "I'll book a flight as soon as possible."

"Thank you. After the helicopter left Rawlins, Hugh took it upon himself to drive to Denver, which is above and beyond."

No, that was total brownnose behavior—a typical Hugh response because he'd do anything for Renner, his boss.

"And he's agreed to stay at the hospital until you get there."

Oh, *hell* no. "As soon as I have my flight info, you can call Renner's foreman and let him know I'm on my way, so there's no need for him to stick around." Did that sound harsh? Harlow didn't care. She could not deal with her father and Hugh Pritchett both on the same damn day.

"I know we've both had issues with Dad, but he was really scared," Tierney said. "I've never seen him like that. It actually scared me."

Harlow closed her eyes. "He's less of an ass to you since you're the vessel bringing forth the long-awaited grandson."

"That's not it. But Dad and I have reached a place where he can live with my life choices."

"I'm not holding my breath that'll ever happen with me."

"Your passion for what you do, Harlow—he doesn't discount it, even when he doesn't understand it," Tierney assured her.

That much was true. When her passion for service trapped her in a nightmare situation last year, he'd done everything in his power to get her out of it. She did owe him for that.

"Leaving at a moment's notice won't be an issue?" Tierney prompted.

"Not since I'm here on sabbatical."

"Do you think you'll get to Denver tonight?"

When her admission didn't register with her sister, Harlow decided to keep any explanations about recent career developments in her life to herself. "Flights leave LAX every couple of hours. You'll need to let the hospital staff know I'm on my way."

"No problem."

"Look, I'll probably be in the air when he gets out of surgery, so promise me that if the worst happens"—she knocked on the wooden window frame to ward off bad luck—"you won't tell me over text or through voice mail."

"I'd never do that."

Harlow breathed a sigh of relief. "Good."

"Love you, sis."

"Love you too."

Two hours later, Harlow had scored the last standby seat on a flight to Denver.

After boarding the plane and taking her seat—next to the bathroom in the last row—she slipped on her noise-canceling headphones and closed her eyes, hoping Michael Bublé's smooth vocals would soothe her ragged thoughts. Or better yet, lull her to sleep.

But her mind had other ideas. Like reminding her of the first time she'd seen one gruff cowboy named Hugh Pritchett.

Dammit. She did not want to think about him or that summer. But her brain had already rewound the clock and the memories rushed back . . .

Chapter Two

Three years earlier . . .

$\mathcal{W}$*elcome to Muddy Gap, Wyoming. Population . . .*

Harlow squinted at the sign. Looked like someone had shot out the number of residents. That didn't bode well.

But with her arrival the population was one more than yesterday. Maybe they'd get a new sign.

She drove through the impressive entrance to the Split Rock Ranch and Resort and parked her Prius in the nearly empty lot. She climbed out, stunned by the pocket of beauty surrounding the Western resort. After traveling through miles of prairie and farmland en route from Chicago, she'd hit the High Plains desert and the near desolate Wyoming landscape. This wasn't what she'd expected.

The massive building ahead of her was gorgeous and yet didn't detract from the view. Her sister tore out the front door and down the stairs, practically throwing herself at Harlow.

"I'm so happy you're here," Tierney said on a choked sob. "I've missed you so much."

"Samesies. And stop crying or I'll start calling you Teary Tierney instead of Tenacious Tierney."

Tierney stepped back and wiped her eyes. "Sorry. A year is too long for us not to see each other. Promise me that won't happen again."

"I promise," Harlow said offhandedly as she was busy staring at her big sister's big belly. "How's baby Tenor?"

"We're fine." She grinned and smoothed her palms over her baby bump. "I love your nickname for the womb dweller."

"I seriously hope you're considering my suggestions for baby names."

"Jackie Jackson or Jack Jackson? Not happening."

Harlow stuck her tongue out. "Spoilsport. Tierney, this place is amazing." She rubbed her hands together. "I'm betting my digs are equally awesome. I can't wait to see them."

"Now?"

"Yeah. Why not?"

"Don't you want to see where you'll be working first?"

"No. I drove straight through, so I'm seriously close to going comatose."

Tierney's gaze sharpened. "You didn't stop at all?"

"Just for gas and more energy drinks." Harlow squeezed Tierney's hand and felt her anxiety lessening a little.

"Good thing I didn't plan a big 'Welcome to Wyoming' meal for you later tonight."

"Very lucky for me, since you're a horrible cook."

"I'm better than I used to be."

Harlow raised both eyebrows.

"Okay, fine, Renner does most of the cooking."

"Where is my handsome brother-in-law?"

"With the foreman down at the barn." Tierney pointed to Harlow's car. "Got room for me to ride along so I can show you the fastest way to get to the cabin?"

"Yep. I travel light, as you know."

They climbed in the car and Tierney had her drive by the row of trailers that made up the employee quarters. After dwelling in a tent for six months, Harlow would've been fine living there. But Tierney had insisted her baby sister move into the small cabin that she and Renner had recently vacated, since they'd moved into their new family-sized house.

She followed Tierney up the river-rock-paved sidewalk and checked out the landscaping. Very minimalist—but not due to Tierney's black thumb. She'd learned water was scarce around here. Since she had experience utilizing native flora and fauna on some of the projects she'd worked on, she approved the resort's choice to incorporate native plants, grasses and rock. Not only was it better ecologically; it showcased the uniqueness of the vegetation rather than using sod to cover up the natural beauty.

Harlow followed her sister into the cabin. The cozy space was all Tierney: elegant without being fussy. A compact kitchen. An open living area.

Tierney pointed to a closed door. "The bedroom and bathroom are through there."

"This place is perfect, T." She hugged her sister from behind. "Thank you for letting me stay here, but you didn't have to leave the furniture. I would've been fine with a camp cot and a beanbag chair."

Tierney sniffed like she didn't believe her. "We bought all new furnishings for the new house. Baby-friendly stuff. I doubt that glass coffee table could withstand a toddler smacking toys onto it."

"True."

"Lots of happy memories in this house," Tierney said softly.

"No wild parties to taint those memories, I promise."

"I'll never forget the look on Dad's face when he walked in on you and ten of your friends from the homeless shelter doing karaoke."

"He's never had much of a sense of humor, has he?" Harlow paused. "Things are better?"

"Some." Tierney sighed. "He's been checking in on me a couple of times a week since I told him we were pregnant."

"Really?"

"I know it's hard to believe. Part of me wants to tell him it's too late to take on a fatherly role in my life when he couldn't be bothered when I *needed* a father."

Harlow said nothing. Her relationship with their father had been much different—although not better by any stretch. Gene Pratt hadn't had the same expectations for Harlow that he had for his brainiac daughter, Tierney.

"After all the shit Dad pulled when the resort was getting off the ground, Renner has every reason not to want to have anything to do with him. But he claims the biggest reason he won't cut him out of our life is because of me. And surprisingly, Dad respects that Renner is a bigger man than he is."

"You're so lucky. Not only does Renner worship you—he stands up for you."

"And my baby daddy is also one hot cowboy who fills out a pair of Wranglers to perfection."

"Also true. Too bad he doesn't have any brothers."

"Come on. Let's walk down to the barn so you can say hello to him before you sack out."

The steep decline had Harlow gripping Tierney's arm in case her pregnant sister lost her footing.

No surprise that Renner met them at the bottom of the hill, his assessing gaze on his wife. "Darlin', maybe you oughten be comin' down the hill in your condition."

"I'm fine. Harlow had a death grip on me."

"I'd never let anything happen to her," Harlow assured him.

Renner's gaze finally moved from Tierney over to Harlow. His quick half smile didn't reach his piercing blue eyes. "Good to see you, Harlow."

They'd met only four times and Harlow had gotten the impression that Renner didn't care for her. "You too, Renner." Harlow was about to say something else when her gaze was drawn to the big man exiting the barn.

He ambled toward them, his cream-colored cowboy hat angled down, keeping his face in shadow. His arms hung by his sides as his booted feet kicked up dust. He stopped beside Renner and finally looked up.

Her stomach cartwheeled. With his rawboned facial features and penetrating brown eyes, this guy epitomized a steely-eyed gunslinger from the Wild West.

But his gaze didn't remain on Harlow long. After a quick once-over his focus returned to Tierney. The hard line of his mouth softened. "You ain't supposed to be hoofing it down here. That's why Renner got you a damn golf cart."

Tierney scowled. "Stop treating me like I'm a delicate flower. Both of you. I would've had to walk all the way back *up* the hill to get the golf cart, since we drove down to the cabin."

Renner looked at Harlow. "Did you get settled in okay?"

"Not yet. At least I know where I'm going now." Her gaze returned to the man standing beside Renner. The lower half of his face was covered in dark blondish red scruff that stretched down his long neck. When she glanced back up at his eyes, the man was flat-out scowling at her. "Is there a reason you're glaring at me?"

"You've got pink goddamn hair."

"So?"

"So you look like you stuck your head in a cotton candy machine."

"Ooh. Nice one. Not very original, though. Next time try to work in a Pepto-Bismol pink reference instead."

"If you didn't want people lookin' at you, then you oughten dye your hair that wacky color."

She ignored his comment and looked at Renner. "And who is this charming redneck-cum-hairstylist?"

"Hugh Pritchett. He's the livestock manager and my right-hand man." Renner lifted his chin to Hugh. "This is my sister-in-law, Harlow Pratt. She'll be workin' at the Split Rock this summer."

Just then another guy exited the barn. He stopped, grinned at her and hustled up the hill. When he reached her, he thrust out his hand. "You must be Harlow. Tierney's told me all about you. I'm Tobin Hale. I do all the crap jobs around here that no one else wants to do."

"It's nice to meet you, Tobin."

He squinted at her and smiled. "The Mud Lilies are gonna love you with that wild-ass hair."

"What are the Mud Lilies?"

"It's a group of the best ladies you'll ever meet." Tobin dropped his voice to a whisper. "They're all retired and widowed, but that don't stop them from bein' the biggest troublemakers in the county."

"I can't wait to meet them."

"Unless you're meeting up with them tonight, they ain't gonna see your pink hair. No offense, Harlow, but that's gotta go if you're working here," Renner said.

Good thing she'd planned for that. "I assume you want the piercings out too?"

"I'd have her leave in the nose ring, Ren," Hugh drawled. "That way if she gets outta line, you can attach a chain to it and use it as a come-along."

Harlow's mouth dropped open. "Was that supposed to be funny?"

He shrugged those broad shoulders.

Tobin stepped between them. "Ignore Hugh. His ex-wife got his sense of humor in the divorce settlement." He looked over at Renner. "I know the boss will want his wife to put her feet up, so I'll show you around the rest of the place."

Flirting was second nature to her; she thought nothing of smiling up at Tobin as she threaded her arm through his. Such a cutie with that glorious grin, not to mention the devilish twinkle in his eyes. "Lead on."

"My pleasure."

She glanced over her shoulder at her sister—the only one of the trio who showed any amusement. "See you later."

"We've got a nine a.m. meeting to go over job expectations," Renner said.

"I'll be there with bells on."

❧

Of course she'd overslept. Twenty-some hours in the car without a break, and add in the cocktails she'd knocked back last night in an effort to get to know her new coworker Tanna, and she'd crashed in her clothes. Luckily her backup alarm was loud enough to wake the dead.

Her brother-in-law chewed her ass for the lateness, warning she'd get no special treatment because of her family ties. The work at the resort wouldn't be hard—nothing like the time she'd spent digging latrines in

Haiti. The hardest part for her would be peddling accessories and other junk to people who likely had a closet already crammed with clothing, jewelry and scarves. But her views on excessive consumerism wouldn't be welcome around here. And she wouldn't do anything to jeopardize this job and her true purpose for being in Wyoming.

Keeping an eye on her sister.

Since she and her father were worried about Tierney's first pregnancy— due to a family history of childbirth complications, which had killed Tierney and Harlow's mother and their maternal grandmother—when Tierney mentioned the Split Rock needed temporary summer help, Harlow had begged Tierney to give her the job. With her father's blessing, she claimed Daddy had cut her off again. Given their past history, Tierney had no problem casting their father in the villain's role. She offered Harlow the job without hesitation . . .

✐

When the flight attendant announced they'd begun the descent into Denver, Harlow shut down the memory and prepared herself to see her father at the hospital.

After Harlow deplaned at DIA, she headed straight for the taxi stand. Inside the cab she turned on her phone, hoping she didn't have a single message.

No texts. No voice mail.

Good.

She quickly texted Tierney and received an equally fast response.

Dad made it thru surgery. He's in ICU recovery. Call me right after you see him, okay?

Harlow responded with *K.*

She palmed her phone and looked out the window. Darkness had fallen, so all she saw was the blur of lights as the taxi sped down the freeway. She'd been in such a hurry to leave that she hadn't had time to check on the possible aftereffects of a heart attack resulting in emergency bypass surgery.

She opened the Internet search app and typed in WebMD. It'd become her secret addiction during her stint in Africa when she'd sworn she'd contracted malaria—despite being vaccinated. She'd run through the checklist of symptoms on the medical site, but hers didn't match up, so she accepted the truth: She'd gotten the flu.

That's when she'd become a WebMD junkie.

Harlow knew exactly what terms to plug in to get the most focused results. As she scoured the text, she became increasingly more frustrated because she didn't know the level of heart attack her dad had suffered. So the recovery time could be anywhere from a couple of days to an entire year.

A year.

Surely her proud father wouldn't insist one of his daughters become his caretaker during his recovery? Because with Tierney's responsibilities to her financial consulting business, as well as to her daughter—Isabelle—the new baby and Renner, the "take care of Dad" responsibility would fall squarely on Harlow's shoulders.

Except the man had more money than god. He could afford to hire professional help.

The cab pulled to a stop beneath the hospital awning. Harlow paid the cabbie and hauled her suitcase out of the trunk, her phone in her hand.

The receptionist at the visitors' desk smiled at her. "How may I help you?"

"My father, Gene Pratt, was brought here via helicopter from Wyoming. He's been in surgery in the cardiac unit. I just flew in and don't know what floor he's on."

"Hang on a second and I'll pull up that information for you."

As Harlow waited, she drummed her fingers on the countertop. Then she just happened to glance across the room and she saw him.

Every inch of his six-foot-three-inch frame vibrated with tension. His big hands were propped on his jean-clad hips. His wide shoulders nearly cast his shitkickers in shadow. As always, he'd pulled his cowboy hat down low enough that only the bottom half of his face was visible.

His lips were compressed into a thin, disapproving line.

"Ah, yes, here it is," the receptionist said, garnering Harlow's attention. "He's on the second floor in the cardiac wing. Are you familiar with how to get there?"

"No, ma'am."

"Follow the corridor to the second set of elevators. They'll take you to the cardiac unit. I'll let the charge nurse know that you're on your way."

"Thank you so much." If she'd had the energy to sprint to avoid Hugh, she would have attempted it. But his long-legged strides allowed him to cut her off before she'd made it past the first set of elevators.

"Why are you dodging me?" he demanded.

His deep voice still had the power to send a shiver of want down her spine. "I'm here to see my father, not you. You did your good deed, so now you can go."

"Harlow. I need to talk to you."

Harlow gave herself a quick reminder not to fall prey to this man's visceral pull before she glanced up to meet his eyes.

Pointless advice as it turned out. The one-two punch of lust whomped her in the gut. Why couldn't the man look like hell? Why did he have to look like he'd stepped out of a Western film with his perfectly groomed beard and piercing brown eyes shadowed beneath the brim of his well-worn hat? He even wore a crisp white shirt and dark blue Wranglers—both of which looked as starched as his attitude.

"Christ almighty, woman, how is it possible you're even prettier than I remembered?"

Don't fall for it.

But she wasn't immune to his compliments, especially since they were so rare. The heat in his eyes indicated he was happy to see her. However, the hard set to his jaw indicated he knew the feeling wasn't mutual.

"Hugh. I appreciate you sticking around. But since you're not family"— she pointed to the sign on the wall regarding visitation limitations—"you can't accompany me to the waiting area upstairs." She turned to go.

"Hold on." He set his big hand on her arm. "I'll be right here if you need anything."

"I won't need anything from you."

"And don't even think about tryin' to sneak past me," he warned. "I've always had a strange kind of radar when it comes to you."

"Then that radar should be telling you to get far away from me as fast as possible."

Hugh's lips twitched. "I'll take that under advisement."

She shook off his touch and dragged her suitcase to the elevators, refusing to look his way again. But she felt his presence, felt his eyes roving over every inch of her body like a caress, just like they used to.

Used to. Remember that.

Once the doors opened on the second floor, Harlow straightened her spine, preparing herself for whatever shape she'd find her father in.

Chapter Three

Well, you fucked that up.

No shit. And no goddamned surprise.

Hugh shuffled back to the reception area, unable to keep defeat from weighing on him as he lowered his sorry ass into the closest chair.

Three years had passed since he'd last clapped eyes on her and the first thing he did was snarl at her. Jesus. Talk about a class act.

At least you didn't insult her hair like you did the first time you met her.

That thought brought a quick smile. Remembering the fire flashing in her big blue eyes. Remembering how she'd gone sandal to boot with him, arguing with him.

Remembering . . . everything about Harlow Pratt.

In an effort to get his mind off the past, he rifled through the stack of magazines on the table beside him and scowled. He'd never be bored enough to waste his life reading about celebrities' love affairs and their dietary preferences.

Dietary preferences. Bunch of weird fucking diets where they'd eat twigs and clay but not meat.

That brought his mind back to Harlow. He hadn't been surprised to learn the girl was a vegetarian. But he had been surprised by his immediate pull toward her when they first met. Beneath the punk Barbie look, she had a pretty face, and bee-stung lips that begged for a kiss. Add in her breathy voice, the curvy body, and he'd wanted her with an ache he couldn't understand.

Harlow Pratt was miles away from the usual type of woman that attracted him—a million fucking miles away.

So he'd tried to stay away from her while she was working at the resort. If their paths crossed, he'd become tight-lipped. Not speaking to her, not looking at her physical fineness, generally ignoring her.

But Harlow didn't like being ignored. She'd nicknamed him Grumpy—which secretly amused him—so he'd started calling her Harlot, which hadn't amused her at all, but the attention had given her a reason to tease him at every turn.

Every turn.

Every day.

And goddammit-all-to-hell if it didn't work.

Back then he'd been going through the motions for so long he'd forgotten the simple joys of give-and-take between a man and a woman. He'd never had much use for flirting. But Harlow changed that. She'd changed everything.

A wave of sleepiness rolled over him. He tossed the magazine aside and pulled his hat a little lower. Maybe he could sneak in a catnap.

But he couldn't get Harlow off his mind. He'd been thinking about her all day. How she'd wormed her way into his life three years ago whether he'd liked it or not. He drifted back to that time and the place where they'd left antagonism at the door for the first time . . .

⤖

That summer had been rife with changes—few of them good. As Hugh sat in Buckeye Joe's again, annoyed by everything again, he wondered at what point a young man became a crabby old man.

When the current music and entertainment trends baffled him? When he'd rather stay at home than go out and deal with crowds? When spicy foods gave him indigestion?

No. He was a healthy twenty-eight-year-old man who wasn't getting laid regularly and that made him really fucking crabby.

"What's your deal?" Tobin asked him. "You look ready to punch something."

"I just wish we would've gone someplace else." He tipped up his beer and drank, letting his gaze take in the Buckeye. "Same people here every time. Same lack of women every time."

"Then let's head into Rawlins next week."

"Cool. And then on the 'Welcome to Wyoming' road sign, let's spray-paint 'Horny and Desperate' as the state's new slogan."

"Ain't that the truth," Tobin said. "It bugs the fuck outta me to imagine I might live the rest of my life without a woman in my bed every night."

"After havin' my ex bouncing in all the beds in the county except for ours, I'm fine sleeping alone. Doesn't mean I don't need a warm body next to me once in a while to give my hand a break."

Tobin nearly spit out his beer. "Jesus, warn a guy. You never say shit like that." He leaned closer and scrutinized Hugh's face. "You weren't doin' the Mud Lilies' stargazer shots and you're totally hammered right now?"

"Nah. I'm just restless. I'm used to bein' on the road. I know Ren is all het up about Tierney's pregnancy, but there's no reason why I shouldn't be out there running the events." Hugh nudged him. "Pointless to talk about. Let's play pool."

They took their time playing, since no one else was hot for the table.

"Women," Tobin stated out of the blue. "Is that why you miss bein' on the road so much?"

"Partly. I mean there are always women at the events lookin' for a hookup. There isn't a single woman in this bar I'd consider hooking up with."

Just then Harlow Pratt made a total liar of him by walking in right as those words left his mouth.

Tobin was taking a shot, allowing Hugh time to give Harlow a thorough head to toe. She'd worn a lacy blouse the soft pink color of her lips. Jeans. Flip-flops. She had her hands in her back pockets and she looked around.

Looking for familiar faces.

He frowned. She'd come to the bar alone? Why'd she think that was a good idea?

As she walked away from the front door, four different guys approached her. Two, Hugh knew from spending so much time in here, were married. The other two were dirtbags.

Tobin prompted him to take a turn, then looked to see what'd caught Hugh's attention. Grinning, he set down his cue and headed right for Harlow. Her happiness in seeing a familiar face even made Hugh smile.

Of course Tobin brought her to their table. "Look who I found."

Hugh grunted.

Harlow rested her elbows on the table. "Heya, Grumpy."

"Harlot."

"Ugh. Don't call me that."

"Like you callin' me Grumpy is any better?"

"Can we leave Grumpy and Harlot at the Split Rock tonight?"

"Sure."

"You want me to get you something from the bar, Harlow?" Tobin asked.

"Just water."

"The Split Rock bartender didn't wander into the Buckeye to drink on her night off?" Hugh said skeptically.

"That wouldn't be smart, since I'm also driving. I just needed to get out and be among people I don't have to wait on." She eyed his beer. "Why are you here?"

"Tobin dragged me."

"That's the only reason? You're not here to dance?"

"Why? Are you offering?"

At that moment Emil Pharris marched up to the table, bold as brass, and tapped Harlow on the shoulder.

Harlow turned. "Yes?"

"You wanna dance?"

When Harlow opened her mouth to deny him, Emil said, "Come on, prove me right. I got a drink ridin' on you not bein' too stuck-up to dance with me."

"I'll pass."

"So you *are* stuck-up."

"Maybe she won't dance with you because she's with me."

Emil's eyes snapped to Hugh. Then back to Harlow. "You and this starched shirt are together?"

"For this dance we are." Hugh stood and offered Harlow his hand. "Come on, darlin'."

Tobin returned with two beers and Harlow's water. "Whoa. Where you goin'?"

"Emil was sniffing around, so I nipped that shit in the bud. We'll be back." Hugh kept his hand on the small of Harlow's back as he directed her to the dance floor. When he pulled her in, clasping her right hand in his left, the scent of her perfume teased his nose. Damn. She smelled good. He glanced down at her; her eyes were blazing at him.

"Don't do that again."

"What?"

"Speak for me. Act like you're rescuing me."

What the hell? "You'd rather be dancing with Emil? He's a fuckin' letch."

"No, I didn't want to dance with him, but I didn't want to dance with you either."

"Aw. Now I'm hurt." He paused and locked eyes with her. "Why don't you wanna dance with me?"

"Because Emil was right about one thing. You are a starched shirt. And I doubt you can dance like I do."

"And how's that?"

"Dirty."

"You don't say."

She did a shimmy twist move with her hips. Her thighs brushed his, her belly rubbed over his belt buckle, her boobs pressed into his chest and a section of her hair teased the side of his face. "Very, very dirty," she whispered.

Fuck. Me.

Then she did it again.

When she peered up at him, her eyes held a smug look. She'd known exactly how she'd affected him.

Hugh wasn't sure what possessed him to clamp his hands on her ass, and dip his mouth toward her ear. "That was a nice tease. So, darlin', I *am* gonna make you prove you can be dirtier than that."

She bobbled a step and then recovered.

So she wasn't totally unaffected by him. Good to know.

"Dirty dancing isn't like a lap dance. One person doesn't stay still while the other person does all the work. You want me to prove it, cowboy, you'll mirror my moves."

"Bring it, dancin' queen."

Harlow laughed in a low, throaty, sexy way he'd never heard from her, which was as potent as the sway of her body. "Hands on my hips."

He took his time moving his hands over her curves, closely watching her face as he did so. She leaned in closer, which he took as a positive.

She slid her hands under his armpits and gripped his shoulders. "Lesson one: Listen to the beat of the music. Slow and sultry? Hard and driving? Happy and bouncy? Dance to it like you'd fuck to it." She swung her hips from side to side in small motions. "Follow me. That's it."

He slid his leg between hers.

That startled her. "Why am I not surprised you're a natural at being dirty?"

Hugh just smiled.

"Now watch me roll my belly."

Harlow put a deep arch in her lower back and let it move up through her spine until their chests touched.

"Now you do it."

Flexibility wasn't his strong suit, but no fucking way was he missing out on this. He had to snap his hips harder at the start. The motion of their bodies *was* like fucking. Fully clothed. In front of a roomful of people.

He didn't give two shits who watched. While he had this hot honey showing him all her moves, he'd damn well enjoy every second.

"You're good at belly rolls."

He pressed his thumbs into her hip bones and she released a surprised gasp. "Like that?"

"Mmm-hmm."

"What else you got to show me?"

Harlow spun around and rubbed her ass into his groin. She met his gaze over her shoulder. "Pretend you're doing the limbo, just working your lower half."

"Never done the limbo in my life."

"It's not that fun actually. *This* is way more fun."

They swayed a few more times and the song ended.

Harlow slowly straightened up and faced him. Her cheeks were flushed. Her hair had gone a little wild. She'd dug her teeth into her lower lip as if trying to stop herself from saying something.

Feeling less like a grumpy old man than he had in a long time, he put his mouth on her ear. "So admit you were wrong, doll."

"Wrong about what?"

"Wrong about me not bein' dirty enough for you."

They locked gazes, the heat shimmering between them.

A tap on his arm had him jerking upright so fast his hat tumbled to the floor and the past vanished.

The young, wide-eyed receptionist stepped back. "I didn't mean to startle you. I just . . ."

Hugh reached for his hat and settled it back on his head. "Sorry, I was"—*lost in a boner-inducing memory*—"half-asleep. What did you say?"

"I wanted you to know you don't have to sit down here." She dropped her voice. "Your friend made it sound like you couldn't go to the upstairs waiting room, but it *is* a public space."

"Why're you tellin' me this?"

"Because you remind me of my dad. He's a rancher too."

Christ. He must really look like death warmed over if this young girl thought he was old enough to have a daughter her age. "I appreciate it"—he briefly glanced at her name tag—"Cherise." He pushed to his feet. "I reckon your daddy is right proud of you."

She nodded. "He wants me to get an education and not marry the first cowboy that trips my trigger."

Hugh stiffened. He'd heard similar words—from his ex-wife's father.

"Thanks for the heads-up. I'll get outta your hair now." Energy renewed, he booked it down the hallway at a good clip. The elevator door opened, and medical personnel spilled out. Must be close to shift change, so no one paid him any attention.

But when he saw the nearly empty waiting room in the cardiac unit, he knew he'd draw attention, so he strolled right up to the desk.

An older African-American woman glanced up from a file folder. "Yes?"

"I'm here with Gene Pratt's daughter, Harlow. I'll just be waiting over there for her."

"Fine." She refocused on her paperwork.

That was it?

Huh. Guess they had other things to worry about besides who was taking up space in the waiting room.

He'd barely settled in, elbows on his knees, reading yet another stupid magazine, when he heard the angry snap of flip-flops across the carpet come to a stop right in front of him.

"If you don't leave right now, I'm calling security to have your ass thrown out," Harlow snapped.

Hugh stood slowly, tossing the magazine aside, and intentionally looming over her. "You're hanging on by a thread, doll."

She just looked at him.

He recognized sheer will was all that kept her vertical. "I've got strong enough arms to hold you up. Would it be so bad to lean on me? You can tell yourself I'm the only one here and you didn't have a choice."

"Never thought you'd be the type to take advantage. Oh, right, that's what you do—take advantage and then you leave. Why don't you mix it up this time and just leave first?"

Her direct hit sliced him open, but he kept cool. "I never thought I'd see my fierce girl lookin' so damn lost."

Harlow blinked at him, confused that he hadn't fired off a zinger. Then she shocked them both when her entire body sagged and she whispered, "I am."

"You are what, darlin'?"

"Lost."

That did it. Wordlessly, he pulled her against his body and held tight until she settled.

She gripped the back of his shirt with such force he heard a seam start to rip. He didn't care. It took every ounce of restraint not to kiss the top of her head. Instead he allowed himself to breathe her in.

Hugh had no idea how long they stayed like that, but he knew the second she intended to retreat.

So he let her. But he continued to hold her hand, towing her to the two chairs facing each other in the corner.

"Did you see your dad?"

She nodded. "He wasn't awake, but they let me sit with him." She jammed her free hand through her long blond hair. "The doctor can give me some answers tomorrow."

"No one told you what's goin' on?" he said with surprise.

Harlow's tired blue eyes met his. "No. They've just said he's stable, recovering after coronary bypass surgery, and the first few nights are crucial. They said if I wanted a face-to-face with the doctor, he'll be here early to make his morning rounds."

"It's a good thing I rented a room down the block. You'll be able to get a couple of hours of shut-eye before meeting the doctor."

"I'm staying here."

"Harlow. You need—"

"I said no." She snatched her hand from his. "You don't have the first clue about what I need." Her angry eyes said, *And you never did.*

"Swallow your damn pride and be reasonable. You're exhausted and sleeping here in a chair ain't gonna prove nothin'."

"I've slept in way worse conditions than a padded chair in a temperature-controlled building. And it's not pride that's keeping me from accepting the invite into your bed, nor is it me trying to avoid the temptation of wanting to fuck you in that bed after your oh-so-generous offer of shared sleeping arrangements."

He waited. Kept his mouth shut.

"I need to stay here so they don't have to track me down if something goes wrong."

"Fine. I'll ask the nurse to grab us some blankets."

"There is no 'us,' Hugh."

He leaned forward. "That's something we need to talk about, but right now I'm here as a family friend."

"You'd do the same thing if Tobin's dad was in there? Get him a blanket and a pillow and tuck him in?" she said skeptically.

"Yep."

"Go get them, then, if it'll make you feel better. I have to call Tierney anyway." She sidestepped him and hightailed it to the corner farthest away from him.

Her ass bounced nicely when she flounced off.

Stop staring at her ass. And close the fucking hope chest that you'll ever get the chance to put your hands on it again, bud. You screwed the pooch with her. Big-time.

But that's why he was here with her. For a chance to set things right between them.

Hugh scrubbed his hands over his beard, which had gone past annoying to downright itchy. He'd feel a thousand times better if he could take a five-minute shower. But since Harlow wasn't going back to the hotel, neither was he.

He had to start somewhere in proving to her that he had changed.

Chapter Four

*H*arlow watched Hugh amble toward the desk as she called her sister. She wasn't at all surprised Tierney answered on the first ring.

"How is he?"

"No changes since you spoke to the head nurse hours ago."

"How are you?" Tierney asked.

"Tired. Worried. Annoyed that Hugh is still here."

A pause. "Wait. Hugh is still at the hospital?"

"Right beside me in the cardiac waiting room." So what if she'd given in and taken the hug she'd needed so badly? It was a momentary lapse. She didn't want—didn't need—anything else from him. Tierney knew nothing about Harlow's past with the gruff foreman. She had to tread lightly not to raise her sister's suspicions. "Look, Tierney, I hate to ask this, but Renner needs to call Hugh back to the Split Rock."

Another pause. "Renner and I both thought Hugh would be on the road back here as soon as you reached the hospital, since Renner is shorthanded this week with Tobin being gone."

"That was my thought too, but he booked a hotel room."

"I'll talk to Renner about it. Do you have a hotel room?"

"Not yet. I'm crashing here in case someone needs to get ahold of me."

"Good plan. Text me if anything changes?"

"Will do. Love you."

"Love you too."

Within a couple of minutes she saw Hugh reach for his phone in his front shirt pocket. He stepped away from the desk to take the call. His back straightened and he turned to look at her.

Harlow held her ground and his gaze. She had nothing to feel guilty about. She didn't want him here.

The conversation was short. Hugh slipped his phone into his pocket, pushed his hat back and scratched his forehead.

It was too much to hope for that he'd become his pissy self and storm to the elevators. No, instead he headed straight for her, his gait measured, his eyes blazing. And he didn't stop until the tips of his boots connected with the toes of her flip-flops.

"Dirty pool, Harlow, havin' my boss demand I get back to the ranch ASAP."

She rolled her eyes. "As if I have any control over Renner Jackson."

He snorted. "You don't, but Tierney does. And you're her beloved baby sister, so it ain't all that hard to connect the dots."

Harlow took a page from his book and said nothing.

"I'll leave, if that's what you want."

"I do."

"We'll deal with the rest of this later."

Not likely.

He stood way too close, watching her way too intently.

She bristled. "What are you waiting for? A good-bye kiss?"

"You didn't give me one when you left three years ago; I doubt your offer is sincere now."

"You're right."

After Hugh walked away—and she shamelessly watched that fine cowboy butt purely on principle because she'd felt *him* eyeballing *her* ass—she grabbed the bedding from the counter and settled in for the night.

She slept fitfully and lightly, but thankfully she didn't dream or get thrown into memories of the past.

"Miss Pratt?"

Harlow blinked and sat up, confused about where she was.

"Dr. Mazur is here. He'll speak to you about your father."

Right. She was in Denver. She untangled herself from the blanket. "Thank you."

"Follow me."

They went through the set of double doors and cut sharply to the right. The nurse stopped in front of a room, knocked twice and waited until a doddering man opened the door.

"Come in."

Surely that wasn't the doctor who'd performed the surgery? He was ancient.

As soon as she entered the room, Harlow forgot about everyone and focused on her dad. He still looked horrible. Alive, according to the blips and beeps of the machines around him, but very much like he'd danced with the devil yesterday and barely bested him.

"When will he be awake?" she asked.

"Later today or tomorrow. So for now let's go into the hallway and get the medical stuff out of the way."

"Can I record this? Or will you be able to explain it to my sister over the phone?"

"Record it if you prefer; that way you can go back and listen to it too."

Dr. Mazur went into a long-winded explanation of the need for the emergency coronary bypass surgery, due to problems with Gene Pratt's blocked arteries, which had caused the heart attack. The doctor detailed the six-hour surgery itself, the incision in the chest cavity, the removal of the healthy blood vessels in her father's leg and how he'd implanted them to replace the four damaged arteries in his heart. Then he listed the medications, along with the side effects from the surgery as well as the drugs. He said he'd personally discuss "crucial and nonnegotiable lifestyle changes" with her father. Then he mentioned recovery time. Six to twelve weeks. Minimum.

"Any questions?"

"Not that I can think of now."

Dr. Mazur patted her shoulder. "Get some rest or fresh air. He'll be out of it for a while yet. And you'll be sick of this place soon enough because you'll be stuck here for at least a week."

"Thanks, Doctor."

When her dad woke up on day three, Dr. Mazur had cautioned her about the possible issues her father might be dealing with, such as temporary loss of memory, partial paralysis, confusion and pain that could lead to unreasonable anger. So when she walked into the room, she wasn't sure what to expect.

But it completely caught her by surprise that her dad smiled and said, "Angel baby," on a short wheeze of breath.

Tears filled her eyes when she heard the term of endearment he hadn't used in years. She went to his bedside and clasped the hand he held out. "Daddy."

"I'm happy you're here. Happy you think I'm human enough to warrant your attention as a humanitarian cause."

She smiled because for a change his teasing wasn't mean in nature. "You sure know how to grab our attention."

Fear flashed in his eyes. "This incident didn't send Tierney . . . ?"

"No, she's fine. The baby is fine. Isabelle is fine. We're all fine except for you. Renner is making Tierney stay at home, which is why I'm here."

"Good man, putting his foot down. We both know that she needs to take it easy."

"So do you, Dad. You had a close call."

"Would you have missed me if I would've died?"

Startled by the abrupt question, she stammered, "I d-don't think—"

"Answer me." He paused. "Please."

"Why are you asking me this?"

"Because I realized I want to be the kind of father you'll miss and I know I'm not. I've always been more concerned with earning money than my daughters' love and respect. I need to earn that right."

Shocked by the direction this conversation had taken, Harlow just stared at him.

"I need to make amends to you and your sister. This scare has taught me something. I want to be the grandfather to my grandkids that my grandfather was to me."

Then he drifted off to sleep.

None of the doctor's warnings had prepared her for her father having a complete personality change. Now Harlow wondered if she should really be worried.

❦

Day four, a surly man had replaced her contrite father. But she understood fear was partially responsible for his attitude, since he'd suffered a bout of heart arrhythmia.

She'd waited in the hallway while the medical team worked on him after the episode. Once the room emptied of all medical personnel except the doctor, she approached the bed. "Dad?"

"Don't look at me with pity, Harlow."

"Your eyes aren't open, so you don't have any idea how I'm looking at you."

"I can feel it." He shifted in his bed and winced. "Fuck."

She froze. Her dad never dropped the f-bomb.

"Sorry. I just feel so damn old and helpless."

"What can I do?"

He opened his eyes. "Track down my cell. I'll need to make some calls."

"You had it when you arrived here?"

"No. I had it in the car in Wyoming. I gave it to Hugh. He was supposed to bring it and check it as a personal item for me."

Hugh. She hadn't thought about him in, oh, ten minutes. Why hadn't he mentioned the location of her dad's cell phone when he was here?

Because you threw him out, remember?

Right.

"I'll check on it. Anything else?"

Dr. Mazur approached them. "It's time to discuss rehab options. I'll send Charlie in. He's our coordinator—"

"It might be a little much for my father to think about now. I'm sure he has plenty of options when he returns to Chicago."

"I'm not going back to Chicago."

Startled, she looked at her dad. "What?"

"I had a near-death experience. Do you think I'm eager to lock myself in a business tower and deal with more work?"

"Yes, because that's who you are."

"Then it's past time for me to change, isn't it? This was the wake-up call I needed."

Change? What was he talking about?

"There's no reason I can't do my rehab in Wyoming."

Harlow calmly faced the doctor. "Did he sustain brain damage? Because this man is acting nothing like my father."

Dr. Mazur shrugged. "If a man says he needs to change, he likely does. It's not unusual for people who've had a taste of their own mortality to decide to take a different approach to their lives."

"Exactly," her father said triumphantly. "I need a different approach. What better way to recover than to be around my family?"

"I'll let you sort out the details," the doctor said. "We'll forward your records to wherever you end up. We'll keep you in the ICU just to be on the safe side as far as surgical problems the next couple of days."

After the doctor left, Harlow demanded, "Have you lost your mind? You can't go back to Wyoming."

"It's perfectly rational to recover at the Split Rock, since I already have a room and my things are there."

"Dad. The Split Rock is a resort, not a rehab hospital."

"It'll be cheaper than a rehab hospital. Two meals a day and daily house-keeping? If I hire a nurse to drive in every day from Rawlins or Casper, it'd still be cheaper than returning to Chicago for recovery."

"But . . ."

"What?"

"Chicago is your home. You have friends there. A life there. And the medical facilities are top-notch."

"I took all that into consideration, but I'm determined to recover among family."

Determined. Aka—in Gene Pratt–speak—*I'm a stubborn bastard and the subject is closed.*

Harlow stood. "I'll see if I can't find your cell phone."

And the closest bar.

🙢

That night when she returned to her hotel room, she cracked open the minibar. She didn't bother dumping the tiny bottle of tequila in a glass; she poured it directly into her mouth. Then she filled the ice bucket from the machine on her floor. She crafted cocktail number two: gin and ginger ale on the rocks. She sipped that one, since the only food she'd consumed all day had come from the hospital vending machine.

She flopped in the chair and stared at the ice cubes in her glass. As soon as her dad had woken up, he'd begun dictating to her as if she were his secretary. Which should be the height of hilarity, since her father had refused to give her any position—even in the janitorial department—at his company, Pratt Financial Group—PFG. But what really had her questioning his soundness of mind? Hearing him say she needed to choose between a black, silver or white Lexus SUV to drive when they left for Wyoming. He'd placed a black one on hold, but if she preferred another color, it was fine with him. There'd been no need to ask why he chose a Lexus. Nothing but the best—and usually most expensive—for Gene Pratt.

Her phone rang and she answered it. "Yo, sis, what up?"

"My curiosity. Did Dad have a brain transplant?"

Harlow snickered. "Ooh, that one's much nicer than my original thought that they discovered his heart was dead and black when they opened him up and they retrofitted him with a real one."

"Omigod, that is not funny, because it's entirely a possibility."

"So what weirdness did the emperor bestow on *you* today after he got his cell phone back?"

"Let's see, he called Janie and booked the room he was staying in at the Split Rock for the next twelve weeks—and sweetened the pot by adding a hundred dollars per night to the price, which of course Janie couldn't pass up. Then because he couldn't get a room for his personal assistant, he's renting one of the employee trailers for her."

The drink stopped halfway to her mouth. "Wait. *Karen* agreed to come?"

"Yes. Evidently he's promised her that she won't be his nursemaid, but she'll continue in her capacity as his assistant, helping him get his affairs in order so he can retire properly."

"Fuck. Me. He's serious about retiring?"

"Apparently so. Oh, and he's graciously offered Karen to me to handle the accounting at Split Rock when I'm on maternity leave." She snorted. "Like that'll ever happen. I'd turn it over to you long before her."

Harlow had to admit that stung. Numbers weren't her forte, but she had other skills—valuable skills—according to all the relief agencies and humanitarian organizations she'd worked for over the years. But, as usual, Harlow let the remark go without comment. "What else?"

"You're aware Dad rented a trailer for you?"

Oh, hell no. "Why?"

"Claims he wants you close by so you can help him during his recovery and help me with Isabelle after the baby arrives."

"He doesn't get to decide that for me! And I can't believe you agreed to it."

"Harlow, he kept mentioning the word 'family' and the phrase 'wasted years.' As pregnant and hormonal as I am, I'm easily susceptible to visions of family dinners gathered around a holiday meal as we look at each other with adoration, so give me a break."

Her sister had spent years trying to win their father's approval. Now that he'd shown a glimmer of humanity, had Tierney immediately reverted into that daddy-pleasing girl? And if so, what could she do about it?

Nothing. She just had to make the most of it.

"Fine. I'll go along with it for a few weeks just to keep his health on track, okay?"

"Okay." A pause. "You've been with him for five days. Do you really think he's changed?"

"I don't know. He's less . . . emperor-like, all these plans for his stay at the Split Rock notwithstanding." But she didn't trust him. Deep down she worried this "one big happy family" thing was another one of his power plays; the man was a master at them. "The true test will be if he's an arrogant asshole when he's recuperating."

"I hope they load him up on prescription drugs that'll knock him out for most of it."

"Me too."

"How long before he's discharged?"

"Two days."

"I'll let Karen know. She isn't coming until Dad's out of the hospital and settled here. She said he'll remember twenty other things she needs to bring along, so she'll wait."

"That's why she gets paid the big bucks." Harlow took another sip of her drink. "Is the ever-efficient Karen lining up home health care?"

"I am. Or I should say I did. Remember Lainie? Hank's wife? She's a nurse and she's agreed to take him on. For a week anyway to see how it goes."

"That's lucky."

"Very. I have another place in Casper as a backup plan."

"I'm staying in the employee trailers for the short amount of time I'm there?"

"Since Hugh bought my cabin, his old trailer has been empty, so I'll have housekeeping get it ready for you."

She'd loved that small cabin. Hugh had probably turned it into a man cave. "All I need is a bed and a shower for the short time I'm there, so that'll work."

"Harlow. Are you all right?"

"I'm hungry and drinking. But other than that, I'm fine. Why?"

"You've said 'short amount of time I'm there' numerous times. It sounds like you're already planning to leave and you're not even here yet. Makes me wonder what really happened three years ago that chased you away so fast."

She forced a laugh. "You've read too many mysteries, sis. An opportunity arose and I took it. That's all. You always said I was flighty and would go whichever way the wind blew. I'd think you'd be more surprised that I stuck around as long as I did."

A long pause ensued. "Do I really make you feel that way?"

The last thing Harlow wanted was to be at odds with her sister. So she rapped on the desktop. "Hey, room service is here, so I gotta run. I'll talk to you tomorrow." After that, she hung up.

Harlow dropped her head back and closed her eyes. Choosing to stay at the Split Rock and help Tierney out with the baby and spoil her niece sounded like heaven—except that her father had orchestrated everything so that he hadn't given her a choice.

But she'd made her choice the second she got on that plane.

You'd be facing either his recovery or his funeral. And there's no way you'd leave your pregnant sister to deal with either of those scenarios alone.

Brooding was pointless anyway.

Which was why she never understood why Hugh did it. But he'd always done it so well. His thoughts masked by his hat. Or his silence.

During the first month she worked at the Split Rock that summer three years ago, she'd learned that accusing him of brooding unlocked the part of him that wanted to prove her wrong. And she still remembered the first time he'd revealed any melancholy and vulnerability . . .

⤖

After the weekly staff meeting, Harlow had remained behind the bar at the Split Rock to clean up. Why were employees always the messiest customers?

Hugh and Tobin had stuck around afterward, speaking in low tones. She'd tried eavesdropping on their conversation, but they really didn't want to be overheard, so she'd given up and finished her closing duties.

Once Tobin left, Hugh had hung around, nursing his second beer of the night.

He looked up when she leaned against the bar. "I suppose you're throwin' me out."

"Actually, I could use a drink."

"I noticed you weren't knocking them back like everyone else."

"Neither were you."

He shrugged. "I'm not much of a drinker."

"But you're a helluva dancer."

Hugh smiled, but didn't look at her. "You been to the Buckeye lately?"

"No. It's not really my scene." She pulled out the house gin—she preferred Tanqueray, but drinking top-shelf booze for her one allotted employee drink per night struck her as taking advantage—and poured two shots in a glass, then squirted in tonic before adding four squeezed limes. "Mind if I sit next to you?"

"Sit wherever you'd like, since you're letting me stay."

Harlow took the corner seat to his left. She took a sip of her drink and exhaled.

They drank in silence. Her mind had drifted off to her last phone call to her dad regarding Tierney and the baby's health. As always she'd had nothing new to tell him. As always that made both of them very happy.

She'd glanced up from her drink and caught Hugh watching her intently. Her belly flipped. His brown eyes were just so . . . soulful.

He said, "You're quiet."

"Sounds like you think that's unusual for me."

"It is. Usually you're so . . ." He paused and drank. "Animated."

"You seem to be more brooding than usual yourself."

He grunted.

"Got a problem you wanna share with your bartender?"

"Yeah. There's this woman I work with. She's such a pain in the ass. Always reminding me I'm not a little ray of sunshine. I'm at a loss for what to do."

"She's obviously trying to get into your pants. I'd coldcock her." She sipped her drink. "Or hot cock her. That's probably what she wants."

Hugh laughed softly. "Why do you say shit like that? To shock me?"

"'Cause I gotcha to smile, cowboy."

His smile stayed intact. "That you did."

"Why are you so melancholy? Is it your birthday and no one baked you a cake?"

He shook his head.

"Your favorite cow became a steak?"

"Jesus. No."

"Come on," she cajoled him. "You know you want to tell me."

Hugh looked at her. "Eight years ago today I got married."

Not what she'd been expecting. "You here celebrating? Or mourning?"

"Is it weird to admit a little of both?"

You sweet, sad man. "No. It's not weird."

He picked at the label on his beer bottle.

Harlow watched him, wishing she knew what thoughts were churning behind those serious brown eyes.

So she decided to ask him.

"All right, since you were tripped up by the ties of holy matrimony, but you managed to cut and run, tell me why your wife is now your ex."

"Why do you care?"

"Because I have a secret desire to be wife number two," she whispered, "and I'm looking for hints."

Hugh smiled. "You'd have to get me to the altar first and that ain't ever happening again."

"What was so bad about her besides that she got your sense of humor in the divorce?"

His eyes bored into her. "You really want the whole ugly truth, Harlow, or are you just sittin' here, killin' time, feelin' sorry for me?"

Harlow dismissed his defense mechanisms. Hugh was closed off, but he'd extended a hand toward her in friendship more than one time—only to yank it back. And today, she wanted to hold on. "I'll remind you that *you're* killing time on *my* time. But since I don't want to sit here and drink alone, I'll change the question. How'd you get into the livestock business?"

"Oddly enough, my marriage and my career are tied together."

"Really? Now you have to spill the whole story."

"If I tell you, you gonna explain why your hands are callused and your nails aren't perfectly manicured? And why you have about six outfits total instead of a vast wardrobe? Those things don't jibe with the entitled princess you pretend to be. Because, sweetheart, I know princess behavior firsthand."

He'd picked up on that? "You show me yours first. Life story. Sordid details welcome."

"I'm from Kansas, same as Renner. Summer after I graduated from high school, Ramses Ashland hired me to work in his stockyards. The job paid well, but the downside was bein' on call twenty-four/seven, since I lived in the bunkhouse on the ranch. I worked like a dog and was grateful for the job, but it drove home the point I didn't see myself in the cattle business long term."

Harlow choked on her drink. "So, uh, how's that working out for you?"

"Hush. You wanna hear this story or not?"

"It depends. Will you let me provide completely made-up color commentary?"

"No. Although it might make it a more palatable tale. To me anyway."

"Fine, I'll make the witty comments in my head only. Go on."

"Ramses' only daughter, Cleo, hadn't set her stilettos on the Ashland Ranch and Stockyards the first two years I worked there. After the golden child graduated from college, she sowed her oats all over the globe, before reluctantly returning home to Kansas." He shot her a warning look. "Not a single *Wizard of Oz* reference."

Harlow mimed zipping her lips.

"Although Wicked Witch does fit her."

"Hilarious. I was hoping you'd compare her to the Cowardly Lion. Or the flying monkeys."

"Here's where it gets confusing." He actually squirmed. "Cleo took one look at me and claimed it was love at first sight."

"Why is that hard to believe? You are a hulking hottie with that unattainable aura. That's very appealing to some women." *It's appealing to me.* Her attraction to him had thrown her into flux. Hugh wasn't a movie-star-handsome cowboy. He wasn't much of a conversationalist except about ranch and cattle matters. But something about him fascinated her in a way she couldn't explain. So she did understand why a woman would believe that nameless something was love at first sight.

"As a naive twenty-year-old kid, I didn't stand a chance against her tenacity and sexual wiles. Cleo chased me. She seduced me. She decided it was time to get married. And I was the lucky one she'd chosen to be her groom."

No sarcasm there.

"Ramses gave his baby girl whatever she wanted. And she wanted me. Before I knew what hit me, we were married and livin' in the house her daddy bought us as a wedding present."

"The marriage sucked from day one?" Harlow asked.

"Nah. The first year was decent. But then when she still wasn't pregnant by our second anniversary, she reverted to her partying ways. She'd stumble home at three a.m.—not giving a damn that I had to get up at five to check cattle. That's when she shed her skin and became mean as a fuckin' snake."

She didn't have to prompt him to continue. Which had her wondering how long this had festered inside him.

"She threw it in my face that she went out because I was boring as hell. She complained to her daddy that I ignored her, which made my working hours as miserable as the hours I spent at home with her. She also complained I didn't make enough money. Ramses gave me a raise once a year, but it wasn't enough to keep Cleo in the style she was used to." He snorted and sipped his beer. "I couldn't fuckin' believe when she admitted Ramses gave her an allowance. A twenty-seven-year-old married woman still expecting Daddy to foot the bills."

Her coworkers at the Split Rock assumed that Harlow was a trust fund baby because her father, Gene Pratt, was originally involved in financing the ranch and resort. Now that she'd perpetuated the lie that Daddy had cut her off and she'd had to get a real job, it wasn't like she could say, "Just kidding. I have less than a thousand bucks in my checking account. I'm here to keep an eye on my sister." But if Hugh saw any correlation between his ex-wife and her, he didn't mention it.

"I know I should've walked away, because it was pretty goddamned obvious I couldn't afford her. But by then I was twenty-two years old and determined to be the kind of provider Cleo needed. I figured more money would fix our marital problems. So I found a second job. Given my work experience with stock, Renner hired me on the spot. Within a month I was the stock manager for Jackson Stock Contracting. Since rodeos were weekend events, I didn't miss work at the stockyards. But I was gone every weekend from the middle of May until the end of September."

"Did Cleo miss you at all?"

He glanced up sharply as if he'd forgotten Harlow was there. "Oh, she complained that I was never around. It makes me a dick, but I took great pleasure in tellin' her that I was working to give her every silly thing she desired."

"And how'd she take that?"

"'Bout like you'd expect. It made me such a fuckin' tool to hope she'd come to her senses and admit she didn't need material things; she'd rather have me."

That broke her heart right in half. "Didn't happen?"

"Nope. Happened that I had to choose between working at the stockyards and working for Renner. By then I knew she was sleeping around and I just wanted to get the fuck away from her. So I did. But bein' on the road . . ." He blushed and fiddled with his beer bottle. "I wasn't taking care of myself. Cleo pushed nasty and cutting to a whole new level when she saw that I was getting fat. When Renner offered me the chance to relocate to Wyoming, I took it."

"Did she even consider coming with you? It could've been a chance for you two to start over."

"A tiny part of me hoped for that. We'd been married four years. We had a history—most of it shitty to be sure. So when I asked her to come with me? She laughed and swore she'd never move to the land of tobacco-chewing sheep fuckers. And she immediately filed for divorce. So yeah. By the time I walked away from her, I didn't have a sense of humor or a sense of self beyond bein' Renner's foreman. Might make me a pussy to admit this, but she fucked me up in so many ways, I only started to come out of it in the last couple of years."

Harlow knew that any sign of sympathy would piss him off. It shocked her how much he'd opened up to her and she didn't want him to close down. Because she knew he wasn't the type of guy who told that story to just anyone who asked.

"Well? Say something," he demanded.

"I'd have to work really hard at being a worse wife than that. And even given the antagonistic tendencies between you and me, I don't think I'm up for the challenge of outdoing her awfulness."

His posture relaxed. "Throwing in the towel so soon?"

"What can I say?" She shrugged. "I'm a quitter."

"Yeah? Me too."

Before he made good on his promise to ask about her conflicting personas, she said, "You and Tobin were deep in conversation after the meeting. Is everything all right?"

"Fine. Just making sure we're on the same page on what needs doing around here. I'll be hitting the road the next couple days."

"You're gone a lot."

"A lot more now that Renner ain't comin' along."

"Does that bother you?"

He grinned. "Nope. I live for it. I love crisscrossing the country when rodeo and county fair season is in full swing."

"Renner mentioned he was tired of that on-the-road life."

"He's got a beautiful wife waiting for him at home, missing him. I might feel the same way were I in his boots, but I'm not." Hugh slid off his chair and threw his empty bottle in the trash. "Thanks for the beer and the ear, bartender."

"Anytime."

The phone buzzed, bringing her back to the present. She hadn't thought about that summer for a long time. But it appeared her brain was determined to dredge up every memory she'd held on to.

She poked the button on the phone for room service. Might as well enjoy the few extra perks while she had the chance, because the time in Wyoming with her father would test her.

Chapter Five

"*Y*ou're living up to your Grumpy nickname today," Tobin said.

Hugh snorted. "Three damn years since anyone has called me that."

"To your face," Tobin shot back with a quick grin.

"Fuck off."

"You have to admit 'Huge' is a much better nickname."

"Only if we're talking about my dick. And you and me ain't ever havin' that convo," Hugh said with a shudder.

"No shit."

Renner poked his head into the office. "Hugh? Got a sec?"

"Sure." He dropped his boots to the wooden floor and pushed out of his chair.

His boss stood in front of the farm door that opened into the main part of the barn. He pointed at something as he spoke to three-year-old Isabelle, propped on his hip.

"What's up?"

It struck Hugh that Isabelle looked very much like her aunt Harlow with her white blond hair and enormous blue eyes. He offered her a soft smile. "Hey, darlin'. You hanging with Daddy today?"

She nodded somberly. "Baby is making Mommy sick."

Hugh's gaze snapped to Renner. "Is Tierney all right?"

"Tired. She does too much. So Mama is resting and me'n my girlie are goin' swimming."

Isabelle looked up at him. "No sharks in the pool, Daddy?"

Renner kissed the top of her head. "I promise there are no sharks in the pool, baby girl."

Hugh mouthed, "Sharks?"

"It's the last time we ask Tobin to babysit. He filled her head with all sorts of scary sh—stuff."

"I want Aunt Harlow to babysit me," Isabelle declared.

"Too bad Aunt Harlow has been babysitting Grandpa, huh?"

Harlow had been back at the Split Rock for almost two weeks. In that time Hugh had had two conversations with her. Her avoidance of him had gone from cute to frustrating. He felt Isabelle staring at him. "Do I have something on my face?"

She frowned. "You don't look like him."

"Like who?"

"Grumpy from *Snow White*. How come that's what Aunt Harlow calls you?"

Renner laughed. "That's a question for another day. But speaking of Harlow . . . would you run up to the lodge and let her know Tierney is resting and I'm takin' care of Isabelle?"

"No problem." Finally a boss-mandated reason to corner that wily woman. "I'll head up there right now."

"Thanks."

Hugh returned to the office to tell Tobin he was leaving.

Tobin had his boots propped up on his desk, his arms folded over his chest, and had tipped his hat over his eyes. He didn't budge when Hugh's boot steps sounded across the wooden flooring.

Everything was low-key here. If Tobin needed a short nap, it was from him starting chores at dawn. Hugh quietly stacked the paperwork he'd been poring over in the file folder and dropped it on Renner's desk.

Of the four desks in this cavernous office space, Renner's stayed the cleanest. Not because the man was a neat freak, but because the majority of his work hours were spent at the lodge, where he shared space with his wife. This "barn office" was Hugh and Tobin's domain. The extra desk gave frequent visitors like Fletch, the veterinarian, and Ike, the cattle broker, a place to work.

At first he thought Renner had gone off the deep end when he'd sold his holdings in Kansas to purchase land in nowhere Wyoming. He'd worried about the man's sanity when Renner admitted he planned to build a larger, hardier herd as well as run the Western resort.

One thing Hugh had never questioned was Renner's drive to be able to do it all and do it well. Renner had guaranteed he would double Hugh's salary and dangled possible shares in the business as an added incentive to relocate.

He'd started his life over in Wyoming without a single regret.

Until Harlow.

As Hugh walked past the swimming pool, devoid of Split Rock guests—likely the reason Renner was taking Isabelle swimming—his thoughts scrolled back to the time that summer night three years ago when he'd encountered Harlow at the pool . . .

After he'd finished a late night in the barn office, he dragged ass up the hill. Working on paperwork wasn't his idea of fun. As he started to cut around the pool and head to his trailer, he noticed the pool gate was wide open—a serious breach of the rules. Acting as resort security wasn't his idea of fun either, but someone had to shut the gate.

He paused with his forearms on the fence. The sharp tang of chlorine wafted to him on the summer breeze. The light from the bottom of the pool reflected upward, creating wavy, silvery patterns across the water. He watched the movement of the shadows across the concrete, taking in the peaceful sight.

He hadn't seen Harlow, perched on the edge of a chaise, until she said, "So it isn't music that soothes the savage beast, but water?"

His startled gaze zipped to her. "I've gone from Grumpy to Beastly?"

She laughed. "You looked beastly when you first walked up, but less so now."

"And here I was hoping the darkness hid my big, nasty teeth. Sadly, there's nothin' I can do about the claws and the horns."

Another soft laugh. "Keep it up, and you'll convince me you aren't Grumpy either."

Hugh smiled at her. "Why're you swimming so late?"

"I just closed the bar. I'm restless. I thought a swim might take the edge off."

I know what'll take the edge off . . . and there's only one part of you that needs to get wet for it.

He was such a fucking pervert.

Harlow stood up from the lounge chair and sauntered over to him. She'd wrapped herself in a towel, making it impossible to get a peek at that tiny red bikini she usually wore. Yeah, knowing that made him a perv too. "You worked late. And you seem tense. Maybe you should join me and we'll take that edge off together."

Fuck yeah.

Clutching the towel with one hand, she reached up and ruffled his hair. "You had straw or something trapped in there." She didn't drop her hand; she merely moved her fingers down to pet his beard. "It probably seems silly, but I didn't know beards were so soft. I assumed the hair would be coarse. Like on your arms and legs and chest." She continued stroking. "Or between your thighs."

"You've been wondering what my pubic hair feels like?"

"I don't know why I said that." Her wide blue eyes locked on to his. "Would you believe me if I said you're the only one I say such outrageous things to?"

"Nope."

Harlow ran the backs of her knuckles across the edge of his beard. "What does it feel like when it's wet?"

Jesus. His dick was now fully hard from her teasing touch and words. "Harlow—"

"Sorry." She dropped her hand. "I'm big on tactile sensations."

"You don't say."

Her eyes danced with mischief. "You too?"

"Yep." Hugh leaned over the fence. "What's the softest thing you've ever felt?"

"Bunny fur. You?"

Was there anything softer than the dewy petals of a woman's pussy? Nope. But not something he'd share. Now if she asked about the hardest thing? He'd drop his britches and show her his cock. "I'd agree with fur."

"That's not what you were thinking."

He lifted a brow. "You a mind reader?"

"No. But you had a dirty gleam in your eye that I really like."

He stared at her. This woman confused the hell out of him.

"Come swimming with me," she urged. "I promise I won't tell anyone you were having fun, so you can maintain your brooding cowboy vibe."

"I don't brood."

"Then prove it. Be daring and do something out of the norm. Come swimming with me."

"I don't have a swimsuit."

"Neither do I. But no one else is around." She unhooked the towel and it hit the pool deck.

Then Harlow was standing in front of him completely fucking naked.

"Skinny-dip with me. Ditch your clothes and your inhibitions and jump in with both feet."

Her body was beautiful. What would it be like to touch and taste such perfection?

Heaven.

"Hugh?"

His tongue seemed stuck to the roof of his mouth.

"Ah, I'm getting a little cold standing out here in just my skin."

Hugh couldn't look her in the eyes. "Then you'd better get in the water and warm up. Don't forget to shut off the lights and close the gate when you're done. Night, Harlow."

He wandered to his trailer in a daze. Had he really just seen—and fucking turned *down*—a chance at putting his hands on that fan-fucking-tastic body of hers?

Yes.

You're not a pervert; you're an idiot.

He'd ditched his clothes and climbed in the shower, letting the warm water fall on him as he jerked off furiously, imagining that he'd had the guts to take her up on her offer.

∽

Hugh shook himself out of the memory and entered the main reception area of the Split Rock.

Before his eyes had fully adjusted from the blinding brightness of the sun to the dark hallway, he nearly knocked Harlow on her ass as she barreled toward him.

He clasped her upper arms to keep them both from hitting the carpet. "Whoa, there. What's your rush?"

When Harlow's gaze snared his, he saw her baby blues were damn near indigo from anger. "I'm in desperate need to find a bigger pillow to smother my father with."

"I thought you hated violence," Hugh drawled.

"I thought so too, but apparently even a pacifist has limits and I've reached mine. Now move it or I'll practice my first act of violence on you."

"C'mere, slugger." He towed her around the corner, crowding her against the wall, blocking her from view of the guests. His body cast hers in shadow and being this close to her reminded him of how small she was. "Take a moment and settle down."

"You just love manhandling me, don't you?"

"Yep." But he noticed she wasn't attempting to flee from him for a change. "What's Daddy doin' that's ruffled your pretty feathers?"

"Being a bigger pain in the ass than usual. It's not my fault he's stuck in his room. He's bored, but he doesn't 'feel like' reading, watching TV or working on his laptop." She let her head fall back. "And I didn't pack my tap shoes for this trip because I didn't think I'd need to entertain him."

Hugh laughed.

Harlow looked at him strangely.

"What?"

"You laughed. You never laugh."

"Not true. I laugh around you because you crack my ass up."

That earned him a sweet smile. "At least you think I'm funny. I'm sure not tickling my dad's funny bone today."

Hugh's brain stuck on the word *bone. Why, yes, sweet darlin', I'd love to play a little slap and tickle with you, and then bone you to take your mind off of all your troubles.*

"I get that he hates being cooped up," she continued. "But it was his choice to come here and not return to Chicago to recuperate. Since Tierney is busy gestating baby number two, I bring his granddaughter to visit and play games with him every day. Lainie is here three times a week doing his rehab. Renner's even roped Tobin and you into stopping by." Her gaze hooked his again. "Mandated visits from the boss, I assume?"

"I don't mind, Harlow."

For the first time since they'd been in the hospital in Denver, she touched him, placing her hand on his chest. His heart skipped a beat. "I appreciate it. He's a difficult man on his best days and those have been few and far between." She wrinkled her nose. "So I don't put much stock in his claim that he's missing all his *lovely lady friends* in Chicago. That was today's complaint, by the way, that sent me over the edge."

"Maybe he is some kinda ladies' man."

"You did not seriously just say that to me. Eww. That's not something I ever want to picture." Harlow broke eye contact and dropped her hand from his chest. "Anyway, thanks for keeping me from committing patricide. I'm feeling much calmer."

"Good." He tucked a flyaway section of her hair behind her ear. "How much longer are you gonna avoid me?"

"Hugh—"

"I haven't pushed because you've got a lot of family stuff on your plate. But that don't mean I'm giving up." He slid his hand around the left side of her neck, resting his thumb on the pulse point beside the hollow of her throat. "I wanna spend time with you."

"Doing what?"

Fucking you until you can't move without remembering my body on yours. "Ah. Normal date stuff."

"Such as?"

"Such as you come over and I cook you supper. Then we'll play cards. Or we'll sit in front of a fire pit. Or we'll go horseback ridin' in the moonlight."

"What if I'm not interested in any of that?"

"Then I'd go with my first choice of stripping you bare, tyin' you to my bed and acquainting myself with every single inch of this wicked, sweet body of yours."

Beneath his thumb Harlow's pulse pounded double time at his last suggestion.

He lowered his head and placed a soft kiss on that spot. "Anything you wanna do, hippie-girl, tame or wild," he murmured against her skin, "I'll make it happen." Then he stepped back, knowing he'd probably gone too far.

The heat in her eyes morphed into a challenge. "Tell you what. If you can round up some *lovely lady friends* to keep my dad company a couple of days a week, I'll agree."

"To what?"

"Anything you wanna do, cowboy, tame or wild," she cooed in that breathy, fuck-me-now voice.

"No foolin'?"

"Not even a little bit. So what do you say?"

That's when Hugh realized Harlow was confident he couldn't deliver.

Wrong.

So wrong.

And, damn, was it ever hard not to grin like an idiot, because he totally had this one in the fuckin' bag. "I accept your challenge."

"You do?"

"Yep. So we have a deal?"

"If you can deliver? Absolutely we have a deal."

"Done. Let's officially seal it."

She offered her hand.

He laughed. "Nice try. But you know that ain't gonna fly with me."

Harlow opened her mouth to protest and Hugh swooped right in. Taking the kiss he wanted. No sweet peck or gentle tease. He devoured her. Twisting his tongue around hers. Sucking on those full lips. Tasting the heat and need that was Harlow. Giving her back that same fire. Reminding her that the desire between them hadn't cooled one fucking bit in the past three years. If anything, it burned hotter than ever.

Her lips clung to his even after he eased back.

When their eyes met . . . Damn. It was all he could do to not toss her over his shoulder and run like hell to the closest bed.

She scraped her fingers over his beard. "Your kisses still drive me wild."

"Same here, doll." He placed his hand over hers, turning her palm to nip the base of her thumb. "I'm supposed to tell you your sister is resting and Renner is with Isabelle."

"Oh. That's good. It's hard to be upbeat with Isabelle when my mood is crap."

He kissed the center of her palm and reluctantly dropped her hand. "Make sure to tell your dad he'll have a visitor tomorrow. A female visitor. That way he knows to slap on some cologne and wear pants."

"Confident, aren't you?"

"No. Just determined to make this situation easier on you."

Her eyes softened. "My, my, stock boss Pritchett. You learned to sweet-talk a little in my absence."

"Like it?"

"No. I always preferred your dirty talk." She sidestepped him and walked away without a backward glance.

Hugh shook the lust from his brain and pulled his cell from the leather holster on his belt. He scrolled through his contacts and hit Dial.

Tobin answered with, "S'up, Hugely Grumpy?"

He snorted. "Need your help."

"Name it."

"You still in the office?"

"Yeah."

"On my way."

✐

He'd kissed her.

But she could admit it hadn't been as much of a surprise as the first time he'd put that warm and skilled mouth on hers.

Harlow paused outside her father's room, still needing a minute to find her balance. Because Hugh certainly had always excelled at catching her off guard.

Especially back then. She'd never known where she would run into him. Or what his mood would be. But she'd never forget the first time he'd kissed her three years ago . . .

✐

Normally Hugh wasn't around the lodge unless Renner forced his presence. So it'd surprised Harlow to see him on a perfect summer night sitting on the bench between the lodge and the barns, watching the sun drop behind the rock as he drank a beer.

Her decision whether to sneak away or approach the bear was out of her hands when he turned and looked at her. Then he'd scooted over in invitation.

Harlow swung a leg over the log bench and sat next to him. "Hey. I never see you hanging out here where you might have to talk to people."

"I talk to people plenty when I'm on the road."

"When did you get back?"

"Two hours ago." He sipped his beer. "Why? Didja miss me?"

"Yes, like you'd taken a piece of my soul with you."

Hugh snorted. "See why I don't seek out human company? Animals don't talk back."

"Did you miss me?" she asked sweetly.

"Yeah, I was hopin' to run into you so I could return that piece of your shrieking soul because that fucker is annoying," he deadpanned.

"Damn, Grumpy. How much have you been drinking? That was actually funny."

"I try."

"So do you crack jokes when you're using your cattle prod to torture livestock?"

He lifted a brow. "Torture livestock?"

She bumped him with her shoulder. "Kidding. Since Renner became my brother-in-law, I'm better informed about the care men and women in the world of agriculture bestow on their animals. I don't just spout off a knee-jerk response about cruelty to animals."

"Huh. That didn't sound sarcastic."

"It wasn't. I've learned not to blindly believe in organizations' propaganda. Some people never bother to check the legitimacy of the organizations' claims."

"And you do?"

"That's what I do, Hugh." She laughed. "Didn't mean to make that rhyme."

"So you ain't a PETA person?"

"Some of their ideas are sound, but some of them are so whacked-out . . ." She shook her head. "While I love animals, I'm far more interested in the betterment of humans."

Hugh stayed quiet.

"Bored with me already? I know you think I'm a hippie, who's all, peace, love and pass the bong. So I'll go and get started on those hash brownies."

"Stay." He clamped his hand on her knee. "Talk to me. I did miss you."

The heat of his hand left a hot imprint on her skin. His words caused a hot flutter of hope. "What do you want to talk about?"

"Tell me about your causes."

"Huh. That didn't sound sarcastic."

He laughed. "Smart-ass. It wasn't."

"Okay. What do you want to know about them?"

"I want to know about you. Why do you do it?"

Harlow tamped down her annoyance, reminding herself this was a teaching opportunity for her and a chance to open his mind. "I do it because I believe one person helping another person can make a difference."

He nodded.

"I give my time to humanitarian agencies that are not affiliated with a specific religion or political persuasion. While missionaries have done some incredible things, others have done serious damage to indigenous peoples' beliefs. I don't think a starving child needs to profess fealty to a certain god to get a damn sandwich."

He choked on his beer.

"But I also think Third World countries that rely on secular organizations with values that aren't in line with their beliefs are creating larger problems."

"Such as?"

"Wars, for one thing. Then it's a lose-lose situation for everyone involved." She slipped her ponytail holder free and shook out her hair. "Even attempting to pick up the pieces after war is tricky—so I avoid the groups that specialize in rebuilding. I choose shorter assignments."

"Why?"

"Keeps attachment at a manageable level. I've seen friends get sucked into that 'the earth is a village' mentality. They become too attached and can't be objective—they believe in their indispensability. That's the whole purpose of why I volunteer. Many of the places I go . . . things have been done a certain way for generations. If we can show them little changes that will increase their standard of living as well as their longevity, then our work is done and it's time to move on." She felt him staring at her, practically with his mouth hanging open. "What? Is my bleeding heart showing?"

He shook his head.

"Then what?"

"Just surprised."

"That I use my head for more than a place to put my hat?"

"Ouch. Nice shot at the guy actually wearin' a hat," he drawled.

Harlow smirked. "If the Stetson fits . . ."

Hugh laughed.

"So why were you looking at me like you'd never seen me before?"

"Maybe because it's the first time I've seen you beyond the antagonistic, opportunistic brat you present yourself as."

"Is there a compliment in there?"

"Why, darlin'? Do you need one?"

"Yes, especially since you saw me *naked* at the pool two weeks ago and didn't offer me one then."

"My damn tongue was hanging out so far I couldn't speak."

Delicious warmth spread through her. So what if he'd been drinking? She'd bask in his compliment. See if she couldn't prompt him to offer more. "Maybe you oughta open your mouth so I can see if the silver side of your tongue is still up."

"You're flirtin' with me, hippie-girl?"

Harlow cocked her head. "Be honest, cattleman. Isn't that what we've both been doing since the moment we met?"

Hugh seemed to consider that. Then he grinned. A grin that managed to be sexy, naughty and shy. Sexy and naughty fit, but the gruff demeanor and the squinty-eyed Eastwood stare had never hinted at shy.

Nevertheless, the potency of Hugh's smile turned her mouth as dry as Wyoming dirt. She swallowed hard. And that appeared to amuse him. It also encouraged him, and he leaned close enough that the brim of his hat cast a shadow over her.

"Why?"

"Why what?"

"Why me? Tobin wants a piece of you—and I don't mean that in a crude way."

"How do you mean it?"

"He's a good guy. He'd treat you like gold."

"Is this your way of warning me that you'd treat me like crap?"

"What if I said yes?"

Harlow laughed. Then she swiped his bottle of beer and took a long pull. "I'd say I never pegged you for a liar."

"You tryin' to goad me into proving you right? Or wrong?"

"Neither." She passed the beer back to him and watched as he drained the remainder. Why did it seem so intimate that his lips were on the same spot hers had just been?

When he continued to stare at her, Harlow stood. She wanted to leave things on a good note. "Thanks for the conversation and the beer. Maybe I'll see you tomorrow."

She'd made it about three steps before a strong arm banded across her middle, yanking her back against the solid wall of his chest. She might've heard the clink of the beer bottle hitting the ground, but any coherent train of thought vanished when Hugh's mouth brushed her ear.

"Why are you running?"

"I'm not running."

His soft chuckle reverberated in her ear, shooting a hot tingle straight down her spine. "You think I haven't imagined havin' that hot fuckin' mouth of yours on mine? You think I haven't wanted every inch of this soft, curvy body pressed against me?"

"You have?" she said, her voice barely a whisper.

"Yes. But I sure as fuck ain't gonna act on it and take the kiss I want out here where anyone can see us."

His words—his intent, his problem—weren't lost on her. He wanted her; but he didn't *want* to want her. "Let me go. Wouldn't want to ruin your reputation by being seen with me."

That startled him and his hand fell away.

Harlow seized her chance to escape. She ran up the hill toward the lodge. She'd surround herself with people, knowing Hugh wouldn't track her down. No matter how strong the attraction was between them, no way in hell would she be his—or any other man's—dirty little secret.

Before she'd cleared the side of the building, she was spun around and pushed up against the wall.

The ferocity blazing in his eyes wasn't from anger. But she had less than two seconds to contemplate Hugh's look of lust before his hands were framing her face and his mouth was crashing down on hers.

Passion poured from him. In the hungry and wild way his tongue invaded her mouth. In the authoritative manner in which his body imprisoned her. In the utter control he took in kissing her.

His way.

Harlow blindly reached for some part of him—any part—that would hold her up. Because if seeing Hugh grin at her turned her knees weak? Kissing the man turned her entire body boneless.

Her fingers connected with the waistband of his jeans and she gripped the denim tightly, inadvertently pulling him closer.

He growled. The sound vibrated from his chest into her mouth and down to her core, spreading his nonverbal admission of need throughout her body.

His mouth commanded hers, yet his big hands remained both firm and gentle. The fixed grip of his fingertips on her head and the tender stroking motion of his thumbs over her cheekbones were overwhelming.

Neither of them wanted the kiss to end, so it went on and on, in greedy, wet glory that consumed them both.

Eventually their need for air forced them to break apart. Harlow kept her eyes closed as she angled her head away from temptation.

"Fuck," he muttered against her cheek.

"What?" she managed to wheeze.

"That ain't gonna be enough."

She knew that. She just didn't know what she—they—could do about it.

"Got nothin' to say to that?" Hugh murmured, and the deep rumble of his voice vibrated in her ear.

Harlow looked up at him and the top of her head bumped into his cowboy hat. "I'm thinking we're better together when we don't talk."

"Can't argue with that." He slanted his mouth over hers for another very hot, very long, very thorough kiss.

The night might've progressed differently if a passel of kids hadn't burst out the door, setting off the emergency exit alarm.

Hugh had released her so quickly she worried she might've caught on fire.

And then she was staring at his back as he walked down the hill. Frustrated, she yelled, "Who's running now?"

That didn't even put a stutter in his step.

As she'd listened to the emergency alarm shrieking, she'd decided to take it as a warning sign herself and vowed to stay the hell away from Hugh Pritchett.

✐✐

You'd be wise to follow that same advice now.

No kidding.

She shook her head to clear it. Next time she'd have more fortitude when Hugh put his lips close to hers.

Speaking of fortitude . . . she inhaled a deep breath and opened the door to her father's room.

Chapter Six

*E*arly that evening Hugh, Tobin and Ike sat across from the Mud Lilies at Buckeye Joe's.

A disgruntled group of Mud Lilies. Not even a round of zombie killers had sweetened their sour moods.

Garnet turned an accusing eye on Tobin. "I thought you invited us because you were bringing us a new flavor." Her gaze moved over him, Hugh and Ike. "You three are the same damn flavors we've seen all year."

Tobin leaned forward. "Miz Garnet, with all due respect, I said we were asking you here because we needed a *favor*, not to offer you a flavor."

"I know what I heard, Mr. T." She shook her finger at him. "And I ain't seen none of that dirty dancin' like you see on that TV show you promised me neither."

Hugh took in Garnet's outfit. She looked ready for an episode of *What Not to Wear*, not *Dancing with the Stars*. She'd worn acid green and bright pink cowgirl boots, athletic socks that reached the base of her bony knees, a pleated white tennis skirt and a pink sequined headband that pushed her hair up like Don King's. But the crowning touch was the black satin tank top with *Disco Sucks* written in rhinestones across the front.

Miz Maybelle had opted to one-up her friend in outrageous clothing by donning a purple zebra print muumuu. She elbowed Garnet. "You're supposed to wear your hearing aid when you talk on the phone, remember?"

Before Garnet lit into her, Pearl slammed her camo-gloved hand on the table. "I'm missing a new episode of *The Forensic Files* because I thought we were here to meet some new young men."

Ike lowered his beer bottle. "New young men? Why would you need them when you've got us?"

"Well, dumplin', you can't deny that there used to be twice as many of you," Tilda said sweetly. "Bran was the first to fall after Hank. Then Abe, then Kyle. Doc Fletcher and Eli are tied down. Devin got hitched. Even Max finally made an honest woman outta Kylie last year. So there used to be ten or eleven of you young bucks hanging around us all the time. Now there are only you three." She tilted her head and her beret nearly slid over her face. "And where's Holt? I ain't seen that boy in a coon's age."

"That's because he works too damn hard," Bernice declared.

"So we ain't good enough for you anymore?" Ike demanded.

Vivien mediated. "Of course you are. But there's not nearly enough of you. We liked coming here and being outnumbered by strapping young men, pretending we had you wrapped around our fingers. Everywhere else we go we're surrounded by women. Widows, mostly."

"Backstabbing biddies is what most of 'em are," Garnet tossed out. "They wouldn't know fun if it chomped them on their fat arses."

"All y'all except Bernice are widows," Tobin pointed out.

"But, sugar lump, we're *fun* widows," Tilda said.

No argument there. "Which is why you lovely ladies were the first ones who came to mind when I needed to ask a favor," Hugh said.

"What kind of favor?" Pearl asked skeptically.

"You all know that Tierney and Harlow's father, Gene, has been recuperating at the Split Rock. He could use some pretty new faces to keep him company for an hour a day or so."

Silence.

Harlow had been wrong; he sucked at this sweet-talkin' bullshit.

Sherry Gilchrist, Kyle's mother and part owner of the Buckeye, sauntered over. "Why so glum, chums?"

"Because our handsome friends have asked us to play nursemaid to that dickhead who almost destroyed the Split Rock," Bernice said with a bitter edge. "I'm shocked that you would even ask us. I'm outta here." Bernice stood, shouldered her suitcase-sized purse and stomped off.

Hugh, Tobin and Ike exchanged a look.

"Oh, she's full of poo," Miz Maybelle said. "She's using your request as an excuse to leave because they're running marathons of *Tabatha's Salon Takeover* and *Blow Out* and her DVR is busted."

Tilda, Garnet, Pearl and Vivien all nodded in agreement.

"Fill me in on what I missed," Sherry said. After the ladies finished, Sherry shrugged. "I'll do it. No problem. Because unlike *some* people"—she aimed a reproving look at the other women at the table—"I appreciate what you boys have done for me and I'm happy to repay you any way I can."

Boys. Hugh snorted. He'd hit the thirty-one mark last month. He hadn't been a boy in years.

But Sherry wasn't finished. "And I expected better outta you Mud Lilies. These guys have helped you out whenever you've asked. They're always just a phone call away."

It was the first time he'd seen the feisty group look remorseful.

"If you don't do it for them, do it for Tierney and Harlow. Remind yourselves that it could be *you* one of these days, stuck in a room due to an unexpected health issue, annoying your children and begging for visitors." Then Sherry smirked. "Plus, due to Mr. Pratt's ultimatums and shortsightedness, you all became part owners of a successful Western resort. Won't it feel good to rub that in his face? In person?"

The ladies didn't speak. They exchanged looks and head nods. One at a time they put their hands in the middle of the table like an athletic team before a game. Pearl yelled, "Break," and then said, "We're in. I'll coordinate the scheduling of what times work best for each of us."

"None of the times can conflict with our reserved hours on the range," Miz Maybelle reminded Pearl.

"Jumping Jehoshaphat, I know that! The sheriff made it very clear we're not allowed there without law enforcement supervision."

"Reenact William Tell with a cantaloupe and a forty-five, just *one* time, and everyone looks at you sideways. It's not fair," Vivien complained. "It wasn't like I missed."

Then the ladies all started talking at once, tossing out their various activities—kickboxing and yoga classes, billiards practice, tatting lessons, daily devotionals and preservation society meetings—for consideration in scheduling.

Hugh grinned. Harlow would be shocked that he'd upheld his end of the deal so fast. And Gene Pratt wouldn't know what the hell had hit him when these ladies started showing up.

"So what gives, Hugh?"

He glanced up. "What do you mean?"

"Why're you calling in favors?" Tobin asked. "Is this something that Tierney asked Renner to do and he passed the buck on to you?"

"No. This has nothin' to do with either of them. Harlow is frazzled by her dad's demands and I figured a few fresh faces visiting him would take some of the stress off her."

Tobin eyed him with suspicion.

Hugh changed the subject and addressed Ike. "Where are you off to next?"

"Colorado. A longtime customer is selling off his entire herd. His wife recently died and he's done in. Poor guy." He paused to take a drink. "What about you? Isn't it about time for that rodeo near your hometown?"

In the last two years Renner's first business, Jackson Stock Contracting, had pared down the number of rodeo events it supplied stock to. Since Renner had gotten married and become a father, he hated being away from home. When Renner decided not to bid on any new rodeo events last summer, Hugh had kept his mouth shut, figuring it was a temporary situation. But they'd contracted for even fewer rodeos this year. The longer this lull went on, the harder it was to pin Renner down on his future plans for the stock contracting company that Hugh had a stake in.

"Yeah. The county fair and rodeo in Phillipsburg, Kansas, runs almost a week. Renner will have to miss it this year because of the new baby, but I'll arrange help."

"Your folks still live around them parts?" Tobin asked.

"Part of the time. The year after I moved to Wyoming, Dad sold the feed store to my cousin, and Mom sold the house to my sister and her husband. Now Mom and Dad live in an RV and are spending their retirement seeing the country."

"You have a sister?" Ike said. "Huh. Never hear you talk about her."

"That's because her and me ain't speakin'." Hugh swallowed a drink of beer—hard to do through his clenched jaw. He had that reaction every time he thought of Mary.

"You know I'm gonna ask why."

"She sided with my ex-wife and said she didn't blame her for refusing to move to Wyoming." A partial truth anyway.

Tobin whistled. "Harsh, man. So your ex must live around there too."

"Yep. I tend to stick close to the stock at the fairgrounds. Their shit is a lot easier to handle than Cleo's."

"I don't doubt that," Ike drawled. "Lemme know if you have any hands back out. I could tag along and help."

"Thanks. Speaking of helping out . . ." He looked at Tobin. "How's Flint workin' out?"

Ike frowned. "Who's Flint?"

"Jaxson Flint. Dodie the cook's grandson," Tobin explained. "He's helping out over the summer doin' whatever needs done at the lodge and ranch. Since his first name sounds the same as Renner's last name, we call him Flint."

Hugh smirked. "Kid didn't think 'Jaxson of all trades' was funny."

"That's because you scared the piss out of him, Huge."

"Fuck off, Toby."

Tobin scowled—he hated that nickname.

"How old is this kid?"

"Twenty. Why?"

"Since the Mud Lilies will be around the Split Rock regularly, you might wanna warn him about them. They look harmless and grandmotherly—"

"But in their cases looks are deceiving."

"Right." Ike lowered his voice. "I'd be afraid they'd wanna test him out as their new *flavor*."

Tobin choked on his beer.

Which of course drew the Mud Lilies' attention.

"What're you boys whispering about us?" Miz Maybelle demanded.

"Just wondering if you ladies are staying here to whoop it up. Or if you're done and we can mosey on home," Tobin lied with a smile on his face.

"Well, if there's no dirty dancin', I'm ready to leave." Garnet stood. "Who's with me?"

"I am." Miz Maybelle stood. "It's early. Let's head into Rawlins. Gotta be something going on at the Blue Lantern."

"Hot damn!" Garnet clapped her hands. "I was afraid I'd wasted this great outfit tonight."

Tobin shook his head at Hugh, warning him to say nothing.

"I suppose if you're headed into town, I'll tag along," Tillie said.

Pearl pushed to her feet. "Might as well count me in."

"You all know very well that I'm the only one with a vehicle big enough to haul all of us, so I'll drive," Vivien said.

That eased Hugh's mind. Vivien was the youngest in the group and usually the voice of reason. Unless she had a firearm in her hand. Then she became Dirty Harry.

"You ladies have fun."

Garnet got in Tobin's face. "Remember our deal, Mr. T."

"Always on my mind, Miz G. But be smart and safe tonight, just in case, okay?"

She patted his cheek. "I will." Then she let out an ear-piercing whistle. "Get a move on, Lilies."

After they left, Hugh asked Tobin, "What deal you got cooking with Garnet?"

"Between us? If she gets arrested, I bail her out."

"What're the odds of that?"

"All bets are off when it comes to her," Tobin said. "But I owe her, and that sweet crazy woman won't let me forget it."

Hugh didn't ask for specifics—he'd be better off not knowing. "You ridin' back with me?"

"If Ike's up for a game of pool, I'll stick around."

"I'm game," Ike said. "I can run you back out to the Split Rock after."

He looked between them. "You two never hang out. You guys havin' a bromance I didn't know about?"

"Call it what you like, but Ike and I are the last two single guys in the group."

"I'm single," Hugh reminded them.

Tobin shook his head. "Not for long. Once Harlow comes around to your way of thinkin', you'll be a couple. The way you refused to be last time."

Hugh blushed. "How the fuck did you know about that?"

"See what I mean, Ike? No one up at the Split Rock gives me a second thought unless they want something from me. But I ain't invisible or blind." Tobin paused. "I saw you two making out a bunch of times. I also saw you sneaking into Harlow's cabin one of the last nights she was here."

Panic arose. Who besides Tobin knew that? Renner? Tierney?

Relax. Tobin keeps shit to himself. Case in point: You didn't know he'd seen you and Harlow together until tonight. Damn near three years later.

"Once you pull off this favor for Harlow, you'll be back in her good graces. Before long she'll be in your bed. Sooner than later." He clapped Ike on the back. "So get used to seeing me'n Ike hanging out."

In his truck, on the way home, Hugh thought of the phrase *good graces* and snorted. After their first explosive kiss, he'd run—a stupid response, since he'd been the one to initiate the kiss—and he'd gotten on her bad side. He remembered when his perception of Harlow began to change three years ago, except it hadn't mattered because he'd let fear rule his actions . . .

No doubt about it, he never should've stopped to sit on that log to enjoy the sunset. Then he wouldn't have heard Harlow speak with such passion about her life choices. He wouldn't have seen her in a different light. He wouldn't have pushed her up against the wall and kissed her like she was light, air and water. He wouldn't have run from her and kick-started the doubts he thought he'd buried since his divorce.

He'd been manipulated by a woman like Harlow before, enjoying their banter because it seemed natural. But then he remembered that's exactly how things had started out with his ex. Funny, sexy teasing that had led them straight to the bedroom. The nastiness hadn't come until later—but it *had* come. Her vile words had sliced him to the bone and left his confidence shredded at her feet.

No. He'd been there, done that, and he wouldn't ever put himself in that position again.

But all his mental resilience vanished two weeks after the kissing incident when he witnessed Harlow's genuinely sweet and thoughtful side. Proof positive she was nothing like his ex-wife.

He'd been sent up to the Split Rock early in the morning to grab office supplies. The door to the employee break room was open and he heard crying, which had given him pause.

"Don't worry, Yvette. I'll take care of it," Harlow said.

More sniffles. "You can't. It's not your problem, Harlow. I appreciate that you filled in for me the day I got sick, but this time is different. Dave will understand. We'll just do it another time."

"Bull. You two deserve time away. It's my day off. It wasn't like I had anything special planned."

Yvette said something he couldn't hear.

Then Harlow's throaty laughter rang out. "Trust me; it's much easier to wash sheets and towels in an industrial-sized washing machine than beating the bedding against a rock, which I know from personal experience."

Hugh couldn't figure out what was going on.

None of your business, man. Move on.

So he'd done that. Hustled past the room without stopping. He'd loaded up the supplies he needed and returned to the barn office.

But he'd returned to the lodge four hours later, shocked to see Harlow, wearing a housekeeping uniform, mopping the floor in the great room.

What the hell?

Then a guest had stormed up to her, right across the freshly mopped floor. "Excuse me, but it's after one o'clock and we still haven't had house-keeping services today."

Harlow looked up. "What room are you in?"

"Eleven."

"I apologize for the delay. I'll be right up to do that."

"See that you are." The woman continued to berate her. "I'm less than impressed with the staff in this place, considering what we're paying for a night's stay."

Harlow said nothing.

Hugh had a burst of anger. This was exactly why he'd stayed away from the guests, bunch of entitled-acting assholes.

The woman stormed off.

Harlow dragged her bucket back to housekeeping.

He followed her. But he ducked into the doorway when he saw her pushing the housekeeping cart down the hallway toward the elevator.

This shit made no sense. Harlow worked in the clothing store and in the bar—not in housekeeping. He wandered into Janie Lawson's office. A harried-looking Janie nursed a baby while she talked on the phone.

Yikes. He didn't need to see that. He backed out before she noticed him.

Then he reminded himself he had plenty of his own shit to do, without worrying about what weird things were going on up at the lodge. He reminded himself what Harlow did or didn't do wasn't his concern.

Since it'd been hotter than hell in his trailer that night, he'd worked late in the barn office, finalizing the details of travel arrangements for upcoming rodeos. When he'd made the trek back to the employee quarters around eleven thirty, he saw a flash of white blond hair out by the Dumpster. By the time he got there, Harlow was tossing in the last bag of garbage.

"You're not supposed to be out here alone."

She jumped and whirled around. "Because people can sneak up on me like you just did?"

"Yep." He frowned. "What're you doin' out this late?" And why was she wearing the bartender uniform? Hadn't he heard her tell Yvette it was her day off?

"Tonight's guests were a bunch of drinkers. I'd still be serving if there weren't complaints about noise and disgruntled guests asking why the bar hadn't closed at ten o'clock like it's supposed to."

"Does that happen a lot?"

She shrugged. "The customer is king. If guests want to stay and drink past closing time and no one complains, the bartender stays."

"Is Renner aware this is happening?"

"I doubt it."

"What about Janie?" he demanded. "She's the GM."

"Janie is only back part-time and she's crazy busy with Harper and Tierney both being gone. Being sleep deprived with a newborn, she's missed a few things, so bringing up the issue about a few guests wanting to drink late in the bar isn't a priority." Harlow yawned. "Look, as much fun as it is to have you chew my ass about doing my freakin' *job*, it's been a long day and I have to be back at it bright and early tomorrow morning."

"Why? Are you covering for Yvette tomorrow too?"

She stilled. "What are you talking about?"

"I saw you today, Harlow. Mopping floors and then hustling to room eleven to provide housekeeping services. And before that, I overheard you talkin' to Yvette. So tell me what's goin' on."

Harlow squared her shoulders and narrowed her eyes. "If I tell you, you have to promise to keep it to yourself."

He'd make no such promises if she was doing something stupid, but he nodded anyway.

"Today is Dave and Yvette's anniversary. She rented a cabin as a surprise for Dave, so he could do some fly-fishing. But when Janie posted the schedule, she'd forgotten to give Yvette the time off. There's a no-refund policy for the place Yvette rented and they've both worked hard this summer and they deserve a special night away. So I said I'd fill in for her today and tomorrow. No big deal."

But it was a big deal. Janie needed to know she'd screwed up. Renner needed to know Janie had screwed up. And they both needed to be aware Harlow had stepped up.

Then Harlow was in his face. "I know what you're thinking, Hugh Pritchett, and I promise I'll be an even bigger pain in your ass if you go running to Renner with this."

"It's his business, Harlow. He deserves to know."

"No. He deserves to enjoy time with his wife and his new baby daughter. You aren't going to pop that bubble of happiness for him. The one little mix-up in staff scheduling has been handled."

"So you'll work yourself to exhaustion?" he demanded. "Let the guests berate you for whatever they want? And the management that caused the screwups is none the wiser?"

She lifted her chin defiantly.

"You've covered for Yvette before. Anyone else? Tanna?"

"Why do you care?"

"I don't fuckin' know, okay? It just pissed me off to see that woman chew you out today because her room hadn't been cleaned on time. And now I find out it's because you—"

"Because I'm what? Incompetent? Or do you think I'm afraid to get my hands dirty?" She poked him in the chest. "Let me tell you something: I'm perfectly capable of cleaning a few hotel rooms and mopping floors. I've lived in places where I've built sleeping areas from nothing but scrap wood and palm leaves, and I had to scrub bedding and mosquito netting every day to ward off poisonous insects, spiders, snakes and frogs."

Hugh wrapped his hand around her poking finger. "Don't assume I intended to insult you."

"Why *wouldn't* I assume that? You're always insulting me."

"Back atcha, babe. But people in charge should know that you're doin' more than your fair share to help out."

"Because most of them assume I'm doing less? That I'm just coasting along collecting a paycheck because I'm Tierney's little sister? I'm some kind of too-good-for-real-work trust fund baby? Wrong. I know what I do to help out. I don't care what others think. Yvette needed my help and I offered. No big deal."

"No big deal, she says. I'm betting it was a big deal to Yvette and Dave."

"So what are you gonna do?"

"I can think of a couple of things I'd like to do to you," he murmured. Then he curled his hand around the back of her neck and brought their faces within kissing distance.

This is wrong. Let her go. You know better than to get mixed up with her.

"Are you waiting for me to make suggestions about what I'd like you to do to me?"

"Smart-mouth." He sank his teeth into her bottom lip and she moaned. That moan did him in.

But Harlow was the one who fused her mouth to his. Who kissed him like she'd been starving for him. And he responded in kind, clamping his other hand on her ass, needing to feel her body pressed against his.

He wasn't sure who broke the kiss first. He did remember their mutual shock at making out like fucking teenagers by the goddamned Dumpster. But even then they were reluctant to move apart.

"I wondered if you'd do that again," she said softly.

I hadn't intended to. "Harlow—"

"I get it, okay? This isn't a convenient attraction for you." She disentangled from his arms.

And he let her.

"Thanks for your concern about me being overworked, but I can handle it." She laughed softly. "I can handle that much better than I can handle you."

Hugh stood there like a dumb ass and watched her walk away because he didn't know what to say . . .

⤞

As he parked in front of his cabin and the memory faded, he realized that uncertainty still held true with Harlow. She tied him up in all kinds of knots. But at least this time he'd managed to be proactive instead of reactive.

He just wished he could be there to see the look on her face when the Mud Lilies started to show up as Gene Pratt's entertainment.

Chapter Seven

$\mathcal{T}$he next afternoon Harlow was in the office with Janie Lawson, the general manager, when Miz Maybelle appeared, looking younger with her gray hair colored a soft mink brown and styled in an artfully messy array. She wore a flowing summer dress, not her usual muumuu.

"Well, Miz Maybelle, don't you look lovely today?" Janie gushed.

Miz Maybelle blushed.

"Have I forgotten about a shareholders' meeting?" Janie prompted.

"No. I'm here to spend a few hours with Gene Pratt. So if you could tell me what room I might find him in, I'd appreciate it."

After Harlow picked her jaw up off the floor, she managed to say, "Why are you here to see my father?"

"Hugh mentioned Gene could use some female company and we have agreed to visit him every day."

"Who's we?"

"The Mud Lilies, of course. We set up a schedule and we're all taking a turn at entertaining Gene. Today's my day."

"But that's—"

"Very sweet of you," Janie inserted. "And how fun for Gene to get some of the local history. He's a history buff, isn't he, Harlow?"

She just blinked at Miz Maybelle in complete confusion.

"It's all right, dear. We'll take care of your father in the afternoons so you're off the hook."

"Are you sure? He can be a little"—*assholish*—"prickly."

"I've dealt with my share of prickly men."

"You don't need me to run interference?"

"No, honey. I have years of experience in handling a man who's cooped up and cranky." Miz Maybelle smiled coyly. "I'm long past needing a chaperone when I entertain a gentleman. So there's no need to check on us. We'll be fine."

"I'm sure you will be," Janie said. "Gene is in room four."

"Thank you." Miz Maybelle turned on her kitten heel and left the office. Harlow stared after her, dumbfounded.

"Harlow? Are you all right?" Janie asked.

"I have no idea." She looked at Janie. "What just happened?"

Janie cocked her head and eyed her. "The Mud Lilies know your father is a handsome man, so it isn't a chore to spend a few hours a week with Mr. Debonair. But I want to know why Hugh approached them on your behalf."

"Are you sure Renner didn't ask Hugh to do this for Tierney?"

Janie laughed. "Tierney isn't the one who's stuck with Gene Pratt. You are. So I have to wonder why Hugh would stick his neck out and ask the Mud Lilies for assistance—god knows that'll cost him big down the line—when the two of you were constantly at each other's throats when you worked here before."

Heat bloomed on her cheeks. "You were on maternity leave for most of that time, so how would you know that?"

"Because I get my hair done at Bernice's Beauty Barn."

Like that was any kind of answer.

"Your point is?" Harlow asked coolly.

"I don't care if you and Hugh get involved. You're both adults. But I would caution you not to play with him."

When had she become some sort of femme fatale? How would Janie and everyone else react if she told them *Hugh* had been the love-'em-and-leave-'em jerk in this scenario?

Harlow stood. "Thanks for the advice. Later." She hustled out and didn't pause when she heard Janie call after her.

She took a minute to gather her thoughts before she walked into Wild West Clothiers. She'd stopped in a couple of times since she'd landed at the Split Rock again. The place still held that funky, cool Western vibe.

Harper waved at her from the front counter while she talked on the phone.

During her summer stint working here, Harlow had preferred bartending in the private bar far more than selling clothing. Tanna Barker, the woman she'd worked with, had the knack for retail sales that Harlow hadn't.

Harley, the other employee at Wild West, wandered out from the back room and grinned when she saw Harlow. "Hey, if it isn't my near twin."

With both of them being blond-haired, blue-eyed, both from Chicago and with similar names, they were easily mixed up. A fact that Harley complained about all the time. Evidently in a moment of pregnancy-related amnesia last summer, Harper had introduced Harley as Harlow to Harper's sister Liberty— and the former soldier still called her by the wrong name.

"Girl. Haven't seen you in a couple of days. Is your dad driving you to drink or something?"

Harlow laughed. "Not yet. But close. Tierney's been super tired, so I've been watching Isabelle."

"Tired will be her life," Harper said, skirting the edge of the counter. "Going from one to two kids is more of a shock than going from two to three kids."

"How is it having a houseful of boys?"

"Awesome. I have the best of all worlds. The boys are either with Bran or at day care for part of the day and then I'm home with them the rest of the time." Harper hip-checked Harley. "I thought I'd have to close the store when Zinnia quit. Little did I know her sister, Harley, was an amazing replacement. I don't know what I'd do without her."

Harley offered her boss a tight smile. "At least in the last year you've gotten my name right."

"Oh, pooh. That was *one* time."

"Wrong. Half the Mud Lilies still call me Harlow."

Harley seemed to have way more resentment about the name mix-up than warranted. Harlow muttered, "Guess that's my answer."

"What was the question?" Harper asked.

She hadn't meant to say that out loud. "I planned to ask if Wild West Clothiers needed part-time help. Not out front," she clarified. "In the back unpacking boxes or getting shipments ready. But that'd just confuse the Harley and Harlow issue even more."

"Add in Harper, and all we need is to hire a Hannah and a Harmony and it'd be chaos."

"Don't forget a Haven," Harley added.

"Or a Haley."

Harper raised her hand. "All these H names are giving me a headache with a capital H."

Harlow snickered.

"Why would you be looking for work? Aren't you here just to take care of your dad?" Harley asked.

Harlow shrugged. "Mostly. And I'm here for whatever Tierney needs. Now that Dad has entertainment in the afternoons, I have free time. Might as well put it to good use."

"Man, I'd totally be napping by the pool every afternoon if I had free time," Harley said. "I thought your family was loaded and you didn't have to work."

"My dad is loaded. That doesn't mean I am."

Harper looked at her strangely but didn't say anything.

"We should meet at Buckeye Joe's one of these nights," Harley said. "We could pretend to be twins. Nothin' more fun than getting the local cowboys riled up."

"I thought you were engaged?" Harlow said.

"I am. Gets my man all riled up too." Harley winked. "Gotta love a man who'll come after you with everything he has."

Those words sent ice into Harlow's soul.

She backtracked to the door. "I'll think about it. Nice seeing both of you."

"Later, Harley," Harper teased.

Harlow walked down the deserted hallway. Only after she'd hit the sunshine and fresh air did she feel like she could breathe again. She slid down the metal door and sat on the concrete. Wrapping her arms around her shins, she pressed her forehead to her knees and inhaled several long breaths.

Why did everyone treat her like she was some kind of man-eater? Or a cocktease? Why did everyone look at her and assume she was a heartbreaker? That she'd somehow emasculate the guys she dated?

Her counselor's words echoed in her head: *You were a victim, Harlow. He preyed on you. Repeat after me: This is not my fault.*

As much as she didn't want to remember when Hugh had accused her of being a cocktease, she'd gladly revisit that memory if it knocked the other, uglier ones back down into the dark hole where they belonged. Her thoughts drifted to that scorching summer day when she'd finally stood up for herself . . .

⤸

Sweat trickled down her spine. She closed her eyes, trying to think cool thoughts as she fanned herself with a magazine. Why was her cabin so freakin' hot? She'd opened all the doors and windows, hoping to catch a breeze, because the wind always blew in Wyoming.

Except today.

"Harlow?" The voice that echoed through the screen door was guaranteed to heat her up.

"Come in. It's open, but I'll warn you it's hot as sin in here."

Hugh wandered in and stopped in the middle of the room. The big, bad cowboy looked wary. Like she might shed her clothes and attack him.

His sexy scowl and prim attitude annoyed her. She'd had enough of his hot and cold behavior. For the last two weeks after the Dumpster incident, she'd treated him politely but coolly whenever they'd crossed paths. She was tempted to ask, "What's brought you into the lair of the seductress? Aren't you worried about compromising your virtue?" Right. She defined *seductress* in her running shorts and a camisole. Instead, she cut to the chase. "Why are you here, Hugh?"

"I was sent to remind you there's a Split Rock shareholders' meeting in an hour."

"So? I'm not a shareholder."

"But you are a bartender. Renner wants you there."

So much for her day off. But at least the lounge was air-conditioned. "I'll be there."

Hugh looked around. "Why's it so damn hot in here?"

"Because I was practicing Bikram yoga."

He blinked at her.

"Sorry, I guess that's not a joke that a non-yogi would get. It's hot in here because the air conditioner crapped out."

"Did you call Dave?"

"Yes. Evidently it's supposed to be his day off too and he's in Rawlins with Yvette."

"He'd come back if you told him it's an emergency."

Harlow frowned at him. "But it's not an emergency. It's just hot."

"The hell it's not. You could roast marshmallows in here."

"It'll cool down when it gets dark."

"That's hours away." He sighed. "Fine. I'll take a look at it. Where's the mechanical room?"

She showed him to the tiny closet beside the back door.

With no time to wash her bartending uniform, she sprayed it with Febreze. She hung it by the front door. Too hot to change here; she'd get dressed at the lodge.

Feeling sluggish, she walked to the sink for a glass of water. All she'd managed to accomplish today was grocery shopping, since she'd gotten tired of living on peanut butter and celery the past two days. She wasn't thrilled working six days a week. After her former coworker Tanna had gone off to stage a comeback in her barrel-racing career, Harlow worried everyone had forgotten hawking clothing and slinging drinks at the Split Rock wasn't her chosen career. Just a pit stop.

Since Tierney had had no issues delivering Isabelle, and her mental well-being and physical health were excellent, Harlow wondered why she was still in Wyoming. She could pinpoint exactly when her restlessness had started: when Tanna finally wised up and let Fletch know how she felt about him. It'd driven home the point that Harlow wouldn't be so lucky to meet her soul mate here.

Heavy footsteps sounded behind her.

She spun away from the sink and faced Hugh. "Did you fix it?"

"It's beyond my repair skills. I did manage to shut off the hot air blasting from your fan, which was why it's so damn hot in here."

He'd ditched his long-sleeved shirt and wore a ribbed tank top that revealed an impressive amount of chest hair as well as his muscular arms. His skin glistened with sweat, which made the shirt stick to his spectacular pecs.

Hugh said "blah blah Freon" and "blah blah iced-over copper tubing," but Harlow had zeroed in on a smudge of grease on his belly that looked like an arrow pointing straight to the Promised Land.

The man was so yummy. She'd like to follow the rivulets of sweat down the front side of his body with her tongue. And then with her teeth.

When the silence registered, she looked up.

Hugh had propped his hands on his hips.

"Umm, sorry. What did you say?"

"I asked if you wanted me to drop my pants so you could get an eyeful of my junk, since you're standin' there licking your damn lips while lookin' at my crotch."

"I am?"

"Don't pretend you haven't been eye-fucking me since I walked in here." Then he loomed over her, his hands gripping her upper arms. "You get off on bein' a cocktease, don't you?"

Cocktease? Harlow wrenched herself from him. "If anyone is a cocktease, it's you."

That startled him. "How do you figure that?"

"You kissed me first."

"You were dirty dancing with me before that."

"Yeah? What about when you kissed me again?"

"That was a few weeks after you dropped your towel and bared your naked body to me, Harlow."

"And then you kissed me again."

Silence.

"That one was all on you. I did nothing to provoke you into kissing me with my evil temptress ways."

His jaw tightened. "Fuck."

"I liked it better when you were insulting me. At least I knew where I stood."

"I haven't done that since you first got here."

"Exactly. Now whenever we try to have a conversation, it ends up with you kissing me and running away. You've done that what? Three times now? I didn't ask you to come to my house. But you're here, with fewer clothes on than I've ever seen on you, so, yeah. You're built and I happen to like chest hair a lot. Big surprise I'm gonna look at you."

He said nothing.

"So here's what's gonna happen." She slid her hands up his muscled chest, stopping to sweep her thumbs over it before she curled her fingers around the back of his neck. "This time, I'm kissing you first."

She pulled his mouth down to hers. But she didn't devour him; she acted every bit the cocktease he accused her of being. She wet her lips and glided them across his. She placed a kiss on each corner of his mouth. Then when his mouth fell open slightly, she paused and let his breath mix with hers. Building up to the moment when her tongue darted in to lick the inside of his lower lip. Back and forth, deeper and deeper until she felt the scrape of his teeth on the bottom of her tongue. She did the same teasing maneuver on his upper lip, licking and teasing until he whispered, "That tickles."

"What about this?" She flicked her tongue in until it met his.

His answer was a deep groan.

That's when she gave in and kissed him with all she had. Dueling tongues, moans exchanged every time she changed the angle of her head to keep him guessing. To keep him chasing her mouth.

Hugh's hands were everywhere. One twined in her hair. The other squeezing her ass, then slipping around to grip her hip. Sweeping up the sides of her body before cupping her breast. Tweaking her nipple. Moving up to trace her collarbone, his fingertips lightly dusted over her bare shoulder. He switched hands, maintaining a firm grip on her hair, reversing his path down the other side.

Harlow imagined him dragging his lips down her body. His beard scraping against every inch of her skin.

The kiss slowed, almost to the point where it stopped completely, allowing them to gaze into each other's eyes. Then the greed rose again and they were lost in the wet heat of hungry mouths, shared breaths of explosive passion.

Her brain urged her to stop before she couldn't. She ripped her mouth free from his and took a step back.

His eyes were dark. His hands were clenched in fists at his sides. "What?"

"This time I kissed you first."

"I got that."

"Then get this." Harlow sidestepped him. "This time I'm the one who's running away first." She snagged her uniform off the door and walked out . . .

⁓

"Are you all right?"

Harlow's head snapped up and the memory vaporized.

Lela, from housekeeping, paused twenty feet down the sidewalk. "I'm fine," she lied, and forced a smile.

"It's really hot right here."

Harlow noticed both of Lela's hands gripped her purse straps in one place so she could use it as a weapon if she had to. Not a stranger to violence. "All the better to stew in my own juices."

Lela looked like she didn't know what that meant. "If you're sure you're all right, I'd probably better get."

"See you, Lela."

That surprised her. "You know my name?"

"Why wouldn't I?"

"Oh. I just thought . . ."

"Do you have me mixed up with Harley?"

"No." She blushed. "Sorry. Never mind."

"Did you assume I was a rich bitch who takes for granted the work you do?"

Her face turned even redder. "It—I—was wrong to assume. I mean, you've never been anything but nice to me, Harlow. I'm so sorry."

"No worries. I'm just trying to figure out what I've been labeled around here. See you tomorrow."

With a wave, Lela lumbered off.

Harlow figured if Tierney or Renner needed her, they would've called or texted. She cut down the hill and around the wall that kept the employees' quarters from view of the Split Rock's paying guests.

She walked the plank toward her trailer and stopped when she saw Tobin on his deck surrounded by a bunch of plastic boxes. "Hey."

He glanced up and smiled that knockout smile. "Hey, yourself."

"What're you doing?"

"Tomorrow is my day off and I'm goin' fishing."

"So this is all fishing stuff?"

"Yep. Rods. Reels. Hooks. Lures. A net. Knives. Pliers. I haven't picked up the bait yet."

"Do you fish from a boat? Or are you into fly-fishing?"

"I'm using a friend's boat. Too far to drive to get any fly-fishing in, but Bran Turner is takin' me the next time I have two days off in a row." He held something between his fingers that looked like a piece of fuzz. "This is a Turner fly. The craftsmanship is amazing."

Harlow made a noncommittal noise.

Tobin looked at her. "What're you up to?"

"Nothing much. Checked in with Wild West Clothiers. Chatted with Harley."

It was Tobin's turn to make a noncommittal noise.

"What?"

"Harley ain't my favorite person. She gives me a bad vibe." He shrugged. "I don't know how else to explain it."

"I don't know her, so it bugs me that apparently some people think we're interchangeable, since our names are similar as well as our appearances."

"You're not even close to interchangeable," Tobin muttered.

"So I'm not being overly sensitive about her comment that I'm loaded and don't need to work?"

"Nope. Dick comment and presumptuous on her part, which is typical for her."

She rested her shoulder on the side of the trailer. "I have to ask you something, Tobin, and I want you to be honest with me. Do I come off as spoiled and entitled?"

He appeared to weigh his answer. "Honestly? You did have 'rich girl' complaints—"

"Define 'rich girl' complaints."

Tobin scratched his jaw. "You talked about all the places you'd been and where you wanted to go next."

True, but they didn't know that when she was traveling, it was to spend time in the slums in India, Haiti and Rio.

"And you were pretty obsessed with Tierney's pregnancy, almost like you were jealous and wanted what she had." Tobin's green-eyed gaze hooked hers. "But I figured it was a sibling rivalry thing, since she was your sister."

"Nice save."

He laughed. "But in all seriousness, something has changed with you. You haven't started passing out pamphlets, so you haven't gotten religion or sober."

Harlow smirked. "Be a sad thing if I *hadn't* changed in the last three years."

"I hear ya. I'm getting stagnant after five years at the Split Rock. The cattle business is making money and Renner is real good about spreading that around. But I'm still livin' in the same dumpy trailer. Still hitting the bar with the few of us guys that're single."

"You're still at the Mud Lilies' beck and call."

"Yep. What's it say about me that I'd rather hang out with them gals than women in my generation?"

It says you're a sweet, thoughtful guy and I could've saved myself a world of hurt if

I'd done the smart thing and fallen for you. "I don't imagine there are many women your age around here."

"The downside of livin' in the least populated state in the country," he said dryly. "But what do I have to offer a woman anyway? I don't have a house, or even land to promise to build a house on."

"That stuff—or maybe I should say the *lack* of that stuff—shouldn't matter to a woman who wants to be with you. You should be enough."

"It matters to me, though." Tobin refocused on the fly tie. "So the short answer to your question is no. I don't think you act entitled. Anyone who says that is making snap judgments." He paused. "Especially women like Harley who say shit outta pure jealousy."

Seriously no love lost for her.

"Did Miz Maybelle show up today to visit with your dad?"

Her eyes narrowed. "How did you know about that?"

Tobin looked up and grinned. "Hugh dragged me along to the Buckeye for moral support when he asked for the Mud Lilies' help."

"He asked all of the Mud Lilies?"

"Yep. And they all agreed. Yet, you don't look as happy about that as I thought you'd be."

"I was thinkin' the same thing," Hugh drawled behind her.

Her heart jumped into her throat and she whirled around. How had the big man with the loud boots snuck up on them? "I'm not unhappy. Just surprised."

His eyes cut to Tobin. "Mind if I steal her for a bit?"

Tobin looked at Harlow in silent question. Then whatever he saw in her eyes had him say, "Fine by me. I need to get on the road anyway if I wanna make camp before dark."

"You're leaving tonight?"

"Gonna take full advantage of my day off."

"Have fun. And thanks for . . ."

He smiled. "Anytime, Harlow."

She started toward her trailer, two doors down from Tobin's. She dug her key out of her pocket and unlocked the door.

Hugh followed her in. He gave a quick look around. "Hasn't changed since I lived here."

"I'm not exactly the 'add homey touches' type, since I don't plan on staying long."

"You'll be here long enough to fulfill your end of the deal. Which was *anything I want*."

"Anything within reason," Harlow amended.

"Meaning what?"

"Meaning I won't drop to my knees right now and give you a blow job." His neck flushed red. "I wouldn't squander my *anything* option on that."

"I was such a bad lay last time, you assume I don't give very good head either?"

Hugh stalked closer. "What makes you think you were a bad lay?"

"I don't know. Maybe the way you couldn't get your pants on fast enough after you finished fucking me? Or maybe it was the look of disgust you leveled on every naked inch of me as you slipped on your boots." She paused, hating how her stomach roiled. "Oh right, it was when you said nailing me was a big mistake that wasn't ever happening again."

He dropped his gaze to the floor. "I was an ass."

"No, Hugh, you were a soul crusher," she said softly.

His head snapped up.

"And don't look at me like you aren't fully aware that those harsh words were what sent me packing."

"I'm aware of the nasty shit I spewed, Harlow. Fully aware. I wish I could take back every word. I've wished that for three goddamned years. I swear I thought you'd come back or I never would've left things the way they were."

"When and why would I have come back here?"

"For Isabelle's first Christmas."

"Our family has never been big on holidays." Why was she explaining all this to him? "It doesn't matter now."

"It does matter," he insisted.

"Why? To alleviate your guilt?"

"Nothin' will ever alleviate the guilt." His eyes searched hers. "I left you a voice mail."

"Four months after I left."

"That's when I learned you wouldn't be coming here for the holidays. But it don't change the fact that I reached out to you."

"And what an earth-shattering voice mail it was. *Shit, Harlow, I'm sorry. I fucked up. Come back.*"

Two dots of color bloomed on his cheeks. "I said what I needed to. And it must've stayed with you, because you can still recite it, word for word, years later."

"I can remember it because the entire message, Hugh, was under ten words." She covered her face with her hands and remained that way for several breaths before she looked up at him. "What did you think would happen with that single voice mail?"

"That we could start talkin' again. Like we did before that night went to hell."

"So you called me because you wanted us to be friends?"

He shook his head. The heat in his eyes . . . Dammit. She shouldn't recognize it, to say nothing of feeling the flutter in her belly at seeing it.

"What about now? You want to be friends now?"

"No. It seems you expect me to leave you be. I'm not doin' that. No way, no how."

In all of his explaining, she had yet to hear an apology from him. Then he said, "I'm sorry. Really sorry. It was embarrassing to realize I'd picked up that kind of nastiness from my ex. I was so ashamed of how I acted and what I said. I still am." He paused. "Is there any chance you'll forgive me?"

They stared at each other until Harlow looked away. She didn't answer because once again Hugh had confused the hell out of her. So she did the mature thing and changed the subject. "It might've been a little misleading when I said I'd do anything if you could find female visitors for my dad."

"You only said that because you doubted I could deliver."

"Yes, but you did deliver and I'm grateful. So I'll uphold my end of the deal, but within much narrower parameters than you might be expecting."

"More narrow than I just want to cook you supper and hear everything you've been up to in the last three years?"

"That's it?" she asked skeptically.

Those dark brown eyes read *For now*, but he said, "Yeah. That's it."

Say no.

"Fine." Dammit. Why was her mouth doing the opposite of what her head told her to do?

"Good. Then dinner at my place tomorrow night. Around seven?"

"Don't forget I'm a vegetarian."

"I remember. And I've been watching you for two weeks just to make sure."

"Sounds creepy."

He smiled. "Maybe it is. It'll be creepier yet when I admit I've been planning this for three years." He stepped forward and kissed her forehead. "So I'm really lookin' forward to dinner."

He walked out.

Harlow wondered when she'd lost the upper hand. But the biggest part of her feared she'd never had it in the first place.

Chapter Eight

*T*hree raps sounded on his door.

Hugh wiped his hands on the dish towel and exhaled a long breath. He ran his hand over his hair. No hat to hide under tonight.

Nerves will get the best of you if you let 'em. Take the bull by the horns and do what needs done.

He opened the door.

The early evening sun backlit Harlow, dressed in a long white skirt that hugged every curve. A gold-and-white top left her shoulders bare.

"Hugh? Can I come in?"

"Sure. Just stunned by how angelic you look."

"That almost sounded like a cowboy sweet-talkin'."

"You sound skeptical, sweetheart."

Harlow patted his cheek. "That's because I am." She brushed past him close enough that he caught a lungful of her perfume.

He followed her, enjoying how her ass swayed in that clingy material.

She spun around abruptly and caught him staring. But she didn't rip into him with her usual feminist indignation and he swore she could practically read his thoughts.

Yeah, I know you're more than sexy curves and soft womanly parts. But I'd be doin' you a disservice if I didn't show my male admiration for those attributes that make you so beautifully female.

Hugh smiled. "Like I said. You're lookin' good. Can I getcha something to drink?"

"Do you have white wine?"

He didn't know fuck all about wine, except that Harlow used to drink it, so he'd asked the cashier in the liquor department for a decent bottle of red and one of white. "There's a bottle of each in the fridge, so go ahead and open the one you want."

"Are you having some?"

"Nah. I'll stick to beer." He pointed to the lone wineglass on the counter. "I think that glass is yours anyway. It was in the cupboard when I moved in."

"It'd be Tierney's. I've never owned any wineglasses. If there were kitchen things left, they were hers too, not mine. I've never seen the need to haul all that kinda crap along with me, since I move so often."

"You don't have a place in Chicago that serves as your base to return to, since that's your hometown?"

"No. After I went to college, Dad moved out of the apartment I grew up in. When I came back to town, which wasn't often, I stayed with Tierney. Then she left, so I was pretty much homeless." She sipped her wine. "Why'd you buy this place?"

"It's convenient. I spend enough time outside that I don't wanna do yard work. Dave maintains this outside so it blends in with the rest of the buildings around the lodge. The size is perfect. I don't need much space." He popped the top on his bottle of Budweiser.

"What's that scowling face for?"

"Thinking about my ex-wife. She never would've lived in a place like this."

Harlow looked around and smiled. "Too bad. It's so homey. Although I admit I wish you would've kept the wallpaper."

"Did you put your stamp in here someplace?"

"Just one thing."

"What?"

She laughed. "Not telling you because you'll think it's stupid. You probably already tore it down."

"Show me."

With a smirk on her lips, she spun around. Her flip-flops smacked against her heels as she walked into the bedroom. She flicked on the lights and stopped at the edge of the king-sized bed before she looked up. "The hook is still there."

"The canopy was your doing?"

"My one princessy thing." She cocked her head. "I imagine you don't believe that, so I'll say I was used to living under mosquito netting and it made me feel safe. Did you check the drawers for a tiara after you moved in?"

Hugh got toe-to-toe with her. "No. But I was hopin' to find a pair of your lacy drawers in the drawers. Does that count?"

"In your dreams, cowboy." She put her hands on his chest and pushed him. "How did we end up in your bedroom first thing?"

"Just lucky, I guess." Since she'd touched him first, he took that as a sign touching was okay. He curled his hand beneath her jaw and tilted her face up. He just stared at her. A challenge was there in her blue eyes. Her soft pink lips parted. In anticipation?

She said, "Don't make a big production out of it."

"Out of what?"

"Kissing me. Just do it. That's what you're waiting for, isn't it?"

Hugh angled his head closer. And closer. Until their breath mingled. "Just want to get it over with?" He barely brushed his lips over hers and he felt hers tremble. "Fast and hard, in a burst of passion, and then it's done? Kinda like the night we fucked?"

"You consumed me that night, Hugh." Her soft exhalation drifted into his mouth and he could almost taste her. "You devoured me and then spit me out when you'd had enough."

"I'll never get enough of you, Harlow. I knew it then. I know it now. So if you want me to devour you this time, say the word."

"What word?" she murmured against the corner of his mouth.

"Please." He pressed a full-on kiss to her lips. "Devour." Another longer mouth-on-mouth connection. "Me."

"Yes. Please devour me."

He planted his mouth on hers fully and settled in.

Kissing Harlow was a fucking benediction.

He'd never appreciated the power of a kiss—even when he had kissed her before, it had never been like this. Not with the conviction of a man who knew what he wanted.

More than just one kiss. More than just one night.

Harlow's fingers flexed into his chest.

He bit back a growl at how quickly her flesh yielded to his as he adjusted her head to dive ever deeper into her succulent mouth.

That's when she pulled away.

And he let her—after he pressed his mouth to hers one last time for a soft kiss before leading her out of the room. "Hungry?"

"Starved." She paused. "What did you cook?"

"Grilled portobello mushrooms, baked potatoes and a tomato salad." Hugh glanced at her over his shoulder. "All vegetarian."

"Will they revoke your membership to the cattlemen's club for making a meatless meal?"

"I never considered that. Guess it'll have to be our little secret, doll."

"I guess so." She picked up her wineglass.

"Have a seat."

Hugh loaded the food on the table and sat across from her.

"Why don't I know if you're a good cook?"

"You worried?"

Her noncommittal shrug made him laugh.

"I ain't a bad cook. It wasn't my own cooking that turned me into a lard ass, though. It was bein' on the road, eating fried food three meals a day."

"So it wasn't you eating your troubles away after your divorce that packed on the pounds?"

"Nope. That's when I finally lost the weight. The irony isn't lost on me either," he said dryly.

Harlow filled her plate and waited while Hugh did the same.

After she praised the food and they ate in silence for a while, she broke it. "So, Hugh. What do you do for fun?"

He chewed a bite of the grilled mushroom. Not bad, but he wished it were a filet. "Checking to see if I've changed my boring ways?"

"You still bothered by my 'You wouldn't know fun if it bit you on the ass' comment from when we first met?"

"Mostly it bothered me because it was true. It still is to some extent."

"Why's that?"

"I work ten to twelve hours a day. When I have a day off, I hang around here anyway. Damn good thing Tobin and I get along so well." He took a drink of beer. "We joke that we're married to the job, which practically makes us married to each other. God knows we spend more time together than most married couples."

"Which means you don't want to hang out with Tobin after the workday ends."

"Him'n me and Ike and Holt are the only single ones left in our group. Holt is working all over the state. Ike's a local, so he has family around here. Which leaves . . . me'n Tobin."

"Are you regretting moving away from your friends and family? It's a pretty isolated existence."

"That's part of the reason why my wife is now my ex-wife. The isolation would've made her crazier yet. Her idea of hell was livin' in the middle of nowhere, bein' away from friends and shopping."

"And your idea of hell?"

Hugh looked at her. "Talking about my ex-wife with a beautiful woman I'm havin' dinner with." His gaze dropped to her plate and he was surprised to see it was empty. He still had half his food. Jesus. Had he been yammering on that much?

Harlow's fingers brushed his forearm. "The meal was so good I'm afraid I ate like I'd never seen food before. Thank you."

That gentle stroking on his arm was unconsciously erotic. He lowered his head, hiding his eyes so she couldn't see how deeply her simple touch affected him. He mumbled, "You're welcome."

Then the warmth of her hand was gone. "If you don't eat up, I might just finish yours too."

"Then you might not have room for dessert."

"There's dessert?"

He looked up. "Yep."

"What is it?"

"A surprise."

A funny look crossed her face.

"What?"

"Why are you being so . . . ?"

"So what, darlin'?"

"Charming."

Hugh leaned over the table. "The first time around, you musta missed out on the fact that I *am* charming. So I'm just showing you what's always been there." He picked up her hand and brushed his mouth across her knuckles. "I'll give it to you straight. I wanna spend time with you for as long as you're here."

"Why?"

She really wasn't going to make this easy on him.

It's no less than what you deserve for how you treated her last time.

"Because there's always been something between us. Even when one of us didn't want to own up to it. I let my fear get the best of me three years ago, Harlow. I screwed up with you." He felt heat creeping up his neck. "When I think back to how I acted like an eight-year-old boy, saying stupid, mean shit . . . only way it could've been more obvious that I liked you was if I'da yanked on your ponytail or pushed you in the mud."

Harlow's lips curved. "Renner did that to Tierney when she first came here to oversee things. It's more like she fell in the mud after he scared her, but she ended up in a puddle in one of her fancy suits."

"So you saying if I would've pushed you in the pool that night I caught you skinny-dippin' . . . ?"

"I would've held on to you for all I was worth and dragged you under with me."

He swept his thumb over the inside of her wrist. "I wouldn't have put up much resistance. A hot, naked woman squirming against my wet body? That's my idea of heaven."

"I'm not going to sleep with you tonight," she blurted out.

Hugh couldn't help but grin. "Damn. There goes my dessert plan. Now I'll have to rustle up ice cream."

"Eat your dinner, cowboy, and stop thinking about eating me."

Oh, hell yeah. His dick stirred at the prospect of that. "Sorry, but I can't stop thinking about tasting those sweet lips."

Her baby blues flashed when she realized what lips he meant.

So he pushed his luck a little. Bringing her hand to his mouth, he kissed the base of her knuckles between her index and middle fingers. Then locking his heated gaze to hers, he pushed the tip of his tongue through the split V of her fingers. Flicking his tongue in and out, back and forth. Licking softly. Then gently nibbling.

"You're pulling out all the stops, aren't you?"

"Yeah, darlin', I am. I've been waiting to get the chance to make it up to you." He nipped at the fleshy skin between her thumb and index finger. "But if you're still leery, then I can pull back and let the heat smolder a little longer until we're ready to combust. I want you to trust me. And I want you to know that I won't run scared this time."

Harlow's other hand shook when she picked up her wineglass. After draining the pale liquid, she peered at him over the rim. "And if I said 'Get over here, push my dress up and put that sweet-talkin' mouth between my thighs' . . . ?"

"I'd get fabric burns from my jeans I'd be on my knees so damn fast."

She laughed. "Just checking."

He shoveled in the rest of his food without tasting it. Then he cleared the plates and grabbed the bottle of wine. "More?"

"No thanks."

"Did it suck?"

"Not at all. But since Tierney is ready to pop and I'm on tap for Isabelle duty, I limit myself to one glass."

"I know the circumstances ain't been ideal, but it's a huge load off Renner's mind that you're here to take care of the precious."

"Yes, it's a shame the darling little girl suffers from lack of attention." She slid her chair back. "I need to move around before the food and wine make me sleepy."

"I have to head down to the barn."

"Okay. Then I'll just go back to my trailer and let you—"

Hugh pressed his mouth to hers to keep her from babbling. "I wasn't tryin' to get rid of you. I want you to come with me."

"Okay." She shoved her cell phone in the pocket of her skirt.

He opened the door for her and followed her out.

The evening air held a chill and his gaze moved over Harlow's bare arms. "Did you bring a coat?"

"No. I'm fine. I've always been hot-blooded." The instant she said it, she amended, "Not that way."

"I beg to differ." He clasped her hand in his, and pulled her arm against his body. "Rocks are slippery in them kinda shoes."

Harlow stopped and stared at the sign:

NO RESORT GUESTS BEYOND THIS POINT

"Has there been a problem with unauthorized guests?"

"There was before we put the sign up. Lots of people think the barn is some kinda petting zoo."

She gasped dramatically. "It's not? Then I'm leaving right now. You know how much I love feeling bunny fur."

"As long as it's still attached to the bunny," Hugh said dryly. He pushed open the barn door and towed her inside.

Her nose wrinkled, but she didn't comment.

He'd been around these scents for so long the smell didn't even register with him. He led her down the center of the barn, keeping a tight grip on her hand.

"I'm surprised there's still a dirt floor in here. I'd expect a fancy operation like this to have upgraded to concrete."

"Fancy operation?" he repeated.

"In the countries I've worked in, everyone was a farmer or involved in agriculture in some way. The shelters they built to protect their animals had palm-thatched roofs, support poles made out of whatever they could scrounge up and dirt floors."

"Ah." Hugh scraped his boot across the dirt. "This whole area is almost solid rock beneath us. The contractor had to use dynamite to get down far enough to set the footings. The lodge is built on the one section of the land that was level and had the least amount of dirt work. So when building the barns, Renner chose metal over traditional wood, because metal can withstand the drastic shifts in temperature. The ground is a living thing, and keeping the flooring dirt is better for the animals too, because that's what they're used to in the field."

Harlow looked thoughtful. "So the people in the Third World countries aren't behind the times as much as we'd imagined."

"Nope. By and large dirt is best." He glanced down at her bare toes peeking out from beneath her long skirt. "But dirt is hell on manicures."

"Pedicures," she corrected. "But since I prefer to go barefoot whenever possible, a little dirt don't hurt."

Hugh recognized that she'd mimicked him, but it didn't bother him. He bent down and kissed her soundly right on her smirking mouth. When he pulled back, he saw her eyes were shining with pleasure.

She reached up and touched his beard. "It's softer than I remember. Have you always had this?"

"I'd originally started growing it to hide the weight I'd put on. After I lost the weight, I kept it." He captured her hand with his and kissed the center of her palm. Then he resumed the leisurely stroll.

Harlow was craning her neck to see inside the pens. "Where are all the animals?"

"We don't have any right now that need doctoring. A couple of heifers got into the bull's pasture and will calve out of season that we're keeping an eye on."

"So no baby horses?"

"Not this year. Tobin's been wanting to breed Dream Killer, since she's a helluva bucker. But he's waiting to see what Renner does with the rodeo stock contracting side, since she's one of the reasons we get rodeo contracts."

"What's the other reason?"

"BB, our bull."

She laughed. "The one that Tierney stole?"

"Jesus. Your sister was crazy to do that. But it was goddamned funny."

"She's always had a better sense of humor than people have given her credit for." Harlow shot him a sideways glance. "I suspect people who know you say the same thing about you."

Hugh shrugged.

"What's that?" She pointed to a closed door in the far back corner.

"Tack room."

When he opened the door, she said, "No one locks their doors around here. I find that really bizarre."

"Says the girl from Chicago."

"Theft happens outside of big cities." Harlow walked into the room. "I'd think with all these saddles and other leather stuff you'd want to lock it up." She wandered to the workbench and tilted her head to look up at the rafters. "I love the scent of leather."

Right then, all the warm, happy feelings he'd had since she'd shown up on his doorstep tonight shifted into lust. Especially seeing the material of her skirt clinging to every curve, her long hair playing peekaboo with the smooth skin of her bare shoulder. He moved in behind her and curled his hands around her hips, pressing his lips to the ball of her shoulder. "Fuck, woman. I'm tryin' really hard to take this slow."

She turned her head, rubbing her cheek against his. "But?"

The warm, earthy scent of her landed another shot of lust straight to his dick. "But I wanna hoist you up on that bench, push your skirt up and eat my dessert."

Her lips grazed his ear. "So do it. Show me what you've been fantasizing about doing to me for the last three years. And you'd better make it good."

A challenge? He could work with that. He nudged her head to the side, demanding access to her neck. The heat of her skin warmed his lips. The taste of her, the scent of her, intoxicated him. He slid his right hand down and cupped her pussy through the clingy fabric of her skirt, gliding his middle finger over her slit. "I want you wet when I taste you." He nipped her earlobe. "So wet that your juices coat my face and your sweet honey runs down my throat." He nuzzled the slope of her shoulder, letting his soft facial hair follow in the wake of his mouth. "So wet, when I wake up, I still have the scent of your pussy on my beard."

"When you talk like that . . ." She shivered when he blew in her ear.

"Turn around and gimme that mouth."

Harlow wheeled around so fast his teeth nearly smacked into her forehead. But then her arms were wreathed around his neck as she pulled his head down for a ravenous kiss.

He detected a hint of wine as their tongues swirled and stroked. She pressed her pelvis into his, rubbing against his cock. If he hadn't already been as hard as a two-by-four, that sexy little test to gauge his reaction to her would've given him wood. Iron wood.

Hugh propelled her backward until her butt met the workbench. He ripped his mouth from hers, clamped his hands on her hips and lifted her onto the metal surface.

"Oh. That's cold."

"This hot ass of yours will warm it right up." He dropped to his knees. Fisting the hem of her skirt in his hands, he pushed the material up her legs until it was ruched at her hips. Her panties were a thin strip of white fabric that he wanted to tear off with his teeth, but he tugged them aside. "Arms behind you and spread your legs."

She widened her knees, but she kept one hand on his head.

Hugh looked at her. "Think you'll need to direct me, darlin'?"

"No. But I want to touch you."

"Fine, but keep that hand outta my way or I'll break out the ropes." He angled his head toward the wall. "Plenty to choose from."

Interest flared in her eyes.

His hands were so large and her hips so narrow that he could open the glistening pink flesh of her sex with his thumbs and still palm the curve of her ass.

He placed a kiss on the soft blond hair running in a small strip down her mound, taking a moment to just breathe in the musk and sweet scent of her. Then his tongue darted out to tickle her clit before following the split of her sex to the warm, wet opening to her body.

She released a soft sigh.

Jesus. Her cunt had a citrusy tang. He wanted to fucking *bathe* in her juices and found himself growling against the heated core of her. Licking. Lapping. Sucking. Gliding his tongue through her folds. Suckling her pussy lips. Then starting over again from the top.

Harlow's breathing changed to short, fast pants, but besides that, she didn't make any noise.

But he knew by the way her hand clenched in his hair and how her thighs quivered that he was getting to her.

God knew she—this—was getting to him. His skin was damp. His cock dug into his zipper. He flexed his fingers against the lush flesh of her ass, his heart beating double time as he drove her toward that apex of pleasure.

She yanked his hair hard as she started to come.

Her soft, breathy "yes, yes, yes" spurred him to keep going after the last pulse faded. "One more, doll. I wanna feel you come on my tongue."

A groan echoed above him, followed by a resounding sigh.

He chuckled against her moist flesh. That put-upon sigh didn't ring true and she knew it. Was she trying to save face for being so responsive to him?

Too. Fucking. Bad. He'd enjoy every moment of making this woman come apart. He didn't tease or drag it out. As soon as she could take direct contact on her clit, he focused on that swollen pearl, priming it, plumping it. Flicking his tongue over it until she detonated.

When she absentmindedly patted his head, he dragged openmouthed kisses away from her wet sex.

He nuzzled the insides of her thighs as she floated down from her second orgasm.

When Harlow didn't speak, he looked up at her, her head angled back and a secretive smile on her lips.

"You okay?"

"Better than okay."

Hugh rolled to his feet and placed a possessive kiss on the side of her neck. He set his teeth on the cord that met the strong edge of her jaw.

A buzzing sensation vibrated beside his wrist.

"Hang on," she said in a throaty rasp. She dug through the fabric of her skirt until she came up with her phone. "Hey, what's up?"

He backed off when her body tensed.

"Of course I'm ready. I'll grab my bag and be right there." She set the phone down and touched his face. "Tierney's water broke, so I have to go."

His eyes searched hers. "You don't seem happy about that."

"I am. It's just . . ." She blew out a long breath. "I know Tierney's been through childbirth before, but so had our mother. Her complications didn't manifest until two months later. By then it was too late. I know medicine has come a long way in three decades, but I worry about her just as much now as I did last time. I stuck around for two months after Isabelle was born just to make sure she didn't . . ."

Then it clicked with him. He'd overheard part of her conversation with Tobin when he said she seemed a little obsessed with Tierney's previous pregnancy. "That's what never made sense to me before. Why you were here. Your dad didn't cut you off. You just told Tierney that so she'd offer you a job. That way you could keep an eye on her."

"Yes. This time Dad said he'd stay here. Evidently my mom had an early labor with me and he thought Tierney might follow the same pattern when they put her on bed rest. Thank goodness she didn't and I hope . . ."

I hope you stick around an extra two months this time too.

Selfish? Yep.

"Your worries are understandable." Hugh straightened her skirt and kissed her forehead. "You want me to take you to their house?"

"Thanks, but I'll drive. It's not like Dad will need the car."

Just as Hugh moved to help her down, she leaned in and kissed him in a friendly peck. "Thank you for a great night, Hugh."

Feeling dismissed, he managed, "Anytime."

Chapter Nine

*T*he next afternoon, Harlow was seriously dragging ass.

Isabelle had been sound asleep when she'd arrived at the Jackson house. But Harlow hadn't slept at all until Renner called with the news of Rhett Jackson's arrival into the world and that mama and baby boy were doing well.

The phone call had woken Isabelle and she'd insisted that Aunt Harlow sleep in her bed. It'd taken multiple stories to get the little girl to fall asleep.

Then Isabelle had woken up out of sorts because neither Mommy nor Daddy was around. It'd been a rough morning with tantrums and constant repetition of the word *no*.

For a change of scenery, Harlow drove to the Split Rock to check on her dad.

While Isabelle and Grandpa played Go Fish, Harlow snuggled into the plush chair. The TV droning in the background served as the perfect white noise and Harlow fell asleep.

A little finger poking her arm jolted her back to awareness. "What?"

"You snore like a bear, Aunt Harlow."

She smoothed Isabelle's curls. The sweet angel's eyelids were drooping. "Whatcha need, bug?"

"Cookies."

Right. Isabelle needed a nap. But maybe Harlow could sneak a cup of coffee while she searched for cookies. She pushed herself out of the chair and when her cell phone buzzed, she opened the picture message from Renner. Her heart melted and her eyes misted at seeing her sister's big grin as she cuddled her red-faced baby.

"What is it?" her dad asked sharply.

"A picture of your daughter and your grandson." Harlow walked over to the bed and handed him the phone.

Her dad's eyes were a bit watery. "She looks good," he said softly. "Happy. Healthy." He looked up at Harlow. "She called me this morning to assure me everything had gone fine."

Harlow squeezed her dad's forearm. "I'm glad. I don't suppose you slept any better last night than I did."

He shook his head.

"I wanna see!" Isabelle said.

"It's a picture of your mommy and your baby brother, Rhett."

Isabelle squinted at the image. But she didn't say anything. She just stared and then yawned so widely her face disappeared.

"You look tired, Isabelle."

"No! I wanna watch cartoons."

"Crawl up here and we'll watch *Dora*," her dad said, without missing a beat. Which shocked Harlow, quite frankly, his being attuned to his granddaughter when he'd never been that way with either of his daughters.

Take it for what it is: a sign people can change.

After settling Isabelle with her blanket and adding a protective layer between the squirmy three-year-old and her father's incision, Harlow returned to the chair. What were the chances she'd fall back asleep? Slim. So once Isabelle and her dad were both sawing logs, she quietly left the room.

She popped into housekeeping to tell Lela and Yvette to wait until later to tidy up her dad's room. Of course they wanted the details on Tierney's baby, so she ended up staying longer than she'd intended. On her way to the kitchen, she ran into Hugh.

Those brown eyes of his lit up at seeing her. He quickly dragged her around the corner, backed her against the wall and kissed the holy hell out of her.

The man kissed her with such a sense of . . . need. Every time he put his mouth on hers, he kissed her as if he might not get another chance, so he'd make every kiss count.

He pulled back and smiled. "Hey."

"That was a pretty nice *hey*."

"Been thinkin' about you." He adjusted his stance and lowered his head, running his lips down her neck from her ear to her collarbone. "Wanting you. Fuck, woman, I want you."

The gruffness of his words was in direct contrast to the soft puffs of breath against her skin. She flattened her palms on his chest and pushed him back. "Hugh. Stop mauling me in public."

"You'd prefer I do it in private?"

"No. I prefer you don't do it at all, especially not right now."

He stiffened but gave her some space.

Harlow started to walk away, but he snagged her hand, pulling her back. "What is goin' on with you?"

"What is going on with *you*?" she retorted. "We had one date and you think that entitles you to act like we're together?"

His nostrils flared as he gifted her with a head-to-toe inspection. "I told you I wasn't gonna hide that we're involved this time."

"Oh, so I don't get a say?"

"What's that supposed to mean?"

"You fucked me and dumped me last time. So if we do get involved, maybe I don't want anyone to know this is just us hooking up."

Hugh loomed over her. "No."

"Excuse me?"

"I said no, Harlow. It'll be more than a fucking *hookup* between us."

She stood on tiptoe and got right in his face. "No, it won't be. In fact, it won't be a problem, since there won't be hooking up of any kind between us."

Before he could put that magic mouth on her and try to convince her otherwise, she backed up, sidestepped him and hustled away. She had no idea where she was going except away from him.

Then she heard, "Harlow. Over here."

She stopped and saw Janie Lawson, Harper Turner and Lainie Lawson standing together in the middle of the great room. She wandered over.

"We were just talking about you," Janie said.

"What did I do now?" She had a moment of panic. Had they seen Hugh drag her around the corner?

"Oh, pooh, don't be paranoid," Harper said. "We know that you took care of Isabelle last night, but we thought it might be better if the three of us take turns watching her."

"Isabelle loves playing with the boys," Janie said. "I'm done for the day, so I could take her with me, and Renner could pick her up later tonight on his way home from the hospital."

"But—"

"And since Harley is opening tomorrow, I'll be home with my boys, so Renner could drop her off at our place in the morning when he's on his way back to the hospital," Harper said.

Harlow looked between the three of them. Did they think she was incapable of taking care of her own niece for a couple of days? God. Clearly they had a high opinion of her.

Lainie set her hand on Harlow's shoulder. "We all know how trying it can be to take care of a three-year-old—the terrible twos have nothing on willful three-year-olds."

"Amen to that," Janie said.

"Brianna loves having another girl to play with, so tomorrow afternoon when Harper goes in to work, she can leave Isabelle with me. That way you can do whatever you've been doing in the afternoons and we'll take care of Isabelle."

Whatever I've been doing in the afternoons?

Did these women really have no idea she'd been happily spending as much time as possible with her only niece? Did everyone think she was some flighty girl that flitted from flower to flower and shirked adult responsibilities?

"Enough," Renner called out, startling all of them. He moseyed over and pointed at Janie, Harper and Lainie. "I'm gone one goddamned day and the three of you decide to take over my daughter's childcare schedule?"

Harlow froze.

"Well, we thought Tierney would prefer—"

"Tierney made her preferences clear to me and to Harlow. Harlow is taking care of Isabelle. Period. And if you think different arrangements needed to be made, then you take it up with me, since I'm Isabelle's father. You don't just decide you know what's best for my kid. And you all know how pissed off you'd be if someone did that to you."

All three women had the grace to look abashed.

"I trust Harlow with Isabelle. Tierney trusts Harlow with Isabelle. Just because Harlow don't have kids of her own don't mean she don't know kids." He snorted. "Any of you aware that Harlow worked in an orphanage in Croatia for six months? She was in charge of eighteen kids, not just for a few hours a day, but twenty-four hours a day."

It shocked her that Renner sounded *proud* of her.

"We made a decision to keep the interruptions in Isabelle's life at a minimum, which means she stays at home in familiar surroundings, 'cause god knows her little world will be turned upside down when we bring Rhett home."

"I'm sorry," Harper said softly. "I was just trying to help."

"We all were," Janie added.

"Without bein' a dick, if we want additional help, we'll ask for it."

"Understood." Lainie offered a small smile. "Sorry, Harlow. I didn't mean to question your abilities."

Renner flung his arm over Harlow's shoulder. "Come on and take me to my girlie. Her mama and I are missing her something fierce."

She steered him down the hallway toward her father's room. "Thank you. I know it might've looked as if they were railroading me, but I promise I'd never allow any changes to Isabelle's schedule without talking to you and Tierney first. I was just trying to come up with a more polite way to tell them to back off than telling them to fuck off."

Renner chuckled. "I know that. But it pissed me off to see them bein' their usual pushy-ass selves. I love it on the business side, but when it comes to seein' them do it to my family? Not so much. I'm sure they meant well, because they're all caring women, but their execution left a lot to be desired, huh?"

"Yeah."

"How was my baby girl last night?"

"Restless. I ended up sleeping in her bed. Then she was up early. She had a meltdown before lunch, but I attribute it to her being tired. We came to visit Grandpa. She curled up with him to watch cartoons and conked right out. It's been an hour since I left the two of them. I was about to head back to check on them when I was waylaid by the tiger moms."

Renner stopped outside the door and ran his hand through his hair.

"How are *you* doing, Daddy?"

"Tired as hell." He smiled. "But I haven't been lugging a baby in my belly the last nine months, so I ain't complaining none, because Tierney is the one who has that right."

"So everything went okay?"

He rolled up his shirtsleeves. He had finger-shaped bruises on both of his forearms. "No nail gouges or scratch marks this time for me. It went faster for her, but she had back labor for half of it, so she was in a lot of pain." He briefly closed his eyes. "It fuckin' killed me to see her like that. Even knowing she'd gone through this before, I just felt so damn helpless watching her go through it again."

Harlow's heart seized at hearing the distress in her brother-in-law's voice.

"But then, immediately after she pushed our son out, she was fine. Fine," he repeated, as if trying to convince himself. He looked at her. "She's an amazing woman and I'm the luckiest man in the world."

She threw herself into his arms and hugged him tightly. "I'm so glad Tierney found you, Renner. You've given her everything in life she's ever wanted."

He patted her back. "Thanks, Harlow. And no offense, but I'm already dealing with a hormonal wife and a distressed daughter. I need you to be the one female in my world to stay on an even keel, okay?"

She nodded.

"So before we see if Goldilocks and Papa Bear have awoken, let's go over the plan for the rest of today."

"Hit me."

"I know you're dyin' to see the baby, so I thought if you wanna head into town and spend time with Tierney and Rhett in a bit, I'll do daddy-and-daughter stuff with Isa. Then I'll bring her back into town with me so she can meet her baby brother and see her mama."

"Then what?"

"If you wouldn't mind hanging around in town while Isa's visiting the hospital, when we're done, you can pick her up and come home with her. Feed her, bathe her and tuck her in. I'll be home later tonight."

"You're not staying in the hospital?"

Renner shook his head. "Tierney won't rest if I'm there and she needs it. I've got stuff to handle around here in the morning, but I can bring Isabelle with me. They're planning to release Tierney and Rhett late tomorrow afternoon." He glanced over his shoulder. "But we're keeping that on the down low to give Tierney time to settle in at home before people start dropping by."

Harlow remembered after Isabelle's birth a steady stream of well-wishers showed up at Renner and Tierney's place, adding to their happiness but also to their exhaustion. "Sounds like a plan." She rubbed her hands together. "I can't wait to get my hands on that baby boy."

"I figured." Renner knocked twice before he opened the door to Gene Pratt's room.

"Daddy!" Isabelle shrieked, and started to launch herself off the bed.

Renner raced to catch her. "Whoa there, be careful," he said, scooping her into his arms. "I'm taking you to visit Mama in the hospital and we don't need a trip to the ER beforehand."

Isabelle placed her hands on her daddy's cheeks. "I missed you."

"I missed you too, baby girl."

"You didn't make me waffles today."

"Waffles tomorrow morning, I promise." He kissed her forehead and nuzzled her blond curls.

"With whipped cream and sprinkles?" Isabelle pressed.

"As many sprinkles as you wanna dump on. You just can't tell your mom."

Isabelle giggled. "K."

Harlow felt herself getting weepy again. What was up with her crying at the drop of a tissue lately?

"Hey, Gene. How you feelin' today?" Renner asked.

"Blessed that Tierney is doing well. Happy that my sweet Isabelle kept her grandpa company for a bit." He winked at his granddaughter. "We'll have milk and cookies next time."

"Any chance you'll be heading to the hospital to see your daughter and grandson?"

He shook his head. "My executive assistant, Karen, is coming tomorrow, so she and I will need to catch up on business things. So I'll wait to see him—them—until they're home. But feel free to keep those pictures coming."

"Me'n Grandpa took a selfie and sent it to Mommy."

Harlow laughed. A three-year-old and a sixty-five-year-old snapping selfies.

"I'm sure your mama appreciated that, because she misses you." Renner kissed Isabelle's forehead again. "We're gonna git. See ya."

After they left, Harlow snagged the walker and brought it to her dad. "You ready?"

"Can we skip the walk today? I'm tired."

"Nope. You just had a nap."

"Then I'm not using the walker. Get me the cane."

"Sure." His incision had healed enough that he didn't need either, but forcing him to use the rehab tools ensured he'd take a slower pace. "It's a gorgeous day. I thought when we finished, you could wait out on the patio for your daily dose of mud."

Her dad smirked at their code name for the Mud Lilies.

It still threw Harlow, seeing this easy side of her rigid father. Before, he'd rarely smiled unless it was his Snidely Whiplash type of grin and that had always scared her.

"Give me a few moments to lose the invalid look."

His need for an impeccable appearance hadn't changed. "No problem. I'll wait in the hallway."

Harlow closed her eyes, devising a plan. It'd be a short PT session today. The hospital was thirty minutes away and she was anxious to see Tierney and meet Rhett.

Suddenly a shadow fell over her and she opened her eyes.

Hugh's hands were beside her head on the wall. And he was too close for comfort. "What?"

"I fucking hate it when you walk away from me when I'm talkin' to you."

"We were done talking, Hugh."

"No, we haven't even started." He paused. "Is that all you see this as? A hookup?"

She sighed. "Are we back to this? Then, yes, if we ever have sex—which is looking less likely the more you push me—it'll be no strings, no promises, no guarantees of a repeat. I can't make it any clearer than that."

His response resembled a growl more than a word.

"Harlow?" her dad said from the other side of the door.

"Right here."

But Hugh elbowed her aside to hold open the door so Gene could hobble through.

"Thanks, Hugh. I'm surprised to see you here."

"I've been hanging around hoping to continue my earlier conversation with Harlow."

What in the hell was the man doing? She stepped between Hugh and her dad. "We finished that conversation."

Her dad sent her a sideways glance. "Doesn't appear that Hugh's done talking."

"Since your daughter won't listen to reason, maybe if I make my intent clear to you, she'll be more inclined to believe I'm serious. See, I acted like an ass to her a few years back. And she believes that jackass thing I did defines the type of man I am. It doesn't. Not then, not now."

Omigod. He was *not* going there.

"I'm not a wham-bam kind of guy. Since your daughter and I are involved, there'll be no sneaking around. Just giving you a heads-up, so you're not surprised when you see us together. All. The. Time."

And . . . he went there.

"Also, we'd appreciate it if you kept this to yourself. With Renner and

Tierney dealing with a new baby and other matters, we'll tell them about our relationship when things settle down for them. All right?"

Then Hugh flashed her a challenging grin.

Her dad looked at her, concern in his eyes. "You sure about this, Harlow?"

She sent Hugh a cool look. "Yes, I'm perfectly happy keeping all of this our little secret, since there's nothing to tell."

"You let me know when you get it sorted out," her dad said.

Then she addressed Hugh. "Don't you have cows to kill or something?"

His gaze narrowed.

"Come on, Dad. Let's get your PT done."

Harlow managed to put the whole pushy way Hugh acted out of her mind while she tended to her dad. After she settled him and Vivien on the patio with a bottle of pinot grigio, she drove into Rawlins.

For the next two hours she laughed and cried with her sister as they marveled at the newest addition to the family. She listened to Tierney talk of babies and day care and preschool issues. Made the appropriate noises when Tierney questioned whether she should work as much with two kids. By the time Tierney got around to asking Harlow specifics about her upcoming plans, Renner arrived with Isabelle and she dodged the questions.

But she didn't have that same luxury of blocking out the Hugh situation as she killed two hours in the grocery store, waiting to take Isabelle home.

Okay. Break it down. Why would Hugh work so hard to try to convince her he wasn't a love-'em-and-leave-'em asshole?

One, he wanted to have sex with her again.

Duh—no-brainer there.

Two, he liked spending time with her because they had so much in common.

She snorted out loud at that idea.

Think, Harlow.

But nothing came to mind.

So it was just about sex between them.

She could work with that—or around that in this case. She'd let him think he was wooing her, convincing her that theirs was a real relationship. Truth was, they were both stuck at the Split Rock. Him by choice. Her by circumstance. There were worse ways to spend her time than skin to skin with a hot cowboy who wanted to prove he could satisfy her between the sheets.

Chapter Ten

$\mathcal{T}$he numbers weren't adding up.

Nothing added up today.

Hugh dropped the papers on the table and leaned back in his chair. His concentration was for shit.

And he placed the blame squarely on the hot-bodied blonde he couldn't get out of his mind.

Why would he want to hide their relationship? And why was that what she preferred?

It'd taken guts for him to march up to Gene Pratt and announce his intentions. Hugh might've looked calm on the outside, but his insides had been quaking like an aspen.

Maybe it bothered him that Gene hadn't seemed to care one way or another. But he imagined apathy was a far sight better than the treatment Renner had received when he and Tierney announced they were involved.

Four soft raps sounded on his screen door. Hugh squinted at the clock. Who'd be dropping by at ten o'clock at night? An emergency always warranted a phone call first.

"I know you're home, Hugh," Harlow said through the screen door. "I can see you sitting at the table."

"Come on in."

She opened the door halfway and slipped inside. Then she frowned at the door before facing him. "I didn't notice before that you fixed the squeak."

"Damn thing drove me crazy."

"It served a purpose. Then again, it's probably never worried you to live alone in a secluded cabin among a different set of strangers every week, being that you're a big, strong manly man and all."

Hugh cocked his head. "Am I supposed to take that as a compliment or an insult?"

"Just stating a fact. When I lived here, I *wanted* the door to squeak. It was my alarm system."

"Did you have many problems with breaking and entering?"

"No, because my squeaking-door alarm scared would-be burglars off."

He grinned. Then his smile faded. "Why're you here, Harlow?"

"To apologize for being snippy with you today."

"Snippy?" *Count to ten, man. She's here. Don't fucking blow this.* He exhaled a long breath. "Darlin', snippy is when you ask me to do something for you, I don't do it in your time frame, and you snipe that you may as well do it yourself."

"That's actually a dead-on definition."

"You were plain damn defensive with me when we were alone and when I talked to your dad." He paused. "Why?"

Harlow twisted her fingers together in front of her. "Because I felt guilty, all right?"

"You felt guilty about what?"

"About what happened in the barn. I shouldn't have let it go that far."

"You telling me you regret me goin' down on you?"

She looked at him, her cheeks the same luscious shade of pink as her lips. "At the time? No. But in the aftermath . . ."

"You decided the next time you saw me, you'd give me what-for about it?"

"No, Hugh. As soon as you saw me, you dragged me off and kissed me like it was your right. It caught me off guard. Last night, immediately after you rocked me on the tool bench, I had to leave. Today my focus was split between worrying for my sister and taking care of a three-year-old. I haven't had time to process *anything* that happened between us." She straightened her posture. "But rather than giving me that time, you took matters into your own hands. You told my father that you and I were together—before you even asked *me* if we were."

Goddammit, she was right. He was always fucking up with her.

Harlow ran her hands through her hair. She looked tired and stressed. And he hated that he'd willingly and willfully contributed to that.

Rather than demand, "So we're not together?" he said, "I'm sorry."

She studied him in silence.

"Harlow. Talk to me."

"Do you have any booze? Besides beer? Or wine?"

"Maker's Mark." When she didn't shudder, he said, "Want a slug?"

"Please."

"Have a seat. I'll bring it over." He grabbed two lowball glasses from the cupboard along with the bottle. He poured them each two fingers of whiskey and carried the glasses to the living room.

Harlow sat on the couch, her knees pulled up to her chest. She held out her hand. "Thank you."

"No problem." He didn't ask if he could sit by her; he just did.

She sipped and swallowed. Sipped and swallowed. Then she leaned forward and set her glass on the table. "I'm still lost, Hugh."

He waited to see if she'd tack on anything else. When she didn't, he said, "What can I do?"

"I don't know if there's anything anyone can do."

That's when Hugh had a lightbulb moment. Harlow had felt lost before she'd gone to Denver to deal with her father's health crisis. Before she'd returned to the Split Rock. Before he'd kissed her and pressured her for more.

While he felt relief that her detachment wasn't aimed solely at him, her guardedness concerned him, because that wasn't Harlow's nature at all.

"My father's assistant, Karen, is coming tomorrow."

He rolled with the subject change. "How well do you know her?"

"Nothing about her besides that she answers Dad's private office line when I call him. Or she forwards the call through when he calls me. Tierney knows her. Or she used to know her when she worked for PFG. Anyway, Tierney says Karen is the epitome of efficiency."

"High praise coming from Tierney."

"Right? And what bugs me? It seems like my dad was more excited about Karen coming than Tierney's baby being born. I don't get that at all."

"Can I play the dumb-man card?"

"Sure."

"Men don't get excited about babies unless they're ours. And even then . . . when a baby is just a screamin', cryin', shittin' blob? Not a huge fan."

She laughed softly.

"Gene does fine with Isabelle, though?"

"Way better than he ever did with me or Tierney, according to my big sister."

"There's your answer. He's more comfortable around older kids."

"I suppose that could be true." She smirked at him. "I suppose that's not a dumb-man answer." She picked up her glass and scooted into the corner of the couch. "Do you fall into that 'babies are gross' mind-set?"

"Yep. Do you think babies are *all that*?"

"Yes."

"All babies?" he said skeptically. "Or just friends' and your family's babies?"

"All babies. I did a stint in an orphanage in Croatia. Heartbreaking, but I got to feed and comfort them. The instant I put one of the older abandoned babies back in a crib, that's when it turned fussy, which proved there's a biological need for constant close contact between parent and child. Being held close was the ultimate comfort for them. They couldn't get enough of it." She studied the amber liquid in her glass. "And at the opposite end of the spectrum were the kids who'd never had any close contact. Even their food was delivered without human interaction. The bottles were rigged above their beds like with animals at feeding time. So skin-to-skin contact was literally painful for them."

Hugh curled his hand over her knee. "I don't know how you come to terms with some of the things you've seen, hippie-girl. I imagine in your shoes I'd feel more than a little lost too."

He watched in horror, his stomach churning, as Harlow's tears fell and dotted her jeans.

Fuck this. "Drink up," he said gruffly.

She raised her tearstained face. "What?"

"Finish your damn whiskey and come here. Your tears are gutting me."

When Harlow continued to stare at him, he plucked the glass from her hand and put it on the coffee table. Then he hauled her against his chest and stretched them out on the couch.

"Hugh, I'm not ready—"

"I'm not doin' nothin' but giving you some of the physical comfort you need, sweetheart."

She debated about fifteen more seconds before she snuggled into him, using his biceps as a pillow.

He closed his eyes, at a complete loss to process how right this felt. He'd never held her like this, the front side of her body tucked against him, where they touched in a long line: chests, bellies, hips and legs.

"Thank you," she said softly.

Hugh said nothing. He just kissed the top of her head.

It wasn't long before Harlow was out. Her steady breaths drifted over the collar of his shirt. It humbled him that after the disaster that'd separated them for three years, here she was. Trusting him enough to fall asleep in his arms.

Let this be the start of something. Give me a chance to prove I can be the man you need.

As Harlow slept on, Hugh's thoughts raced forward and back as he didn't want to mess with what he had going on in the present.

But as hard as he'd tried to block it out, his mind returned to the one night they'd ended up in bed. He didn't want to remember what an ass he'd been in the aftermath of sex that'd rocked his world. So his memory scrolled back to how they'd become comfortable with each other again after Harlow had kissed him and run out of her own house . . .

⌒∕⌒

Hugh understood that Harlow had done the right thing in leaving him hanging. Although that worried him they'd never get back to even a basic friendship. He tried to tell himself that her cold shoulder was the sign to stay away from her. But he couldn't. He'd never met a woman like her. He'd never genuinely liked a woman as much as he liked her. And he could admit his earlier comparisons between Harlow and his ex-wife were rooted in fear. In reality, Harlow and Cleo weren't even the same species.

So a week after she'd given him a taste of his own medicine, he'd wandered into the Split Rock bar after closing time and yelled, "Truce."

At first Harlow eyed him like a three-dollar bill and then a smile bloomed on her face. "Truce it is, cowboy. You want a beer?"

And that had been that.

They'd done a lot of talking after that. Some flirting. No kissing. He'd loved hearing her yammer on about her niece with such pride, awe and love. She'd complained a little about her job and the slowdown of the summer season. He'd relayed a few of the raunchier stories of life on the road. He'd followed those up with minor complaints about his workday. Normal things. He'd gotten into the habit of hanging around while she closed down the bar. Then he walked with her outside to where the path split and they went their separate ways. Sometimes she'd just appear in the barn if he was working late.

But that night, he'd shown up at her cabin later than normal and found her beating the crap out of a pillow she'd rigged up as a makeshift punching bag.

She'd been wearing spandex shorts that hugged her ass and a sports bra that allowed him to see her flat belly and the sexy curves and muscles in her back.

Her outfit made him hard.

Her sweat-coated skin made him hard.

Her aggressive behavior made him hard.

There was no way in hell he could've stayed away from her that night. Being the smooth fucking operator that he was, he told her if she needed an additional outlet for her anger, she could use him.

And she had.

The trip to the bedroom and the clothes removal were a blur. They'd been so frantic for each other there was little foreplay besides hungry kisses and eager hands as he put on a condom.

Then they were naked in her bed and he was inside her. It was fucking fireworks. It was a choir of angels. It was heat and need. It was everything he'd heard sex could be but hadn't believed.

She'd come twice, clawing at his back, panting in his ear, and he'd managed to hold off until her second orgasm ended.

Afterward, he'd been breathing too hard to do much but flop on his back and try to find a sense of balance. Because that? That had changed things.

Harlow, being sweet, wonderful, open Harlow, had snuggled into him. She'd whispered, "I think I've been half in love with you since you told me about your ex-wife. But after this? Now I know I'm crazy in love with you."

He'd never experienced such a crippling sense of panic. Love? What did he know about love? What the hell did *she* know about love? And why would such a free spirit boldly confess her love after they'd fucked each other stupid? It was just sex. What more did she want from him?

Then he'd thrown himself out of bed and started yanking on his clothes. He hadn't even removed the condom. When Harlow spoke again, he'd said the first things that'd come to his mind. Awful words, none of them true, but he'd needed distance and time to sort things out.

Harlow had given it to him. She left the next day.

He just hadn't expected it'd be three long years before he'd see her again.

But he was older and wiser and he'd be damned if he'd make the same mistake twice . . .

∞

Something soft tickled his nose and he turned his head away. His chin smacked into a solid object.

"Ouch."

He glanced down to see Harlow looking up at him. "Hey. Sorry."

"I guess we both fell asleep."

"You have any idea what time it is?"

She shook her head. "I don't really care. Do you?"

"Not when I've got you here with me like this."

Harlow pushed up and fused her mouth to his in a sweetly seductive, but somewhat unsure, kiss.

She didn't move her hands or her body and neither did he. They just allowed the heat to build and expand. After a bit, she kissed a path to his ear. "I want you. I don't want to talk about it. I just want to climb on and ride you until we're too tired to do anything but sleep."

He wasn't fool enough to question it. "I've gotta move to get a condom. Shit. I don't think I have any."

"I'm covered, so don't worry about it. And I haven't been with any-one . . . in a long time."

Floored, he said, "You trust me?"

"Yes."

"Why?"

"Because if you'd turned into a manwhore in the last three years? You'd have a stash of condoms and you wouldn't be chasing after me so hard to try and make things right."

He grabbed her chin to garner her full attention. "You're sure this is what you want?"

"Yes, I'm sure." She paused. "Are you?"

"Like you even have to ask me that, darlin'. I've never been so sure of anything in my life." *Whoa, there. Slow down.* "I haven't been with anyone in a long time either."

"Then we both need this, don't we?" she said softly.

"I'm willing to wait."

"I don't want to wait. I don't need a big sweeping romantic gesture. After last time . . . We don't need the pressure. Let's ease into it. Make out like teenagers on this big couch. See where it leads."

Hugh understood there was more to why she needed to be in control. It went deeper than what'd gone wrong between them in the aftermath last time. She was wound so tight he feared one wrong move, one wrong word, would send her scurrying away. He'd never done any sort of role-playing, but he was willing to try for her because she needed to get out of her own head. "Okay. But we have to be quiet because my parents are in the next room."

Her eyes widened, and then she smiled slyly. She slid out from under his arm and pushed him onto his back. Couch cushions flew onto the floor and she straddled him, groin to groin. Then she started popping the buttons on his shirt.

He ran his palms up the tops of her thighs. "I'm gonna want those nipples in my mouth."

"Gimme a second." Her hands were all over the hair on his chest. "I remember this. And this happy trail." She traced the line of hair bisecting his belly that disappeared under the waistband of his jeans.

His fingers busied themselves on the buttons on her sleeveless blouse. Beneath that, she wore a tube top. When he tried to slip the shirt off her shoulders, she caught his hands.

"Let me." She tugged the tube top down to her waist, baring her breasts.

"You have the sweetest tits," he said on a groan as he urged her forward, taking a nipple into his hungry mouth.

Harlow braced her hands against the arm of the couch and stretched over him so her tits were right in his face.

He laved and sucked and teased, watching goose bumps ripple across her supple skin, hearing her soft moans as he did something she liked. Given her obsession with his beard, he spent a lot of time just rubbing it on her, like a cat.

Harlow didn't sit still as he focused on her chest. She rocked forward and backward, grinding her crotch over his cock. Forward with a hip thrust at the end. Backward with a side-to-side slide.

The more she toyed with his cock, the harder it got. He started to have that crazed need for full skin-on-skin contact. He wanted the barriers between them gone. He tugged on her skirt. "Off."

She pushed upright, pulling her nipple from his mouth. Then she yanked the stretchy material down her legs and whipped it behind her.

Jesus. She wasn't wearing underwear.

"My turn." Then she planted kisses from his forehead down between his eyebrows, on the tip of his nose, on his mouth, his chin, his Adam's apple, the hollow of his throat.

Hugh stroked her hair as she nuzzled his chest. His heart raced—something she was fully aware of when she wrapped her lips over his left nipple and sucked.

She moved back up to nibble on his neck, but kept her hand in place, alternately ruffling her fingers through his furred chest and sweeping her thumb across his nipple. "You smell so good. Like sunshine."

Thankfully he'd showered or she'd be singing a different tune.

"I know you feel good inside me. Even though it was only that one time, I still think about it." She paused. "Do you?"

"All the fucking time." He angled his head to nuzzle her shoulder.

Harlow looked at him, desire shining in her eyes. "I want to feel like that again."

"Lift up." He raised an eyebrow. "Unless you think you can get my clothes down without help?"

"I'd probably knee you in the family jewels and that'd put an abrupt end to tonight."

"You'd better let me do it."

She pushed up while he shoved his jeans and boxers down to his knees. "You wet enough to take me?"

Harlow got nose to nose with him. "Touch me. Find out for yourself."

Snaking his hand between them, he followed the curve of her mound down to where she was soaked. He pushed two fingers into her dripping cunt and swallowed her cry in a kiss.

Fuck yeah. She was ready. He plunged in and out a few times to be sure, dragging his fingers against the inside wall in a long tease that had her gasping before he slid them out completely.

Your move, sweetheart.

Warm fingers circled his shaft and she canted her hips. Then holding his cock straight up, she lowered herself until he filled her fully.

A soft hiss escaped her mouth and she looked at Hugh.

He cupped his hand around her face. Tracing the shape of her mouth with his fingertips—the same fingers that had been inside her.

She lightly sucked on the tips, watching his reaction.

"Sexy as fuck, darlin'."

Harlow began to move on him. Torturously slow, but he knew it wouldn't last because he could feel her heart racing. He could see the need for more in her eyes.

Would she ask for it?

"Hugh."

"Yeah, doll? Tell me what you need."

She grabbed his hand and put it on her ass. "Help me move."

"You surely don't need my help, 'cause you move like a fuckin' dream, but I can do this." With both hands on her ass, he lifted her supple body after she'd lowered. Christ. She was so fuckin' tight and wet and hot he didn't think he would last.

"Oh. That's good." Her confidence grew with every plunge and retreat.

He managed to keep the rhythm, even when she made the unconsciously sexy move of letting her head fall back as she rocked her pelvis forward. The beautifully curved line of her torso and the gentle bounce of her tits would drive any man to distraction. He'd been dreaming of this for far too long to not savor every second.

"More, please. Touch me."

Hugh slipped his right hand between her hip bones, his thumb moving up and down on her clit, giving her the friction she needed.

Harlow became so frantic in her movements Hugh wondered if she even remembered he was there.

But it was heady stuff, being in the front row when she climaxed. Feeling her pussy pulsating around his cock, seeing her soft gasps turn into a smile of satisfaction when the clouds of pleasure cleared.

She finally opened her eyes and looked down at him. "Sorry I zoned out. But, damn. You make my body hum." She leaned down so they were face-to-face again. "Now it's your turn. Fuck me, Hugh. Fuck me in the way that'll get you off. I want to see you."

He surged up into her. "Kiss me. Ride me hard. I'm almost there."

Her mouth collided with his, her body pushing and grinding, working him harder than she'd worked herself.

Then *bam!* The work paid off. His balls went tight, his cock jerked hard against her snug walls and he poured his seed into her, each jetting pulse hotter than the one before. A ripple of gooseflesh started at the nape of his neck and flowed outward, sensitizing every inch of his skin. He broke the kiss and sucked in extra air, since he'd gone dizzy.

Harlow stiffened and moaned into his ear. With the extra tightening of her pussy, he knew she'd come again.

He grinned. Hard not to feel cocky about that.

They remained locked together like that. Her breath in his ear, his hands on her ass. Hearts thundering. Sweat cooling. The only way it would've been more perfect was if they were naked.

Finally he roused himself from the postorgasm laziness and placed soft kisses down her jaw. "Harlow."

"Mmm."

"I need you in my bed. And I ain't letting you out until morning."

"Hugh—"

"Look at me."

She tilted her head back.

"Make no mistake where I'm comin' from. You just rocked my fuckin' world. But it's *our* world now. We *are* together—in bed and out. I promise I won't run out. I promise I won't say stupid shit. I promise this is the start, not the end. So please"—he kissed her—"sleep next to me for the rest of the night."

"Why is this so important to you?"

"So when I wake up, feel your heat and softness next to me and hear you breathe, I know you're real and not just another damn dream."

She smiled. "Okay. But I didn't bring pajamas."

"Don't worry. I got ya covered."

Chapter Eleven

*H*arlow would've been happy sleeping on top of Hugh the whole night with his cock wedged inside her. She'd waited for that thickness to soften, but he'd stayed hard. She'd expected him to start things up again, setting her on fire with his kisses, becoming insistent with his touches, but he'd held back.

And she wasn't sure if she was happy or embarrassed that he'd known she needed to be in control.

After they'd separated, she ducked into the bathroom to clean herself up. The lights were off in the bedroom and Hugh had already climbed between the sheets.

She paused at the end of the bed.

"What?"

"You're on my side, cowboy."

He grinned. "We could sleep in the middle, darlin', with me on top of you."

"Wouldn't be a whole lot of sleeping going on."

"True."

Harlow undressed quickly and nearly tripped over Hugh's clothes scattered across the floor. She slipped beneath the covers, scooting her butt into his groin.

He pulled her closer, so her face rested half on the pillow and half on his biceps.

She should've pulled away when he'd started trailing his fingers down her left arm. His sweeping caress shifted to her hip and then up her left side. Gooseflesh spread as he stroked the eight inches of raised skin between the bottom of her rib cage and her hip.

"Whoa. What's this?"

"A scar."

"What happened? I don't remember it bein' there before."

She refrained from reminding him that it'd been pitch-black the last time they were naked together or that he'd left so fast afterward he hadn't looked at any specific parts of her.

"Harlow?"

"It wasn't there before."

"How'd you get it?"

"Long story."

"I've got time."

Harlow rolled away from Hugh's questing fingers. Perching on the edge of the bed, she snatched the first article of clothing she touched. She slipped on Hugh's shirt and walked out of the bedroom.

In the kitchen, she gazed out the window above the sink, trying to remember the dreams and plans she'd had three years ago as she'd stood in this very spot.

You had no idea the dark turn your life would take. You were so naive running from here, thinking you'd find something better.

Harlow prided herself on her ability to look at situations from all sides. Being here with Hugh now, seeing that he had suffered remorse after his treatment of her, gave her the sort of closure she'd needed. And in that closure, she'd found *her* truth; she'd left here because he'd hurt her feelings. Hugh wasn't a horrible person. He was just a man who'd made a mistake and had admitted as much. And she could admit she'd been wrong too, to paint him and the past with such a wide brush.

She wondered how he'd react when she told him the truth of what she'd gone through. He wasn't the type of man to ignore the signs and just let her be. Complete honesty on her part would show her how much he'd push for more—she just wasn't sure if she could handle the retelling tonight. Even putting it off a day would leave her better prepared.

For what? Aren't you most afraid that he'll look at you and see you as weak?

She turned on the cold water tap and filled a glass. A mouthful of the cool liquid loosened up her tight throat.

"Harlow?" Hugh said behind her, startling her. "You okay?"

A soft, sweet lover's inquiry, not the demanding tone she'd expected. "I'm fine. I needed a drink."

"Bullshit. Tell me how you got that scar and why you fucking ran when I asked about it."

Ah. There was the harsh tone. She took another sip. Swallowed again. "Because I don't want to talk about it."

His angry breaths fluttered her hair.

"Why won't you look at me?"

Harlow whirled around so fast water splashed on Hugh's chest. "Because it's none of your business. When I say I don't want to talk about something? Guess what? I'm not kidding." She brushed past him and returned to the bedroom, snatching up her clothes.

Before she registered what was happening, Hugh picked her up, then tossed her on the bed. He crawled on top of her, his weight making it hard to breathe, pinning her wrists above her head with one hand, and curling the other beneath her jaw, almost around her neck.

Keep calm. Keep your eyes closed. Keep your body relaxed.

"Look at me."

"Let me go right now or I'll scream." She couldn't keep the tremor from her voice.

He immediately scrambled off her. "Shit. I'm sorry. I didn't mean to scare you."

But you did.

Harlow stood and quickly put her clothes on. She didn't look at him when she said, "I'll see you later."

"Don't go."

"I can't"—*talk to you about this*—"stay."

"Just tell me . . . Were you attacked? Is that how you got the scar?"

She paused at the door and shook her head.

"Then was it an accident?"

"No. It was self-inflicted." She fled before he could respond.

Once she reached her trailer, she locked the door and headed straight to the bathroom, where she stripped and cranked on the shower. The water nearly scalded her, but it didn't help because she couldn't stop shivering.

She should've kept her distance from Hugh. Not let things get intimate. It was that need for closeness—an intimacy Hugh hadn't been able to give her three years ago—that'd driven her to search for it elsewhere. And she'd found the intimacy she'd craved. Too bad she'd given her trust to a monster.

Harlow remained in the warmth and safety of the shower even after the shuddering stopped.

Can't stay in there forever.

A tremor of fear jolted her and she spun around, afraid since she'd heard Fredrick's voice, she'd see him lounging against the wall, warning her, watching her, waiting for her like he always did.

But no one was there.

After toweling off, she braided her hair and shuffled to her bedroom.

As soon as her heated skin slipped into the cool sheets, her brain simply shut down and everything went dark.

⌒⌒

When Harlow came to, she didn't know how long she'd been asleep or what time of day it was.

But she knew someone was in her room.

"It's just me," Hugh said softly.

"How did you get in? I know I locked the door."

"This used to be my trailer, remember? My key still works."

Guess she'd have to have Dave change the locks ASAP. "I locked the door because I wanted to be alone. I'll let it slide if you leave the key on the counter when you go."

The chair in the corner creaked. The carpet didn't muffle his heavy footsteps as he crossed the room and stopped at the edge of the bed. "See, that's the thing. I can't let it go. I can't let you go, when I know you're hurtin' and hidin' from me."

"Even if it was you that left me hurting?"

A pause. "Especially then. So you might as well start talkin'. I need to know if this . . . fear you have was an issue and I just didn't notice it three years ago."

"No. I didn't have it." She took a breath. "You never scared me. Not then, not now. That said, I knew I never should've gotten mixed up with you that summer. You were so sexy and compelling and raw. A completely different animal from the men in my world. So maybe the fact our differences couldn't ever mesh appealed to me. You saw me as a bit of dandelion fluff floating anywhere the wind blew me. You made me feel unworthy of you."

"As I've repeatedly admitted, I was an ass and I'm sorry. It is fucking killing me that my actions and words caused you to run." She heard him swallow. "Please, Harlow. Somewhere in your travels you ended up with the scar. I want to know how it happened."

Harlow knew she'd have to tell him at some point. The fact he'd calmed down before he'd chased after her showed he had changed. She took a moment to gather her thoughts. "After I left here, I drove to Portland. A new relief agency needed workers for a yearlong job in Laos. The guy in charge, Fredrick, was one of those charismatic men who were born leaders. I had an audition phase of two weeks, working in a local shelter, before he'd determine whether our personalities and work ethics meshed."

"The audition requirement didn't bother you?"

"No. It's actually customary before a long-term contract. Volunteers have to be able to work together. Anyway I passed the audition. Fredrick and I hit it off. I knew his vision would have a hugely positive impact and I wanted to help make that vision a reality. It would've been ideal to have twenty volunteers, but we had to make do with ten."

"When you say volunteers . . . no one got paid, right?"

"No, this was a paid project, although it works out to less per hour than minimum wage. So in this case when I say volunteer, I really mean worker."

"Got it."

"We spent six months preparing. Securing donations. Getting transportation for us and our supplies. Making sure our visas would clear. Brushing up on local customs. Contacting other relief agencies for their experiences."

"I'm surprised to hear that's standard practice."

"Swapping information is crucial. Not only that, volunteers jump from agency to agency. Say an international peace coalition is in a part of Africa for two years. Then a native studies group takes over for their contracted time. It's beneficial to have at least one person familiar with the locals to help with the transition between organizations. So that person who remains behind has to become part of the new organization so there aren't contract violations." She tried to squirm away. "I'm sorry. This is probably boring you."

"Nope. It's interesting to me because it's your life, Harlow. And I'm assuming it's important to how you got the scar."

"It is."

He kissed the back of her head. "I'm listening. Go at your own pace. I'll be right here."

"We went into the situation a little blind, since no other relief organizations had been in that part of the country for longer than two weeks. That right there should've cautioned us. But I was so happy to be part of the mission I ignored all the warning signs."

"Were you also happy to be with Fredrick?"

Harlow hesitated. Part of her didn't want Hugh to know how naive she'd been. Another part of her wanted him to understand why she'd needed to be someplace where her skills—and she—were valued. "Yes. I spent twelve to fourteen hours of every day working with him. Half of our group of volunteers lived together during the six months of prep time. So we were together practically twenty-four/seven. We'd had many of the same life experiences and I believed I'd found my soul mate." She swallowed the bitter taste that admission left in her mouth. "Of course, that's what he manipulated me to believe. He did see the real me—the woman who needed to belong—and he preyed on that. He built me up and I came to rely on his praise too, like it was food and water, like it alone could sustain me. So when he started to tear me down, I believed I deserved his harsh words because I'd disappointed him."

Hugh brushed his lips across the back of her head. He might've whispered *I'm sorry* or it might've just been a heavy exhalation.

"So to keep me on the hook, and starry-eyed about him, Fredrick didn't start a physical relationship with me until we were in the middle of nowhere. At first, it was great. I had everything I'd ever wanted. A man who loved giving back to the world as much as I did, a man I loved and who I thought loved me in return. I didn't want the little things to bother me, so I tended to ignore them."

"What little things?"

"It seemed like all of the other volunteers had something bothering them. Daphne's jealousy about me and Fredrick. Pat's worry we'd jeopardized our health by not having a medical professional along with us. Rialta's concern the locals were resentful and could become violent. All of which I knew were concerns for every humanitarian-based trip. But it did bother me that we were so cut off from civilization."

"If I didn't know firsthand there are plenty of spots in Wyoming that have little to no cell service, I'd ask if there were really places on the planet that isolated."

She couldn't help but smile. "It's a shock to first-time workers to not have technology be a daily part of life. And then there are encampments where the whole point is to introduce the locals to technology. But usually those places are founded by technology companies who are looking for a place to put up a cell tower."

"Darlin', you're getting off track," he said gently.

"Sorry. After two months on-site—at that point I'd known Fredrick eight months and I had a hard-core case of hero worship—I noticed Fredrick had started to speak for me. When we, as an organization, had to make a decision, we stuck to majority rules. Everyone had an equal vote. The first time Fredrick spoke for me wasn't an issue because I agreed with him. The next time, when he said, *Harlow agrees with me*, I argued vehemently and said I did not. He didn't get angry. He didn't belittle me or argue back. So I assumed he understood I had my own opinions that weren't his. But that night, when we returned to the room we shared, that was the first time he hurt me."

Hugh's body went tense behind hers. "What did he do?"

"Threw me face-first on the bed and slapped his hand over my mouth while he fucked me. If I made any noise, he'd shove his palm up higher and pinch my nose shut, cutting off my air."

"Jesus."

"I couldn't use my hands to shove him off me because he'd trapped them. And the entire time he fuck-punished me, he kept up a running monologue about me disrespecting him. How I was nothing without him. And unless I wanted to find myself in the pit, then I'd better not embarrass him again."

"What's the pit?"

"A hole in the ground the locals used to punish bad behavior. Fredrick was our leader. If he put me in the pit, no one—none of my coworkers or the locals—would help me out. After he hurt me ... I tried to hide the bruises on my face with makeup. If any of my colleagues asked, I'd claim it was dirt. I toed the line for a couple of weeks. No beatings, but we hadn't had sex either. And when I'd convinced myself that Fredrick had been under a bunch of stress, and he hadn't really meant to hurt me ... another vote came up. I voted against him."

"What happened?"

"He acted like it was no big deal. We went to bed. Took me a long time to fall asleep because I worried he'd fuck-punish me again." She swallowed hard. "I woke up with him sitting on me, his hand around my neck. He choked me until I passed out. When I came to, I saw he'd scratched me hard enough to draw blood. Five lines of claw marks down the center of my body. Then like before, he flipped me facedown on the bed and held his hand over my mouth. But that time he pinched the skin along my sides hard enough to leave a line of bruises. As he ... hurt me, he rubbed his cock on me and ejaculated on the marks." She'd been so ashamed she couldn't look at him when he tossed her baby wipes to clean herself up. The blood mixed with his sticky leavings and the powdery scent of the cloth had kicked in her gag reflex.

Hugh whispered, "It's okay. You're here with me."

"After he saw me sobbing, he felt so bad he cried. He claimed he felt my injuries as keenly as I did because we were connected in body and soul. He acted so contrite. He even offered to take me to Erika, who only knew basic first aid, so she could make sure the scratches didn't get infected. I convinced myself if he had no issues telling Erika that he'd inflicted the injuries on me, then he must've been telling the truth about passion being the cause."

Hugh didn't say anything.

"I don't even remember at what point I realized I was in an abusive relationship. I started agreeing with him during meetings, hoping that would end his physical demonstrations of his disappointment in me. But he changed the parameters and punished me whenever he felt like it. But even when he hurt me, he assured me that pain was part of his love for me.

"I'm a college graduate. A smart woman who's been around. I knew better than to fall for that bullshit, right? I've taken domestic-abuse awareness classes. I know the signs. I've seen what the cycle of abuse does to women and children. But I didn't believe it could be happening to *me.*"

"What about the other volunteers?" he demanded tersely. "They had to see the marks. They had to suspect what he was doing to you."

"I hid the marks. And I went out of my way to present the 'happy perfect couple' image to everyone. Because if I acted like it was true, then maybe Fredrick would believe it was and he'd stop hurting me."

"But he didn't."

"No. It just got worse."

"How long did this go on?"

"Ten months. At that point I thought if I could just stick it out until the yearlong contract ended, then when we returned to the States, I'd be free of him. But Fredrick informed us he was in negotiations to extend our stay. Anyone could leave if they wanted. I knew that offer didn't apply to me. Most of my coworkers were professional aid workers and seized the opportunity to stay on because an extension was a sign we were doing good work. That's also when I knew I had to do something drastic to get out of the situation."

"Jesus, Harlow."

"You asked if anyone knew that Fredrick was . . ." She paused. "Evidently Erika thought it was odd I wore my hair down all the time. So when Nico and Fredrick hiked to the next village, she took me aside and grilled me. I'd never be a good spy because I cracked within five minutes. She examined me and saw the fading marks. She feared Fredrick would become increasingly more violent, and injure me more prominently to leave permanent marks. She asked if we had sex without him hurting me. I admitted it hadn't been that way in the beginning. But she pointed out we'd been friends for six months before becoming lovers and he'd hurt me for the first time within weeks of us becoming intimate."

"Harlow. Baby. You don't have to tell me—"

"Yes, I do. So the only way to escape would be if I had a believable accident resulting in a life-threatening injury. Fredrick would *have* to allow me to travel to a village with medical facilities."

"Explain *believable accident*."

"Something self-inflicted that could get infected and still be passed off as an accident. If Fredrick pressed me to explain how I'd gotten hurt and why I hadn't told him, I could confess I felt stupid about how it happened and didn't show him out of embarrassment."

"Oh, sweetheart."

"I found a sharp piece of glass and after five shots of the local liquor I sliced myself open, eight inches long and a quarter of an inch deep." She shuddered and Hugh held her tighter. "It was tempting to clean the wound, but I let it be. The next three days were a blur. When my body felt feverish and the skin around the puncture site oozed green, I knew I had a raging infection. That's when I told Fredrick. I screamed when he touched me and then collapsed." The unholy gleam in Fredrick's eyes when he'd witnessed her pain still gave her nightmares.

"He argued against taking me to the village until Erika said she'd carry me herself if she had to. After we made the trek there, the village healer scrubbed out the wound and put me on an IV of antibiotics. I refused morphine because I needed to keep my wits about me. After forty-eight hours the infection had subsided enough the doc could stitch me up. That's when I called my dad."

"Did you talk to him without Fredrick in the room?"

She shook her head. "I was never alone. At our site, he was always there, every time I turned around. I couldn't even shower without him waiting for me. If I even smiled at another man, he accused me of flirting and punished me."

"What did your dad say when you got in touch with him?"

"Since I started going on missions, there was always a chance I'd get kidnapped, so Dad and I had our own set of code words. If I told him to have Ira release the funds, that was code for a ransom situation. If I told him my allergies were back, that meant a hostage situation with nonhostile captors."

"I'd argue that fucker Fredrick had been very hostile to you."

"Yes, but with him it was different than being held by machine-gun- and machete-wielding militia."

He grunted as if he couldn't see the difference.

"Code words didn't matter, because the second I heard my dad's voice, I broke down. I told him I needed emergency medical help and I had to get out."

"Your dad has those kinds of contacts?"

"He's funded a lot of private security corps over the years. After I hung up and looked at Fredrick, I thought he might kill me. He was so infuriated; he smacked me across the face twice and split open my lip before anyone could stop him. The hospital manager removed Fredrick by force and kept me under guard. Within twenty-four hours Erika and I were en route to the U.S."

"Thank god." Hugh kissed the back of her head. "So your dad knows everything that happened?"

"No. He's aware I ended up in an abusive situation with my boyfriend, who was also my boss. I didn't want to talk about it with him; I just wanted the nightmare to be over and to get far away from Fredrick."

"He fucking abused you, Harlow. You should've pressed charges."

"I considered it, but if by some miracle it would've gone to trial, I knew I couldn't face Fredrick in the courtroom. The incidents happened in a foreign country. The burden of proof for the abuse was entirely on me. I had *one* person who knew about it. He had seven people who lived with us for an entire year and saw nothing but the happy-couple facade I'd manufactured. So I was fucked."

"What'd you do?"

"Went to Florida with Erika. I rented a small apartment and sat on the beach as I contemplated my future. I saw a counselor and she helped me come to terms with what happened." Harlow wrinkled her nose. Aida also advised her to transition into the real world of paid permanent—or semipermanent—jobs, versus flying all over the globe to help others. They'd also had in-depth conversations about her relationship with Tierney and her father. She'd questioned if Harlow's need to give everything of herself to others was to show their father she was the direct opposite of him in every way.

"You fall asleep?" Hugh murmured in her hair.

"No."

"Tierney doesn't know what you went through?"

She bristled at his tone. "What purpose would it serve? It's over and done with. She's used to me being off the grid. Plus she had a kid and I know her focus didn't extend beyond the bubble she lived in, in Muddy Gap, Wyoming. It is what it is."

Hugh stayed quiet for so long she wondered if he'd fallen asleep. But his hand on her belly tightened. "Do you blame me?"

She'd thought about it and talked about it with Aida. "Maybe at first. If it'd been the start of something between us instead of the end? Yeah, I did wonder if we could've made it work. But the answer I keep coming back to is no. My time here was temporary. I might've stuck around a few more months, but I wasn't permanent-partner material for you any more than you were for me—then or now. You're rooted here; I'm rootless. I probably would've ended up in Portland anyway, just not as soon as I did."

He sighed. "I blame me. If I wouldn't have been such a dick to you, maybe you would've stayed." He gently rolled her onto her back and loomed over her.

The softness in his face and the regret in his eyes quickened her pulse. "What?"

"I'm so sorry. Even though that won't ever be enough to heal the scars you have that I can't see."

She reached up and stroked the scruff lining his cheek.

He angled his head into her touch.

"I don't want what he did to change how you want to be with me," she said.

"You need to put it in plain terms, Harlow, so there's no misunderstandings between us."

"You're the first man I've been with since Fredrick."

Hugh remained quiet a beat too long. "I don't know what to say to that."

"Don't say anything. I'm just letting you know there weren't any others. It was you, then him . . . now you again. So don't treat me like a victim. Don't mistakenly believe I can only handle sweet, sweet lovin'." She petted his beard. "You're a hard man. You keep your passion buried so deep that when you let it out, it explodes like a geyser. I don't need you to put a lid on it. I need you to be who you are, not who you *think* I need you to be."

"So no need to touch you with kid gloves. You know I'm rough around the edges. Any problem with me bein' rough with you?"

Her pulse jumped, from excitement, not fear. And it was tempting to answer him with a solid no, but if he accidentally crossed a line he wasn't aware of, it'd be her fault, but he'd still blame himself. "No scratching. And, uh, no pinching."

"Not even your nipples?"

She shook her head.

"I've got no desire to hurt you, darlin'. Ever. But you're feisty enough you might need a swat on the ass. Where does that fall?"

"You can use your hand on my butt, but no swats anywhere else. And only your hand. No belts or paddles or hangers." She looked away. "Or cords."

Hugh turned her face back toward his. "You're doin' good. I need to know this. Anything else?"

"I don't like it doggie-style. That's the only way he'd do it after the first time he hurt me. And no choking. Ever," came out on a whisper.

He went still. Then he murmured, "I'd much rather use my hands like this"—he cupped her breast and swept his thumb over her nipple—"while I put my mouth here." He dragged an openmouthed kiss up and down her neck. She shivered and her skin broke out in gooseflesh. "Especially when I can get you to respond like this." He nuzzled her throat.

"Hugh . . ."

"Anything else we need to talk about right now?"

"Ah. No."

"Then we're done talkin'." He circled his fingers around her wrists and pulled her hands above her head, pressing her knuckles into the mattress. "Leave them there."

"Why?"

He placed a kiss on the edge of her jaw. "I don't want interference. So you just relax and let me do a little exploring." His mouth returned to hers. He kissed her leisurely and ran his hand down the center of her torso, over her breast, then detoured to her side.

The side with the scar.

Harlow squirmed and broke the kiss. "Stop. That tickles."

"No, it doesn't. You just don't want me touchin' it."

Dammit.

"Close your eyes." He scooted down and pressed a kiss on her sternum. Then he brushed his mouth over her rib cage, back and forth, but increasing his range with every thorough pass.

Harlow tried to close her eyes. Tried to relax, but he kept surprising her with little flicks of his tongue.

Then his breath connected with the top of the scar and was quickly followed by the warm touch of his mouth. At first he just nuzzled the ridge.

"You don't have to—"

"I don't do anything I don't want to. And I wanna do this, so hush and let me." He glanced up, a sexy challenge dancing in his eyes. "You'd rather I started searching out all of your ticklish spots?"

"No."

"Good. Now let me keep working my way down. 'Cause a smart woman like you can figure out where my mouth is gonna end up."

She moaned. It seemed a lifetime since a man had taken his time with her. Teased and pleased her. She hated that slow and steady glide of his lips and tongue as much as she loved how it increased her anticipation.

"Yeah, darlin'. Let go. Trust me to take care of you."

Had she ever imagined she'd be granting Hugh Pritchett her trust again? No.

But this time he'd earned it.

His tongue followed the full length of her scar. Then he paused and pressed soft kisses over every inch. Twice. Three times. "Any other scars I need to see?"

"The rest are internal," slipped out before she could stop it.

When Hugh scooted up and stared into her eyes, the ferocity she witnessed there stole her breath. He lowered his head and kissed the left side of her chest with such care she knew he was trying to show her if she trusted him, he could heal her heart.

She touched his face. "Don't stop."

"What?"

"Any of it. Make me come with your mouth. Watch me come. Then crawl back up here and let's do it all over again. You show me what you need."

He didn't respond with words. He let his hands and mouth and body answer for him.

No teasing. No drawn-out foreplay. He kissed her sex with long curls of his tongue. Then he pulled the fleshy ridges aside, exposing her folds, her clit, her pussy lips. He fastened his mouth over the whole of her and relentlessly pursued her orgasm until he got what he wanted.

Harlow fisted her hands in the sheets as he sent her over the edge twice.

Then Hugh came over her. Body to body. No sweetness, just pure sexual greed.

But even as his body mastered hers, he kept their gazes locked so she could see every flash of pleasure in his eyes and he could see if any fear entered hers. He gripped her ass, pumping harder with each stroke.

She met every stroke, in tandem. In opposition.

When he came, the whole bed shook. He held nothing back.

She felt like he'd given her everything.

Chapter Twelve

$\mathcal{S}$ince Renner had Isabelle duty until noon, Harlow slept in after Hugh had left her bed to take care of some cow crap.

Her use of the term *cow crap* cracked him up.

It'd made her smile too, particularly when she felt Hugh's laughter vibrating against the nape of her neck. He'd kissed her thoroughly and then he was gone.

When she did awaken, sore in places she hadn't been sore in for a while, she couldn't help but relive the night's events. She decided not to shower; she liked wearing Hugh's scent on her skin.

Harlow purposely tried to keep an extra bounce out of her step when she showed up at the lodge. She wasn't ready to deal with the "You're in such a good mood, you must've gotten lucky last night" comments. But she did snicker when she wondered how Hugh would handle that, because he'd definitely been in a great mood this morning.

The door to her dad's room was open. She paused at the threshold and noticed another desk had been hauled in as well as a printer and a chair. Then her gaze moved to the hospital bed.

A disembodied voice boomed from the closet in the back of the room. "You're recovering, Gene. You don't need to button up into a three-piece suit every day."

"I know I will recover faster if I don't look like or feel like a bum, Karen."

A butterball of a woman with hair the color of burnished steel emerged from the closet. "I can call Greg, your tailor at Bergdorf, and tell him you're in dire straits. He'll have clothing ready within a week, if you can hold off that long."

"Hold off from what?"

"Your garden of admirers."

"How'd you know about them?"

Karen propped her hand on her ample hip. "Janie Lawson filled me in when you were napping."

"I'll just bet she did," he grumbled. "Because you, woman, cannot help but gossip."

"My gossiping always leads to valuable information for PFG." Karen had started toward the bed when she noticed Harlow. She smiled. "Come in—don't just lurk in the doorway."

"I didn't want to interrupt."

"Harlow. I'm glad you're here to save me from this overbearing woman who thinks she runs my life," her father said.

"Who *thinks* she runs your life? Mr. Pratt, I *know* I run your life."

"You haven't met Karen yet, Harlow, have you?"

"Not in person." She offered Karen her hand. "I'm thrilled to meet the woman Tierney waxes poetic about for her mad organizational skills."

Karen ignored her hand and pulled her into a hug. "I'd trade all of it for her head for numbers. Every single pool we had going at the office? That girl won it."

"I'd take the math brain too."

"From listening to your father talk about your mother, seems you take after her with your generosity and helpful nature."

There was a total shocker. Gene Pratt discussing his dead wife with his executive assistant? When he barely spoke of her to his daughters? "I'm not certain of that, but I'll take the compliment."

Karen looked at her boss. "I'll be back in fifteen. Do whatever grooming you need to in that time, because when I return, we're getting to work." Then she smiled at Harlow. "Will you show me how to get to the employee trailers from here?"

141 ᴔ WRAPPED AND STRAPPED

"Sure. Did you drive a rental car?"

"No, PFG bought me a car and I drove it up from Denver. The bellhop parked in front of where I'm staying and he should've unloaded my luggage."

"It's a quick walk. I'll even show you the shortcut." After they'd exited the lodge and started down the rocky path, she noticed Karen wore three-inch heels. Would she dress like that every day? Of course she would. After five years of living in Wyoming, Tierney still dressed in suits and heels for work.

Karen scrutinized the employee quarters as they approached.

Harlow had to wonder what her dad had been thinking, expecting this elegant woman used to working in a high-rise in the middle of Chicago to have no issues living in a trailer in rural Wyoming.

Probably her dad had tripled her salary for the duration.

"Well, this is better than I expected, actually," Karen said.

"It is?"

Karen walked around the square decking in front of her trailer, stopping to brush dust off the pair of lawn chairs. She took in the scenery and tipped her head back to gaze at the sky.

"It's probably not what you're used to." Harlow wasn't sure what'd possessed her to say that, so she amended, "But I've had much worse."

"So have I," Karen said softly.

"Okay, I'm ditching decorum and asking you a bunch of questions, Karen, so get ready."

She laughed. "Let's sit and enjoy the sunshine. It really is quite lovely here."

Harlow sat next to her.

"All right, you want the basic rundown on how I ended up working for your father?"

"I remember it was right about the time I started college."

"Yes. Initially your father hired me out of pity. See, my husband, one of his longtime clients, had a midlife crisis. He found a younger, thinner woman to replace me. I'd spent my life as a corporate executive's wife. I organized and planned and did everything to make my husband's rise to the top his sole focus. I raised our two children without much help from him besides financially. And when he filed for divorce, with no warning, I was out of a job."

Harlow made a sympathetic noise because Karen's husband sounded suspiciously like . . . Gene Pratt.

"Anyway, I met with Gene to discuss my financial situation. My ex-husband had been generous with the settlement. At some point I realized I didn't miss my ex-husband as much as I missed the support I'd provided him in his career. Gene was really the first person who'd told me I had valuable skills because I'd essentially been my husband's executive assistant for years. Gene hired me on the spot."

Harlow's jaw dropped.

Karen smiled. "I see that shocks you. There are many things about your father that would shock you. Anyway, I've worked for Gene ever since that first meeting. We've had a few bumps along the way, primarily regarding his treatment of you and your sister." She sighed. "I saw so much of my ex-husband in him when it came to his dealings with you girls, so it's been a struggle to compartmentalize that for me."

"He tends to"—*marginalize*—"compartmentalize us too. It's always struck me as odd that Tierney couldn't emulate that behavior with him."

"Because you could."

She shrugged. "He didn't have the same expectations for the hippie do-gooder daughter as he did for the brainiac daughter with the multiple finance degrees."

"I know I'm not stepping out of line when I tell you he is proud of you, Harlow. So proud that he's donated to some of the organizations you're so passionate about."

Another jaw-dropping moment. "Really?"

"Yes. But his pride is tinged with sadness because you remind him so much of the woman he loved and lost."

"Dad never talks about my mom."

"It makes you mad that he's spoken to me about her?"

"No." Harlow looked at Karen. "It makes me curious more than anything. About your relationship with him."

Karen didn't look away. Or fidget. She maintained a cool composure.

"Is this where you tell me it's none of my business?"

She laughed. "Oh honey, of course it's your business. Your father suffered a major trauma to his health and you've been dealing with it. Now I'm here, away from everything that's familiar to me, supposedly to help him get ready to leave a business he's spent his entire life building. And if I'm successful in my job, creating a smooth transition for him, then my reward is I'm out of a job. Bit of a catch-twenty-two, isn't it?"

"Yeah. Wow. I never thought of it that way."

"I'm paid to consider everything from every angle. And between us, I do have a selfish reason for agreeing to make Wyoming my temporary work environment."

"Which is?"

Karen leaned forward and her eyes danced with excitement. "I've never been out west. I've always wanted to visit Yellowstone, the Tetons, Devils Tower, the Rocky Mountains, Mount Rushmore, Crazy Horse Monument, the Battle of the Little Bighorn. This place is more centrally located to those sites. So I agreed to work four days if I had three days off in a row to get in my car and explore."

Harlow grinned; she'd never doubted Karen's tenacity, because she'd need to have it in massive doses to sustain working with Gene Pratt every day. "I'm so happy to hear that my father won't be working you to the bone the whole time. And if you want a local day-trip, Tobin is the man to see."

"Thanks for the tip. Who knows? Maybe I'll find a sexy, weathered cowboy to entertain me." She patted Harlow's knee and stood. "I'll take a quick peek at my new place, but the unpacking will have to wait until Gene is visiting with his new lady friends."

"Does that bother you?"

"No, it doesn't bother me. In fact I'm relieved. It gives me more free time." She winked and disappeared into her trailer.

There wasn't anything weird about that conversation. Nope.

What would her dad do if she just started grilling him about her mother? In the past, he'd always closed down.

Harlow wandered back to her trailer and settled in the chaise on the deck, tilting her head to bask in the sun.

Throughout her childhood, there'd been no mention of her mother, Jean. There'd been no pictures. No books or knickknacks. No jewelry or clothes or perfume bottles. It wasn't even until their stepmother had first arrived on the scene that Harlow realized the oddity of it. Barbara had been ready to purge all traces of Jean Pratt, but it'd been done long before she'd moved in.

One afternoon when Harlow had been left to her own devices, she'd found herself in her father's study. The room was off-limits and usually locked. But that day . . . well, an open door had been an open invitation. Most everything in the space was boring old-man stuff. Military and sports memorabilia. A variety of globes and crystal decanters. Leather-bound books. She'd about given up when she saw a box in the closet on the top shelf. She'd pulled it down and it'd weighed more than she'd anticipated, so the box had hit the floor and the contents spilled everywhere.

It was a box of pictures, letters and the pieces of paper that were tangible proof of memorable events in her mother's life. A concert ticket. A service award. A funeral program. She remembered her excitement in finally getting a glimpse into her mother. She'd known she wouldn't have enough time to look at it all, and she wasn't sure when she'd ever have the chance to see it again. So she'd dumped the contents in a garbage bag and replaced the box on the shelf.

Then congratulating herself for her cleverness, she'd spent hours poring over every scrap of paper, every photo, every item, no matter how inconsequential.

She'd learned her mother had lost her mother at a young age.

She'd learned her mother had had an abiding love for animals.

She'd learned her mother had adored her husband and sworn her life had started when she'd met him.

She'd learned her mother smoked.

But she hadn't learned if her mother's life had been fulfilling. Or if she'd had friends. Nothing could tell her what her mother smelled like. Or what it felt like to be hugged by her. Or if her mother had adored her children as much as her husband.

The box contained more than she'd imagined, but less than she'd expected.

So Harlow had put the bag in her closet and forgotten about it.

A few weeks later when she'd remembered the bag, she'd looked for it, but it wasn't there. It wasn't anywhere. Panicked, she'd asked the maid if she'd been in her closet and she learned the truth. The garbage bag containing every personal thing about her mother . . . had been thrown away.

She'd cried herself sick over it for almost a week.

A few months later, her father asked if she'd been in his study. Before she blurted out the truth, Barbara jumped in and berated him about his lousy organizational skills. She said she was surprised he didn't lose track of more papers.

In her father's eyes, she'd seen that he blamed Barbara for the empty box.

Harlow let him believe that. Sometimes she wondered if that guilt kept her from pestering her dad for stories about her mother. She'd destroyed any chance of a Hallmark moment, where her dad tearfully handed her the box.

But that'd also been another defining moment. She'd make memories and share them with those she loved, not hoard them like her father did, or have her life reduced to a small box of meaningless memorabilia like her mother's.

Shaking off the memory, she headed down to the barns to retrieve Isabelle from Renner.

"Aunt Harlow!" Isabelle came at her in a full run.

Harlow caught her. "Hey, bug. Whatcha been doing this morning?"

"Me'n Daddy made waffles with lots'n lots of sprinkles. And then we did baby stuff." Her nose wrinkled.

"Baby stuff?"

"Putting the bassinet in our bedroom. Stocking the nursery with newborn diapers. Finding the baby tub. I got the rest of the list Tierney gave me if you wanna look at it," Renner drawled behind her.

"I'll pass." She turned and looked at her brother-in-law. "Did you get some rest last night?"

"Yep. But I'll be damn glad when my wife is sleepin' beside me tonight."

"I'll bet. Any idea what time you'll be home?"

"Six or so. The doc is doin' rounds late and he's gotta sign off on Tierney before she's released."

Harlow shifted Isabelle on her hip. "I'll take her and hopefully she'll get a long n-a-p in."

"I don't wanna nap! I wanna watch Hugh ride the bull."

Her heart almost stopped. Her gaze moved to Renner. "Hugh is bull riding today?"

"No. We've got a couple of guests who are tryin' it out. Since I won't be here, Hugh is in charge of moving the bulls," he clarified for his daughter, "*not* ridin' them."

"But I wanna watch, Daddy."

Harlow kinda wanted to watch too.

Renner kissed his daughter's pouty mouth. "Aunt Harlow's in charge, baby girl. And if she lets you watch, you will be way on the other side of the chute."

She knew that was more a warning for her than Isabelle.

"Please, Aunt Harlow?"

Twist my arm, kid. "We'll see. Say good-bye to Daddy."

"Bye."

"Next time you see me, I'll be bringing your brother and your mama home."

She scowled. "Don't want the stupid baby in my house."

Renner opened his mouth, but wisely shut it. He kissed Isabelle on the cheek and left without another word.

Harlow opted to let her outburst slide. She set Isabelle down and took her hand. "You stay right by me at all times, understand?"

Isabelle nodded.

They followed the path down to the outdoor arena. Five-foot-high metal corrals surrounded the arena. The walkway around the outside was made up of old planks. There was no place to sit back here, since there was a seating area up by the chutes. She hoisted Isabelle onto the third rung and stood directly behind her.

"Daddy used to ride bulls," Isabelle announced.

"Uh-huh." Harlow squinted across the dirt for a glimpse of Hugh.

"Mama won't even let me have a pony."

Ah. There he was, standing on the upper ledge. Looked like Tobin manned the gate. So who was the guy offering the guest rider advice? Another cowboy hottie to be sure.

Then Tobin pulled the gate open and the bull and rider flew out of the chute.

The guy managed to hold on for about three seconds before he hit the dirt. Tobin raced over to help the guy up, which left Hugh to deal with the bull.

Desire shot straight to her core as she watched Hugh square off against the animal. Waving his arms, yelling, "He-yaw!" in a deep tone that echoed across the arena. She gasped when the bull charged. But Hugh weaved and ran backward toward the gate. The bull trotted past him and he closed the gate.

When he turned around, he noticed Harlow. He hollered something to Tobin and jogged across the arena.

Hugh was smiling when he reached the fence. "Hey. What're you doin' here?"

"Picking up bug. She mentioned you were bull riding, so I had to make sure you . . . weren't."

He laughed. "Nope. I'll leave that to the paying guests." He leaned in and whispered, "And to the young fools who don't have a beautiful woman lookin' at them the way you're lookin' at me."

"Not nice to tell secrets," Isabelle chastised them.

Tingles raced down that side of Harlow's body from Hugh's nearness. "What are you ladies up to?"

"We're goin' to my house and we're gonna play games and read books and make ice cream!"

"And take a nap," Harlow mouthed.

"That sounds like fun. Can I come?" Hugh asked.

"No! No boys."

A little aggression there.

"Shoot. I'll just have to go back to work, then." He paused. "Let me know when you're done tonight. I want to see you."

"Okay."

He shot Isabelle a quick glance. The girl must've been distracted, because Hugh stole a kiss. Then he moseyed away.

She shamelessly watched every boot step.

"Aunt Harlow. Can we go now?"

Only when Hugh disappeared behind the gate did she say, "Yep. Let's go."

⋘⋙

Hugh sucked at playing it cool.

He hauled Harlow into his arms almost before she'd finished the first knock, lifting her off her feet for a hot, wet, hungry kiss. He lowered her back to the floor and planted kisses down the arch of her neck. "Damn, you smell good."

"It's the lingering scent of cookies."

"Huh-uh, darlin'. It's all you." He forced himself to step away. "You want a glass of wine?"

"No thanks, I'm good."

"Tierney and Rhett both back home?"

"Yes. And can I say my sister should've stayed in the hospital another day? She's exhausted."

"They kick new moms out quick, don't they?"

"I don't get that. Anyway, Rhett was screaming; Isabelle was crying; Renner tried to calm Isabelle down, but she only wanted her mommy. So as I waved good-bye, Renner had the screaming baby, Tierney had the screaming child and they both looked ready to scream themselves." She shuddered. "It was enough to put me off ever having kids." She sauntered in front of him. "But not off having sex."

Hugh took her hands and kissed her knuckles. "That won't be an issue for us, since we're not havin' sex tonight."

Her eyes narrowed.

"Before you remind me that you have a say in when we get down and dirty, I'll rephrase that." He kissed her knuckles again. "I don't want it to only be about sex between us. So let's spend time together with our clothes on tonight."

"What did you have in mind?"

"A movie in Rawlins. If you don't load up on popcorn and candy, there's a place that has a decent vegetarian menu."

"You've eaten there?"

"No, but I looked it up online."

She stood on tiptoe and kissed him. "You sweet, sweet man."

"So that's a yes? 'Cause the movie starts in an hour."

"Let's go."

They held hands on the drive into Rawlins. And they talked of the events of their day easily, as if they'd been doing it for years. Harlow told him about Karen and how she suspected she'd been displaced in her duties to her father.

Now Hugh had to worry that she'd pack up and go to some far-flung corner of the world.

Fuck if that was happening. He'd just gotten her back. Since she hated being idle, he'd just have to find something for her to do that made her feel useful.

At the movie theater in Rawlins, they were in the long line for popcorn when Harlow hissed, "Shit," and turned away.

"What?"

"Don't be obvious, but that's my dad and Miz Maybelle at the cash register."

"No way."

"I'm not kidding."

Hugh scooted to the side for a better view. Sure enough, Gene and Miz Maybelle were acting awful chummy. "What do you wanna do about it, doll?"

"He's not supposed to be out of bed and on a damn date! God. If he's been faking his recovery time, I'm going to be so pissed."

"I don't think that's it. He told me that his recovery was going faster than he'd expected."

"Then he should be visiting his daughter and his new grandson, not out at the movies."

"He's not supposed to drive, right? Miz Maybelle picked him up, so he's not really breaking any rules, Harlow. He's probably suffering from cabin fever, so I can't blame him for needing a break. The movies are about the safest place he can be. At least he'll be sitting down."

She scowled at him. "I hope they sit in the middle of the theater so they don't see us."

"We can go and do something else tonight."

"No way. Now I have to stay and keep an eye on them. But so much for your hand job in the back row."

"Playing with fire, darlin', taunting me like that."

She eyed his hat. "You should've left that in the truck so they don't recognize you."

"'Cause no other guys in Wyoming wear cowboy hats except for me," he said dryly.

"Few of them are as sexy as you," she cooed.

He dropped a smacking kiss on her mouth.

"I'm going to follow them to see where they sit."

"You want Junior Mints or Raisinets with the popcorn?"

"Neither. None of that fake yellow grease they try and pass off as butter either."

"No hand job, no candy and now no butter on my popcorn?" He leaned in. "This ain't turning out to be the greatest date, Harlow."

She laughed. "Now who's sorry he put the kibosh on sex tonight?"

⋙

Late the next afternoon Hugh headed up to the lodge. He hoped to run into Harlow, although it'd be hard to act like they were just friends.

Like he hadn't been inside her with his mouth, his fingers, his cock. Like she hadn't turned him inside out with the way she'd given him her trust.

The man who for all intents and purposes had broken her heart and sent her running. Straight into the path of that fucker Fredrick.

He'd kept it together while Harlow relayed what she'd gone through. He'd done well for the most part. Asking if she had any sexual triggers hadn't been as difficult as hearing what they were and why.

Hugh had to stop, lean against the side of the building and unclench his fists. And his jaw. And force even breaths into his lungs, which had seized up in rage.

Think of her softness and sweetness. Think of her resilience. Be humbled that she's chosen you to reclaim the sexual part of herself. Be proud that you can be the man and the lover she needs. That you're able to give her new memories of how making love should be—sometimes raunchy, sometimes sweet, sometimes urgent, sometimes leisurely—but never scary or purposely painful.

But he also needed to show her it was—and always had been—more than sex between them. They'd started building something three years ago before he'd knocked everything back down to the foundation in one manic burst of fear. But from the first time she'd come back into his life when he'd seen her in the hospital, and she'd admitted to being lost, he'd known if she gave him the chance, they could dig through the rubble together and find a new footing.

So he couldn't make a misstep with her.

He scrubbed his hands over his beard and sighed. For all his blustering about not hiding that they were together, he wanted another week of just the two of them reconnecting.

A woman's laughter drifted down the hallway. Laughter he recognized. Hugh followed the sound to Gene Pratt's room.

The door was ajar. He peered inside and saw Vivien and Gene sitting side by side on the small love seat, heads bent close as they watched something on a cell phone. Gene had stretched his arm across the back of the couch and his fingers idly stroked Vivien's shoulder.

Fuck. Seriously? He'd seen Gene make the same move on Miz Maybelle last night at the movies. Down to the gentle kiss he placed on Vivien's temple. Down to the way he murmured into Vivien's ear that had her snuggling into him the exact same way Maybelle had.

Gene Pratt was a fucking player. And it pissed Hugh off that the rich bastard looked to be playing Hugh's friends *and* playing his daughter about how much his health had improved. Before he could storm in there, a manicured hand landed on the door handle and pulled the door shut.

He stepped back and looked at the stout woman with an authoritative manner. Had to be Karen, Gene's assistant.

"Can I help you with something, Hugh? It is Hugh, right?"

How had she known his name? "Yes, ma'am. You can tell me what kind of game your boss is playing with my friends. We saw him last night. Cozied up to Maybelle like he's cozied up to Vivien right now."

Karen cocked her head. "Your friends are adult women capable of making their own decisions and mistakes."

"So it *is* a mistake for any of them to get involved with Gene?"

"Some mistakes are fun and you know while you're making them that they are mistakes. Neither Gene nor your friends are looking for marriage, just for entertainment. So as much as I appreciate your concern, to be frank, it's none of your concern. They all know the score."

"So Miz Maybelle and Vivien know he's taken things farther with them than, say, Pearl, Sherry, Garnet and Tilda? The other ladies who also regularly entertain Gene?" Hugh paused. "Or is it the same with every damn one of them? Because I'm *not* okay with that and I seriously doubt any of the Mud Lilies would be either."

Karen sighed. "He spends more time with Vivien and Maybelle than any of the others."

"And?"

"And believe it or not, he really likes them both. I'd rather not say anything more than that. Gene is my boss and I strive to stay out of his personal affairs."

Right. "You'd have no issue with me mentioning to Vivien after she leaves that I saw Gene at the movies with Maybelle last night?"

Her eyes turned shrewd. "Cut to the chase. What do you want?"

"Jesus. That's not what I—" He snapped his mouth shut. *Let's not be too hasty. Karen has the power to help you get the one thing you want.* "Fine. There is something."

"There always is. Name it."

"Harlow is feeling displaced since your arrival. Gene is telling everyone he's a quick healer. For at least the next week can you make sure Harlow gets time with her dad every day? Make sure she feels she's contributing to his recovery."

"That's it?"

"Yep."

"Done." But Karen wasn't done. She studied him. "I wasn't expecting that. This favor isn't entirely selfless, is it?"

"No. But bein' that you 'strive to stay out of your boss's personal affairs,' let's leave this under the radar where Gene and Harlow are both concerned."

"Of course."

"Thanks." Hugh started to walk away toward the office.

Karen said, "Wait."

He turned.

"You wouldn't happen to have a single uncle or other older family member around here that you could introduce me to?"

Hugh laughed. "Nope. But if you're looking, try the Buckeye."

Chapter Thirteen

"*I*'m not ready for this."

Hugh brushed his mouth over the top of her ear. "Get ready, because we're almost there. And sweetheart, we have been together for over a week now."

"You're such a romantic, insisting we arrive on horseback."

Romantic. He snorted. That'd be the day. "Jimbo needed exercise and we have to come clean with my boss and your sister—sooner rather than later—so we're killing two birds with one horseback ride, darlin'."

"I don't want to hear about killing, Hugh, even in jest."

"My mistake." He placed a soft kiss on the side of her neck. "I *really* like ridin' tandem with you."

"I can tell."

"Shoot. I wanted it to be a surprise. What gave it away?"

"You mean your hard cock digging into my back wasn't a hint?"

He chuckled. "That's it?"

"That's the biggest indication." She leaned back and sighed. "You're good at this ridin' stuff, cowboy."

"Glad you approve. I'm sorry we never did anything like this before."

"If I would've asked you to take me horseback riding three years ago, smarmy you would've put me on a bucking bronc."

"Maybe." He directed Jimbo to the left. The top of Renner and Tierney's house came into view. "But we're goin' forward now, not back."

Harlow was quiet. Too quiet. It meant she was worried about something. "What?"

"What are we going to say to them?"

That wasn't what was really on her mind, but he let it go. "Tierney doesn't know why you left before?"

"No. She suspects something happened, but she's never prodded me too much about it and I've never confirmed it. I don't see what difference the past makes now."

He pressed his lips to the back of her head.

"But I don't want to lie, either."

"We can both admit we were attracted to each other before, but this time we acted on it. That's not a lie."

"And it's not the past I'm worried about, Hugh. It's when they ask our future plans. Whether we see this as something long-term. If I plan to stay in Wyoming, for how long, and what would I do to support myself?"

Hugh stilled. "Those are very specific questions, doll."

"Because I've already had the third degree from my dad."

"How'd you answer him?"

"I didn't. His line of questioning came up late in the day and Tilda showed up. He couldn't wait to get rid of me."

"You don't think your dad . . ." He shook his head. "Nah. Forget it."

"My dad is . . . what?"

"Is doin' all the Mud Lilies?"

Harlow elbowed him. "No way! And that mental image might put me off sex forever, buddy, so watch it."

"Forget I said anything," he breathed in her ear, "because I'm gonna have you in every possible way I can come up with and then some."

He felt her smile against his cheek. "So you're inventive?"

"What I'm lacking in sexual creativity I make up for in tenacity."

She groaned. "Can't you turn this horse around and take me back to bed?"

"Gotta face the music first. And after that, darlin', I'm gonna make you sing." Hugh kicked the horse into a gallop and cut to the corral. By the time they'd dismounted and he'd unsaddled Jimbo and turned him loose, the entire

Jackson family was waiting on the porch. And Hugh didn't miss their exchanged looks when he took Harlow's hand.

"Glad we got a warning call about this," Renner drawled.

Tierney had Rhett cradled in her arms, while Isabelle hung on Renner's leg. She didn't rush toward Aunt Harlow like she usually did.

Harlow was having none of it. "Hey, bug, where's my hug?"

"Mommy's mad at you. So am I."

"Solidarity in all family things, huh? I can respect that." Harlow stopped in front of Tierney, who stood three steps higher on the porch. "You want little pitchers to hear this?"

"You gonna be swearing and sharing raunchy stories?"

"One never knows with me."

Tierney stared at Harlow.

Harlow didn't back down.

Renner patted Isabelle's head. "Isa, sweetheart, you wanna work on that sticker book we started yesterday? You missed a couple of coloring pages."

"Can I color them in marker?" she asked her mother.

"Have Daddy set you up at the breakfast bar." Silent communication passed between husband and wife. Then Renner and his daughter scooted inside the house.

Hugh's anxiety kicked in. Neither Renner nor Tierney had spoken to him directly.

"So you're mad at me," Harlow said to her sister.

"Yes, I'm mad."

"Why? Because I kept something that happens between two consenting adults . . . private? Wow. Totally see where that would cause your concern and justifiable anger."

"You should've been a lawyer," Tierney said.

"Now, there's an insult."

Tierney scrutinized the two of them. She shoved her glasses up higher and absentmindedly patted the baby's bottom. "Fine. Show me."

Hugh looked at Harlow in confusion, but she offered a small shrug like she didn't know what was going on either. She said, "Show you what?" to her sister.

"How it is between you two when it's not insults and dirty looks." Tierney dipped her head to Hugh. "Go on. Kiss her."

"What the hell, T.?" Harlow demanded.

"You cannot expect me to believe that Grumpy"—Tierney inclined her head to Hugh—"and Harlot"—she gave Harlow the same head tip—"have set aside their contempt for one another without giving me a demonstration of how you've both been lovestruck and filled with lust."

"You're joking."

"Not even a little bit. I've heard of this kind of situation before. Where two people who couldn't stand each other each need something from the other person, so they fake being in love and try to fool their family and friends."

"You've *heard* of this?" Harlow laughed. "You mean you've read about it in one of those dirty books you love so much."

Tierney blushed.

Hugh bit his cheek to keep from grinning.

"Regardless," Tierney continued. "I would like to see that Hugh's tongue in your mouth doesn't kick in your gag reflex, Harlow."

"This is so stupid! We don't have to prove anything to you or anyone else. In fact, there's no way I'll do it."

"Harlow."

She whirled on Hugh. But before she could stomp off, he pulled her close, lowered his mouth to hers and kissed her. Not with hunger or overblown passion, but with familiarity. Slipping his hand up to sift through her hair. Letting his other hand mold to the curve of her hip while his thumb stroked her belly.

Harlow melted into him, twining her arms around his neck.

Everything else faded into the background. The world boiled down to the heat between eager bodies and the taste and tease of their lips and tongues.

"Jesus. Do I need to get out the damn hose?" Renner asked.

Harlow eased away first, but she kept her eyes on Hugh's as she stroked his jawline. Then they smiled at each other before they broke apart. "Blame your wife," Harlow said to Renner, who had reappeared on the porch. "She demanded proof that we weren't pulling a prank on you guys." Then Harlow aimed a cool look at Tierney. "Convinced?"

"Yes."

"Still mad?"

Tierney bit her lip. "I just feel out of the loop. I was so focused on my pregnancy—"

"As you should've been," Harlow said softly. "You have plenty of things on your mind besides what your wayward little sister has been up to with the hunky ranch foreman."

"But am I blind that I didn't notice you two had noticed each other?"

Hugh saw that Renner studied his wife intently.

"Did you think Janie was blind when you and Renner were sneaking around?" Harlow retorted.

Tierney glanced at Renner and a devious smirk curled her lips. "Not at all. At first we were constantly at each other's throats and then we weren't because we were too busy trying to get into each other's pants." She laughed. "Okay. I see it from the other side now."

"And we've got nothin' to hide," Hugh said.

Renner opened the child gate on the left side of the porch. "Let's head around back."

When Harlow reached Tierney, she stopped and said, "My turn to hold Rhett."

Hugh had spent quite a bit of time at Renner and Tierney's place. The Western elements found at the Split Rock were absent here. The house itself was traditional: two stories with a wraparound porch that connected to a deck on the back side. Since the location had steep terrain comprising rock on both sides, Renner had constructed a metal staircase that zigzagged down the rock face to the bowl-shaped bottom, the only place with grass.

"I have such house envy, sis. I could sit out here for hours," Harlow said, dropping into the swing.

"I have been. Since Ren put up the awning, we're shaded back here all afternoon. The breeze blows up from the canyon and it's perfect." She smiled softly at her husband and wrapped her arm around his waist.

Renner kissed the top of her head. "I'll open the door so we can keep an eye on Isa."

Hugh sat next to Harlow on the swing, stretching his arm along the back.

Tierney chose a single padded chair across from them. But when Renner returned, he pulled her to her feet, and then situated himself with Tierney on his lap.

"Is everything okay?" Harlow asked.

Renner whispered to Tierney and she shook her head.

Hugh felt Harlow stiffen beside him. Something was going on.

"Seriously, sis, what's up?"

"I'm just more tired than I should be. But I can't sleep. Rhett is a fussy baby"—Tierney shot a wry look at her son conked out in Harlow's arms—"so I've stopped breast-feeding and put him on formula so Renner can take some of the night feedings." Tierney snuggled into Renner and looked at Harlow warily. "Please don't yell at me for going with formula and not sticking with the natural way to feed my baby."

"How is your choice any of my business? You make me sound like some radical who'll turn you in to the La Leche League."

For the first time Hugh wondered if the "hippie-girl" nickname for Harlow bothered her. Harlow lived by her own code, but he'd never heard her try to impose it on anyone. From hearing her talk, he knew the humanitarian organizations she worked for weren't about enforcing their will or a specific belief system on the people they'd elected to help.

Renner said, "I know you and Gene had concerns about Tierney and this pregnancy, Harlow. I'm doin' what I can to help my wife understand that she shouldn't try to do it all. We're partners in this. Which means I'm takin' more time for her and the kids."

"That's good. Ain't like the Split Rock is gonna crumble if you're not there twelve hours a day," Hugh said. "I'll take this opportunity to remind you that you've got a good crew, boss. Let us carry the load. You shouldn't try and do it all either."

Tierney elbowed Renner. "See? Told ya."

"And I'm here for as long as you need me," Harlow added.

Hugh forced himself not to react. When he'd pressed Harlow on her plans, she'd hedged.

"About that." Tierney's gaze winged between Hugh and Harlow. "Is this a long-term thing? Or just a fling?"

"Way to cut to the chase, babe," Renner said with a grimace.

"Fine. Maybe I should've asked if you've told Dad yet."

"Actually, when I knew things were headed the way they were, I spoke to Gene," Hugh said.

Renner raised his eyebrows. "What'd he say?"

"Not much."

"Well, when Hugh said, 'Me'n Harlow are together—get used to it,' there wasn't a whole lot Dad *could* say," Harlow pointed out.

"True."

"Hugh and I aren't labeling this. We're living in the moment. How many moments that leads to . . . we'll see. Right?"

Fuck that. I'm just giving you time to get on board. Hugh knew exactly where this thing between them was leading. But he just kissed Harlow's nose and said, "Right, doll."

Footsteps sounded across the deck and Isabelle stopped in front of Harlow. She glared at the baby. "Put him down. You're *my* aunt and I don't hafta share you with him."

Looked like baby jealousy had struck.

Harlow said, "Take Rhett for a minute," and placed him in Hugh's arms, and then she was gone.

Shit. He tried not to show panic, but he didn't want to be responsible for this baby. Jesus. It was so freakin' small. So breakable in his big, rough hands.

"I'm pretty sure I wore that same look the first time I held Isabelle," Renner said. "Here. I'll take him."

Then Hugh could breathe again. He looked over, but Tierney had gone inside with Harlow and Isabelle.

"Isabelle is actin' out," Renner said. "It's driving Tierney crazy 'cause how are we supposed to discipline Isa for sibling jealousy?"

Hugh had no clue.

"Dealing with all this stuff . . ." Renner sighed. "Goin' from one kid to two kids has been a bigger adjustment than either of us expected. So, yeah, you're right. I need to delegate."

"Just tell me what you need done."

"Between me'n Tobin, the cattle are handled. But Tobin ain't workin' seven days a week. So if you could help out the mornings Tobin is gone, I'd appreciate it."

"No problem. I'm here."

"And this is one wrinkle I haven't mentioned to my wife yet, but the week we're contracted for in Kansas?"

Please don't say you're going to cancel it. "Yeah?"

"I can't go. I can't leave Tierney here with both kids. I've gotta be here for my wife."

Hugh snorted. "I didn't plan on you goin', because you didn't like bein' away from her *before* you two started procreating."

Renner grinned. "No lie. So I'm askin' you to take over the Phillipsburg deal and finish the final scheduling."

"Be happy to. In fact, you *do* remember my main job is supposed to be running Jackson Stock Contracting?"

"Daddy!" Isabelle yelled through the screen door. "I wanna do more stickers."

"Be right there, sweetheart." Renner shifted the baby, who'd started to fuss. "Bet bossy girl demands Daddy put the baby down." With that, he walked off.

Hugh stared after him. Once again Renner had dodged the question.

But maybe if Hugh did a great job in Kansas, it'd convince Renner not to abandon the stock contracting side. He had to at least try to save that side of their business.

⊂∞⊃

Hugh's preoccupation on the ride back to the Split Rock concerned Harlow. Something had changed in the short amount of time Renner and Hugh had been left alone on the deck. Had Hugh's boss expressed displeasure about their relationship?

And she had to think of it in those terms. Renner was responsible for Hugh's livelihood. While she didn't think Renner the type to make the same kind of ultimatums as her father, it could be a difficult work situation.

Back at the barn at the Split Rock, she draped the saddle blanket over the railing to dry while Hugh brushed Jimbo down. She readied a bucket of oats and waited out by the corral.

Hugh ambled out and her heart fluttered. Everything about him was just so quietly commanding.

After the oats were gone, Hugh hung up the pail and reached for her hand.

She gazed into his face and tried to make out his expression, since it was perpetually shadowed by his hat. "What now?"

"You tell me."

"Should we go our separate ways to eat dinner and meet up later?"

He tugged her against his body. "Not really hungry. At least not for food."

She loved the dark glint in his eyes. "Then let's feed that other appetite of yours first."

Next thing she knew, he was dragging her uphill at a good clip. He took the shortcut to his cabin, easily hoisting her over the rock wall. By the time they reached the front door, his house key dangled in his hand and he shoved it in the lock.

The second they were inside, Hugh kicked the door shut and pressed her against it. "You're so fuckin' hot. Havin' this ass"—he latched on to her butt cheeks with both hands—"pressing against my cock as we rode has kept me hard the last three hours."

"Poor hard cock." She reached for his belt buckle as she teased his throat with nipping kisses. "So confined. Let's give him some breathing room."

Hugh groaned when she got the zipper down. He hissed when she slipped her hands inside his boxers and freed him. As she pushed his jeans down his legs, she lowered to her knees.

Sometimes it was all about the tease. Driving him to the edge, backing off and building him up again until she felt his entire body vibrate with the need for release.

But she didn't want that for him now. This time she wanted his pleasure fast and acute. She circled the base of his cock with her hand and pulled it away from his belly, enclosing as much of the shaft in her mouth as she could.

"Fuck, Harlow. That's so . . ." He groaned again. Muttered something she couldn't make out.

She smiled and started to work him, sliding his length in and out. This time she wouldn't use her hands, just the wet heat and suction of her mouth.

His callused hands cupped her face. He gently stroked the hollows of her cheeks, never forcing himself deeper, allowing her to set the pace.

Harlow felt his burning gaze from head to toe. She knew the visual of her on her knees, wanting to do this for him, was an epic turn-on for him.

"So close," he said on a sharp exhalation.

"Faster?"

"Fuck yeah."

She lost herself in the urgency. In the now familiar taste and scent of him. In the way she'd become attuned to the subtle changes in his breathing, in his touch.

He made an inarticulate noise, his cock grew harder against her lips and then he was done. His warm, salty seed spurted against the back of her tongue as she held him in her mouth, sucking and then swallowing until he'd spent completely.

After a minute or so when his body quit shuddering, he dropped his hand back against the door to brace himself.

Harlow pulled back and smirked at him. Even after he'd just come, he was still hard. She kissed the tip of his cock and then the tops of both of his thighs before she looked up.

His brown eyes were soft. Sated. His hand shook a little when he tucked her hair behind her ear. "You love doin' that, don't you?"

"Yes."

"You . . ." He gave her a goofy smile. "Not thinkin' straight yet, but damn. That was . . ."

She rolled to her feet and tugged his boxers and jeans back into place.

He zipped and buckled before wrapping her in his arms. "I never know if I'm supposed to thank you or build a shrine to you."

"A shrine. Definitely. With a chocolate fountain."

He chuckled. "You got time to stick around for a while?"

"Sure. But can I make myself a salad? I am a little hungry."

"There's stuff in there from last time." He paused. "Will it bother you if I heat up a burger?"

"No, that's fine."

They fixed their individual meals and sat at the table to eat. After a quick cleanup—and how thoughtful was it that Hugh brushed his teeth so he wouldn't taste like meat when he kissed her?—they settled in front of the TV to watch episodes of *Fringe*. It'd surprised her to discover his favorite shows and movies were sci-fi, not Westerns.

At one point, she looked over and saw Hugh lost in thought, not paying attention to the show at all. She used the remote to hit pause and waited for him to notice.

Roughly thirty seconds passed before he glanced over at her. "Something wrong?"

"You tell me." Harlow climbed on his lap, her knees against his hips and her forearms resting on his shoulders. "What's on your mind? Did Renner warn you off me because I'm a man-eater who'll break you before I move on?"

Hugh lifted his mouth to hers for an achingly sweet kiss. "No. And I would've told him to back off if he had. 'Cause, darlin', you ain't no carnivore."

"Damn straight. But something is eating at you."

"Two things are."

Getting him to talk tried her patience at times, but she'd figured out he would talk only when he was ready. Better that than him blurting out the first thing that popped into his head.

"The stock contracting side of Renner's business, which used to be his only business, is providing stock for an event in Kansas. Renner always intended to go, but now he won't leave Tierney and the kids, which is understandable. That leaves me shorthanded."

"So you'll have to back out?"

"No, I'll have to round up replacements."

"But?"

"But I'm afraid you'll leave while I'm gone. And I never thought I'd say this, but I'd be willing to back out of our contract if I thought me staying here would keep you around longer."

Her heart just about melted.

Hugh rested his forehead against hers. "I know you don't wanna hear this. You wanna keep everything casual. I get that. But I'm so fuckin' crazy about you, Harlow. Crazy and afraid that I'm alone in feeling this way."

She curled her hands around his face and tipped his head back to look into his eyes. "You're not alone. I'm pretty crazy about you too. But I don't want to define this; I don't want any pressure for long-term plans for either of us. And yet, I want to be with you twenty-four/seven."

A smile bloomed on his face and she swore the heavens opened up.

She shrieked in surprise when he stood, scrambling to get her legs around his waist as he strode toward the bedroom. "Hugh! What are you doing?"

"Takin' you to bed to cement our mutual craziness." As soon as they entered the bedroom, he stripped her completely. Touched her. Teased to heighten her awareness that he knew exactly how to get her hot and bothered. How to make her wet and writhing for him.

Then he pinned her arms above her head and fit himself inside her. He paused to let his full weight rest on her body, pushing it deeper into the mattress, as his big hands traveled from her wrists, down her arms and the sides of her body.

The power he possessed didn't scare her. He was a completely different kind of guy from Fredrick. The rightness of how they were together this time around scared her far more.

Hugh nuzzled her neck. After he kissed her lips once, he whispered, "Crazy about you," and spent the next hour proving it.

Chapter Fourteen

*I*ke's invitation to meet at Buckeye Joe's for a drink caused Hugh some concern. He and Ike were friends, but they never hung out just the two of them. He hoped Ike didn't have some kind of personal problem, because he'd never been comfortable handing out advice.

Since happy hour had ended, the Buckeye wasn't jam-packed. Hugh paused at the end of the dance floor, looking for Ike, since he'd seen his rig parked out front.

Ike waved at him from the far back table.

Hugh nodded at the folks he knew as he made his way to the back of the bar. He pulled out the chair opposite Ike, sat down and said, "Hey."

"Hey. I woulda ordered you a beer, but I figured you'd rather wait for service than drink a warm one."

"Got that right."

Ike lifted his can toward the bar, signaling to a waitress.

Hugh stretched his arm across the chair beside his. "It's no secret I ain't good at making small talk, so what's on your mind?"

"Remember when you were talking about that rodeo in Kansas and you mentioned you might need hired hands to help you out?"

"I do." He paused to thank Susan for dropping off his Budweiser. He sipped and set the bottle down. "Why? You lookin' for work?"

Ike glanced down at his own beer before he met Hugh's gaze. "Yeah, I guess I am."

Hugh waited while Ike gathered his thoughts.

"I've been a cattle broker for a dozen years. Started out doin' it because I liked the challenge. I liked connecting buyers and sellers. I liked bein' part of the ag community."

"But?"

"But, with the way technology has changed things in the past five years, so much of my job, at least the parts of it that got me into this business in the first place, have changed. I've always spent my working hours surgically attached to my cell phone. That never bothered me."

"What does bother you?"

"That I've gone from a salesman to a videographer. I don't even have to meet with folks face-to-face anymore. Buyers or sellers. The sellers upload videos of the stock they're selling. Then the buyers either go to a specific site to view the videos or it's sent as an e-mail attachment."

"They're cutting out the middleman," Hugh stated.

"Basically. Not in all cases. I've dealt with many of these ranchers for years and they're loyal. But they're the older generation. The next generation that's taking over, well, I ain't gotta tell you that they grew up with technology, so it's easier for them to handle their stock sales virtually."

Hugh took another sip of beer. "Without getting into specifics, your income has dropped?"

Ike nodded. "Cattle prices have been at an all-time high, and the volume of the deals I was making offset the losses. But as I'm lookin' to the fall, when I do a huge bulk of my business, my calls are down damn near seventy percent."

"Holy shit."

"Yeah." Ike leaned back in his chair, mimicking Hugh's posture. "I've never been a big spender. No wife, no kids, the biggest chunk of my income goes to traveling expenses and my mortgage. So it ain't like I'm hurting. I can tighten my belt, drink cheaper beer"—he tipped his chin at the Pabst Blue Ribbon can in front of him—"and I'll be fine for a few years."

"So you're *not* lookin' for work?" Hugh asked with confusion.

"I'm lookin' to find a way to keep doin' what I'm doin', working within the Western way of life. That's what I'm missing. The people. The travel."

That's when Hugh realized he had found someone he could talk to about his frustrations with the changes in his own life and professional responsibilities. "I hear ya."

"And feel free to correct me if I'm wrong, but you were on the road a lot for a number of years with Renner as he built up Jackson Stock Contracting."

"Yep. We spent almost seven months outta every year on the road."

"Do you miss it?"

Hugh met Ike's curious stare. "Like you wouldn't believe."

Ike just nodded.

"Look, I know you're affiliated with Jackson Cattle Company—"

"What we're talking about here won't go any farther than us," Ike said. "I just told you I was pretty damn disillusioned with my job. I'd like to think now that we've opened a dialogue, you can be honest with me too. In ways you can't be with your boss or your coworkers."

At that, Hugh upended his beer, turned and caught Susan's eye for two more.

"That bad, huh?" Ike said with a laugh.

Hugh shrugged. "Figured our throats might get dry if we're talkin' about all this."

Neither spoke until the next round had been delivered.

"What's your story?"

"I started out as a hand at a stockyard. Didn't love it—it was just work. A couple years into it, I married the boss's daughter. And even with that dumb mistake, I knew the man wouldn't ever give me a piece of the business. I'd always just be a shit shoveler. So I went lookin' for something else—not any kind of personal fulfillment bullshit, but a job that paid more, because my wife had expensive tastes. Renner hired me. That's when I realized what I wanted to do. And up until he bought the land in Wyoming, that's what I thought Renner's long-term plans were too."

Ike fiddled with the pop-top on his beer can. "Ain't it funny how things change?"

"Don't get me wrong. I like it here. I thought if we were lookin' to provide stock for the Mountain Circuit, we'd probably be better off based out of Wyoming. But instead of growing the stock contracting business like I'd assumed he would, Renner has expended way more effort and money building a cattle company. I never wanted to be in the cattle business like we are. That ain't what I signed on for."

"I figured that might be the case. And don't go thinking that it's obvious to anyone else. It's plain to me because I recognize the restlessness." He paused. "How long's this been eating at you?"

"For the first year, I was dealing with the divorce and learning to be single again. The second year, Renner was focused on the resort and the cattle company. All the while he's learning to be a married man. Then a father. That's when he decided to scale back on the travel. And I would've been fine without him bein' on-site for every rodeo event. But he somehow got it in his head that if he couldn't be there, then it wasn't worth doin'."

"Which you took as he didn't trust you to do the job you'd been doin' all along," Ike said.

"Yep. I coulda understood if the stock contracting end of things was losing him money, but it wasn't. I dealt with the payouts for the day hires. I know what the feed costs were. Fuel costs. Maintenance costs."

"And?"

"And two years ago, with cutting out twelve events, the profit had increased by about five percent." Hugh swallowed a mouthful of beer. "Bear in mind the price of fuel two summers ago was the highest it'd ever been. The venues he dropped from the schedule were small, granted, but those smaller venues are the moneymakers, because you gotta supply less stock, gotta hire less behind-the-chutes help. We can stay on the grounds. There ain't never been a time that staying on the fairground camping areas hasn't led to picking up another rodeo event."

Ike studied him.

Which got his back up. "What?"

"You haven't pointed out any of this to Renner, have you?"

"That's what's bugging the piss outta me. I shouldn't *have* to point it out. This is stuff that Renner used to live and breathe. Now he's much more focused on the room fill/rate ratio at the Split Rock and the calf weight ratio of the hardier herd he's building. I don't care about either of those things. That genetic junk is Tobin's area of expertise. He's happier than a pig in shit jawing on about that with Ren. Christ. It's about the only damn time I wanna wear earplugs."

Ike grinned. "I'll admit I'd be listening in on those conversations." His smile faded. "Well, I woulda used to listen in, hoping I could find something that'd give me an advantage when brokering sales. But now . . ."

"Now what?"

"Now I'm more interested in finding out what rodeo events are coming up and if you've already lined up local stock for the timed events."

Hugh pushed his hat back a fraction and rested his arms on the table. "I'm afraid Renner is so focused on his family and his baby son he hasn't set any of that up."

"Jesus. Ain't that like a week out?"

"Yep."

"See, this is where I come in. I've got contacts all over the place. You say the word, tell me how many calves and steers you need for a two-day event and I'll line it up."

"That'd be a huge load off my mind. Renner's too."

"And," Ike continued, "I'm a damn good hand. So I'd help out behind the scenes and the arena if need be."

"What're your salary requirements?"

Ike considered. "Travel expenses for sure. But I'd be willing to keep the same pay rate as the day-labor hands you hire."

Hugh barely kept his mouth from dropping open. "No kidding?"

"I'm serious about wanting to stay in this lifestyle. It'd be a challenge for me, keeping up those charming sales tactics I'm known for"—he grinned like a loon—"balanced with the physical demands of taking care of livestock rather than just selling them."

"This sounds like a brilliant fuckin' plan. But that's the problem, because I don't know what the boss will say."

"What's your job description?"

"Officially? Manager."

"For both the stock contracting and the cattle company?"

He nodded. "On the cattle side it's only because I was already in place before Tobin got hired. But I have no problem deferring to him. Why?"

"Here's what I propose you do. Then we'll know where to go from there."

Ike detailed the proposal and Hugh admitted the man's knowledge of stock contracting was top-notch. And if he was a betting man, he'd say Ike would give Renner a run for his money on contacts.

"I don't have to tell you most of this stuff. You know it. All's you gotta do is double-check it, present it to Renner and see what he says."

That's what he was worried about. Renner feeling threatened that Hugh was trying to tell him how to run the stock contracting business he'd spent years building.

If he spent years building it, then why doesn't he have the same level of pride in it that he used to?

"I see them wheels churning, Pritchett."

He sighed. "My role has always been second-in-command."

"So? Show Renner you've taken the initiative. Maybe he hasn't asked you to take on more responsibilities because you've never indicated you're interested."

"Fuck. I hate that you could be right." But for the first time in a long time, Hugh felt ready to take the next step.

"You do research on your end and I'll do some on my end. What's the time frame we're looking at?"

"I'd say tomorrow."

"Shit."

"There won't be anyone in the office tonight, so I'll start pulling files and seeing what's what. Then we can reconvene tomorrow afternoon and go from there. The better we have the facts lined up, the more likely Renner is to give us free rein."

Ike held up his beer can. "I'll drink to that."

Hugh touched his bottle to the can. "Me too."

They parted ways soon after.

On the short drive back to the Split Rock, his mind was running in ten different directions. He pulled up to the back of the barn and unlocked the door.

Lights on, computer booted, sleeves rolled up, he got to work.

❧

Harlow was restless.

She'd played with Isabelle; she'd cuddled baby Rhett while Tierney showered. She'd stopped in to see her dad but he'd hung the DO NOT DIS-TURB sign on his door handle—and she swore she heard giggling inside the room.

Probably the TV.

The lodge was full, so she couldn't venture to the bar, or take a dip in the pool.

Tobin had volunteered as DD for the Mud Lilies' hiking trip—and she'd been too afraid to ask why they needed a sober driver after a hike.

Dave and Yvette were cuddled up in front of the TV—not that Harlow had been peeking in their windows, but it was remarkably easy to see inside their trailer.

Note to self: Shut the curtains when Hugh comes over.

And that seemed to be the crux of her problem.

She missed Hugh.

Tonight when she'd seen his truck drive past after six, she pretended it didn't bother her that she hadn't known where he was going.

But it did bother her, because she liked him, dammit. The man was so easy to be with. His presence either soothed her or inflamed her. And she thought he liked hanging out with her too, even if they weren't naked.

Maybe taking a walk around the resort would take the edge off. And if her casual, no-destination-in-mind stroll passed by Hugh's cabin, and if she saw the lights on, she might stop and say hello.

You are so gone over him. And this is exactly what happened to you last time.

So just to prove she had willpower where one Hugh Pritchett was concerned, Harlow purposely headed down the hill on the other side of his cabin.

She parked herself on the sandstone bench and gazed up at the stars. The warm night air, nearly absent of bugs, flowed over her bare arms and legs as gently as a lover's caress.

Hugh hadn't been gentle with her last night. Right after entering her trailer, he'd pushed her face-first against the wall, arms above her head. He'd yanked her athletic shorts to her ankles and ran those rough-skinned hands up the backs of her calves and the outsides of her thighs.

He'd touched her, teased her, in absolute silence, save for their labored breaths. Hers bounced off the paneled wall. His drifted over her body.

Once he'd electrified every inch of her skin, he'd twisted his hand in her hair, pulling her head down until the crown met the wall. While holding her in place, he'd attacked the nape of her neck with hot sucking kisses, plus barely there flicks of his tongue. Then he used his teeth.

Oh god, the scrape of his teeth drove her mad. And he'd come to know the reactions of her body so well that she'd had a tiny orgasm just from the relentless attention he gave the backs of her shoulders and the side of her throat.

The only sound more erotic than the chink of a metal belt buckle hitting the floor was Hugh's guttural grunt of male satisfaction as he impaled her.

Even now, the remembrance of his big hands curled around her hips as he held her in place, methodically fucking her, made her panties wet, her nipples tight and her throat dry.

And it should've bothered her, how he just took her whenever he wanted, however he wanted, but usually she was too busy coming to be PC about things between them. The man had mad fucking skills. He never left her wanting. He never asked for direction. He just . . . knew what she needed and gave it to her without a play-by-play.

Yeah, thinking about how amazingly well he fucked was not easing her restlessness, but giving her skin a distinctive itch that only he could scratch.

Close your eyes. Breathe in the calming sage.

Harlow had found a calmer internal place when the scent of manure wafted to her from the arena. She squinted beyond the tree line and saw a light was on in the barn. Odd. For all the loosey-goosey attitude around here about locking stuff, the barn lights were shut off and the door was always padlocked every night. She inched her way down the hill and skirted the empty corral attached to the left side of the building. Maybe it spoke of her hopeful nature, but everything inside her relaxed when she saw Hugh's pickup parked by the main door.

At least now she knew where he was. Hugh rarely worked at night and she didn't want to intrude. So should she head back to her trailer? Or would he welcome her dropping in to say hey?

All the entrances were buttoned up except the far back door. The hinges squeaked loud enough to wake the dead.

Hugh called out, "Who's there?"

"Just Harlow."

The softer creak of his office chair preceded the heavy strikes of his bootheels as he crossed the wooden flooring.

Then there he was, leaning in the doorway. Looking good enough to eat.

"C'mere, just Harlow."

She sauntered forward, her heart racing.

Backlit from the office lights, Hugh had a larger-than-usual presence. And she fought the urge to run to him.

He didn't appear to move at all until she made eye contact with him. Then she noticed his lips were curved into a soft smile.

"Am I interrupting? I saw the light on and thought I'd check it out."

"You running the night watch now?"

"Just keeping my eyes on you, cowboy." She planted her hands on his chest and rolled on the balls of her feet so she could taste the smirk on his mouth.

The instant her lips touched his, Hugh crushed her into his arms and lifted her until their mouths were at the same level. Then still kissing her with the infinite sweetness she craved, he walked them backward. He didn't release her until he was damn good and ready.

He pulled back far enough to gaze into her eyes. "What?"

"What do you mean, what?"

"You just chuckled in my mouth, woman."

"Oh. That." Harlow pecked him on the lips. "A little Hugh-ism popped into my head and amused me."

"Hugh-ism," he repeated. "Darlin', do I even wanna know?"

"Someday."

He set her down. "So you were just outside soaking in the mountain air and noticed my truck parked down here and the lights on in the barn?"

"No. I knew you left earlier and I was at loose ends. I tried to come up with something to do, but all my thoughts just kept coming back to you." She studied the buttons on his shirt. "And I hope you don't think I'm a clingy freak, but I missed seeing you today."

"Harlow—"

"I know, I know. You have a life. Ranch responsibilities. You probably have fifty other things to do besides hang out with me—"

Hugh pressed his palm to her mouth. "Stop talking and listen to me." She blinked at him.

"I'm crazy about you. I'd blow off my job if I could spend every moment of the day with you. That's the truth. I didn't think you were ready to hear that, but apparently you are."

She nodded.

"I'm not one of those guys with slick words and moves. I'd rather say nothin' than say the wrong thing. So I'll lay it out. I don't have fifty things I'd rather be doin'." He flashed his teeth. "Unless it's figuring out fifty different ways to do you."

Harlow twined herself around him. "After you admitted that, look out. I'm gonna be on you like white on rice."

"Lookin' forward to it." Hugh turned, dropped into his office chair and plopped her on his lap. "I was just about to call it a night anyway."

"Would you've tracked me down?"

"Yep. Then I would've stripped you down and gone down on you."

"I can make it to my trailer in five minutes if I run."

He chuckled against her ear. "No need to rush off. It's a standing offer."

"Lucky me." She looked at his computer screen and the stacks of files strewn across the desk. "What are you working on?"

"A proposal for Renner."

"I hate to break it to you, big guy, but he's unavailable."

"You're in a mood," he murmured against the side of her throat.

She didn't say anything, since she wasn't sure how he'd take it.

"I can feel you thinking. Something on your mind?"

"I know you say I can tell you anything, but this . . . maybe this falls into that gray area known as 'rich girl' problems."

"Wrong. And you know you'll feel better once you get it off your chest."

Just say it. "I'm afraid my time here is almost done."

"Done? Why?"

"My dad is improving every day. Tierney and Renner are trying to figure out how to deal with two kids. I'm so used to being on the go that when everything grinds to a halt, I don't know what to do with myself."

"You're bored."

Harlow tilted her head to the side and looked at him. "Not with you. But this has been building for the last couple of days and like I said, I'm afraid it'll just get worse."

Hugh shifted her around, draping her legs over his hips. His eyes were so somber when he slid his hand along her jaw and feathered his thumb over her lips. "Do you remember when you told me you worry you've lost the need for adventure?"

She nodded.

"And you missed the spark of excitement to try something new?"

Harlow's eyes narrowed.

He grinned. "I ain't circling this back around to sex. But I do wanna ask you something serious."

"Okay."

"In roughly a week I'll be taking off for Kansas to supply stock for the Phillipsburg Fair and Rodeo and I've got a line on a couple of other smaller ones. I want you to come with me."

"You do?"

"Yeah. I'd put you to work."

"Put me to work doing what?"

"Not bein' vague or trying to pull one over on you, but I'd have you doin' whatever I need you to do."

"Hugh. That is completely vague."

He rested his forehead against hers. "I know. I don't find out that information until the last minute. The point I'm tryin' to make is if you don't have objections to working with animals, then I want you to come with me."

"We'd have our own rodeo adventure?"

"Yep. For two weeks."

"And you think I'm capable of handling it."

"Doll, you're more than qualified. And anything you don't know how to do, I'd teach you."

Yes. This was exactly what she needed.

"I know, darlin'. That's why I asked you."

Harlow jerked her head back. "I didn't mean to say that out loud."

"But I'm glad you did." He pressed a soft kiss to the hollow of her throat. "So is that a yes?"

"Am I allowed to have conditions?"

He groaned. "Like what?"

"Like if my dad takes a turn for the worse, I can back out?"

"No, hippie-girl, I'm gonna make you come with me regardless of what happens to members of your family."

She whapped his arm.

"Of course if something like that arises, I'll come up with an alternative. But like I said before, as much as I want you with me for the pure pleasure of havin' your warm, soft body next to mine in that cramped bed for fourteen nights, there won't be much leisure time until we're on the road to the next event."

"And if I don't come along, you'll have to hire someone else?"

"Yep. And this is just between us, 'cause I haven't brought it up with

Renner yet, but Ike would be with us. If I'm doin' Renner's job, someone's gotta be doin' mine and Ike is more than qualified."

"Do you think Renner will have a problem with that?"

An annoyed look briefly entered his eyes. "Doubtful. We're committed to venue and it'd be shitty if we backed out now. Ike wouldn't be staying with us; he'd be driving one of the transport trucks. I'll have to peg Riss to drive the cattle truck for the bulls."

Harlow grinned. "I can't wait. I don't suppose we can go tomorrow?"

He shook his head. "I've got some finagling to do first."

Then Hugh's eyes darkened and he slipped his hands down to the buttons on her blouse. "Enough talking," he said gruffly. "I need me some sugar."

She climbed off his lap and clasped his hands, tugging them to indicate she wanted him to stand too. Trying to move Hugh on her own? She wasn't nearly strong enough.

"Whatcha got in mind?"

First Harlow untucked his shirt. In doing that, she released the clean scent of him, laundry soap and the subtle aroma of pine from his aftershave. She popped the pearl snap buttons on his shirt from the bottom up, happy to see he hadn't worn a tee or a muscle shirt for once. She rubbed her face across his chest, loving that he was such a man with the hair on his chest being as sexy as the hair on his face. Her lips found his nipple and she teased it with soft kisses and tiny tongue flicks.

He hissed.

So while she petted and stroked him with her mouth, her hands zeroed in on his belt buckle. Once she'd pulled the leather clear of the metal, she unbuttoned and unzipped his jeans. His cock was already hard and poking up from the waistband of his boxer briefs. She tugged on the denim until the material cleared his lean hips and muscled thighs and bagged around his knees.

"I like where this is goin', darlin'."

"I thought you might." Locking her greedy gaze to his, she cupped his butt cheeks and slid his boxer briefs to his knees.

"Fuckin' sexy-ass woman." He curled a shaking hand around her face. "You getting on your knees for me, doll?"

"No. I want this fine cowboy butt on the desk, your legs spread and your hands behind you, outta my way." She angled her head and lightly bit down on the inside of his wrist. "Think you can handle that?"

"I'm willing to die trying."

She laughed and kept touching the slope of his broad shoulders and the thick slabs of his furred chest as he scooted into position. Harlow stepped between his legs and rubbed her lips over his. "Look at you. Being all obedient and shit."

His answering grunt turned into a groan when she wrapped her fingers around his dick and pumped.

Hooking the chair leg with her foot, she dragged it over. After sitting down, she scooted closer so his cock was at her mouth level. Harlow gave him one long lick, from root to tip. "Gonna be hard not to use your hands?"

"Gonna be hard to deep throat me without my hands to guide you?" he shot back.

"Hugh. Sweetheart. This bad boy is at least nine inches. There's no way I can get it that deep in my throat."

"Never know unless you try." The humor in his eyes morphed into heat when she rimmed the sweet spot with her tongue. Then she suckled the head.

Yeah. She thought that'd shut him up.

Harlow closed her eyes and gave herself over to the wash of pleasure she got from pleasuring him this way. She loved feeling the hardness of his flesh covered in satiny smooth skin gliding over her tongue. And the trust he placed in her, allowing her to use her teeth and the quick motion of her hand.

And Hugh was a watcher. He didn't close his eyes and let his head fall back as she sucked and stroked and teased. His eyes were glued on the wet, sucking motion of his sex plunging between her lips. Exiting her mouth shinier and wetter than when it went in.

The last time she'd blown him, he'd held her head captive as he moved his hips. He hadn't pushed her too far, understanding a face fucking from a well-endowed man like him was something that had to be worked up to.

"Harlow. Get me wet. Don't swallow. Let the saliva fill your mouth and coat me. Fuck. Yes. Goddamn warm and slippery perfection."

When he kept offering suggestions in that husky tone, she didn't feel as if he were directing her, but praising her for rendering him almost incoherent.

She curled her fingers around the girth, her mouth and hand working in tandem. Sweat broke out on her forehead and trickled down her spine from the nape of her neck. The playful teasing ended as her determination to make this strong man surrender to her kicked in. His sexy growls vibrated throughout her body, increasing the buzz she got from having control of his cock.

"Take me deep a couple of times. Fuck. That's it. Can't hold off."

So don't. Give it to me. Give me all of you.

"So fuckin' hot and wet. Fuck. I'm almost there."

Harlow had reached that last level, her hand jacking him faster and faster as she bobbed her head. Although her panties were soaked, she didn't squirm to try and get friction to get herself off. This was about him and she didn't want to miss out on that fleeting moment when his cock hardened the final bit, followed by his stillness in breath and body. The temporary suspension of time and place right before his taste exploded on her tongue in a salty, musky rush of heat.

"Sweet Jesus. Don't stop."

She sucked hard, yet kept that constant stroking motion of her tongue beneath the cockhead. His body shook and jerked with each spurt. She let his essence fill her mouth, keeping the heat and wetness surrounding his rigid pulsating flesh, until he exhaled. Then she slid his cock into her throat just past her gag reflex and swallowed and swallowed and swallowed.

After a few moments, he said, "I'm never gonna look at this desk the same again."

"Mmm." She nuzzled the happy trail of soft fur that led up to his belly button.

"Harlow. Let me take care of you now."

She shook her head and stood. "While I love your hands on me and all the inventive ways you like to get me off, let me have this. This was for you."

When Harlow reached the door, Hugh said, "You can visit me in the barn anytime, darlin'."

Chapter Fifteen

*H*ugh hated confrontation. Especially when he knew what should be a simple conversation could turn into a big ol' argument.

He'd gone over all his paperwork at least four times. Since he knew sharp-eyed Renner would zero in on any weak point or potential problem, Hugh had made damn sure there weren't any.

Tobin walked in and took the seat across from Hugh's desk. "Hey. No offense, man, but you look about to barf."

"I just might." He breathed in slowly. "I suck at this kinda stuff."

"I disagree."

Hugh's gaze snapped to Tobin's. "Why?"

"When you first got here and you were dealing with your divorce and settling in, you did whatever Ren said without question. But somewhere along the line you started doin' what he paid you to do—which is manage his stock. And I suspect if you'd pushed a little harder, he'd have given you more input on the stock contracting business."

"Seems to be a moot point now."

"Doesn't have to be." Tobin laced his fingers behind his head, the picture of relaxation. "Look, we both know his focus ain't been where it needs to be if he's gonna continue with the stock contracting side. Has he given you reasons on why that is?"

"Not really. What he tells me sounds more like excuses."

"In the meantime, he's doubled the size of his herd. And I think . . ." Tobin shook his head. "Never mind."

"No, go on and tell me. You're here with me every damn day, T. While I ain't complaining, I know that what you're doin' on a day-to-day basis ain't what you signed on for either."

"That's a fact. But Fletch helped Renner see his dream of a dedicated genetics lab and semen-collection facility was just that—a dream. Havin' a place for expansion and actually expanding into those specialized areas of the cattle business were two different things."

"But nothing's changed in the three years since Fletch took Renner to task on that, except that Tanna got a really nice place to train," Hugh pointed out.

Tobin grinned. "Sometimes I wonder if that wasn't Fletch's intent all along."

"Could be. And maybe it makes me a dick for saying this, but I've seen how bein' in a relationship changes these guys. Their priorities change." He had to wonder how he'd change if he and Harlow made their relationship permanent.

"As they should," Tobin declared. "If I ever am lucky enough to find a good woman, I'll treat her like gold. Because in my sad love life, a good woman has been as rare as gold."

In recent months Tobin had mentioned his loneliness and his disappointment that he wasn't in a relationship at his age. Hugh didn't like spilling his guts, and it made him uncomfortable when other guys did it. But it bothered him that Tobin, who was honestly one of the greatest guys Hugh had ever met, was unhappy. And he suspected Tobin's disillusionment would lead him out of Wyoming. Hugh wasn't the type of guy to offer advice—his fucked-up past with Cleo and his uncertain future with Harlow made him the last person who should talk. But he needed to let Tobin know he did care, and to some extent he did understand.

But Tobin beat him to the punch. "That said, I've been lucky that Renner lets me experiment on my own time."

"And on your own dime. I wish you could be around in Kansas when we put CC in the arena to see what he'll do."

"Oh, I know what that sonuvabitch will do. He'll throw the bull riders into the next fuckin' county."

CC, son of legendary bull BB, was Tobin's first foray into genetics. He'd bred the ornery bull with a cow known for her crappy disposition and large calves. The two-year-old bull was making his debut in the rodeo arena this summer. BB's other progeny—DD, Triple E and Double F, all of different dams—were yearlings and their bucking ability hadn't been tested yet. "I'll make sure someone videos at least one of the rides."

"Cool. Anyway, I'm happy to see that," Tobin said, pointing at Hugh.

"See what?"

"You excited about something, Grumpy."

Hugh narrowed his eyes.

Tobin laughed and pushed to his feet. "My pep talk is over. Good luck."

Renner passed Tobin in the doorway. He said, "Got something I wanna run by you, so make time for me later."

"Will do."

When Renner walked by Hugh's desk, Hugh started to gather up his paperwork. He should've expected Renner would want to have this conversation at his desk.

But Renner said, "No need to move. I was just gonna grab a soda. You want one?"

"Unless it's too early for us to have a beer?"

"That's what I was hoping you'd say." Renner returned with two cans of Budweiser and parked himself in the chair. "I miss them late nights, planning and scheming down here while we finished a twelve-pack. Seemed my best ideas always came after a beer or three."

"You've always been the idea man." *Except this time.* He popped the top on his beer and drank.

"I'm hopin' you didn't set this meeting up because you've run into problems?"

Hugh shook his head. "Exactly the opposite. While I was making final arrangements with Phyllis at Phillipsburg, she mentioned two smaller venues, one in Kansas and another in Nebraska, that were without stock contractors for their county rodeos. I did some checking because they sounded familiar, and we provided stock for them seven years ago." He took another drink. "The venues are within our travel parameters. Since they won't conflict with our current itinerary, I went ahead and added them to the schedule."

Renner stared at him without speaking. For as long as he'd known the man, Hugh had no idea whether he was pissed off.

"When you did your checking on these past events, did you find anything in the notes on why we'd stopped providing stock?"

"Yeah. We got the contract for River Run in Missouri for that same week. Since it's three times the size, you booked that one the next year and dropped those two. Since we stopped goin' to River Run two years ago, I didn't see a conflict."

"Did you book the events before or after you read the notes?"

"After. Why?"

"You shoulda cleared it with me first."

And here it was. Hugh pulled the contract out of the file folder and slid it across the desk. "Take a look."

Renner didn't skim the page. He read the entire document before he passed it back. "The terms are generous because they were desperate to fulfill their CRA requirements?"

Hugh shrugged. "Partially. But to be honest, I think since we've mostly been out of the loop that you've forgotten how lucrative stock contracting can be." *There.* He'd said it.

"I haven't forgotten how goddamned expensive travel costs are. Gas was at an all-time high the last two years. That would've eaten every penny of profit."

"I disagree. But that's not an issue right now, since fuel costs have dropped considerably."

"That don't mean I want you signing on for a dozen more rodeos this season," he warned.

"You know I'm gonna get questions on whether Jackson Stock Contracting is out of the business entirely. I'll get approached about bidding next year's events. What I don't know is how you want me to answer any of those questions, Ren."

Renner picked up his beer and drank. He stared at Hugh, but it was more like he stared through him.

Hugh waited. A line of sweat ran down his spine.

"Who all are you takin'?"

"I'll have the final list to you tomorrow. Waiting to hear back, so it's not completely finalized." Half-truth there. "Harlow is comin' along."

"Why? It's not like she's got stock-handling experience."

"Harlow wants the experience, so she'll be a fast learner. Part of the reason she's coming is because we're in a relationship. The other part is she volunteered, which saves on labor costs."

"I'm surprised Gene ain't throwing a fit about her leaving. He's gotten mighty used to her bein' around."

"Well, according to Harlow, he's ahead of the expected recovery time. He's not lacking for entertainment," Hugh pointed out.

"True."

"So if Harlow wasn't coming with me, I imagine she'd be on her way to her next thing."

Renner frowned. "She didn't mention to her sister that she might be leaving soon. Then again, she didn't mention she'd gotten involved with you either."

Like you've got room to talk.

"Is there anything else?"

"I take your nonanswer to mean I'm supposed to hedge when folks ask me about next year's schedule?"

"Yeah." Renner closed his eyes. "I'm so damn tired most days I can't remember what I'm supposed to do next week, say nothin' of next year."

Hugh saw that Renner had hit the limits of what one man could do. Rather than put more stress on him, he tabled the rest of his suggestions.

Renner stood. "Whining ain't gonna get nothin' done. Thanks for handling all this for me. We'll talk more later."

Hugh nodded. He knew an empty promise when he heard one.

⤚✦⤚

"Why aren't we just meeting at your place?" Harlow asked him the next night.

"Because Riss is bringing the cattle truck by to make sure it meets our requirements for transporting our bulls."

"How many bulls are we taking?"

Hugh smiled at her use of "we" and shifted into second gear to take the corner. "Depends on the size of her double-decker trailer. Legally, we can't haul horses and bulls together. And we'll have to leave room to load the calves and steers for the timed events. Some of the bigger contracting companies haul twice what we do, but they don't drive nearly as far. It's a daytrip for them. And competitors are always anxious to try our stock, since it's pretty rank."

"Have you tried any of the stock?"

"Not ours. But I have ridden a bull, and participated in saddle bronc and bareback events."

Harlow leaned across the seat and cooed, "Ooh, did you get a shiny belt buckle to draw attention to that big cock in your Wranglers?"

"Jesus, Harlow. Would you please stop sayin' I have a big cock?"

"Well, you do." She smirked. "I'm proud of it. You should be too."

The woman confused the fuck outta him sometimes. "Let's go." Hugh skirted the front end of the truck and by the time he'd reached the passenger side, she'd already climbed out. "Rule number one, darlin'. You wait for me to help you out."

Harlow got in his face. "Amendment to rule number one, *darlin'*: Women who are capable of opening a door are exempt from waiting for their man to rescue them from the confines of a big ol' pickup truck."

"Got a mouth on you tonight."

"I just have low tolerance for sitting pretty and staying put when I know once we're on the road, and I'm Harlow the hired hand, the rules will change."

She had a point. "Fine. But when you are with me, that means my hands will be on my hand. At all times."

"Got it."

He draped his arm over her shoulder and kissed her temple. "By the way, you look fine as fuck tonight."

She looked up at him. "That's a better compliment than *fine as frog's hair.*"

The door to the Buckeye opened and disgorged a couple of drunken guys and their angry wives, who'd apparently been called to haul their sorry asses home.

Harlow stopped to watch the spectacle.

"Ain't polite to stare, doll."

"If they didn't want people to watch their scene, they shouldn't have caused one." She winced when one guy fell down and his pissed-off wife kicked him in the ass. Then the other couple started laughing so hard they had to hold each other up.

"Come on." He opened the door.

Once they were in the thick of the boisterous crowd, Hugh wished they could've met up with Ike and Riss some other place.

Didn't look like Ike was there yet, so he towed Harlow to a booth by the side door. "I'll grab drinks. What you want?"

"Gin and tonic." She opened her mouth and then shut it.

"What?"

"I doubt they stock Tanqueray, so well gin is fine."

At least she'd been in enough times to know not to order wine.

Hugh headed for the bar. A harried Sherry shouted drink orders while an equally harried new bartender attempted to fill the orders.

When Sherry saw him, she hustled right over. "Hey, Hugh. What'll it be tonight?"

"A pitcher of Bud, three glasses and a gin and tonic."

Sherry stood on tiptoe and peered over his shoulder. "The gin and tonic for Harlow?"

"Yep."

"I assume it's a family thing that she prefers Tanqueray. Give me an extra minute to track down the bottle and I'll bring it out."

As Hugh returned to the table, it bugged him that Gene Pratt might be charming Sherry Gilchrist into sneaking booze in for him.

"You're frowning," Harlow said, leaning across the table. "What's wrong?"

"Is Gene under alcohol limitations during his recovery?"

"One alcoholic drink a week, according to his doctor. Why?"

"It's odd that Sherry knows Gene prefers Tanqueray gin."

"Honey, *anyone* who drinks gin prefers Tanqueray. Besides, it's not the booze the Mud Lilies sneak in that's the problem. It's the cookies, bars, pies and bread." She shook her head and several wisps of hair escaped from her ponytail. "Yesterday, both Pearl and Tilda visited. Pearl tried to act like it was an oversight, but she showed up half an hour early. She and Tilda had words. Dad faked a headache and locked himself in his room, the chickenshit."

Now Gene was messing with Pearl and Tilda too? Maybe he'd done the wrong thing in agreeing to keep Gene's liaisons quiet. But part of him did agree with Karen. The Mud Lilies were grown women. They'd be just as pissed if he meddled, so he was screwed either way.

"Hugh?"

"What?"

"You've got a weird look on your face."

"Just trying to wrap my head around Gene Pratt, who oversees a multitude of multimillion-dollar corporations with PFG, being afraid of Pearl and Tilda."

"When they're pissed off and probably carrying? I would be. Aren't you?"

"When you put it that way . . . yep." He reached out and smoothed back her hair. "You haven't colored your hair like an Easter egg recently."

"Dye your hair pink one time and you're branded for life."

"Garnet followed your lead. Looked like she had pink insulation on her head for a couple of months."

She kissed him. "You can be more creative than the standard 'cotton candy' comparison."

"I try."

Sherry swung by with her tray and dropped off the glasses, pitcher and drink, but didn't stay to talk.

Ike slid into the opposite booth seat. "Man. What is goin' on here tonight? This place ain't usually this busy on a Tuesday."

"Heard 'em say softball leagues."

"Ah." He poured a beer for Hugh and himself. "Who else is coming?"

"Stock transporter."

"You using Al?"

Hugh shook his head. "How's your drink?" he asked Harlow.

"Good. But I know she's been mixing these for Dad, because he's the one who taught me to drink them so limey."

When Hugh reached for his beer, Ike moved it out of reach.

"What the hell, Ike?"

"Why won't you tell me who's driving transport?" Ike demanded.

Hugh said nothing. But Ike knew exactly what it meant.

"Are serious? *Riss?* You hired fuckin' *Riss?*"

"Best driver and stock handler around and you know it. So I'm gonna ask you to try not to be a fuckin' douche bag."

"That's an impossible request, Hugh. Ike wrote the book on douche bag behavior."

Hugh looked up at the freckle-faced redhead who'd reached their table. "Nice to see you, Riss." He squeezed Harlow's shoulder. "Larissa 'Riss' Thorpe, meet my girlfriend, Harlow Pratt."

Harlow offered her hand. "Great to meet you."

"Same here." Riss shook Harlow's hand. "Pritchett neglected to mention a girlfriend coming along on this trip."

"Harlow will also be working as a hand, learning the ropes."

She made a noncommittal noise. Then she grinned. "Pritchett and Pratt. Sounds like a comedy duo. Or a pharmaceutical company."

Ike snorted. "Still as awkward as ever, I see, La-Riss-a."

"Still as much of an asshole as ever," she shot back.

Awkward silence.

"So, did you two used to date and it ended badly?" Harlow asked.

Riss said, "Not fucking ever," the same time Ike said, "Zero fucking chance."

"Ah. So you fucked once. One of you regretted doing the nasty, the other one didn't and that someone got pissed off, resulting in the hate fest?"

Hugh choked on his beer.

Both Riss and Ike looked between him and Harlow suspiciously.

"No?" Harlow continued studying them. "I give up. What happened between you two? We need to know—it will affect all of us in this working relationship."

Putting them on the spot meant he'd finally hear why these two were oil and water.

"Business deal gone bad," Ike said without looking at Riss. "We both got fucked over. Some of us more than others." He showed Riss his teeth, but it no way resembled a smile. "Would you like a beer?"

"While I'm out driving a semi? Uh, no. I'll pass." Riss faced Hugh. "You wanna check out this rig so I know if it'll work?"

"Sure. You gonna bitch if Ike weighs in?"

Riss returned Ike's totally fake smile. "Probably."

"Let's go." Hugh put his mouth on Harlow's ear. "I'm sparing you the rest of the sparring. Hold our seats. If we're not back in ten minutes, call the sheriff, 'cause I'll be dealin' with a double homicide."

"Hugh—"

"Kiddin'." He kissed the hollow behind her ear, breathing in a hint of her perfume. "Be right back."

Riss left first. Hugh followed on her heels and Ike brought up the rear.

Hugh jumped inside the double-decker semi. Checked all the loading ramps and mechanisms to make sure they worked right. "This is your rig? Not a lease?"

"It's mine. I bought it last year at an auction."

"It's great. More than I expected. I'm good with it." He glanced at Ike. "You?"

"You're the boss. Whatever you say goes."

"For Christ's sake. Knock it off. Both of you. I don't need the people I'm relying on to help me run things smoothly to be the cause of drama, angst and bullshit. Understood?"

They both nodded.

"We've gotta be in Kansas by ten a.m. on Friday. That's a fourteen-hour haul, so we'll take off Thursday at noon."

"Where will I be loading? At the Split Rock? Or over at Jackson's paddock where he keeps the bulls?"

"Jackson's. I don't need to tell you to allow plenty of time for us to load up, because these bulls haven't been out since last year."

She whistled. "I'd heard Renner had cut back on events, but I hadn't imagined it'd be that much. This is the first outing? And it's almost the end of July?"

He forced a cheerful note into his voice. "Took us all by surprise. Anyway. We'll load you up first before we get the horses. Then we'll caravan and decide on rest stops as we go." He looked at Ike, leaning against the back wheels. "Anything to add?"

Ike shook his head.

"Any questions, Riss?"

"I'm sure questions will pop up as I'm on the road. But there's nothing else I can think of right now."

"Good." He thrust out his hand. "Thanks for agreeing to do this on such short notice."

"No problem. See you on Thursday." Riss climbed up in the cab. She honked as she pulled away.

Hugh and Ike crossed the road in silence. Before they walked back into the bar, Hugh said, "You gonna tell me what's really goin' on with you and Riss?"

"Sure. As soon as you tell me whether it was you or Harlow who had regrets after the first time you fucked."

"Asshole."

Ike stopped at the bar for a shot and Hugh paid their bar bill.

Hugh turned the corner and saw Harlow wasn't alone. And she seemed annoyed.

His irritation skyrocketed when he recognized the guy encroaching on his woman.

Tort Franklin.

The man didn't look up until Hugh cast him in shadow. "Oh, hey, Hugh."

"Tort. There a reason you're sitting that fucking close to my girlfriend?"

"Girlfriend? Really? Huh." The bull rider took his own sweet time getting to his feet.

"Tort was just telling me that he was the last contestant to ride BB," Harlow said slyly.

"You didn't 'ride' BB," Hugh scoffed. "You got on him in the chute and BB refused to get up, so they gave you a different bull."

"From what I hear, BB's prime days are past anyway." Tort threw back his shoulders, trying to make his five-foot-five stature intimidating. "Not that I'll need to put your stock to the test, since I'm far ahead enough in the standings after Cowboy Christmas to take a break."

Bully for you.

"You sure you don't wanna dance with me, Harlow?"

"Yes, she's fucking sure," Hugh snapped.

"Big man, with the big mouth, I wasn't talking to you."

"And as of right now, you're done talkin' to her. Now beat it before I beat on you."

Tort scowled, muttered something and took off.

Before Hugh reclaimed his seat, Harlow stood. "I want to leave."

"Why?"

"Because I don't like it when you do that."

"Do what? Warn off a jackass who intended to put his wandering hands all over you?"

"I don't need you to bulldoze your way in and pee circles around me, Hugh. You don't own me. I can take care of myself."

"Great. But guess what?" He got right in her face. "When I'm around? *I* take care of you. And that includes chasing off dickheads like Tort who have the reputation of bein' forceful in their attentions with the ladies."

Harlow glared at him.

He glared back at her.

"Aw, am I witnessing a lovers' quarrel?"

Fuckin' awesome. Like he needed to deal with Harley tonight. He faced her and maneuvered himself behind Harlow, drawing her body against his. "No. Just an intense discussion."

"In other words . . . a lovers' quarrel." Harley looked at Harlow. "I saw Tort putting the moves on you before your white knight stormed in and rescued you."

"Actually, I think Tort came to the table because he thought I was you," Harlow said.

Dammit. He really didn't need Harley running her mouth.

Harley fastened her gaze on Hugh's. "Yes, that's been a problem in the past. Not only when I've been mistaken for someone else, but when I've been a *substitute* for someone else too." Then her gaze pointedly moved to Harlow.

Any moment he'd wake up from this bad dream.

Harlow subtly disentangled from him and stepped forward to hug Harley. "That sucks. I'm sure your fiancé only has eyes for you, especially since you look fantastic. Is that outfit from Wild West?"

"Of course. As soon as I pulled it from the box, I knew I had to have it." Harley went off on a tangent about clothes and other shit, assuming she had Harlow's full attention. Harlow wore a look that might've passed as interest, but Hugh recognized it as a mask for her anger.

Directed at him.

Your own fault, dumb fuck. You should've told her.

He didn't trust Harlow's benign expression when she looped her arm around his. "It is sad we don't see more of each other at the Split Rock. We'll have to do that girls' night out that you suggested. I've always suspected we have a lot in common."

Shit. He was fucked. Seriously fucked. Monumentally fucked.

Harley said something as Harlow led Hugh toward the door. His pulse pounded so loudly that's all he could hear.

Once they hit the fresh air, his head cleared. But he knew better than to discuss this in the parking lot of the Buckeye where anyone could overhear them.

He opened the passenger side first and she climbed in without looking at him. Even after he'd started his truck and they were on the road, the silence continued.

Finally at the entrance to the Split Rock, she said, "Drop me off at my trailer."

"Harlow—"

"Fine. I'll walk from here."

And she bailed out.

Hugh rolled down the window and crept along behind her. "Jesus fucking Christ, woman, get back in the goddamn truck."

"No." She stoically marched down the gravel road leading to the employee quarters without acknowledging him at all.

He pulled over and parked, knowing if he didn't catch her before she went inside, she'd lock him out. And as much as kicking down her door appealed to him, he wouldn't do it.

Before she reached the planked walkway, she whirled around and yelled, "You slept with her!"

He didn't respond, due to his shock that Harlow was shouting at him.

"When? How long did it go on?" Immediately she held up her hand. "No, don't tell me. I don't want to know. It doesn't matter." Then she spun back around and stormed off.

"Harlow. Wait."

She wheeled around and marched up to him. "Are you going to tell me you can explain?"

"No need, because it's pretty fuckin' obvious why I slept with her."

That startled her.

He moved in. "It happened over a year and a half ago. Right after she started workin' here. Before I knew she had a boyfriend."

She held up her hands to ward him off. "Stop talking! I don't want to hear this."

"Tough shit. You *need* to hear it and you know it." He slipped his hand around her wrist and towed her down the walkway.

Tobin sat outside his trailer in front of his fire pit. He asked, "Everything all right?" as Hugh dragged Harlow past him.

"Fine and fuckin' dandy," Hugh snapped.

Upon reaching Harlow's trailer, he stepped aside so she could unlock the door.

"You are *not* coming in here," she said snottily.

"Try and stop me."

She made a frustrated noise and stomped inside.

He followed her and locked the door behind them.

Harlow stood in the living room, her hands clenched into fists at her sides.

Hugh squared off against her, his hands on his hips.

"Well? Spit out what I *need* to know."

"Which part do you want to hear first?"

"Were you an asshole to Harley after you fucked her, like you were to me?"

"No." He paused, trying to calm the fuck down. "I was worse to her afterward. Way worse. Because I knew it was wrong from the start. I wanted her to be you and she wasn't. For Christ's sake, Harlow, I even said your name when I was with her. *Your* name. Not hers."

"You did not."

"I did."

"What did she say?"

"She was pissed. But I didn't give her a chance to say anything or nail me in the balls as I got dressed and lit out as fast as possible. I felt guilty as hell. So the next day I went into the clothing store to apologize. Her boyfriend was there visiting. So, yeah, it wasn't like I could out her as a cheater. We never talked about it again."

"Who else knows you fucked her? Renner? Tobin?"

"Tobin. That's it. I'd like to think she kept it to herself, but I have no idea who she might've blabbed to."

"Awesome. That's just great, Hugh. Now she's going to hate me."

Didn't look like it from where he'd been standing. That was another ball-shrinking fear. That they'd get together and compare notes.

"You've said your piece. Now go."

He closed the distance between them rapidly and latched on to her upper arms, gentling his hold when he saw fear in her eyes. "I want you to think on the fact I was so damn desperate for you that I took a woman who reminded me of you to bed. A year and a half after you left."

"You just used her to alleviate your guilt about how things ended between us."

"No, darlin'. I used her because I couldn't have you. At the time she seemed like the closest thing to you—but it turned out she wasn't even fuckin' close. There's never been any woman like you, Harlow."

She closed her eyes. "You say that, Hugh. You say it over and over. But here's what I'm not sure about: Are you trying to convince me or yourself?"

"I hadn't been with a woman since that night everything went to hell with you'n me. After Harley? I've been ridin' the goddamned celibacy train, round and round for a year and a half until you came back into my life."

Her eyes flew open in shock. "Why?"

"Because even with me bein' a dickhead and leaving you like I did? When we were naked, locked in passion and lost in the rush of pleasure that night . . . it'd never been that way for me before. Or since."

She said nothing.

"How about I stop trying to convince you with words and just prove it to both of us with actions instead?" He swooped in, pressing her mouth and her body to his. His hands were in her hair, on her face, moving down to cup her tits, sliding around to grab her ass. He kissed her for an eternity. Until the rigidness in her posture softened. Until she started touching him back in all the ways she'd learned he liked. Then he eased off, and rested his forehead against hers. "I'll go if you want me to."

"No. Maybe you should do a little more convincing," she whispered against his lips. "Nice and slow."

Hugh briefly closed his eyes, glad he hadn't fucked up with her again. "I can do that." He tugged her head back; his mouth followed the slim column of her neck to the hollow of her throat, his desire for her a living, pulsing thing.

"I like your mouth on me."

"That's good, because I like havin' my mouth all over you." Hugh planted kisses up the other side of her throat. He nibbled on that stubborn jaw. Teased her lips before rubbing his beard in the spot where her neck curved into her shoulder.

"I like that you can slow things down when I ask."

"Never doubt that, sweetheart. I can stop. Even when I don't want to."

Her soft laugh vibrated against his lips.

He nuzzled her, but the sweet scent of her skin and the hard pounding of her pulse made him damn dizzy. The smooth skin of her neck affected him like a drug.

"Hugh."

He shifted his focus to her tiny earlobe. Licking the edge, gently tugging on it with his teeth, sucking the soft flesh as if it were her clit. He'd dropped both of his hands to her ass, holding her close but not so tightly that she couldn't step back if she needed to.

"Hey, cowboy," she said, twisting her head, breaking the connection of his mouth on her skin.

Hugh steeled himself against what he might see when he looked into her eyes. But the heat he saw pooled in those blue depths caused his hope to soar. "What?"

"You convinced me the way I needed you to."

Shit. Did that mean they were done for tonight? "Okay."

Harlow placed one hand on his heart and the other on his cheek. "Now I need you to convince me your way."

"What's my way?"

"Physical. Now give me that side of you where there are no words, where it's hard and fast and maybe a little desperate. I want us naked, locked in passion and riding that rush of pleasure."

His cock was totally on board for that. He had to make sure his head made the decision. "You're sure?"

"Positive." Harlow pulled him to her mouth by his beard.

Jesus. He liked that little bite of pain. So he gave it back to her, sinking his teeth into her bottom lip.

Her soft gasp just fueled the fire.

His hands came up and wrenched the top of her dress down, revealing her breasts. "You're gorgeous here. Creamy white and pink." As he plumped and squeezed the small mounds of flesh, Harlow arched into him, moaning loudly when his tongue connected with the hard tip of her nipple.

He kept at her until she turned almost feral in her need for him.

Her hands were frantically yanking his shirt free from his jeans, then pulling hard until the pearl buttons gave way and his shirt hung open. Her fingers were unbuckling his belt. Undoing his zipper.

Through the haze of tasting her, touching her, when he felt her cool fingers stroking his shaft, he realized he'd lose control if she kept that up.

Hugh bent down and hooked his arm behind her knees, bringing them to the floor. His mouth immediately returned to her nipple, nursing vigorously on the right side while he tenderly stroked the swell of her left breast.

Harlow continued to twist and writhe, her eyes closed, her teeth digging into her bottom lip, her hand alternately pulling his hair and pushing him away.

Hugh clasped both her wrists above her head. He sucked her lower lip into his mouth, catching her surprised gasp with his kiss. His right hand slipped beneath the hem of her dress, and trailed up the inside of her thigh until his greedy fingers reached the hot, wet heart of her.

He stroked the rise of her mound over her soaked panties, and then pulled them aside to tease her petal-soft, hot and swollen pussy.

She bucked upward at the first touch and he pinned her leg down with his, as he opened her thighs wider.

Then his mouth attacked her nipples as he slid one finger inside her. Pushing and pumping, stretching her until that moment she canted her hips and he knew she was ready for more. He added another finger, driving into her harder. Deeper. Her wetness coating his hand and the insides of her thighs.

He growled against her breast and finger fucked her, purposely avoiding her clit.

"Hugh. Please."

"Come like this," he panted against her damp skin. "Come like this and I'll make you come again with my mouth."

Three more pumps of his hand and she arched, her cunt spasming around his fingers, and she cried out his name.

Hugh looked up and watched her come apart, his cock jerking against his zipper in anticipation.

When her body went limp, he eased his fingers out and moved between her thighs. He planted soft kisses over her mound, ran his tongue and his beard along the creases of her thighs. He breathed her in, kept her primed even as he allowed her to settle.

She twined her fingers in his hair and attempted to direct him to her clit. He resisted.

She insisted.

He rolled onto his knees and waited until she looked at him.

"What?"

"Put your arms above your head and leave them there."

"But I want—"

Hugh got right in her face. "You want my mouth on you?"

"Yes."

"Then do it."

"God. You are so fierce right now."

"Are you scared?"

She petted his beard and dragged her knuckles along his collarbone and up his neck. "Far from it. I see how fast your blood is pumping right here. I want to press my lips there and taste it."

He angled his head, lightly sinking his teeth into that spot on her throat.

Her fingers tightened on his beard. "Yes. Just like that."

"Harlow," he breathed into her ear. "Put. Your. Fucking. Hands. Above. Your. Fucking. Head. *Now.*"

She complied so fast they *whomped* against the rug.

He allowed a quick grin against her neck before he pushed up and moved back down, placing his big hands on her inner thighs and pushing them wider.

Feeling her eyes on him, he flicked a glance up at her. "Those arms move, I stop. Understand?"

She nodded.

Hugh spread her open with his thumbs. He growled, seeing the glistening pink flesh. Her pussy lips full. Her clit peeking out. He breathed in the scent of her arousal and lowered his mouth.

Harlow kept her hands in place, but her hips jerked up.

After one long thorough lick up her wet slit, Hugh zeroed in on her clit. Swirling the tip of his tongue over the nub until it swelled enough he could get his lips around it. Then he started to suck. And he kept his mouth suctioned to that needy part of her, swallowing her sweet juices as she came in a grinding wet rush against his face.

Fuck. He loved that.

Loved it.

Before Harlow floated down from her orgasmic high, Hugh yanked his jeans and underwear down to his knees and slammed into her still spasming cunt.

She cried out and bowed upward and he fucked her relentlessly.

He buried his face in her neck. Sucking and biting on the delicate skin. He probably left beard burn, but the full access she freely gave him indicated she didn't care either.

When he reached the tipping point, he put his mouth on her ear. "Only with you has it ever been like this."

"Hugh—"

"Say you believe me. Say I proved it to you."

"You did. Yes. Please don't stop proving it."

He bottomed out with the force of a battering ram twice more and then came in a breath-stealing rush. Polka dots danced behind his lids, his hearing went haywire and his body continued to move of its own accord.

If Harlow hadn't hooked her leg around his hips, he wondered how long he would've stayed like that. Then she fastened her mouth to his and leveled him with sweet, teasing kisses.

He looked into her eyes. But he didn't know what the hell to say. He kissed her quickly and retreated. Pulling up his clothing, he stared down at Harlow, still wantonly spread out. He tucked his cock in and smiled at the crazy static mess he'd made of her hair. Zipped up and buckled, he crouched and scooped her into his arms, peeling off her dress completely before he carried her down the hallway to her bedroom.

After he'd slid her between the sheets, she opened her eyes.

"Now I'll go."

She touched his face. "What if I want you to stay?"

"I'd say I'll take a rain check. I hafta be up early."

"Okay."

He gave her one last kiss. "Night, doll. I'll lock up and see you tomorrow."

Chapter Sixteen

For the first time in . . . well, ever, Harlow had her family standing around waiting to say good-bye to her before she left on her latest travels.

It was weird.

Her dad had hugged her for a long time, and asked her to stay in touch. It amused her that during his recovery he'd become proficient with his cell phone, almost to the menace stage with the pictures, videos and memes he shared. As she'd hugged him, she was reminded how frail he was.

"You're sure you want to do this?" Tierney asked.

"I'm looking forward to it. Road-tripping through the heartland."

"Itchy feet," Tierney murmured.

"I can scratch your feet, Aunt Harlow," Isabelle said from her spot on the ground, where she searched through the grass for four-leaf clovers.

"Thanks for the offer, bug, but I'm good."

When an unhappy-animal noise echoed to them, Harlow looked to the source of discontent. Hugh, Renner and Ike were at the loading pens with the semi, loading the bulls.

Tierney had Rhett swaddled and tucked close to her body. She pushed her glasses up the bridge of her nose after giving Harlow a one-armed hug. "I don't know why I'm crying. I wasn't this upset when you went to Haiti."

"That's because you didn't see me off."

"Were you hurt by that? It's occurred to me that's something I should have asked you sooner." Tierney reached out and straightened the seam of Harlow's T-shirt. "Or was it worse having no one to meet you when you came home?"

Harlow shrugged. Confirming her sister's guilt would serve no purpose. Even hearing an *I'm sorry* now wouldn't negate the sense of isolation and disconnection she'd felt then, sitting on a bench waiting for a bus as she saw her friends and coworkers surrounded by loving and supportive family members.

"Although the circumstances haven't been ideal, I've loved having you close by, Harlow. And I . . ."

"And you what?"

Tierney sniffled, but her eyes were dry when she met Harlow's gaze. "I wish we could get back to the closeness and trust we used to have. You used to talk to me and I don't know why you suddenly stopped." Her voice dropped to a whisper. "You went through something bad in the year you were overseas. It kills me not knowing what happened. It bothers me that you didn't give me a chance to be there for you when you've been there for me whenever I've needed you."

Harlow's stomach tightened into a knot. She broke eye contact and turned her face toward the breeze. "Maybe I've finally grown up."

"I hate it when you do that. Cut yourself down, but in such a manner that you think no one notices."

No one does.

"I notice," Tierney emphasized, as if she'd read Harlow's mind.

"That's because you're the nosy big sister."

"Guilty."

And Harlow felt guilty for not letting Tierney know what she'd been through. Even her counselor had encouraged her to tell her sister about it. If not the full details, at least something that'd show Harlow had healed and moved on. She inhaled a deep breath. "I promise when I get back, we'll crack open a bottle of wine and I'll tell you about my lost year in Laos." She paused. "It's not pretty."

Tierney set her head on Harlow's shoulder. "I figured as much." She paused. "Thank you for letting me in."

"It's not easy. I keep everyone out. Especially about this."

"That's where you're just like Dad." She lifted her head. "Does Hugh know what happened?"

"Yes."

Silence. But it didn't feel judgmental.

"Good. I'm glad you could talk to him about it. So is it serious between you and Hugh? You seem to spend all of your time together."

Meaning . . . would this "thing" turn into something important enough in her life to tie her to Hugh, which tied her here? "This trip will be a test of our compatibility outside the bedroom." She shot a quick look to Isabelle, but she hadn't been paying attention.

"Yes, nothing tests the course of true love like being ankle deep in manure as you're both trying to impose your will on a willful animal."

Harlow laughed and gave her sister another good-bye hug.

⤳

An hour later Harlow loaded her cooler in the front of the horse trailer on the floor next to the built-in mini-fridge. She opened the cupboards above the sink and found them empty. Where was Hugh storing his food staples? She glanced up at the low-ceiling area where they'd be sleeping and saw an oversized duffel bag. Even when they'd be living together, she still didn't feel comfortable rifling through his belongings to see what he'd brought with him.

She stepped outside, blocking the bright sunshine with her hand.

Hugh, Renner and Ike were getting ready to load the horses. Riss had already taken off with the bulls. She looked at the truck they were taking to haul the horse trailer—not Hugh's pickup, but a double-cab dually—and decided to check inside. She hopped up on the running board and peered inside the backseat on the passenger's side.

Someone had loaded her case of water and her suitcase. Behind the driver's side was a big black laptop bag with cords hanging out everywhere, a pair of rubber boots and a stack of bedding.

That was it?

He'd assured her he was completely prepared for this trip.

For the next half hour, Harlow stayed out of the way as they loaded the horses. Then the cab jiggled and Hugh climbed in.

He smiled at her. "Ready?"

Are you? "Sure."

He popped the emergency brake, checked the oversized mirrors on both sides and dropped the truck into gear. The long gravel driveway leading to the chutes was at a steep angle, so they inched down the decline with such a heavy load behind them.

Hugh didn't speak until they were on the blacktop. "You're quiet."

"Just watching and learning."

"Any questions so far?"

Too many to name. She adjusted her seat forward. "How far are we going today?"

"Legally Riss and Ike can only be behind the wheel eleven hours a day before they're mandated to rest. We won't be on the road that long, but once we're stopped, it'll be for the required ten-hour break. Why?"

"I'm just wondering when we'll stop for food and gas."

"This truck has a dual gas tank, which oughta get us five hundred miles before we have to refuel and check the animals."

"And get food?"

He shrugged. "Usually whoever is in the lead makes that call. Or we wing it."

Harlow turned to look out the window. She wasn't a "wing it" kind of person. At all. In the years she'd spent volunteering, she'd had to plan for every contingency. She preferred rules and protocol and a detailed itinerary, at least during the travel stages. Winging it would definitely take some getting used to.

"You tired?" Hugh asked. "I kept you up later than I'd planned."

Late last night after she'd packed and tidied her trailer, to try to calm her restlessness—always an issue for her prior to embarking on a trip—she had rolled out her yoga mat. But she couldn't focus on asanas and her balance seemed to be out of whack. Switching to deep breathing and meditation had helped . . . until Hugh walked in.

Normally the man wore jeans and starched shirts. Boots. Either a cowboy hat or a baseball cap. She'd never seen him in a sleeveless T-shirt that show-cased his muscular arms and defined chest. Or in baggy cutoff sweatpants that rode low on his lean hips, providing a peek at the strip of hair that dis-appeared beneath his waistband. It floored her, how much younger he looked dressed like that.

"Looks like we had the same idea," he had said gruffly, stopping at the top of her yoga mat.

"Where have you been?" she asked.

"Fitness center. Me'n Tobin work out a couple times a week. Why?"

"I didn't know that. I mean, you're in great shape . . ."

"But you thought it was natural?"

She'd nodded.

"I lost eighty pounds once I got back in shape after my divorce and I'm never packing it back on, so I work to keep it off."

"It shows."

"Are you done with"—he gestured to her mat, block and strap—"all that?"

"Yes. I'm just cooling down."

Hugh had stalked over to her. "Gonna be a problem if I heat you back up?"

Little did the man know that the look in his eyes had already done that. "Ah, no."

"Good." Then he'd pounced on her.

They'd rolled around on the floor, kissing like crazy, laughing as they wrestled to see who'd end up on top.

Hugh won.

So he'd fucked her on the yoga mat, first with her hands and feet on the floor, her legs spread wide as he held onto her hips. Then he brought them onto their sides, him stretching out behind her, bringing her top leg over his and entering her from behind. Sucking and biting on the nape of her neck, nibbling on her ears, tweaking her nipples, grazing her clit with his callused thumb, turning her inside out as he slowly worked his cock in and out of her body. Every time she got close to coming . . . he'd stopped and whispered, "Gonna make you wait for it tonight, hippie-girl."

Her belly had done a slow roll when Hugh grabbed the nylon strap she used to assist in her yoga stretches. The cowboy "well versed in ropes" had his own idea how to utilize the strap. He'd tied it around her wrists and looped the ends beneath the leg of the chair. Then he'd wedged the foam block beneath her lower back, holding her hips up so he could bury his face in her pussy, watching her face as he ate her.

And again, every time that tingle started, he'd back off.

She'd loved seeing a different, more playful side of him. Then witnessing his shift from teasing man to intense lover. He'd dragged out the interlude until they were both sweaty. Needy. Desperate.

Their explosive, mutual climax had left them both gasping. Shaking. Stunned. Once they'd found their way back from the orgasmic bliss, Hugh had picked her up and taken her to bed. Wrapping himself around her completely.

"Harlow?"

Hugh's deep voice startled her back to the present. "What?"

"What were you thinkin' about so hard?"

When she met his gaze, she knew he knew *exactly* where her thoughts had been. She smirked. "Taking a nap. I am tired."

He smirked back. "Rest up. You'll need it for later."

"Plan on a repeat of last night?"

"I'm thinkin' on it. But next time we stop, darlin', I'm putting you behind the wheel. Although I plan on doin' all the driving, things happen and I need to know that you can take over if need be."

"All right. It's probably easier than driving a bus."

That took him aback. "You've driven a bus before?"

"In a dozen different countries on roads that were a serious stretch to even be called a goat path."

"Were you ever scared?"

"Once. Along the cliffs in Bolivia. I puked as soon as everyone was off the bus. I'd been so afraid I'd plunge us into a ravine." She popped open the top of her CamelBak water bottle. "But that wasn't as scary as the time the military police pulled us over." She shuddered. "It was bad enough being a passenger and having to press your face in the dirt while eighteen-year-old kids walked around with machine guns."

"Jesus, Harlow. Where did that happen?"

"More than one place. Mexico, Cambodia and Armenia. And before you ask, I've lost track of the number of times it's happened."

Hugh cracked open a Mountain Dew and took a couple of drinks before he spoke again. "How did you ever get started doin' that kinda work?"

"I'm sure you're thinking it's some rich-girl thing to alleviate my guilt for growing up privileged," she shot back.

He said nothing. Didn't even take his eyes off the road to look in her direction.

"Sorry." Harlow blew out a breath. "You didn't deserve that. I just get all sorts of nasty remarks and judgments from so many people who have no idea what they're talking about. And for all the good I've done with the organizations I've worked with, the responses to me doing *that kind of work* are almost always negative. So yeah, I am overly sensitive."

He kept his eyes on the road when he reached for her hand. "I pride myself on not bein' like most folks. And I wasn't tryin' to get your back up when I asked. I'm seriously interested in what makes my woman tick."

My woman. That gave her a secret thrill, so Harlow debated whether to tell him something she'd never told anyone.

"Anything you tell me stays only with me."

No one besides her therapist had ever made that promise to her. "This is a poor-little-rich-girl story. You know my mother died when I was two months old. We had a parade of nannies after that. Some were more memorable than others. I have a better recollection of Rosa, our maid, than anyone else from my childhood besides my sister."

Hugh smirked. "No wonder you speak Spanish so fluently."

"That's probably part of it." She paused. "How did you know I'm fluent?"

"That first summer you worked at the Split Rock, I overheard you talking to some guests. On more than one occasion. I imagine you have to be at least bilingual to do what you do."

"It helps. I know a smattering of other languages, enough to get me by anyway."

"Back to the story," Hugh prompted.

"My dad worked all the time. So we were raised by strangers. I had Tierney and that's all that mattered to me. We lived in this huge apartment. Tierney and I had our own rooms, and each bedroom had a playroom and a bathroom. I remember I didn't like being away from my big sister, the one familiar, constant person in my life. We'd stay in her room one night. And mine the next. Sometimes we'd set up a tent in one of the playrooms and pretend we were camping. She was the greatest.

"One night during the week, our dad was home for dinner. It was such a rarity I remember Tierney being really nervous. And there was a strange woman at the table with Dad. Tierney immediately didn't like her. She said her smile was as fake as her hair color. Barbara had worn a slinky cocktail dress, not exactly appropriate for dinner with children. That was our single introduction to Dad marrying her. She didn't try to be our stepmother. In fact we called her Barbara. The first indication that she was a horrible person was when she fired Rosa. Then she got rid of Beedie."

"Who was Beedie?"

"He was like a butler. He drove us places. Carted groceries in. Helped Rosa." Harlow shot him a look. "Rosa was Mexican. Beedie was black. As soon as Barbara moved in, she hired a white staff. Not only was she racist— she hated homosexuals, and anyone who practiced a religion besides Christianity. And then we learned the hard way that she hated children." She took a drink of water. "She convinced my dad to send Tierney away to boarding school."

"Shit."

"After Tierney left, I was inconsolable. I threw such a tantrum that my dad came home during the day—which was unheard of—in an attempt to calm me. I heard him tell Barbara that it was a mistake to send Tierney away. But that conniving bitch convinced him otherwise. Then after Dad left, she took me into my room and had a little chat with me. She said if I didn't quit being such a spoiled, whiny brat, she'd personally see to it I never saw my sister again."

"And you believed her?"

"I was five years old, Hugh. Of course I believed her. If there weren't age restrictions, Barbara would've shipped me off to boarding school too. With Tierney gone, I had no one." She gritted her teeth and admitted her private shame. "Within a year I'd imprinted my father's wife on my personality. I watched her. I asked to dress like her. I mimicked her way of dealing with people. I craved attention from her. My father thought it was cute that I wanted to be like her."

"Until?"

"Until I succeeded in being as nasty and awful as she was. I was a perfect little sponge that absorbed her racism and her disparagement of the working class. Being like Barbara didn't make her like me more or act any more like the mother figure I craved. Then Tierney stopped coming home—evidently she'd taken a page from my father's book, because he rarely came home either." She paused for another drink. "This story has a point, I promise."

Hugh brought her hand to his mouth and kissed her knuckles. "It's all good, sweetheart. Keep talkin'."

"I started to change when Tierney refused to have a Sweet Sixteen birthday party. I couldn't understand why she wouldn't want to be the center of attention, wearing a dress fit for a princess and being the envy of everyone. She told me she didn't have time for such trivialities. I knew she was a total brainiac, but I didn't know she'd started taking college classes that year. I asked her why and she said one day she would take over PFG and make it more successful than ever. I didn't see why she'd set that goal. Wouldn't she rather be pretty and fashionable than smart and driven?"

"I can just imagine the look on her face when you said that," Hugh drawled.

"Then two things happened. My dad divorced Barbara and I was alone again, trying to figure out who I was. After school one day I was walking with some of my friends when we came across a homeless man. They stood in front of him, taunting him, saying the most horrible things. Normally I would've been chiming in, but when the guy looked at me, I swore it was

Beedie. I bent down to talk to him and my friends took off, leaving me alone with a homeless guy. By then I realized he wasn't Beedie, but it had taken its emotional toll on me. I wondered if Beedie ended up homeless after Barbara fired him.

"I asked my dad and he didn't know or care. So I started watching the other people in my life and I quickly realized they didn't care either. And I hated it. I hated Barbara. I didn't want to be like her. I made a choice to change my life, who I was and who I wanted to be."

"How old were you?"

"Thirteen."

He whistled. "So young to have such a revelation. At that age I was still wearin' Batman pajamas. My biggest goal was convincing my parents to buy me a puppy."

"A puppy figures into this poor-little-rich-girl tale of woe too," she said dryly. "After seeing the homeless guy, I started paying attention to my surroundings. About two months later I literally stumbled over a box of puppies."

"No way. You're pullin' my leg now."

"No, I swear it's true. I picked up the entire box, not knowing what to do with them. I couldn't leave the pups in the cold to starve. I must've looked suspicious because a beat cop stopped me. When she saw what I had, she called a squad car to pick me up. We ended up at an animal shelter." She closed her eyes. The images of those animals packed in cages and crying out for attention still turned her stomach. "Long story short, they needed volunteers. So I took the form home and filled it out. But I knew my dad wouldn't sign it. So I forged his signature."

"Rebel girl."

"It wasn't like I was racking up charges on his credit card. It was for a good cause. That's how I justified it. Anyway, volunteering made me feel good about myself. People relied on me. I learned volunteers are in short supply everywhere. So I found a couple of other causes to support with my free time."

Hugh opened his mouth. Then closed it.

"What?"

"Did you support them with money?"

She shook her head. "That came later. I had limited access to the trust funds that'd been set up for me. And since you haven't asked, but I know you're curious as to why, that's also when I became a vegetarian."

"Any specific reason?"

"We had to dissect fetal pigs, fish and frogs in biology class and it grossed me out. The shelter wasn't a 'no kill' shelter at the time and I hated knowing the animals were going to die. The smell of cooking meat started to make me sick, so I quit eating red meat, pork, chicken and fish."

"How long have you been all about the veggies?"

"Sixteen years. I'll admit it's a lot easier now to be vegetarian than it was as a teen." She swallowed another mouthful of water. "Sorry if I'm boring you and you're rethinking taking me on the road with you."

"Darlin', you're about as far from boring as it gets. And I feel guilty because I oughta know this stuff about you and I don't."

"You know more than most. I think it's time I hear the Hugh Pritchett life story."

"Only if you wanna be put to sleep."

Harlow gave him a sultry look. "The last thing I want to do when I get in bed with you is sleep."

"I'll drive off the road if you start me thinking about us bein' in bed together." He playfully nipped her fingers. "Gonna be tight quarters back there. You're all right with that?"

"It's enclosed and I won't be fighting bugs and reptiles trying to crawl in with me, so yeah." She yawned. "Maybe I will take that nap after all."

❧

Hugh hit the brakes harder than he'd intended and Harlow jerked forward.

"Sorry for the abrupt end to your nap. My depth perception got screwy there for a second."

Harlow stretched forward and squinted at the dashboard clock. "I didn't mean to sleep that long."

"You must've needed it," he murmured. While she'd slept, her head resting on the console between them, Hugh's emotions had run the gamut from shame to pride. Shame for the assumptions he'd made about Harlow and the dismissive way he'd treated her when she first worked at the Split Rock. Pride for all the brave, stupid, amazing, heartbreaking things Harlow had done with her life so far.

Never once in the retelling had she bragged, not even in that self-deprecating style that was annoying as fuck. She'd just laid it out, where she'd been and why. Except Harlow never used the singular "I" when talking about the trips she'd taken. It'd always been "we."

And she hadn't painted a rosy picture of every experience either. She'd been brutally honest about the times she'd feared for her life and about places she'd never return to. He'd found it intriguing that she'd kept politics out of her decisions on where to volunteer her time. Yet, he'd felt her frustration when she spoke of choosing to play political games in order to achieve humanitarian goals.

"What was that noise?" she asked.

"What noise?"

"The one you just made in the back of your throat that sounded like a growl."

"That's because it was a growl. But it wasn't in my throat, darlin'—it was coming from my stomach. I'm starved."

"That's your own fault. I cannot believe you'd embark on a two-week trip and neglect to pack even a loaf of bread and a jar of peanut butter."

"I know." He squeezed the steering wheel. "I knew I'd forgotten to do something, and it didn't hit me until you started asking about food that I'm an idiot. A hungry idiot."

"I'm happy to share what I brought. But I doubt it'll tide a big guy like you over for long."

"You're so sweet, woman. Thank you."

"Where are we?"

"Headed toward two empty pastures that are owned by one of Ike's old clients. We'll dump the bulls in one pasture, the horses in the other. Let 'em stretch their legs. I'll warn ya. We'll be out in the middle of the field, miles away from the house, so there won't be an electrical hookup."

"That sucks. There goes my plan to blow-dry my hair while I'm waiting for my microwave popcorn to finish popping."

He laughed.

Her fingers skated up his forearm.

Immediately tingling gooseflesh shot up his arm and down his side. Hugh felt her staring at him and briefly took his eyes off the gravel road. "What?"

"You laugh more." He knew she hadn't said it to make him self-conscious when she added, "I like it. It seems more . . . you."

"I laugh more around you because you say some funny shit."

"And that's the only reason?"

A pause hung in the air.

Dammit. He should've said what he really felt and not made her ask for clarification. "No, that's not the only reason. I'm happy around you, Harlow. For so long I've felt like I've been holding my breath, waiting to get sucked back under to that dark place. When I'm with you, I see light. I feel like I can breathe again."

He heard her seat belt unbuckle. Then her warm lips grazed his ear. "That is the best thing anyone has ever said to me. Thank you."

Any additional response would be inadequate, so he merely smiled.

Hugh put the truck in park and killed the engine. He unbuckled and turned to root around in the back of the cab until he found what he needed. "Don't say I never gave you nothin'," he joked.

The amber-colored dashboard lights sent a soft glow across Harlow's face. "What is it?"

"A headband with a headlamp. You'll be using it a lot, since we'll be moving stock at night. There's never any guarantee there'll be yard lights on at the rodeo grounds."

She pulled the Velcro straps apart and settled the headlamp in the center of her forehead before reattaching the straps. Then she gestured to his headband. "So, cowboy, you wear that over your hat?"

"Nope." He removed his cowboy hat and set it brim up on the backseat.

He slid the headband down, letting it dangle beneath his chin. "Let's get Ike unloaded."

Hugh waited for her in front of the truck, gauging how far the truck's headlights reached and whether he should crank them to high.

Next thing he knew, Harlow had invaded his space completely. "Look at you. Sexy beard, faded flannel shirt, ripped jeans, scuffed boots and a look of concentration. If the headlamp was a pair of goggles, you could pass for a hipster master brewer, out searching for the perfect organic hops for your heirloom beer recipe."

He laughed at her assessment as Ike ambled over to them. "Glad someone is havin' fun. What's the plan?"

"Pull into the pasture, unload and check the water supply. Repeat with trailer number two."

"You manning the gate?" Ike said to Harlow.

"Yes. I just need to make sure there are no gate-crashers, right?"

"Right."

The gate was a bunch of old wooden posts strung together with barbed wire. Such a pain in the ass, how it dragged across the dirt almost sideways and closed with another loop of wire over the top of the fence post. Hugh had gotten spoiled. Every fence around the Split Rock and the Jackson Cattle Company was new.

The horses were anxious to get out. The hard part would be getting them back in the trailers tomorrow.

Then Riss parked the semi. Bulls were always more stubborn about moving and even the prospect of lying down in sweet Nebraska grass didn't entice them to move it along.

Hugh fought a grin, seeing how wide Harlow's eyes got when Riss brandished the cattle prod. All she had to do was stick it through the slats and without it touching a single hide, the bulls scampered out.

Ike and Hugh pulled up the loading ramp and closed the rear doors, sliding the locking bars in place.

Riss wandered over to Harlow. "You got your rope ready for tomorrow to help us catch some bulls?"

"No, but I did bring a red cape."

Hugh laughed and slung his arm over Harlow's shoulder. "Night."

"What do you mean, night?" Ike demanded. "Bulls ain't getting taken care of?"

"I'll let you and Riss sort it out."

"Renner never left this kinda stuff for us to handle," Riss said snottily, as if that'd get him to turn around and grab a pitchfork.

"Ren never had a hot blonde to share his horse trailer. I do."

He ignored the muttering from both Riss and Ike.

It was good to be the boss.

Chapter Seventeen

$\mathcal{H}$arlow wiped her forehead with the inside of her wrist. Being in the dusty pens since the crack of dawn had been exhausting and now she was about to melt from the sweltering heat.

She and Hugh were headed back to the horse trailer after spending the morning wrangling livestock. Although it was two in the afternoon, and her stomach growled, she couldn't think about food until she cleaned up.

Hugh was washing up in the sink in the kitchen, so she slipped into the dark bathroom. She flipped on the lights, took one look at herself in the bathroom mirror and screamed.

Hugh hauled ass into the bathroom. "What's wrong?"

"Look. At. Me."

He seemed puzzled. "I am." He moved in behind her and stared at the top of her head. "Did you find a tick or something?"

"Ticks? I have to worry about *ticks* too?"

"Ticks. Fleas. Mites. Flies. Mosquitoes. The not-fun part of working with livestock."

"So is there a fun part?"

His gaze met hers in the mirror. "Darlin', what is goin' on with you? You look like you're about to cry."

Harlow had never been a crier. She hadn't considered herself vain. She wasn't a stranger to working in the muck. She'd sweated in the jungle. She'd trudged through the desert. And she'd never cared about her hair—besides that it stayed out of her face. Heck, she'd even used mud as a protective sunscreen. But looking at herself in that moment? With her hair plastered to her scalp in places with mud—she refused to even consider it could be any other substance—and sections of her hair not coated with hay dust stuck straight up as if she'd shoved her finger in a light socket, she was near tears.

Her face was so filthy, her eyes and teeth were neon white. She looked like one of those vaudeville performers wearing blackface.

"Harlow. Baby. You're scarin' me."

She let her chin drop to her chest, wishing her hair would cover her face. "I didn't mean to scare you. I'm fine."

Hugh wasn't buying it. He didn't gently turn her around. He wrapped her tightly in his arms; then he set his chin on top of her head, making it impossible for her to escape.

After several long moments, she squirmed. "Thanks for the hug. But you can let go of me."

"Nope."

She bristled. "I need to get in the shower."

"Well, I wasn't gonna say anything, but since you brought it up, you *are* smelling a little rank."

Harlow burst into tears at that point.

"I didn't mean it. I was kiddin'." He released her and spun her around before picking her up and plopping her on the vanity. Then he was right in her face. "Please stop cryin'. I'm sorry. That was a bad joke. You don't smell."

She tried to keep her head down to avoid his eyes. "You're right. I reek."

Hugh trapped her face in his hands, forcing her attention. "Talk to me. No bullshit. What is goin' on with you?"

"Look at me. No, wait, don't. Because I'm a mess." She wasn't even a hot mess. She was just a plain old dirty mess.

"You've spent hours in the pens. When you get done with that, you ain't gonna look like you stepped outta the spa."

"I know that. I just didn't expect I'd look like I'd been wrestling in mud and pig shit."

A silent moment passed. Then Hugh's soft, warm lips were on hers. He held her face in place so she couldn't twist away. Kissing her with the utmost tenderness, despite her ragged appearance.

Harlow sighed into his mouth.

"Do you trust me?" he murmured against her lips.

"You know I do."

"Sit right there. Don't move. Don't open your eyes."

She heard the cabinet door open. She felt him reach around her ass and cop a feel before he turned on the water.

He stepped back and she immediately missed the heat and the comfort of his body against hers. "Still with me?" he asked softly.

She nodded.

"Good. Keep them pretty eyes closed." His hand moved beneath her jaw. He pressed a warm, wet washcloth against her forehead and gently dabbed at her skin.

"Hugh? What are you doing?"

"Ssh. No talkin'. Just let me take care of you."

After that, she couldn't hold her tears in any longer. This sweet, gruff man had so many more important things to do besides administer to his freaked-out girlfriend. But here he was. Cleaning her up with such tenderness it made her ache.

Harlow had to bite the inside of her cheek to stop her lips from trembling. He'd swipe the warm cloth down her face. Rinse the washcloth and then repeat. Wipe and rinse. Wipe and rinse. After he finished with her face, he started on her neck. And after he finished with that, he moved on to her arms, wiping her off with a long, wet sweep of the cloth, up and down the length of her arm. From the inside of her wrist to the tip of her elbow. Rubbing the webbing between each finger, followed by a gentle rub across her knuckles. Each fingernail. When he finished with her hands, he kissed the tips of her fingers, one at a time as if he were trying to imprint the shape of each one on his lips.

She was glad he'd demanded that she keep her eyes shut. It allowed her to concentrate on the loving care with which he tended to her. He didn't tell her she was beautiful. He showed her. By cleaning her with a deft and delicate touch. As if she were a precious piece of art. As if she belonged to him and it was his duty and privilege to take care of her.

The water had cooled by the time he finished.

Then she experienced the same tight feeling in her chest when Hugh very carefully, very thoroughly kissed every inch of her face. His lips followed the edge of her hairline from her forehead to the curve of her cheek. Soft-lipped kisses from the middle of her eyebrows to the corners of her eyes. Soon he parted his lips to more fully taste her. After a thorough kiss, he bestowed a quick peck on the end of her nose, before giving her one longer press of his mouth against her lips. It was a mere tease of breath and warmth at the corners of her smile. Because by the time he finished, she was definitely smiling. Her head buzzed. Her heart was full.

Hugh tugged off her boots and lifted her into his arms. She buried her face in his neck, breathing him in. The scent of his skin was soothing aromatherapy, as well as a potent aphrodisiac. And she wanted—needed—to imprint his scent on her. So she would get a whiff of him no matter where she was, no matter what she was doing, and know that she belonged to him.

Irrevocably.

He hefted her up the stairs to the bed without missing a beat and laid her on her belly. The sheets were cool against her fevered skin. He tucked a pillow beneath her cheek. He kissed her temple and whispered, "Sleep. I'll be right here when you wake up."

She wanted to protest, and invite him to join her, but as soon as she closed her eyes, everything faded away.

❧

Hugh's phone rang. He cursed and fumbled with turning off the ringer so as to not disturb Harlow. He quickly and quietly stepped outside. "Pritchett."

"Do you always answer your phone that way?" his mother demanded.

"Pretty much. Especially when I'm on the road or in the sun and can't read the caller ID."

"So you would've ignored my call?"

"'Ignored' is a harsh word, Mom. I'd let the call go until I could properly focus on speaking with you."

She snorted. "Who you been taking sweet-talkin' lessons from? Because you sure didn't inherit the ability from your father."

Hugh slumped against the trailer. "How is Dad?"

"He hates being retired. He gets up in the morning and finds something to putter around with. Then depending on which campground we're in, he has coffee with his cronies, or he plays horseshoes."

"How about you? How're you doin'?"

"Not much changes with me, son. You know that." She paused. "And you've gotta know that I didn't call to bore you with my aches and pains from old age."

"I figured."

"I looked at the calendar and realized you're probably in Kansas."

"Yep."

"Doesn't seem possible it's rodeo time again."

"I take it you and Dad won't be here this year?"

"We'd consider making the trip if we could spend time with you, but your boss is a slave driver."

"Renner is a good guy. But he's not here. He put me in charge. So I've been busier than normal."

"Too busy to see your sister, Mary, I imagine."

Hugh counted to ten. "I'd be fine seeing her, just as long as I don't gotta talk to her."

"Hughley. Alphonse. Pritchett."

Fuck. He hated his fucking name. Why hadn't his parents named him something simple like Jim? "What? If you called to chew my ass about Mary, you can save your breath and hang up now."

"I hate that you two are still at odds. How much longer is this gonna go on?"

"Until she apologizes and admits she was wrong."

They both knew that wouldn't happen anytime soon.

"Will you be traveling a lot this summer?"

"Nope. Renner didn't sign on for hardly any events this year, since his wife was pregnant."

"Didn't seem like you were on the road as much last year either. That had to make you happy."

Sometimes he wondered if his mother knew him at all. "Not really. I like the craziness of rodeo season. I'm too damn busy to get bored."

"You got good hands?"

"We've only brought half of the stock we normally do. Ike, a cattle broker from Muddy Gap, is driving one of the transport trucks. Riss, a truck-driving ranch gal Renner's used in the past, is handling the double-decker transport. And Renner's sister-in-law, Harlow, is with me, learning the ropes."

"With me," his mom repeated, "as in with you . . . how?"

"As in her head is on the pillow next to mine in the horse trailer at night and during the day she's in the pens with me."

"Well, this *is* news."

"Bet that changes your mind about coming to see me at the rodeo, doesn't it?" he teased.

Hugh's phone beeped. "Got another call, Mom. Good talking to you." He hung up and clicked to the other line. "Pritchett."

"Hey, it's Renner. Just checking in to see how things are goin'."

"Good." Hugh started to pace. "No problems so far. Ike knows a lot of people. He'd give you a run for your money in the schmoozing department."

Renner laughed.

"But he ain't afraid to get his hands dirty either."

"I'm still wondering why he signed on. Don't get me wrong—I'm grateful he did, but it don't make much sense."

Ike's issues with his path in life weren't Hugh's to share. "I'm with you, Ren. But I ain't lookin' a gift horse in the mouth."

"And Harlow? Tierney hasn't heard from her except a couple of picture messages."

"You know Harlow. She's doin' what needs done, without complaint."

The odd pause on the line lingered.

"You still there?"

"Yeah. I just can't quite wrap my head around you and Harlow together, let alone workin' stock together. We've been friends a long time, Hugh. Happy as I was to see you rid your life of Cleo, the divorce knocked you low. In the past five years I've not seen you with another woman. When you decide to emerge from your shell and enter the dating world again, Harlow is the first woman on your radar? It's just a fun, opposites-attract, she-was-convenient, temporary thing, right?"

"No. I'm crazy about her. And before you further insult what I feel for her, you should understand I fucked things up with her three years ago. I won't make the same mistake twice."

"You two were together before?" Renner said with complete surprise.

"Sort of. And no, she didn't tell Tierney then and *you* can't tell her now. How much she shares with her sister is entirely Harlow's call. Me'n Harlow have some history between us. But for once in my life I'm not lookin' back. I'm lookin' forward."

"Fuck. You cannot spring this shit on me." He lowered his voice. "And I'm *not* supposed to tell my wife? Dick move, asshole."

"You've made plenty of dick moves over the years, so suck it the fuck up, cupcake, and keep your mouth shut."

Renner laughed—but it wasn't with amusement. "Sounds like we need to talk when you get back. Right after I punch you out for the cupcake comment, jackass."

Hugh was still grinning as he hung up.

⊸◦⊸

After he checked to make sure Ike was attending the meet and greet with the rodeo committee, he returned to the horse trailer. The humid scent of shampoo, body wash and Harlow met him at the door. Her scent always made him hard.

What were the odds she'd still be naked?

Just then she emerged from the bathroom. Dressed.

Damn.

Hugh's gaze took in the flowing floral halter-top dress that brushed her beringed toes and exposed her sexy back. She'd left her white blond hair in loose waves that fell just above her breasts.

"You look good enough to eat, doll. Why don't you scoot onto the table, pull up that dress and let me eat my fill?"

"Because once you get your face between my thighs, you tend to stay there a while." She smirked. "Not that I'm complaining. But you need to get ready. The banquet starts in fifteen minutes."

He started to stalk her. "We can be late."

Harlow stood her ground. "No, we cannot, because I hate being late." She slid her hands up his chest, then cupped his face between her palms. "Thank you. For earlier."

"You're welcome."

"I just . . ."

He kissed her furrowed brow. "I know."

"How did you know?"

You were hurting and it wasn't only about being dirty. It was about needing TLC and not knowing how to ask for it. And for me, it was about you finally letting me be the man who gives you what you need, without hesitation.

"Hugh?" she prompted softly.

He brushed his lips over hers. "I'll get myself cleaned up so I don't look like a bum next to my gorgeous woman."

After a quick shower, he ran his hands through his damp hair. He trimmed his beard, tempted to shave the damn thing off for the summer. What would Harlow think? She'd never seen him without facial hair. But she loved feeling his beard all over her hot little body and that was worth the occasional itch.

As he exited the bathroom, towel wrapped around his waist, he called out, "Darlin', did we—" He froze, seeing Riss standing in the kitchenette with her mouth hanging open. "Sorry. I'll just—"

"Don't leave on my account," Riss said, her gaze firmly on his chest. "Holy pectorals, Batman. I had no idea you"—she pointed from his damp head to his bare feet—"had all that going on under your baggy clothes, chute boss Pritchett."

Hugh blushed.

Harlow stepped in front of him, squaring off against Riss. "Eyeballs off my man, or I'll have to hurt you."

Riss looked amused until she realized Harlow wasn't joking.

His cock started to stir at witnessing Harlow marking her territory. "Something you needed, Riss?"

"She was trying to skip out on the welcome banquet," Harlow answered. "I was about to tell her it wouldn't kill her to ditch her trucker's overalls for one night."

Hugh covered his laugh by clearing his throat.

"Besides, you'd rather hole up in your cab and do what? Eat beef jerky and watch Netflix? Come with us. Eat real food. Have a real conversation. Your bunk will be fine without you holding it down for a few hours."

Riss glared at her. Then she jammed her hands through her mass of wild red hair. "Fine. But I ain't wearing a dress. And you'd better not ditch me with Ike."

"I fully expect these guys will ditch us, which is why I need a familiar face around so I'm not drinking alone."

She grinned. "Why didn't you just say that in the first place?"

Harlow reached over and opened the door. "Out. And keep your eyes on the floor and off my man."

"Later, PITA. See ya, hot-bodied Hugh."

He might've heard Harlow growl, which was sexy as fuck. Then he realized what Riss had said. "It doesn't bother you that she's calling you PETA?"

"Not PETA the organization. PITA, short for 'pain in the ass.'"

"Doll, that ain't much better."

"I've been called worse. Way worse." She smacked his ass. "Now get moving."

Harlow slipped her arm through Hugh's as they crossed the campground to the enormous tent. They wore lanyards that denoted their place in the rodeo world. "So will you be trying to round up business for Jackson Stock Contracting for next year's rodeos?"

"I wish."

She stopped. "Okay. That's like the third or fourth time you've made that cryptic comment. What's going on?"

Hugh looked around as if he was afraid someone might overhear him. "We'll talk later."

"Give me a hint."

"I get on the road and realize how much I miss it. Renner doesn't. In the last two years I've had the feeling that if he could get rid of the stock contracting side, he would."

"He doesn't like to venture far from home. Which I understand."

His eyes searched hers. "You, Miss Wandering Feet, understand the appeal of home?"

Harlow had been so thankful he'd opened up she'd said the first thing that came to mind. But Hugh's comment was justified. "No. You're right. I don't understand." She tugged his hand. "Tell me about this welcome party."

"Two things you'll want to be aware of before we walk in there. One, guys are gonna hit on you, so don't be surprised if I make it crystal fuckin' clear that you're mine."

Mine didn't have the same connotation when Hugh said it as when Fredrick had said it. She could hear the difference now.

"Two, people will ask you about Jackson Stock Contracting curtailing the number of rodeos we're working. Don't explain about Renner and Tierney having a new baby. Don't talk about the Split Rock. Don't mention the cattle company. Just tell the truth—you go where you're told."

She didn't like that Hugh felt he had to spell out her response for her. But she also understood that Renner had entrusted him with the business and he was just doing his job. "No problem. Anything else?"

"Nope. Stick close."

The instant the tent flap opened, they walked into a wall of sound. She sent Hugh a sideways glance and saw his jaw tighten.

He directed her to the bar. "Budweiser and . . ." He tipped his hat at her expectantly.

"Tanqueray and tonic."

The bartender laughed. "Honey, the best gin I've got is Gordon's."

"In that case I'll have a margarita on the rocks." She looked at Hugh. "What?"

"Won't they take away one of your tie-dyed shirts, hippie-girl, if you admit you prefer top-shelf booze?"

"Funny." As soon as she held the mixed drink, she leaned over. "It'll put a black mark on my feminist card if I let you pay for the drink and I've got no problem with that."

Hugh smiled at her and dug out his wallet.

As they made their way through the room, several people snagged Hugh's attention and he stopped to talk. After he'd introduced her as his lady, she tuned out the conversation. It was so much more interesting to people watch. Rodeo queens were easy to pick out. Gotta love women confident enough to wear tiaras.

A mass exodus started when the buffet opened.

Ike joined them at that point, looking snappy in a cream-colored button-down shirt, a black leather vest, gray jeans and beat-up black cowboy boots. In a sea of hats, he'd opted to keep his head bare. Harlow thought to herself it'd be a shame to cover up all that wavy blond hair with a hat anyway.

She took the chance to study Ike while he conferred with Hugh. Although he had to be in his late thirties, he still sported the boy-next-door/captain-of-the-football-team clean-cut look. Tall and slender, he was built, but not bulked up. His face was always smooth-shaven. Dimples bracketed his smiling mouth. His eyes, the oddest shade of blue green, were way more somber than usual. It gave her a weird feeling when she noticed both Hugh and Ike scanning the room.

When Hugh caught her watching him, she said, "What's going on?"

"Some folks here I'd rather not get cornered by." He smiled, but it didn't reach his eyes. "Ike's mapping out exit strategies."

She could read him well enough to know he'd just told a little white lie. Why? "Who are you avoiding?"

"I'll tell you later."

"Tell me now. I don't want to get ambushed and end up face-to-face with your ex-wife."

His look of horror was almost comical. "Actually, my ex-wife's father—my former boss—is here."

"Are you afraid she's here someplace?"

"Afraid? No."

"What does she look like, so I can keep an eye out for her?"

"An evil sea hag."

Harlow laughed.

"Laugh, but, darlin', I'm not joking. She's even got a wart. She claimed it was a mole, but I always knew the truth." He put his hand on the small of her back. "Let's get in line."

Ike and Hugh were roped into a conversation with the guys behind them. Harlow hated to be rude, but she checked her phone for messages from her sister. Their dad had gone to the doctor today and she was anxious to hear how the appointment had gone.

Someone bumped into her as she was looking down at her phone. She looked to the side and saw the bumper was none other than Riss.

Riss, who looked nothing like the foul-tempered, overall- and ball-cap-wearing truck driver. She'd tamed her wild corkscrew curls into a sleek bun at the base of her neck. She'd donned a peasant blouse the color of emeralds, white skinny jeans and jeweled sandals. She'd even put on mascara. Thick black lashes made her green eyes stand out. Riss hadn't bothered to try to cover up her freckles, but she'd slicked peach lipstick on her lips.

Riss bumped her shoulder into Harlow's again. "Close your mouth, PITA—you're catching flies."

"Holy crap, Riss. You clean up good."

"Just because I don't ever wear shit like this doesn't mean I don't know *how* to wear it."

"And you don't smell like axle grease, which is the real bonus," Ike said behind them.

"Bite me, asshat," Riss snapped.

When Harlow tried to balance her drink while getting her small purse open, Riss said, "I'll hold that," and snatched the margarita from Harlow's hand. Then she took a healthy swallow.

"Do you know anybody here?" Harlow asked.

Riss shook her head. "This venue is a long haul for us. Most stock contractors tend to stick to their own circuits that are only ten-hour drives one way, tops."

"You think it's unusual that Jackson is providing stock for an event so far away?"

"Yeah. But Renner was based out of this area at one point, so in that context, it's not that unusual. Although I heard people talking. Not trash-talking, but since this ain't my first rodeo like it is for *some* people"—Harlow snickered—"I've been paying attention. Jackson's lack of contracted venues this year hasn't gone unnoticed." Riss grabbed a plastic plate from the stack and cut in front of Harlow.

Harlow eyed the buffet table. She passed by the stack of barbecued pork sandwiches. The beans were dotted with chunks of bacon. She slid a baked potato onto her plate and passed by the cold cuts plate. The iceberg lettuce didn't look too bad, so she piled that on, adding veggies from the relish tray. She snagged a couple of lemons from the beverage station and waited for Hugh.

He frowned at her plate. "If you're still hungry after this, I'll unhitch the truck and take you to town."

After she'd voiced concern about his lack of groceries, he'd in turn voiced concern that it'd be slim pickin's for her in beef country at meet and greets like this. "Thanks. I'll be fine." She smirked at the three sandwiches on his plate and the pile of beans. Ike's plate looked the same. "I'm sure there will be plenty of lettuce left over."

"Let's sit back there." He led them to a long banquet-style table.

Riss set her plate across from Harlow. "I'm getting a margarita. You want another one?"

"Sure."

"I'll take a Coors Light if you're offering," Ike drawled.

"I'll never offer you anything, dickhead." She wheeled around and headed to the bar.

"Pretty clothes and a pretty face still don't mask her ugly attitude," Ike said. "Christ, Hugh. You have shit taste in friends."

He set down his sandwich and offered Harlow a grin. "Just think, darlin'. We get twelve more days of this."

Chapter Eighteen

*H*arlow had survived the first rodeo event and they were off to the next.

They'd pulled in early enough to unload the livestock and eat someplace besides the fairgrounds. Music drifted from the tent behind them where the welcome-to-the-rodeo dance was in full swing. For the past couple of hours she and Riss had bonded over margaritas and their shared love of old movies. So far they hadn't made it inside the tent. They stood outside as Ike and Hugh talked with several rodeo competitors and she and Riss drank.

Over the last few days Hugh had kept his promise by keeping a hand on her at all times. He may as well have tattooed *TAKEN* across her forehead. She snickered. Maybe a better placement for it would be across her ass.

Hugh's warm breath teased her ear. "What's so funny, doll?"

"Nothing."

"You havin' fun?"

"Yes. Are you?"

"Be havin' more fun if we were naked."

She buried her face in his neck and murmured, "You are insatiable." Not an exaggeration. Hugh needed that physical connection every night. Sometimes in the morning. Sometimes at noon.

"You'll tell me if you get tired of the same old, same old, right?"

"You mean sex in missionary?"

"Yeah." He kissed and nuzzled her cheek. "I'm not the most inventive guy between the sheets."

"You don't need to demonstrate you've studied the *Kama Sutra*." She trapped his face in her hands and forced his head up. "You are an amazing lover, Hugh. You've never left me wanting. You always make me feel wanted and that's sexier than you doing me on one leg while I swing on a trapeze."

"You kill me, darlin'." He pressed his forehead against hers. "Thanks. And I do want you. Every second of every day. I don't wanna overwhelm you. But that's what this is for me. Overwhelming."

"For me too." She opened her mouth. Closed it.

"Spit it out."

"You mean the lust between us is overwhelming." *Please don't ruin this and say your feelings for me are overwhelming.* She'd caught him looking at her sometimes with the oddest expression on his face, and she'd been too chicken to ask what he'd been thinking about.

Hugh retreated. He placed a kiss on her ear. "Yeah. What else would I have meant?"

Wow. That almost sounded . . . sarcastic. And maybe a little sad.

"Maybe you two could quit whispering and playin' grab ass and contribute to the conversation," Ike suggested.

"Sure." She shifted away from Hugh slightly only to have him haul her back against his side. "What are we discussing?"

"Scheduling. You'll be all right managing the calves and steers tomorrow?"

"Managing. Like scheduling their massages?"

Ike rolled his eyes. "Like getting them from the pens to the chutes. Usually there are riders assigned to each area so if one takes off, they run it down."

"So I won't be hoofing it after them if they make a break for it?"

Hugh snorted beside her. "No, because *you'd* let the animals go, imagining them livin' free in the wild and not eventually headed for market."

"That *is* a beautiful image. You know me so well."

His eyes were dark with what resembled regret. "Yeah, doll, I do."

"Then after the timed events," Ike interrupted the odd moment, "you'll check their food, water, all that."

"Sounds completely doable for a stock novice."

"You're getting better. There's hope for you yet."

Hugh and Ike moved on in their conversation and Harlow tuned them out. Riss refilled their margaritas. "I feel like causing trouble. After we're done here, let's go pick a fight with the townies."

"Townies," Harlow repeated. "And they'd be?"

"The teased-hair, tight-clothes, caked-on-makeup local girls who live in town and slip on pseudo-Western wear once a year during the rodeo to pretend they're country." Riss slurped her drink. "I wanna pound some faces in."

"Which is exactly why you *won't* be out of my sight tonight, La-Riss-a," Ike warned.

"Oh, bite me, dipfuck. You ain't my daddy or my keeper. I do what I want."

The cowboys next to Ike snickered.

A woman stopped in front of their group. Her eyes scrolled down Hugh's body from hat to boots. "I heard you were here."

Hugh's body stiffened. His jaw tightened so fast and hard Harlow swore she almost heard a bone crack.

Harlow looked at the woman. "Brittle" best described her posture as well as her attitude. Her long brown hair was curled at the bottom and teased at the top, beauty-queen-style. She'd slathered on too much makeup and her eyes were an aquamarine hue not found in nature. She was all curves in her tight, low-cut Western shirt and gaudy jewelry—although Harlow suspected she wasn't the kind who'd wear cubic zirconia.

"I've walked past here a couple of times because I didn't recognize you, Hugh, without your beer gut and double chin."

Hugh said nothing.

Why was he letting this woman speak to him this way?

"How do you know Hugh?" Harlow asked.

The woman gave her a derisive once-over and laughed. "Baby girl, did your mama give you permission to stay out past ten o'clock tonight?"

"Excuse me?"

"Aw, ain't you polite? But keep your trap shut while the grown-ups are talking," the woman said with a sneer.

And . . . it was on. "You're absolutely right, *ma'am.* I was raised to respect my elders. Would you like to sit down while you're insulting us? I'm sure walking around on this hard ground is painful for your aging joints."

Riss made a hissing you-got-burned sound.

"Still surround yourself with losers, I see," the woman said to Hugh.

"Nah. I took an upgrade after I left you, Cleo. Not surprised you don't recognize class."

Cleo. Now the woman's nastiness made sense. Harlow squinted at Hugh's ex-wife. She wore every one of the six years she had on Hugh. She looked like a tool. A nasty tool.

"The man can say more than 'yes, dear' and ask for fries with his Extra Value Meal," Cleo retorted.

"What do you want?" Hugh asked.

"Like I said, I'd heard you were here. I mostly wanted to see you so I could point and laugh." She cocked her head, sending her hair over her shoulder. "It's a good thing Hugh lost all that weight or else he'd crush this bony, boyish body of yours."

Harlow gasped, "You're Hugh's ex-wife?" with total sarcasm.

"Took you that long to put it together? You ain't the smartest cookie in the package, are you?"

No, but I'm the toughest cookie, bitch, and I'm about to take a serious fucking bite outta you and see how fast you crumble.

"You know, I do see her resemblance to an old sea hag," Harlow said in an aside to Hugh. "But I was expecting her hair to be stringier. And it looks like she got the wart removed."

Cleo slapped her thigh. "Gotcha one that likes sarcasm and thinks she's funny. Sugar, did you learn them nasty barbs from watching MTV?"

"I'll take the compliment that you think I'm jailbait, but, *sugar*, I'm older than I look. Then again, just about anyone has aged better than *you*, I imagine."

"Did you and Hugh meet at fat camp? You seem like one of them former fat girls who got skinny like you got Jesus."

Harlow laughed. "What's next? You insult my bra cup size? But I guess if I paid for my tits"—she pointed to Cleo's chest—"I'd feel obligated to make sure that's what people were looking at too. And I'll admit, it does take attention away from your crow's-feet."

Cleo stepped forward. "Can you back up that big mouth?"

"With what? My fists? Why would I fight you?" She leaned back against Hugh and sipped her drink. "I've already got him. And honestly, I should be thanking you."

"For what?" she snapped.

"For being so shallow. If you hadn't made marriage to you intolerable, he never would've moved away. He never would've seen beyond the veil of misery his life had become with you in it. He never would've started over. And he and I wouldn't have met."

Hugh bent his head and kissed the side of Harlow's neck. That simple act spoke more of their intimacy than a full-blown make-out session.

Not that that wouldn't have been loads of in-your-face fun too.

Cleo was so mad she couldn't speak.

Good.

Hugh clasped Harlow's hand and started to lead her away.

Ike draped his arm over Riss's shoulder, neatly blocking Cleo, allowing them to escape.

Hugh was wound so tight Harlow thought if she touched him just right, he'd vibrate like a tuning fork.

They passed the event tent—guess dancing wasn't happening—and didn't stop until they reached the back of the empty grandstand.

Hugh pushed her up against the cement wall. He whispered hoarsely, "You fucking undo me."

Then he took her mouth in a kiss so hot and possessive she figured she'd see body-shaped scorch marks on the cinder blocks behind her.

He kissed her. And kissed her. And just when she thought they'd break free for air, he kissed her some more.

Harlow let him build her up and turn her inside out with just the power of his mouth. The potency of this connection between them grew stronger every hour of every day they spent together.

He slowed the kiss to gentle smooches and the gliding whisper of his wet lips against hers. Then he buried his face in her neck, his hands flexing on her hips.

Goose bumps skittered across her damp skin with his every exhalation. She had one hand resting against his heart, the other hand gripping his hair.

Finally he spoke. "I need you."

"You have me." She nuzzled his ear. "Any way you want me."

Immediately Hugh grabbed handfuls of her skirt and tucked the material behind her lower back. No gentle easing aside of her thong. The man twisted the delicate fabric around his thick fingers and ripped it free.

His face remained nestled in her neck as he unbuckled his belt and undid his jeans. The way his rough-skinned knuckles grazed the soft swell of her belly caused her stomach to pitch. His silent need stoked hers and her body responded.

Hugh lifted her leg, opening her stance and bracing her against him all at once. He didn't ask permission. He just did what he wanted.

She loved that about him.

His fingers slid down the crack of her ass. He adjusted the angle of his cock, aligning the head with the entrance to her body.

Then he paused. His entire body shook.

Harlow had figured out his silence at times like this was from being too clogged with emotion to know what to say.

"Show me. Don't hold back."

The growl that rumbled out as he impaled her hit the mark between necessity and carnality.

Fisting her hand in his hair, she held on as he fucked her with everything he had. Each powerful thrust slid her shoulder blades against the wall. But the scrape of the cement behind her hardly registered. Her mind and body were focused on the raw passion and power he'd unleashed on her.

His harsh pants and soft grunts burrowed into her ear like the sweetest music. The pulsing of her blood had synchronized to the fast and primal way he branded her, marked her body with his own.

And while she'd known this hard fuck was for him, in the end, it was for her too. Her orgasm came directly on the heels of his.

Then he stilled as his cock jerked violently inside her.

His lips found hers. The kiss conveyed everything that words couldn't. The intensity gave way to sweetness. To gratitude.

Harlow had heard the phrase *and in that moment everything changed*, but it'd never resonated with her—until now.

She loved him. Crazy to think that she'd ever hated him.

He gently lowered her foot to the ground and righted his clothing before adjusting hers. He picked up her thong, but she couldn't read his face.

After another kiss on her neck, he clasped her hand in his and pulled her away from the wall.

Framing his face in her palms, she forced him to look at her. "That definitely wasn't same old, same old."

He smiled, but didn't speak.

The walk to the horse trailer took forever. But that was fine, since neither of them seemed to know what to say.

Hugh felt ill as soon as he caught sight of the scrape marks on Harlow's shoulders the next morning.

Jesus. What had he been thinking? Practically goddamn rutting on her in a public place?

You were thinking she was fierce and loyal and snarky and sexy as fuck as she jumped into the snake pit with the queen viper.

You were thankful that Harlow was yours and you needed to prove it. To her. To yourself. To any motherfucker who happened by.

But still, the fact her skin had been abraded, and she hadn't mentioned it during or after, bothered him. He never wanted her to revert to the woman she'd been with her abusive ex—taking whatever he dished out without complaint so it'd just be over.

When he confronted her about the scrapes, she'd played it off as if it wasn't a big deal. He'd dug out the first aid kit and tended to her anyway.

In gearing up for the afternoon rodeo, he'd gotten stuck waiting for paperwork outside the fairgrounds offices. To kill time, he watched the women running barrels in the arena.

Hugh smelled the perfume that reeked of Cleo before he saw her. She sidled in next to him and propped her boot on the lowest metal railing.

"Your fuck-toy is a bitch," she said without preamble.

The woman waiting in the alley for her turn to practice reminded Hugh of Celia Gilchrist. In recent months he'd seen more of Sherry, Kyle's mom, than he had of either Celia or Kyle, because he spent more time at the Buckeye. Although Kyle had officially retired from bull riding, he had a great eye for rank stock. Hugh had found a couple of bulls he'd like Kyle to test, so he'd make that a priority when he got back to Wyoming.

"Not talking to me?" Cleo demanded.

"You offering an apology?"

She snorted.

"I don't know what you want from me, Cleo. You show up last night and insult me. When my girlfriend defends me, you jump her. And now the first fucking thing you say to me is a nasty barb directed at her. So, yeah, I got nothin' to say and I ain't interested in playing your games."

"You're not interested in seeing your daughter?"

Hugh let out a sharp bark of laughter. "Jesus. Give it up already. Tallulah ain't my kid."

"Then why have you refused to submit to a paternity test?"

"Because I hadn't fucked you in a goddamned *year* when you filed for divorce. A year in which you told anyone who'd listen that you couldn't stand to look at your fat-assed husband, let alone allow me to touch you. And then three months after our divorce is final, you tell me you're three months pregnant? Math ain't ever been your strong suit, but thankfully it *is* mine."

"I think—"

"I don't care what you think. Maybe you oughta worry about bein' a good mother to that girl, since it's plain even *you* don't know who the kid's father is." After the divorce Cleo had continued to fuck with him. Telling his sister, Mary, that he'd abandoned her when he'd found out Cleo was pregnant. That'd caused a huge rift with his sister. It infuriated his parents that Mary blindly believed Cleo's lies, because they knew Hugh would never abandon his child, no matter how much he despised the child's mother.

"Let me finish. I think—I know—I screwed up with you. I was frustrated that you were gone all the time. I know about all the buckle bunnies that hang around cowboys and their 'what happens on the road' excuse that gives them free rein to fuck whoever they want. I figured you'd become just like them."

"Bullshit. *I* never had a problem with fidelity. That was all on you. And I'm pretty sure it started *before* I took the job with Renner. Besides, this is all old news and I've no desire to rehash it. Ever."

"You don't give an inch, do you?"

"Nope. With you an inch turned into two hundred fucking miles."

"It's different with her?"

"Very. But she ain't up for discussion." He stepped back. "Do everyone a favor. Stop stirring shit. Makes you look petty and jealous."

"And how's my behavior make *you* look?" she demanded haughtily.

"Like the smartest man in the world for getting as far away from you as I could."

"Hugh?" the fairgrounds secretary shouted from the doorway. "Got your paperwork done."

He didn't give Cleo a second look as he walked past her. And he knew he wouldn't give her a second thought.

⁓

Harlow rode herd on the animals better than Hugh had expected. They were in the same vicinity during the rodeo and it gave him a huge sense of satisfaction to look over and see her.

Since she was better with technology, and wasn't behind the chutes during the performance, she taped CC's arena debut on his phone and sent it to Tobin. And judging from the bull riders' reactions, the buzz was about to start.

Once the evening rodeo ended, they loaded up and were back on the road. They'd drive to the midway point tonight, give the animals a day to rest and then hit the blacktop the following morning. Then they'd head to the five-day event in Phillipsburg. They weren't the only stock contractors for a rodeo that size, but it'd be tricky making sure the animals weren't overused. Because after that gig ended, there'd be only two rest days before the last three-day event.

"What're you thinking about so hard?" Harlow asked.

Hugh sent her a sideways glance. "Getting you naked."

"Liar. You have a completely different look on your handsome face when you're horny. It's a look I'm *very* familiar with. So what's got your brow furrowed?"

"Just goin' over scheduling in my head. We didn't run into any problems, which usually means there'll be some at the next event."

A beat passed before Harlow said, "You love this, don't you? Being on the road in a different town every day, dealing with different challenges every day."

It'd be smarter to downplay it. Shrug and say it was just another job. But he liked having someone to talk to about this stuff. Because he had no one to talk to about some of it. "Yeah. I do. How could you tell?"

"You just seem . . . happier. That's not to say you're a malcontent at the Split Rock—your nickname Grumpy notwithstanding—but you treat the cattle side of Renner's business as just a job. Without sounding stupid or making you feel self-conscious, what you're doing now is more a vocation."

Hugh grabbed his insulated mug and swallowed a slug of coffee. "I don't know whether to be pleased that you see that or scared."

"Pleased, definitely. Because you know I'd never share those observations with anyone else, especially not my brother-in-law. But I have to ask, because I've always considered Renner an astute guy, do you think *he* sees that about you? Or at least senses that you miss it?"

"That's probably why he changes the subject every time I bring it up."

"Ah. Well, you'll have a lot to report on when we return from this time away."

Another small thing that bugged him. Renner hadn't called every night to see how things had gone. In the past if Hugh was running an event, Renner demanded details almost as soon as they'd loaded the last bull.

"And I disagree with your assessment about not running into any problems, cowboy. Running into your ex-wife was a problem."

"For her, maybe. Not for me. And definitely not for you, darlin'."

"Riss said she saw you talking to her today. She track you down to give you what-for?"

Of course someone had seen them talking; he'd be wise to remember there were eyes everywhere at these events. "I probably should've mentioned I saw her. Trust me—it was an oversight, not me tryin' to keep something from you."

Harlow reached for his hand. "That wasn't an accusation."

"I didn't take it as such."

She didn't press him for details, which was likely why he laid out the whole dirty mess that'd happened right after their divorce. Again, it'd felt damn good to get some of that shit off his chest.

Harlow didn't jump right in and offer platitudes; she considered her response before she voiced it. That was another way she'd changed in the last three years. So when she did finally speak, her question threw him.

"Did you want to have kids with her? You were married young. And if she would've gotten pregnant that first year, you'd have a ten-year-old kid right now."

"This'll probably sound weird, but I never saw us havin' kids together. Even when she was obsessed about getting pregnant. I was never disappointed at a negative pregnancy test. And I can't honestly say if we would've had a kid if I'd still be with her or not. It might've changed her for the good, but after the rumors I've heard that she's hardly ever with the kid she does have, I'm so fuckin' thankful I never had to make that decision."

"Me too."

Hugh lifted her hand to his mouth and kissed the inside of her wrist.

Afterward they didn't talk again for a while. He'd look over and see the amber glow of the dashboard lights reflecting in her hair and silently marvel at how beautiful she was in any light.

Hard to believe it'd been only six weeks since she'd come back into his life. Because he was starting to realize he didn't know what he would do without her.

Chapter Nineteen

$\mathcal{T}$he first four days at the Phillipsburg Rodeo were awesome.

She'd finally found her groove with the grind of moving, feeding, moving, feeding, loading, feeding, unloading, feeding the rodeo stock. She'd even chased the bulls into the trailer and hadn't freaked out. Hugh had rewarded her very well for that.

There wasn't as much downtime as she'd expected, which made her happier than if she had hours to kill. While the living quarters in the horse trailer were nice, she preferred to be out among the people.

Between Hugh and Ike it seemed they knew everyone, so they'd had four very social gatherings after the rodeo ended every night. Laughing, drinking, telling stories. She'd seen yet another side of Hugh. Laid-back and charming. And she'd been relieved that his charm hadn't appeared only after he'd emptied a bottle, since he rarely drank more than two beers a night.

Hugh also made sure they had plenty of one-on-one time. Lots of naked and sweaty one-on-one time. They'd christened nearly every vertical and horizontal surface in the living quarters—including during an intense interlude in the horse trailer itself, where Hugh had demonstrated a creative use for an eye-hook and a flank strap. He'd tied her hands above her head to the eye-hook and used the flank strap around her lower back to swing her body into his as he slowly, methodically fucked her.

And yet even after he'd blown her circuits on a nightly basis, he didn't roll over and start snoring. He wanted to talk. They discussed everything under the sun and moon, well into the wee hours of the morning. Part of her worried they bared all so easily because they both understood their time together had an end date. If they didn't share right then, they'd never get the chance to.

Plus, he was always doing sweet little things for her. Showing up at the farmers' market first thing in the morning to stock up on her favorite fresh vegetables. Taking the time to explain ag and rodeo things without making her feel like a greenhorn. Giving her a piggyback ride through the muck when she mistakenly wore flip-flops instead of boots.

Telling her every day she was beautiful.

Reminding her every day how much he appreciated her help.

Asking her opinion and never assuming or arguing when it contradicted his.

Proving he was a man of his word as well as a man of action.

Showing her affection in public and lust in private.

And pissing her the fuck off today.

The day had started out well enough—hot shower sex. In the past ten days she'd become a huge fan of small showers, as there were so many more possibilities to get dirty and creative when you were in a confined space.

Then Hugh had actually agreed to eat breakfast with her: granola and Greek yogurt with organic fruit and honey.

When she'd asked his plans for the day . . . that's when it'd gone downhill.

"I have a cattlemen's thing. It'll take all day."

"I'll come with you."

Hugh stared into his coffee cup.

"What? Don't you want me to come? Had enough of my company?" she teased.

He squirmed. "Not exactly."

"Then what is it *exactly*?"

"The cattlemen's luncheon. It's men only."

"You're joking."

He looked at her. "No. It's one of those things they've been doin' this way for years."

"So cattlewomen—and I've met quite a few of them this week who've taken over the ranch after their husbands have passed on—are excluded because of gender?"

"In this case, yes. Do I agree with it? No."

"Then don't go. The only way to change things is to protest them."

A frown pulled his eyebrows together. "Not that simple, hippie-girl. This luncheon is by invite only. In all the years Renner and I worked this event, we were never invited. I have to go. I'll make great contacts."

"With a bunch of sexist men," she shot back.

Hugh stood. "I figured you'd have this kinda reaction." He put on his hat.

When he paused by the door, she said, "What? You expecting a goodbye kiss?"

"No, because that'd be reasonable and it's clear that's beyond you at the moment."

"You can kiss my ass, Hugh Pritchett!" she said to the slamming door.

Damn him.

She stewed for a while. Paced. After she saw her anger had cost her an hour, she decided to take a different tack. She took out the bottle of Fireball and poured a generous slug in her 7Up. She stirred and sipped.

And coughed. Holy crap. Fireball was not for the faint of heart.

Although the horse trailer was cool, she couldn't stand the thought of remaining there by herself. She dumped more Fireball in her drink before she stepped outside.

Still humid. Bugs buzzed around her face. She considered whether she should just kick back and sulk where it was cool and bug free.

"Harlow!"

She spun around at the sound of Riss's voice.

Riss jogged toward her. "Been wantin' to talk to you."

"Why?"

"Defensive much?"

"Sorry. Hugh decided to vie for the 'prick of the year' award today, so I'm a little testy."

"He's off at the Buckaroos' thing?"

"As far as I'm concerned, he can stay there all damn night," Harlow said.

"The men-only thing pisses you off too, huh?"

"Yes! I'm just supposed to sit inside and wait for him? Maybe I should be cooking a four-course meal, darning his socks and listening for the click of the lock so I can bring him his pipe and slippers the minute he graces me with his magnificent male presence."

Riss laughed. "Oh, girl, you are gonna fit right in."

"Fit in where?"

"See, while the guys take off for their daylong 'men only' retreat, some of the women put on a spa day." Riss leaned in. "Don't let the name 'spa day' fool you. These ladies use it to fool everyone who's not invited."

"What's it take to get an invite?"

"I just happen to have two invites." Riss snatched Harlow's cup and knocked back a big gulp.

Harlow felt less like a lightweight when Riss started coughing.

"Jesus, woman. You *are* mad at him with that much Fireball in your drink."

"I hate sexist shit. *Hate* it."

"So you're against objectifying hot, young cowboys?"

"Don't know. I've never tried it."

Riss looped her arm through Harlow's. "Let's give it a whirl."

Harlow let Riss lead her to the back of the arena where an enormous tent had been set up. A couple of cowboys sat outside the front entrance. The sign on the tent flap read:

~SPA DAY~
by invitation only

"Ladies. Something we can help you with?" the blond cowboy cutie on the right asked.

Riss dug in her front pocket and pulled out two tickets.

The dark-haired cowboy on the left grinned. "Excellent. Do either of you have a cell phone on you?"

Shoot. Harlow had forgotten it on the counter. She shook her head and saw Riss shaking hers. Then Riss added, "But if you really want to be sure, bright eyes, maybe you'd better frisk me."

The blond cowboy stood and opened the tent flap. "You're trouble, Red. So I'll definitely be lookin' for you later."

This was not a side of Riss she'd ever seen before, which caused her to wonder what she'd gotten herself into.

The atmosphere inside the tent resembled a carnival. The areas were blocked off from the front entrance, but she could hear music, and smell something sweet.

A woman, around sixty, manned a small table. She smiled. "Welcome to spa day. I'll need you to sign a waiver."

Harlow automatically asked, "What for?"

"First timer," Riss said, grabbing a pen and signing.

"Ah. The waiver is for protection of the spa day coordinators. This just states you won't discuss anything that you see or participate in here, with anyone who wasn't here."

"Like *Fight Club*," Harlow said.

"Exactly! The second part of the waiver states you won't hold spa day coordinators responsible for any decisions or actions you may choose to participate in."

Harlow frowned.

"Just sign the waiver," Riss said.

"Fine." Harlow signed.

"Great! There are two bars. One for girlie drinks and one for shots."

"Let's go there first." Riss started to drag her off.

"Wait. I don't have any cash."

"Don't worry. It's all paid for."

"By who?"

"By the coordinators' husbands. See, the women got tired of being excluded, so to keep the peace, and their wives happy, the original Buckaroos gave the women money to run the spa. It's a mutual 'don't ask, don't tell' policy." Riss grinned. "But the ladies know the Buckaroos aren't having nearly the wild time we are. The most risqué thing they get is hot young waitresses dressed up like cowgirl cheerleaders. And we get this." She pointed to the first booth, which had an impressive selection of sex toys, lubes, body frosting and amateur BDSM gear. "Ask any question you want. Sheena is an expert in the pleasure business."

Don't blush. "Let's come back. I wanna do some shots first."

"Now we're talkin'!"

The bartender pouring shots was one of the hottest men Harlow had ever seen. On the top he was shirtless to show off all his gloriously cut muscles. On the bottom he wore jeans, fringed chaps and a rather large, well-placed belt buckle. He peered at her with startling blue eyes beneath the brim of a white hat. He grinned. Damn. That sexy-shy grin reminded her of Hugh.

Do not think of that man right now.

Sexy bartender said, "Hey darlin', what's your pleasure today?"

Hey darlin' reminded her of Hugh too.

Dammit. Maybe booze would block him out.

"I'll have a tequila shooter and my shy friend will have the same," Riss said.

Shy? She wasn't shy. Time she proved it. Harlow set her elbows on the bar. "Actually, *darlin'*, I'll stick with a shot of Fireball."

"I figured you might be the *fiery hot at first, but sweet and warm* type," he drawled.

Oh. My. God.

Riss whispered, "Told ya this would be fun."

They touched glasses and downed their shots.

Harlow was proud she didn't hack up a lung, but the trade-off was searing the lining of her throat.

"Another round?" Mr. Sexy Smile asked. "Gotta limit you to two shots an hour, so most of the ladies do 'em back-to-back."

"Sure, cowboy, hit us again."

By the time Harlow and Riss reached the next booth, recklessness had replaced wariness. "What's this place?"

"A makeover station," the woman who looked like a drag queen inserted.

"Oh, I don't know . . ."

"Honey, this is to teach you how to make over more than your face."

Intrigued, Harlow took a seat. For the next fifteen minutes she learned how to shave and wax hearts, flowers and even a kitty cat on her "love bump." Dolores, the makeover artist, dusted sugar-flavored glitter across Harlow's cleavage.

"Trust me, honey. Your man gets a whiff of you smelling like cookies and his mouth is gonna be all over you."

Riss clasped Harlow's hands and leaned closer, a somber look in her eyes. "We've been friends long enough that I feel I should come clean with you about something."

"Okay." *Friends long enough? Don't point out you've only known each other for two weeks.* "What is it?"

"You ever heard that song 'Tequila Makes Her Clothes Fall Off'? That's me. So you'll probably see way more of my tits and ass today than you'd like. So fair warning to look away 'cause I'm trying all of the nipple rouges."

Sure enough, Riss pulled down her shirt and scooped her boobs out of her bra. Then she worked down the spectrum of colors to find the hue that'd make her nipples "pop."

"Ah, I'll just get us a girlie drink while you're browsing," Harlow said. And fled.

The girlie-drink bar was also manned by an amazing-looking cowboy with a to-die-for body. "Hey, sugar. What's sweet enough for you today?"

She squinted at the chalkboard to read the drink names and descriptions. "I'll have a Lick My Clit and Spank Me Hard."

"Sounds like my kinda party." He winked and mixed the drinks.

By the time Harlow reached the makeover stand, Riss had moved on to the rope-tying demonstration. A dozen women formed a half circle around yet another smokin' hot cowboy as he bound a volunteer's wrists to a bedpost. Volunteer number two was tied to a chair.

"I need one more volunteer before I take a quick break."

Harlow expected Riss's hand to shoot up—not for Riss to grab *her* arm and throw her hand up in the air, shouting, "Over here!"

The cowboy's mesmerizing eyes moved over Harlow. "Come on down; don't be shy."

"I'm not shy." She handed Riss her drink.

"So tell me, you got a man who knows his way around ropes?" cowboy hottie asked.

"Yes."

"Lucky lady." He bent Harlow over and tied her left wrist to her left ankle. "This'll give you movement and he can maneuver you around however he likes."

Harlow waited for him to do something else, but that appeared to be it. He addressed the audience. "Please try this at home, ladies."

After he untied her, she wandered over to Riss.

Riss said, "You're welcome."

"For what?" Harlow swiped her drink back and drained it.

Riss smirked. "For giving you something new for you and Hugh to try."

Harlow smirked back. "Hugh already has an active imagination and he has much better rope-tying skills than that guy."

"Go, you!" Riss offered a fist bump.

"What booths haven't we been to yet?"

"There's the massage booth, but since it's hotties with fast hands giving the massages, the line is long. Oh. There's the Kama Sutra lounge, where you can see a cowboy host and his girlfriend act out positions from the book."

"Really?"

Riss hip-checked her. "Thought Hugh had an active imagination."

"He does. I just wanna watch live porn."

"Me too! Let's do it."

Thirty minutes later, Harlow said, "Even Bendy Wendy couldn't get into some of those positions, so now I don't feel uncoordinated."

"Me neither."

They found the food booth, which contained a chocolate fountain and every possible delicious morsel on earth to dip in chocolate. While they stuffed their faces, and laughed their butts off, they continued to knock back drinks.

So then when the cowboy hosts erected a portable stripper pole and performed a routine that had Harlow whooping and hollering, she was selected to try her hand at working the pole.

Evidently she'd done a good enough job—*Thanks, Dad, for insisting on those ballet lessons!*—they asked her to stay onstage to help teach.

Her somewhat drunken ego shouted, *See? You're a natural! You'll make a great teacher.*

After that demo, the music started. At some point half the tent had turned into a dance floor.

By that time almost every woman was tipsy, if not outright hammered. But it was a fun kind of hammered. They sang at the top of their lungs and danced like no one was watching, because no one cared about anything but cutting loose. And while a few women whirled around the dance floor with the cowboy hosts, most of the ladies danced together.

Harlow felt freer. Lighter. Happier. She'd been part of something amazing. She actually got teary-eyed when the DJ played "Time of My Life" from *Dirty Dancing* as the last song of the night.

Gigi and Madge, the coordinators, took the microphone to remind the ladies that what happened at spa day stayed at spa day.

She and Riss stumbled out of the tent. "Shit. It's dark out now. How long were we in there?"

"Seven hours."

"Damn. Time flies. That was some fun."

"I'm not ready for the night to end. Are you?" Riss asked.

"Nope. What's next?"

Riss got right in her face. "How drunk are you?"

"Midpoint between hammered and tipsy. Why?"

"'Cause there's one other thing we can do tonight. But I'll warn ya, it's not for the faint of heart."

"I'm in."

Riss's eyes went wide. "Without me even tellin' you what it is?"

"Yep. I'm gonna be more like you, Riss. Daring and crazy fun."

"Hot damn, Harlow, you're my new BFF. Let's go."

They'd just reached the area where the campers and horse trailers were parked when Harlow saw Hugh headed their way, looking unhappy. She didn't think he'd seen her, but she yanked Riss behind a fifth wheel anyway.

"What the hell, Harlow?"

"*Ssh*. I saw Hugh and I think he's looking for me."

"Of course he's looking for you. You're a fuckin' hottie and he's been away from you all day. Plus, he knows you were mad and he thinks you've been waiting around, so he's been dreaming up dirty things to do to you to get back into your good graces."

Harlow blinked at her.

"What?"

"You're exactly right! You have to hide me from him because he'll swoop in and hit me with his sex mojo—then I won't care that I'm missing out on the 'not for the faint of heart' thing. And I have to do it. *Have* to."

"You sure?"

She nodded vigorously. Whoa. Her head spun.

"Okay. Come on. I know a shortcut." Riss grabbed her hand and they dodged and weaved through campers and horse trailers, until Harlow wondered if they'd gotten lost. Then . . . they were right back behind the arena.

Harlow spun around slowly. "I'm not that drunk. There used to be a tent right here."

"They have to pack up fast because people get snoopy." Riss waved at someone. Then she said, "Stay here. I'll be just a minute."

"Fine. But bring me a drink. I'm thirsty," she said to Riss's retreating back.

"I'm thinkin' you've probably had plenty to drink," Hugh drawled behind her.

Harlow screamed and spun around. She slapped her hands on his chest. "Don't sneak up on me like that, you big jerk!"

"Darlin', I've been following you for the last ten minutes. You should've noticed me."

"I was paying attention to Riss because she didn't ditch me today like *someone* I know." She forced herself to drop her hands and step back. "Why were you following me?"

Hugh didn't allow her to retreat. He moved in closer. "'Cause I missed you." He reached out and twisted a section of her hair around his index finger. "I hated that we had words before I left."

"I hated that you took off for some mysterious man meeting and expected me to just wait around for you."

His eyes sharpened. "So whatcha been doin'? Drinkin'?"

"Yes. I mean *no*. I've been doing woman stuff. You wouldn't understand."

"Still pissed off at me?"

"Yep. So why don't you skedaddle your hot little Wrangler butt on back to the horse trailer and see how *you* like sitting in there alone waiting for me?"

He raised an amused brow. "And what will you be doin'?"

"Hanging out with Riss."

"That still don't tell me what you're up to."

"That's because it's none of your business."

"Losing my sense of humor about this, Harlow."

Riss rejoined them. "Hugh. Fancy meeting you here." She snickered and mouthed, "I told you so."

Hugh focused on Riss. "So maybe you can tell me what your plans are for tonight, since Harlow's acting a little—"

"I am *not* drunk," Harlow retorted.

"I was gonna say you were acting a little vague."

"That's because we're not sure what our plans are," Riss lied.

"Uh-huh." Hugh locked his gaze on Harlow's and her pulse spiked. "You're headed over to the old arena."

"So what if we are?" Harlow couldn't admit she had no idea where they were headed.

"Not happening. Especially if you've been drinkin' all day."

Harlow cocked her head at him. "It's cute how you think you can tell me what to do."

"Cute?" he practically bellowed.

"Ah, Harlow. If we're gonna do that *thing*, we've gotta go."

"What thing?" Hugh demanded. "'Cause there's only two things that go on over there and if you think you're participating in either one—"

"Maybe I'm participating in *both* of them."

"Like hell."

"Ha! What are *you* gonna do about it?"

Riss grabbed Harlow's hand and started to lead her away at a good clip.

"Harlow! Get back here!" Hugh shouted.

When it seemed like Harlow was waffling, Riss increased her iron grip. "Let it go."

"If he locks me out of the horse trailer tonight, can I crash with you?"

"Of course. But, honey, I wouldn't worry about it because we both know he's gonna be in the arena watching with the rest of the crowd."

"Watching what? Uh, Riss? What did I sign on for?" A tiny feeling of panic set in. What had she been thinking? Blindly agreeing to an activity not for the faint of heart?

You weren't thinking, dumb ass. Booze and a dare equals regrets or disaster.

Riss stopped abruptly and faced Harlow. "You, my brave friend, signed on for topless steer riding."

"What! But I can't—"

"Yes, you can. And more importantly, you *have* to now."

"Why?"

Riss got right in her face. "First, because it takes balls to ditch your shirt and get on a steer and you need to prove to yourself you can do it. Second, you start letting Hugh dictate to you? Might as well start bringing him his pipe and his slippers . . . in your teeth . . . on your knees."

When Riss put it that way . . .

"Besides, you won't be alone. I'll be right there beside you."

"You're competing?"

"Of course. I've won it the last two years, and I'm looking for a three-peat before I retire."

"Now I understand why you rouged your nipples," Harlow said dryly.

Riss grinned and looked down her own shirt. "They *will* stand out more in the pictures, won't they?"

"Pictures?"

"Get a move on, PITA."

There wasn't as much chaos behind the chutes as Harlow expected. She did knock back a shot of whiskey with the other contestants beforehand— just to be sociable. The hardest part for her wouldn't be letting her boobs flap in the wind, but exposing her scar.

So when the youngest contestants revealed their perfect perky tits, Harlow's worries lessened. No one would be leering at her tits and watching her ride.

Except for Hugh.

That thought sent a curl of desire spiraling through her as she took off her shirt and bra. It'd be interesting to see her man's reaction.

"Harlow," Riss hissed. "Pay attention. It's almost time."

"Sorry." Harlow draped her clothing over the top of the corral.

Then it was mass chaos. They put the steers in the pen and they had five seconds to choose one and climb on before the gate opened.

She threw her leg over the animal closest to her. She didn't have time to worry about the scratching sensation of the steer's rough hide on her bare skin. The gate opened, the animal bolted and Harlow held on for dear life.

Inside the arena the contestants bounced off one another like pinballs. Riders were already hitting the dirt. Steering the steer was impossible, but the play on words made her laugh.

The boisterous laughter spooked the animal and it put on a sudden burst of speed, forcing Harlow to loosen her grip. When the animal went to the left, her body went to the right. One second she was on the steer; the next she'd flipped ass over teakettle and hit the dirt. She couldn't help but watch as Riss rammed her closest competitor right before she hit the finish line. In first place.

Harlow pushed to her feet and jumped up and down with excitement for her friend.

Riss bailed off the steer and raised her hands above her head in victory. Then she made a beeline for Harlow and hugged her.

Okay. She'd never been naked chest to naked chest with another woman before. She tried to act cool. But it was weird.

The guys in the stands seemed to enjoy it, as they were calling out suggestions for what they could do next—although the Hokey Pokey suggestion was bizarre.

They turned to walk back toward the chutes and who should Harlow see walking toward her?

Hugh.

With her shirt squeezed in his fist. And that look in his eyes.

Uh-oh.

Chapter Twenty

*H*arlow's first instinct was to run.

So she did.

Of course Hugh gave chase.

The only way she knew that, at first, was because the spectators were encouraging him to catch her.

She booked it toward the steers grouped in the far corner of the arena. Once she was in the midst of them, she spun around to check if Hugh had given up.

He paused on the edge of the herd. A wild look danced in his eyes and an evil grin curled his lips. He draped her shirt around his neck and advanced on her.

That's when she noticed her lacy black bra hung out of his back pocket.

"You think you're safe in there, hippie-girl?"

"Back off, Hugh," she warned.

He laughed. *Laughed.*

"You are in a whole mess of trouble." He advanced, his gaze on her chest. "Half-goddamned naked." When she stepped to the side, so did he. "Showing everyone what belongs to me."

Harlow froze.

"What? You don't like me tellin' you that you're mine? Because you are. And if you doubt that?" He grinned. "I'm gonna take all night to prove it to you."

Her stomach cartwheeled. "Hugh, stop."

"Not a fuckin' chance."

The herd moved, so Harlow moved with it.

"Don't make me come in there after you. It's gonna just double your punishment if I gotta keep chasin' you."

And unlike with Fredrick, when Hugh stated she belonged to him, Harlow realized she wasn't afraid. When Hugh warned her that he planned to punish her, she knew in her heart that he wouldn't do anything to hurt her.

The whoops and hollers from the spectators were still going strong and that just added fuel to the fire burning in Hugh's eyes.

She was ready to make him work for it—for her. She darted to the left.

So did Hugh.

"Give it up."

"No!"

"Last chance to come to me of your own accord."

"Or?" She sidled to the right.

Hugh stopped. He clapped his hands loudly and yelled, "He-yah!"

The steers scattered, leaving her unprotected.

Moving faster than she'd ever seen, Hugh was on her.

Her surprised scream when he imprisoned her arms behind her was lost in his hungry mouth on hers.

Through the blood whooshing in her head, she heard a cheer rise behind them.

Hugh kissed her, one hand fisted in her hair, holding her head in place for the onslaught of his mouth. His other hand circled her wrists as he pressed her body against his.

He ended the kiss far sooner than she liked.

Then he eased back and stared into her eyes. "Don't fight me on this."

"On what?"

"You came into the arena your way. We're leavin' *my* way."

Before she demanded clarification, he released her.

Hugh pulled her shirt from where he'd draped it around his neck. He dropped the shirt over her head. But when she twisted up to put her arms in the sleeves, he murmured, "I get to do that part."

Her belly flipped when his hard-skinned hands landed on her waist and began an achingly slow ascent. His thumbs swept over the indentations beside her belly button and the expanse of skin between, his fingers flexing on her sides, then pressing into her lower rib cage.

His eyes—oh god, those warm brown eyes were positively molten.

"You're feeling me up in public."

"Yep."

"Stop it."

"Nope. You saw fit to flaunt these pretty tits to everyone in the arena. I'm just showing them—and reminding *you*—that *I'm* the only man who ever gets to touch them like this."

The warning, the possession, in his voice made her burn.

His hands stopped below the swell of her breasts to stroke her nipples. Over and over. Until the tips were rock hard and she shivered and moaned. In public.

Dammit. What is wrong with you? You're letting him touch you like this in front of an audience.

Harlow opened her mouth to protest, and again, Hugh cut her off with a kiss. A short kiss, but one that inflamed her.

He pulled away and said, "Mine," against her lips as he squeezed her breasts harder than she expected.

After threading her arms through her short sleeves, Hugh rested his forehead against hers and jerked her arms behind her back and quickly tied her wrists together. When she tried to twist free, she realized the tie had some give to it. Like elastic. "You did *not* just tie me up with my own bra straps!"

"Why, yes, darlin', I surely did."

Her scream of outrage was muffled against Hugh's ass, since he'd shoved his shoulder into her belly and she'd become airborne in a fireman's hold.

Loud cheers and a round of applause echoed to her as he started walking across the arena.

"Let me down!"

Hanging upside down, with her head bouncing against his butt, she didn't hear his response.

She wiggled and thrashed. Her hair was full of static and sticking to her face so she couldn't see anything. She rather stupidly tried to kick him, which resulted in four hard whacks on her ass.

The crowd cheered again.

Talk about humiliating.

Even more humiliating? She saw Hugh raise his arm as he waved to the crowd.

Waved.

Jerk. She tried to bite his ass. That backfired big-time when she felt his teeth sinking into the back of her thigh.

Harlow gasped. That should not feel good! That should not make her hot and wet.

It should not make her hotter and wetter when he smacked her ass four more times.

And he should not be rubbing his fingers on the inside of her thigh like that, as if the smug bastard knew how his swats, nips and manhandling affected her.

When the ground changed from soft to hard-packed dirt, she knew they were out of the arena.

But Hugh didn't slow down. If anything, his pace increased.

Her heart thundered when she imagined what he'd do to her when they were behind closed doors.

❧

At first, when Hugh arrived in the arena and saw Harlow milling about in the pen with the other female "contestants," his head had threatened to explode. What the hell was wrong with the woman that she'd refused to heed his warning?

His blood pressure skyrocketed when he watched her take off her shirt and her bra like it was no big deal.

No big goddamned *deal* to be bare-chested in an arena full of drunken, horny guys.

He almost jumped over the railing, into the pen, and dragged that defiant—and half-goddamned *naked*—woman out by her hair.

Ike had stopped him. "Whoa there, buddy. What do you think you're doin'?"

"Getting her the fuck outta there," he snarled.

"I wouldn't. Unless you really wanna humiliate her."

Hugh glared at him. "What the fuck are you talking about?"

He gestured to the people surrounding them. "You see any of these guys acting prudish and pissed off about their women flashing their tits? No. They're proud. Look at that dude." He pointed to a twenty-something guy who was yelling encouragement to his girlfriend while she hammed it up. "No one is holding a gun to these women's heads. They chose to participate. *Harlow* chose to participate. And I know you don't wanna hear this, but you've gotta let it run its course."

"Jesus. There's no fuckin' way I can be proud of her for takin' off her goddamned shirt in public."

"Don't punch me, but, man, you oughta be proud. She's a fine-looking woman. I'm usually a fan of big tits, but those smaller ones of hers are—"

"Stop lookin' at her!"

Ike laughed.

Proud. Right. Harlow had a great body, but it was his to enjoy, just *his*, no one else's. His hungry gaze roamed over her, starting at her delicate collarbones and the smooth flow of her chest muscles above the swell of her tits. Then there were those sweet little nipples. He bunched his hands into fists as he stared at her exposed body. He could practically feel the jut of her rib cage beneath his palms as he followed the long line of her belly down to the flare of her hips. He'd spent hours exploring every freckle, mole and mark on her skin.

Every mark.

Even the one she'd tried to hide from him. The one she'd hidden from the world.

But here she was, strutting around, her girl bits on full display, not trying at all to cover up the scar she'd called her private shame.

Sweet darlin' mine. How far you've come.

The true scope of Ike's words resonated with him. Harlow had to do this. Even though he didn't like it, he couldn't act all big, bad Neanderthal boyfriend and drag her ass out.

At least not until the competition was over.

As soon as it ended, he would go in to get her.

And he had.

Now it was time to claim his prize.

"Hugh. All the blood is rushing to my head."

He liked the vibration of her voice against his backside. "We're almost there."

They hadn't run into anyone on the way back through the campground. He dug his key out of his pocket and unlocked the door before he lowered Harlow's feet to the ground. Since she probably felt woozy, he set her against the side of the horse trailer and pressed his body into hers to keep her upright.

She blinked those big blue eyes at him and he was totally lost, completely gone for her. He fit his mouth over hers and kissed her with the tenderness he couldn't access earlier. She made those sexy little mewling noises that drove him crazy.

His mouth wandered down her neck. Across her collarbones. "Woman, why do you smell like cookies even after you were skin to hide with a steer?"

"It's body glitter."

"I like it."

"Are you going to untie me?"

Hugh used his teeth on the cord straining in her neck as she gave him full access to her sensitive skin. "Yeah, I'm gonna untie you."

"Are you really mad?"

He hated the hesitation in her voice. In that moment his plans changed. He cupped her face in his hands, forcing her to look at him. "Maybe at first I was. But I'm not now. And those few smacks on the ass are it as far as punishment." He kissed her. "Let's finish this inside." He reached around and untied her hands.

She still seemed wary after they were in the horse trailer and he'd locked the door.

So again, he changed tactics. He let his eyes rove over her with hunger. "I'm gonna fuck you. You want me to use my limited seduction moves on takin' off your clothes? Or can I save that for when we're naked and on the bed?"

There was that heart-stopping smile. "I'll strip and you do the same, cowboy. I'll meet you up there."

"Deal."

Thirty seconds later he saw that fine ass of hers shinnying up the ladder. Thirty seconds after that, he joined her.

She hadn't bothered crawling under the covers. But she wasn't watching him crawl across the mattress either. She stared at the ceiling, lost in thought.

Hugh circled his hand around her ankle and followed the lean length of leg up to her hip. "Did you have fun tonight?"

"Honestly?" She grinned at him. "It was crazy fun. Something I've never done. But I probably wouldn't do it again."

He chuckled. "Smart of you to pick a steer without horns."

"I wish I could claim I'd done it intentionally, but I can't."

Straddling her knees, he placed his hands by her hips and pressed a kiss on her belly button. He slid his mouth across the trembling muscles of her abdomen to the start of her scar. He traced the length of it with his tongue. Then he kissed the bend in her elbow and continued his journey upward. "You're so beautiful." He kissed her biceps. "So strong." He kissed the upper swell of her left breast over her heart. "So fierce."

"This isn't going to be hard and fast, is it?"

"Nope. But trust me, it's gonna be hot." He kissed the ball of her shoulder. "Intense." He followed the curve of her neck with his mouth and stopped at the hollow below her ear. "And very sweaty."

She groaned.

Hugh completely lost himself in her as he committed every inch of skin to memory. He filed away her soft sighs, the surprised gasps, the little purrs, knowing he'd go back and relive every sexy, sweet, needy sound she'd made for him.

He did discover her most sensitive spot. Who knew constant caressing of the backs of her knees could reduce her to a shuddering, begging, wet mess?

He did.

A sense of elation filled him when he rolled her over on her belly, shifted her to her knees, hiked her hips into the air, and she didn't stiffen and say no. Her relaxed posture, her heavy breathing, assured him that she was in this passionate moment with him, not in the past.

Harlow's wet pussy eased the way for his cock as he slowly pushed inside. He lowered his body over hers, his chest plastered to her back, since they were both as sweaty as he'd promised. She turned her head to the side and he brushed her hair free so he could see her beautiful face.

Hugh set a deliberately sensual rhythm, long strokes, interspersed with short jabs. He whispered hot things. Dirty things. Sweet things. He kissed her neck, bit her neck, licked her neck. He did the same to both of her shoulders, amazed as always by her response to him. Asking for more.

So he gave it to her.

Only when they both teetered on the edge did he increase the power of his thrusts—steady, but nowhere near the force with which he usually fucked her.

His balls had drawn up almost at the start. How he'd kept himself from coming, his cock clasped in her tight pussy with the scent of her hair in his lungs and the taste of her skin on his tongue, damn near constituted a miracle.

He reached between her thighs and dragged his thumb up and down her clit. She whimpered and rocked her pelvis into his hand.

"That's it, doll. Take it. You've earned it."

Harlow came with a hoarse cry.

Her cunt's contractions pulled his orgasm right out of him in long, slow, endless pulls he felt all the way to his toes.

Hugh collapsed on her, his head in a fog. Only when it cleared a bit did he realize what he'd done. His instinct was to scramble off her.

But Harlow reached back and clamped her hand on the back of his thigh. "Stay. I like this." She paused. "Thank you."

"For?"

"For showing me how it should be. For being you and giving me exactly what I needed, your way. It was perfect. Feel free to put me in that position anytime."

He nuzzled the back of her neck, so in love with her, it took every ounce of restraint not to shout it out. Instead he whispered, "It'd be my pleasure."

Chapter Twenty-one

They'd finally reached the last rodeo on their itinerary.

During the last two weeks Harlow hadn't had much downtime. Having it now, pretty much all at once, sucked. She'd even asked the local Red Cross staff if she could help pass out water to the attendees and vendors, since it was so blasted hot. They'd assured her they were fully staffed.

She sighed.

"What? That's like the fifth time you've heaved a dramatic sigh, PITA."

"I never ever say I'm bored."

"But you're bored."

Harlow looked at Riss. "You're not?"

"Of course I'm bored. But I don't have a fine man in my bed to ease the nighttime boredom, so I amuse myself during the day by watching the men work and playing my fantasy fuck game." At Harlow's confused look, Riss clarified, "It's like a fantasy sports game, except I'm imagining bedroom games. And just how I'd audition each potential player. Which ones I'd want double-teaming me." She shrugged. "Everyone needs a hobby."

Just then a young girl of about ten approached them. She had a stack of flyers in her hand.

Harlow manufactured a polite response that, no, she wouldn't like to join evening services at the cowboy church.

"We're having a chili cook-off," the ponytailed girl said, and passed over a flyer. "Winner gets a hundred bucks and a year's subscription to the *Shelbyville Gazette*."

Harlow scanned the rules. "This isn't sponsored by the beef council or the pork producers?"

"No, ma'am. The newspaper has been holding the cook-off for twenty-five years. You just bring your chili to the hospitality tent at four o'clock and it's automatically entered."

"No entry fees?"

"No, ma'am. Although there is a canned-goods food drive, if you wanna donate to that."

Harlow smiled at the girl. "Thank you for the information." Suddenly she knew how to cure her boredom. She said, "Later, Riss."

She rifled through the cupboard as soon as she entered the horse trailer, inventorying the canned goods. She'd planned to make chili during these two weeks, so she'd stocked up on basic ingredients. After laying everything out, she plugged her phone into the stereo system, listening to Vitamin String Quartet while she prepared her entry.

Hugh hadn't returned during her cooking spree, which'd taken just over an hour. Good thing, since she appeared to have used every pot and dish he owned. She covered the pot and set the stove to simmer.

Her phone rang with Erika's name on the caller ID. Harlow had stayed in Florida for six months after escaping Fredrick. She'd changed her phone number, but after doing that, she realized what a mistake it'd been. In cutting off Fredrick, she'd also cut off everyone else. She'd managed to reconnect with some people through e-mail and it'd been a while since she'd talked to her friend.

"Erika!"

"Harlow, how are you?"

"So good to hear from you. Girl, what is going on?"

"The big news is I got my master's degree this spring!"

"Congrats to you. That is awesome. So how many companies are beating down the door to hire you?"

She laughed. "None. But I've had a couple of great interviews. If nothing pops by this fall . . . well, I can always go back to HDI for a few months, right? It's not like I'd be tempted to make it my full-time job now that I have options."

Harlow chose not to be offended by Erika's jab. Her association with relief agencies was a full-time job for her. HDI—Humanitarian Diversified Incorporated—was an organization that provided a place for workers to check for paying jobs. Both she and Erika had found Fredrick's mission through the HDI website.

"What are you doing?" Erika asked. "Still in gangland LA?"

"I wasn't in gangland. The seminar was held at Bleeker, so I was perfectly safe in the dorms."

Erika was quiet. "You really did it. Took that intensive seminar. I'm proud of you."

"Thanks. I needed to be with people who'd been in similar situations. Although hearing some of their stories really drove home the point it could've been much worse for me."

"So are you ready to get back into the thick of helping the less fortunate across the world?"

"Bleeker offered me a full-time teaching position," she blurted.

"What? Get out. That's amazing."

"Shocking is more like it. But they said I've had more experience with various organizations than all their other staff combined. Which freaked me out, because when did I get that old?"

Erika huffed, "*Puh-lease*. You've been serving the greater good in some capacity since you were what? Fourteen? Do you have any idea of how many places you've been in all those years?"

"No," she answered honestly. "I'd have to look at my passport."

"The point I'm trying to make is you are *perfect* for this, Harlow."

"Even if I don't have a teaching degree? I mean, my two-year degree in international relations from a community college no one's ever heard of is less than impressive." The only reason she'd gone to school there was that travel and volunteerism had been requirements in the curriculum.

"Listen to me, as I'm an expert with a newly minted master's degree and no job. You have life experience teaching. That's what's important. The students will flock to your classes to learn from your experiences instead of listening to a tenured professor who did one three-month summer stint on an Indian reservation in the U.S. over twenty years ago."

"You have a point. I did end up leading two of the seminars after I mentioned my experiences in Cambodia. Seemed more people showed up for class those days."

"And it helps that you're a super hottie. Gonna have a lot of hipsters hot for teacher, babe."

Harlow groaned. "Erika."

She laughed. "When do you start?"

"Not sure. My dad had emergency heart bypass surgery and my sister had her second baby, so things have been hectic."

"You're in Wyoming?"

"I was. Right now I'm in Nebraska, helping out my brother-in-law." Which wasn't a total lie—since she worked for Hugh and he managed Jackson Stock Contracting.

"Of course you are. Anyway, as glad as I am to talk to you and hear your good news, I did call for a reason." She paused. "Rialta called me."

Crap. If she'd heard from her, that meant . . .

"They're back in the States. All of them."

Panic set in. *He's nowhere near you, because he doesn't know where you are.* "Erika, you can't—"

"Tell Rialta or anyone else from our group where you are. I'd never do that. I'm the only one who saw what he was capable of. I just wanted you to be prepared because we both know he'll try and contact you."

She closed her eyes. She'd dreaded this. She'd especially dreaded it after talking about it in the seminar because the consensus there had been the same: She'd done the right thing in escaping and moving on.

"Lemme ask you this, Harlow. In the seminar, how many victims pressed charges against their abusers?"

"In all the classes I've taken the last six months? Three. All three cases were dismissed. You can imagine those women were messed up by it. Abused and then ignored by the system that was supposed to hand out justice. At least I don't have that extra baggage."

"Amen, sister. It sounded to me like everything went to hell after we left. Only four of our original ten finished the contract."

"I'm not surprised. Look, I'd love to talk to you about this"—such a total fucking lie—"but I need to get to this potluck thing."

"Oh, sure, I understand. It was good catching up, Harlow. Take care. Keep in touch."

She mumbled, "I will," and ended the call.

Then she opened the cupboard and pulled out Hugh's bottle of Maker's Mark. She removed the cap and drank two big gulps straight from the bottle. Warmth spread like magic. The tension in her shoulders lessened. Normally she preferred yoga to relax, but it helped to know whiskey would do in a pinch.

Fredrick. What could he ever say to her that would excuse what he'd done? Nothing. Not, *Sorry.* Not, *I was addicted to power—it's like crack.* Not, *God has forgiven me—why can't you?*

But her biggest fear? Would be that he'd downplay what he'd done. Claim she'd overreacted. Or worse, claim she'd embellished what he'd done to her.

One more slug and she shut down that train of thought.

Why had she told Erika about the teaching offer from Bleeker? She hadn't mentioned it to anyone else. Although surely it was something her sister and her father would be happy about. Harlow in an academic environment instead of a hostile one? But part of her feared they'd point out that she didn't have the credentials to take on that kind of a job—not in a cruel way, at least not on Tierney's part. Her dad was still a wild card when it came to career directions.

But what about Hugh? He'd asked her several times what her future plans were and she'd been vague because she'd loved this time away. She wanted to bask in the moments they had together now. Them getting to know each other on a different level. But it didn't change the fact it was still on Hugh's level. His comfort zone. She had to wonder how he'd fit on her turf instead. Where she had the expertise and experience and people looked up to her for leadership.

The timer dinged on the stove. She had ten minutes to get to the hospitality tent.

She added a dollop of sour cream and stirred the chili one last time. Then she placed the pot in the cardboard box she'd rigged up with a towel in the bottom. In the bathroom she smoothed out her hair and freshened her makeup.

It was a challenge carrying the hot pot while closing and locking the door. Harlow hoped she didn't trip on the way. Scorching hot beans on her white dress wouldn't be cool.

Inside the tent, a dozen people waited in line. Men and women, which surprised her. From what she'd seen, traditional male and female roles in agriculture were alive and well in the Midwest. When she'd mentioned that observation to Hugh, he pointed out that if tradition worked for people, he saw no reason to tell them they were living their lives wrong.

That'd been the first time he'd gotten snippy with her since the Buckaroos snafu. She'd retreated, even knowing it was dumb to worry he'd belittle her or punish her for her opinion.

Hugh had sensed her fear. He'd held her, soothed her, teased her and ultimately made love to her to calm those fears.

"Next."

Jostled out of the memory, Harlow set her box on the table.

"Name?"

"Harlow Pratt."

The woman passed over a plastic bowl. "Your entry number is on the bottom of the bowl. Fill the bowl with six cups of your chili and leave the bowl on the table. You can put your pot with the extra against the far tent wall. Good luck."

"Thank you." Harlow followed the instructions and found out the winners wouldn't be announced for an hour. So she went looking for Hugh.

She saw him directing a bunch of hands and she waited to approach until he'd dismissed everyone.

His lips stretched into a big smile when he noticed her.

Harlow jogged the last few steps between them.

"Hey, darlin'." He dipped his head and then those smiling lips were on hers.

Someone yelled, "Take it behind the barn, Pritchett," which only made him grin wider.

"What have you been up to today?"

"Moping, mostly. I'm feeling displaced as your number one stock hand."

"Like I told you, I've gotta use these guys since it's a paying job for them."

"I understand. Will it sound sappy if I tell you I miss being behind the scenes with you?"

"It makes you sweet, my hippie-girl. And I can't wait to eat you up." He nipped her lower lip. "Later."

She brushed dust off his shoulders. "I don't want to hang out in the horse trailer tonight, so should I go to the rodeo?"

"I suppose you could, but I wouldn't want you sitting by yourself."

"Because you don't think I can handle myself?"

"I believe you'd handle yourself just fine, Harlow. But you're a pretty woman, doll, and you'll attract attention. I've got a full day tomorrow, so I can't be beating the fuck outta the guys hitting on you tonight."

"Funny."

Hugh stared at her.

Right. He wasn't joking. "Then I'll take a page out of the Hugh Pritchett handbook and wear a hat pulled low over my face, a baggy flannel shirt, jeans and scuffed-up boots. I'll scowl at anyone who looks at me."

"Funny."

Ike strolled up. "You guys eat yet?"

"Nope. Where you headed?" Hugh asked.

Ike said, "Tofu Shack," with a straight face.

Harlow pushed him. "Jerk."

Ike laughed. "Thought maybe that'd get you to eat with us."

"I ate while I was cooking, so you guys go ahead."

Hugh looked at her curiously. "What did you cook?"

"Chili."

"Chili?"

"Yeah. My chili is awesome."

Ike said, "Tell me you didn't do what I think you did."

"Well, that's a pretty broad statement, Ike."

"You know what I'm talkin' about. Riss said you disappeared just after noon."

"What do you think she did?" Hugh asked Ike.

"Did you enter the chili cook-off?" Ike asked.

Why was Ike acting so pissed? "Yes, I did."

Hugh's eyes narrowed. "What kind of chili did you make?"

"My delicious three-bean chili."

"Meat in it?"

She shook her head. "It's so good it doesn't need meat."

"You entered vegetarian chili at a county event in beef country," Hugh stated.

"The rules did not *specify* it had to be a meat dish. And besides, what kind of backwards place doesn't have a vegetarian category?" she demanded.

"The kind of backwards place that relies on livestock as their livelihood." Hugh pushed his hat up and sighed—a sure sign of his agitation. "What if everyone stopped putting hamburger in their chili?"

"We'd be a healthier nation with more cows?"

Ike scowled at her. "Really fuckin' funny, Harlow." He looked at Hugh. "She's your girlfriend. You can deal with this. But without meat I'm sure her chili won't make it to the final round, so it won't be an issue. Let's hope anyway." He walked off.

Harlow looked at Hugh in total surprise. "What is his problem?"

"It's my problem too, Harlow. You entering that cook-off was basically a big 'fuck you' to this event."

"No, it wasn't!"

"You don't have an agenda?"

"Not besides wanting to fill my free time. A girl invited me to enter the cook-off. So I did. That's it. And it's stupid that my entry would upset anyone."

He stepped back. "I'm goin' to get some food."

"You're mad at me and ditching me?"

"I'm headed for the Barbecue Hut. Didn't think you probably wanted to come along."

"I'll pass." She returned to the tent and spent the next forty-five minutes watching people. And when the head judge took the mike to remind everyone the winners would be announced in five minutes, a weird feeling took root.

Third place went to Loretta Palmer.

Second place went to Art Derby.

Harlow sat among strangers when they called off number sixteen—and her name—as the first-place winner. She saw everyone asking one another, "Who's that?"

When she reached the stage, she saw the box piled high with canned goods for the food drive and felt guilty she'd forgotten.

"Harlow Pratt, you are the grand-prize winner. You get a year's subscription to the *Shelbyville Gazette*—the proud sponsor for this event for a quarter of a century—and a hundred-dollar gift card."

"Thank you so much." Harlow moved to return to her seat.

"Oh no, sugar, you ain't local, so you probably don't know how this goes. First question, tell us what about your chili made it so special."

Lie like a motherfucking rug. "Ah. It's an old family recipe."

People nodded.

The judge said, "Where are you from?"

"Chicago."

"The town known for putting its own spin on pizza and hot dogs. So what did you do to put your own spin on that old standby, chili?"

"Well, it isn't what I put in as much as what I left out . . . the meat."

Silence.

"It's . . . vegetarian chili?" the judge said in the type of whisper used to relay bad news.

"Yes."

Grumbling sounded from the audience.

"Disqualify her," came a shout from the back of the room.

From where Harlow stood, it looked like everyone in the audience agreed.

"She bought off the judges," someone else yelled. "I knew Myrtle Petersen was going soft when she allowed chili made with chicken to win last year!"

Mumbles of assent.

"Enough," the judge said. "This recipe won on the basis of taste. So let's congratulate Harlow. Anything you'd like to add?"

"I'm donating the gift card to the food drive."

That didn't even earn her a single thumbs-up from the audience.

Shit.

One of the hired hands helping Hugh out with the stock, named Alton— who'd also entered the cook-off—saw her struggling with her box and offered to carry it for her. Having a local guy help her warded off a few of the evil looks she'd gotten.

When she found Hugh in the audience, he didn't say a single word positive or negative about her win.

Nor did he even want to try her chili.

Jerk.

Yeah, you haven't tried any of his dishes either, so what did you expect?

And rather than annoy him further by going to the rodeo by herself, she stayed in the horse trailer and watched TV.

Hugh woke her up in her favorite way. His mouth between her thighs.

Was it his version of an apology? Did they need to talk about what'd happened earlier?

No, this showed that he was ready to move on. Theirs were differing philosophies and talking wouldn't change either of their minds.

So she relaxed and gave herself over to him.

Once Hugh knew she was sentient, he came at her full force. Pushing her legs over the arms of the easy chair, opening her up to his ravenous mouth. She was used to his passion, but this was something else. He drove her to that knife's edge. Where one more sweep of his tongue over her clit would send her soaring. But each time she got close, he backed off. He'd drag his beard over the insides of her thighs until they trembled. Until that rasp of hair across her sensitized flesh was pleasure with a prickle of pain.

The third time he'd teased her to the point of frustration, she said, "If you don't make me come, I'll take matters into my own hands."

"Won't feel as good as my mouth sucking your clit."

Cocky jerk. "Give it to me, then."

Harlow half expected him to make her say *please*.

But he didn't. He didn't stop, either.

Not after she came the first time. Or the second. Or the third.

After she found her way back to earth after three orgasms, she looked at Hugh to see he'd stripped. His cock jutted out. His chest heaved. His jaw was set. His eyes were beautifully dark with need.

Harlow started to push up, wanting her mouth on his cock, her hands teasing his balls, but he shook his head and brought her hands to his chest.

Hugh liked nipple play, but he was either too shy or too embarrassed to ask her specifically to touch him there.

Then he wrapped her legs around his waist and leaned over her, bracing his hands on the cushion above her head.

That put his chest right at mouth level.

When he surged into her, Harlow slid her hands down to his hips to stop the rapid-fire motion. She buried her face in his chest hair, breathing him in. When he caught the hint she could focus her attention on his nipples if he slowed his thrusts, he adjusted his thrusts to a leisurely glide in and an equally slow withdrawal.

She'd glanced up to see if he was watching her. But his eyes were closed, a blissful expression on his face that remained until after he came. Only then did he kiss her. The level of heat transcended that of a normal kiss, while rooting it in sweet supplication, and she was lost again in how deeply she felt for this man.

The next morning Hugh left without waking her.

After the chili incident, she didn't feel like mingling with the maddening crowd. So she spent an hour doing yoga, a couple of hours looking at the class descriptions at Bleeker to see where her proposed classes would fit for students in the humanitarian studies curriculum. As a guest lecturer, she'd teach the required intro class for incoming freshmen.

Riss stopped by with a message from Hugh that they'd be hosting the workers between the end of the afternoon event and the start of the evening rodeo.

Looked like her contribution would be leftover chili, since it was too late to go to the store.

Late afternoon, Harlow exited the horse trailer with her Crock-Pot of chili. "Where should I put this?"

Riss cleared a spot. "I'll run an extension cord, since we'll have a couple of other hot dishes."

"It's nice that Hugh is doing this."

"Yeah it is nice—too nice—considering this bunch of hands are assholes. I wonder who recommended them."

"Ike maybe?"

Riss shook her head. "He mentioned he thinks these guys are dickheads too."

Harlow withheld judgment. Alton had been great after the chili cook-off yesterday. "We've got how many coming?"

"Eight. Plus the four of us."

"Do these guys bring wives or girlfriends? Do we need more food?"

"Heck if I know." Riss smirked at her. "Throw out a plate of veggies and salad. I doubt the guys will eat any and the chicks will."

"Including you?"

"Hey, I like veggies. Just not as much as steak. Don't worry—we have enough food. I'll finish doing this. You head down to the pens and see when they'll want to eat."

"Sounds like a plan." Harlow grabbed a jacket and a ball cap. Although it was brutally hot, the arena had been exceptionally dusty and she preferred the grime on the hat and the coat and not her skin.

The slack trials put an extra burden on the contractors, wearing out the steers and calves before the timed events tonight. Through Ike's connections they had found another twenty head.

She zigzagged through the corrals until she spied Hugh and Ike. She stopped to admire the view of two cowboys who each filled out a pair of Wranglers like they'd been invented specifically for him. Long-sleeved shirts stretched over broad backs and wide shoulders. The hint of sunburn between the shirt collar and the start of the hairline. Those sexy hats. The languid way they draped themselves over the metal bars oozed confidence.

Hugh turned and looked over his shoulder, as if he'd sensed her gaze. "There's my woman."

"There's my Neanderthal."

"What's up?" He wrapped an arm around her waist and planted a kiss squarely on her mouth.

"Checking to see how much longer before you'll be ready to eat."

"Fifteen minutes. And I'll warn ya it'll be a dine and dash situation."

"Got it."

After another kiss, she returned to their campsite. Alton and two of his buddies were moving food to the larger table.

She and Riss stayed busy, because more people showed up than they'd planned for. But everyone had brought food. By the time she and Riss sat down, there was only one table of guys left.

Riss leaned over. "Shouldn't they be with Hugh and Ike, since they're the hired hands?"

"You'd think so. Maybe Hugh is making them stay and help us clean up."

"I doubt it. Cleaning up constitutes women's work around here." Riss scooted sideways and turned the opposite direction. "I need a beer. I'm going to my rig to grab one." She pointed to Harlow's half-empty bottle of water. "Want another?"

"Yeah. The chili got way hotter overnight." She bucked up and ate the last three bites of her chili and wiped her mouth.

Alton and the other hands gathered around her.

She smiled, ready to demur at their thanks for the food.

"We saw you enjoying your award-winning chili."

"It might've won for hottest batch today, since it was much spicier."

"That can happen when you modify a recipe."

Harlow nodded. "Next time, less chilies."

Alton had a smug look on his face. "Will you leave out the meat next time?"

"This is vegetarian, remember?" She looked at the guys beside Alton, who also had sneering expressions.

"It *was* vegetarian. See, when you was inside mixing up more tofu and shit, me'n Piker improved on your recipe. We added more chilies, bacon fat and some cooked ground veal." Alton looked at her empty bowl. "And it musta improved the taste, since you ate yours all gone. Damn near licked the bowl after your second helpin'."

A sick feeling took root. "You dumped meat in my chili?"

"From the most tender baby calf, so soft the meat melts in your mouth. Almost like it ain't there. But I made sure I added two cups to jazz it up. Because despite the judges picking your stupid recipe as the winner, everyone around here knows that chili ain't chili without meat. So we just put back in what you left out." Alton grinned nastily. "You're welcome."

Harlow watched them swagger away, patting one another on the back. Turning around and laughing at her before they disappeared.

Her belly pitched. Not just an emotional reaction, a physical one.

She managed to reach the bathroom in the horse trailer before the first nauseous wave expelled the contents of her stomach. Tears ran down her face as the acid crawled up her throat and lingered. For the longest time she couldn't swallow it down; she couldn't throw it up.

She hadn't eaten any meat—not a morsel—not even accidentally—for sixteen years. Her body rejected the substance completely.

Her head pounded.

Her gut twisted. The immediate cramping had gotten more painful.

The meat burps were the worst. She gagged with every one.

"Harlow?"

She couldn't even rouse herself enough to answer Riss.

A door slammed, then footsteps, then, "Omigod, Harlow! What's wrong?"

"Sick," she managed.

"I see that." Riss crouched down. "What can I do?"

"Water."

"Be right back."

After Harlow drank a mouthful, she felt queasy again and threw up. Then she rested her clammy head on the cool tile floor until the seesawing sensation in her gut forced her upright and her head into the toilet.

How long that went on for, she didn't know.

Riss said, "You are really sick. I'll get Hugh."

"No. He's busy." She swallowed thickly. "The worst is over, I think." And her body promptly made a liar out of her by shooting out another stream of vomit.

"Harlow, Hugh needs—"

"To do his job. I'll be okay. I just need to"—*have my stomach pumped*—"rest until it passes." She swiped the sweat from her forehead with her forearm. "Can you give me some privacy, please?"

"Okay. But I'll be right outside."

"Thank you."

Riss closed the door.

Harlow heaved again and then curled into a ball on the floor.

⚊

A warm, rough hand moved up her shin. She knew that touch before he rasped out her name. "Harlow?"

"Yeah."

"Darlin', what's goin' on?"

"Sick."

"How long have you been in here?"

"I don't know."

"Can you try and sit up? I'll help you. We'll go slow."

The world spun. Hugh seemed the only stable thing in it, so she latched on to him.

Halfway up, she had to take a barf break.

Hugh held her hair back.

But she couldn't hold back her tears when he sat on the bathroom floor and gently pulled her onto his lap.

"I probably need a breath mint."

"You're fine." He kissed the crown of her head. "You think this is food poisoning?"

She nodded.

"What did you eat that made you so sick?"

"I wasn't trying to make a statement. But I made them all mad."

"Who?"

"Alton."

"Darlin', you're not makin' sense." Then his hands cradled her head and tipped it back so he could look into her eyes. "Tell me what happened."

So she did.

When Harlow stopped talking, Hugh closed his eyes and tucked her against his body.

It should've bothered her that he said nothing. But his silence spoke everything his mouth couldn't.

He handed her a cup of water.

She shook her head. "If I drink it, I'll throw up."

"That's the point. Get it all out of your system."

Harlow drained the water and within a couple of minutes she was hanging over the toilet again. They did that three more times until she kept the water down.

Then Hugh picked her up and carried her to the bench seat in the kitchen across from the bathroom. He crouched in front of her, and tenderly dragged his knuckles down her jawline. "Wanna try 7Up?"

"No liquid in or out for a bit."

"All right." His gaze roamed over her face. "What can I do?"

"You've gone above and beyond." She yawned and clapped her hand over her mouth. "Yuck. I really need to brush my teeth."

He kept a steadying hand on her as she returned to the bathroom. She left the door open and scoured her mouth to the point she tasted blood.

But it helped.

Chapter Twenty-two

*F*or the first time in his life Hugh understood the reason for a rocking chair. The movement soothed the rocker as much as the rockee. At first he worried the back-and-forth motion of the recliner would make Harlow woozy. But she murmured she liked it before she'd fallen asleep. So he kept rocking, now for his own sake more than hers. It kept his murderous impulse on simmer, rather than boil.

That little fucking weasel Alton. Hugh hadn't wanted to work with him, but the stock contractors had no choice when the rodeo committee supplied chute workers. Alton had proven himself worthless and lazy, and Hugh just had to put up with it.

But what he'd done to Harlow crossed the fucking line. He didn't have to put up with that bullshit.

When Hugh realized Harlow had crashed to the point she snored, he shifted and slipped out of the chair. He fussed with the blanket, needing to touch her as he tucked her in.

Then he stood, settled his hat on his head and went to take care of business.

As soon as he stepped out of the horse trailer, Ike and Riss were up, away from the picnic table.

"Is she okay?" Riss asked.

He snagged a beer out of the cooler, draining it in three long swallows before he spoke. "She's sleeping. Hasn't gotten sick for the last hour."

"What happened?"

"Alton happened." As Hugh explained, his rage returned hotter than ever.

"That little cocksucker needs his ass beat," Ike said.

"Yep. So you with me?"

Ike's eyes widened. "I was kiddin', Hugh."

"I'm not."

"But you can't—"

"When it comes to Harlow, I surely *can*—and *will*—do whatever it takes to take care of what's mine." He crushed the beer can in his hand. "Puking her fucking guts out for hours because of him. Fuck that and fuck him." Hugh started in the direction of the after-party tent.

"Wait. I'm coming with you," Ike said, grabbing a couple more beers.

Riss fell into step beside Hugh and he looked at her questioningly. "Oh, hell no, you guys don't get to have all the fun. Harlow is my friend. This asshat fucked with her, so it's my duty to watch you beat the hell out of him so I can give her the play-by-play."

"Fine. But I'd prefer you didn't jump in."

"No problem. I'll stand back and hold your hat." She snaked an arm around Hugh's in a quick show of solidarity.

Ike scowled at her and offered Hugh a beer as they walked.

He declined. He needed a clear head.

Although it was just past midnight, the party still rocked along.

"How do you know he's here?" Ike asked.

"He's the type that'll stick around until closing time, bragging about what he done today." Hugh ducked under the tent flap and started a slow scan of the space. To Riss he said, "You go left; I'll go right. Ike, check outside."

They split up.

By the time Hugh reached the midpoint, he figured Alton had left, since he hadn't seen any sign of Alton's friends. When he looked across the space, Riss pointed to a group of four guys near the side entrance.

Gotcha, you smarmy cockroach.

Hugh's wide grin bordered on psychotic and he didn't fucking care when he moseyed up to the group. Most of them were pretty well lit, but they seemed happy to see him.

How fast that would change.

"Pritchett!" Piker clapped him on the back. "You here to buy a round?"

"Looks like you don't need another."

"I don't stop drinkin' until I pass out," Piker bragged.

Hugh's focus stayed on Alton. At this point he didn't care if the motherfucker was one drink away from blackout drunk; it'd take less effort to lay him out cold.

Weasel-dick Alton had an air of smugness about him. "Didn't think after-parties were your thing."

"They're not." Hugh leaned forward, using his extra six inches in height and fifty pounds in mass to loom over Alton. "I'm here for you. And you knew I'd be comin'."

Alton didn't even blink. "I got nothin' to say."

"Don't care, 'cause I'm gonna be talkin' with my fists anyway. Get your scrawny ass outside."

Alton's friends started to rally around him.

"You fuckers wanna take me on? Fine. But not until I'm done with this fuckin' prick." Hugh sneered at Alton. "You either go outside on your own steam or I drag you out kickin' and screamin'. Choose."

Alton surprised him by walking out the side door without additional argument.

Hugh followed him to the gravel parking lot, on the other side of the tent. He faced off against him.

"So your girlfriend tattled on me. So fucking what? It's really worth a fight to you? Jesus. Get over it. It was a goddamn joke."

"Not a joke to her. Or to me. Since she's been puking her guts out for hours because you fucking poisoned her."

"Poisoned? From eating a little meat?" He laughed. "Then maybe she oughta eat like a normal person and not a fucking rabbit."

Hugh put his hands on Alton's chest and pushed him. "Maybe you oughta mind your own fucking business and not worry about what she eats. It's her choice to be a vegetarian. It's not up to you to change her choice without her knowledge or consent." He pushed Alton again, his anger escalating. "I don't give a shit if you agree with her choice or not."

"You're just pissy because I doubt your vegetarian bimbo princess eats *your* meat."

Hugh's fist connected with Alton's jaw with a loud *crack*.

Alton stumbled back, momentarily dazed. Then he charged. He hit Hugh in the stomach and it knocked both of them to the ground. Alton started out on top and pounded Hugh in the eye first and then the mouth.

Hugh roared. He bucked Alton off like he was a pesky fly. Then he aimed a kick for the middle of Alton's back and missed.

But he was back on his feet.

Another charge. But this time Hugh didn't go down. He brought his elbow into the middle of Alton's back and Alton dropped to his knees. Hugh brought his foot up and kicked Alton in the ribs. "I hope you puke your guts out, motherfucker. And then I hope you piss blood."

Alton fell facedown in the dirt.

Before he could level another kick, an arm banded around Hugh's neck.

Enraged, Hugh twisted his body to face his new attacker.

Piker, that drunken fucker, managed to bring his knee up into Hugh's gut and land a solid jab on Hugh's eye before Hugh knocked him out cold.

Breathing hard, he whirled around to see if any more of Alton's buddies were waiting for their chance to jump in.

But they had all run away.

No one came near him.

Riss and Ike moved in. Riss holding Hugh's hat—she must've picked it up after Alton had knocked it off his head—and Ike holding a wet towel. "What's that for?"

"To clean up the blood, Rocky."

He was bleeding? He hadn't even noticed. "Thanks."

They walked back to the campsite in silence. He hadn't needed an escort, but Ike insisted in case someone tried to jump him.

Turned out two guys were waiting in the shadows. But their bootheels nearly caught fire—they ran so fast—when Hugh started for them.

"Man, give it a rest. You done what you had to. Now go clean up and check on your woman."

Hugh did the minimum amount of disturbing his broken flesh. His lip hurt like a bitch. His ribs were sore. He'd definitely feel worse tomorrow. But he popped some Motrin and gritted his teeth as he lifted Harlow enough so he could slide into the recliner.

She snuggled into him with a sigh and every wild thing inside him settled.

He'd never had this before, the sense he'd found what he needed. The question now was, how could he convince this beautiful woman with the wandering feet and the generous heart to stay with him? That even in just eight short weeks he had learned to be what she needed?

Even if that means letting her flit off to dangerous places without you?

Hugh squeezed his eyes shut against the sudden spike of pain in his head. Thinking about this shit did no good, because it wasn't a problem that could be solved in one night.

At some point his brain fell quiet and he drifted off to sleep.

Soft fingers petting his beard roused him. Waking to Harlow's sweet touch first thing always put him in a good mood. He smiled and immediately winced because it hurt.

"Hugh. What happened to your face?"

"Got into a fight. Don't worry about it. I'm fine."

"Yeah? Try and open your eyes."

He did, but he could see out of only the right one. Just a small sliver of light was visible on the left side. "I probably shoulda iced it last night."

She placed her hands on either side of his head. "What happened?"

"I tracked down Alton and beat the hell outta him for the bullshit stunt he pulled. Piker took offense and got in a few blows. But I can guarantee you they look a lot worse than I do."

Harlow wore a look of shock he'd never seen before.

"What they did went beyond a prank to a violation of your beliefs and your body. I'm not the kind of man to ever let that slide. It killed me to see you so sick. And I knew the sickness was from more than just ingesting meat."

"Did it help?"

"What? Callin' him out on it and beating the fuck outta him? Yeah. It did."

Her fingers traced the swollen bumps on his top and bottom lip.

Hugh watched her process it.

The recliner dipped slightly when she shifted to straddle him and move her hands beside his head. "Were you arrested or anything?"

"No. Hell, we didn't even draw much of a crowd. It's strange to you, but, darlin', that's the best way to handle things sometimes."

"With fists?"

"Yep."

"So am I supposed to thank you for defending my honor?"

Was that sarcastic? He studied her eyes and the wariness he saw turned his stomach. "I'm not like that Fredrick prick, Harlow."

"But that's the thing. I never imagined he'd be like that either. And yet, he was. And now I see that you're capable of something like this."

Fuck. What was he supposed to say to that?

Nothing. Because it's her issue. Not yours.

Hugh had an unexpected sense of loss. The worst part was he feared she'd have this same reaction if this type of thing happened six months down the road.

But it wouldn't be an issue in six months, because she'd be long gone by then.

Talk about a machete to the heart.

"Hugh?"

He forced himself to look at her, hoping she'd attribute the anguish in his good eye to his physical pain and not the emotional gutting she'd just leveled on him. Now would she think back on the swats he'd given her after the steer-riding incident as another example that he was capable of violent behavior?

Heartsick, he managed a gruff "I gotta move."

Harlow paused beside the chair as Hugh stood.

He opened the closet and took down his second-to-last clean shirt. Good thing they'd be headed back to Muddy Gap after the rodeo tomorrow night because he was out of clean clothes with no time to do laundry.

"What's wrong?"

"Nothin'. Why?"

"Our conversation ended abruptly."

"Huh. I thought we were done talkin'." He grabbed his boots and jeans. They'd go another day, since they weren't sporting any bloodstains. "Besides, I gotta get. We'll be shorthanded today and tonight."

"You're shorthanded because—"

"Alton and his buddies won't be workin' the chutes with us."

Her posture sagged. "I never meant for any of this to happen."

"I know. It ain't your fault Alton was a fuckin' menace."

"But you're the one who's paying the price."

Hugh shrugged. "Goes with the territory of bein' in charge. I'll be fine."

"Do you want me to fix you breakfast?"

"Nah. I'll grab something on my way to the arena. And so you know, I won't be back until late tonight." He didn't look at her as he said that last thing. He just closed the door behind him.

Chapter Twenty-three

*S*he had fucked this up.

Big-time.

And she didn't have any idea how to fix it.

Maybe that's a sign you shouldn't. Just let this go and move on. You have a life—and a job—waiting for you in California.

But . . . Hugh was rooted in Wyoming.

If she wanted to be with him, she'd have to set down roots there. She had no doubts that she loved him. She knew he loved her—even though neither of them had found the balls to say it out loud.

But would love be enough?

When they had fundamentally different life philosophies?

Would he consider uprooting his life to be with her?

No.

But have you asked him?

Harlow didn't need to ask. She knew.

Could she give up a great opportunity for him? For love?

No clue.

And the only person she desperately wanted to talk to about it . . . was him. He'd become her everything in a short amount of time.

She'd be a fool if she didn't make the comparison, at least on the surface, to how she'd had these same feelings and doubts about her relationship with Fredrick before it'd gone to hell.

Although Hugh hadn't asked her to wash his clothes or clean up the horse trailer, she spent the entire day doing that. And when she'd finished, twelve hours later, every surface sparkled. The clothes were pressed and put away. She felt cleansed.

There was irony in that too.

Harlow climbed in bed earlier than normal, but it'd been an exhausting day.

The bed dipped sometime later, waking her. She could smell that Hugh had been drinking.

Ask him where he's been.

Not your business.

Would he pretend everything was fine and pull her into his arms?

Some of their most revealing talks had taken place in the dark confines of a bed, when they didn't have to look each other in the eye.

Hugh sighed heavily. Then he shifted and his big hand smoothed her hair back from her face.

See? He's reaching out. Talk to him.

But his hand was gone and he'd turned away.

⤠

The next morning Hugh was up before her. She decided she'd stay in bed until he left.

"Harlow?"

Guess faking sleep wasn't in the cards. She sat up and yawned. "Yeah?"

Hugh stood at the end of the bed wearing one of the four white shirts she'd washed and ironed yesterday. "Thank you for doin' laundry yesterday and cleaning the place up. It looks great."

"You're welcome."

"You didn't have to."

"I know. But I'm just following the cowboy way of doin' what needs done."

He stared at her. "We're leaving after the rodeo tonight."

"Driving straight through?"

"Yeah. And since I'll be in the pens and chutes all day, I'm thinkin' it'd be best if you drove the first leg back to the Split Rock."

"Not a problem. I'll hang around in here and get some rest."

"I wasn't suggesting you lock yourself away, Harlow."

"It's probably best that I stay out of the way."

"Best for who?"

"For everyone. Even when you can use my help now, you don't want it." Hugh didn't bother to hide his frustration. "You didn't offer."

"You didn't ask," she shot back. "And you're paying for that now, aren't you? Doing everything yourself, no local hired hands to help out—because of me." She exhaled. "I came along because I wanted to help you out. I haven't done squat the last three days except clean and do laundry. But I can't even cook for you, so again one thing I should be able to do as a partner, I can't."

"That's all you see yourself as to me now? As a housekeeping service? Or are you usin' that as an excuse to back off because I got into a fight? You think at some point I'm gonna put the hurt on you like he did?"

"That's a crappy thing to say to me."

"But you're not denying it, are you?"

Three knocks sounded and then Ike opened the door and stepped inside. "Hey, we gotta get a move on." He froze at seeing Hugh's angry posture. "Sorry if I interrupted."

"It's a good goddamned thing you did." Hugh plucked his hat off the table and settled it on his head. "I'll see you later. Keep your phone on you. We're getting the hell outta this place as soon as that last bull is done tonight."

"Fine."

"Fine."

The door slammed behind him.

The pillow she threw at the door didn't make the same satisfying crack a dinner plate would have.

ᥰᥱᥰ

With time to kill, Harlow flipped on her laptop for the first time in days. She had twenty-seven unread e-mails, including one from . . . Her blood ran cold at the sender's name.

Fredrick.

Her heart raced and when her vision wavered, she realized she'd been holding her breath.

The cursor blinked on that e-mail. Should she open it?

Her friend Erika's voice snapped for her to just delete it.

Her counselor's voice reminded her he had no power over her anymore. No power. Right.

Prove it. Open the e-mail.

When she placed her hands back on the keyboard, her palms were sweaty. She double-clicked and briefly closed her eyes to prepare herself for what she might find.

Harlow,

It's been a while since I've been in contact. I had no idea the trip had taken such an emotional toll on you and I haven't contacted you in hopes that you've started to heal from the trauma of being so isolated.

"Being isolated wasn't my trauma, you piece of shit," she said out loud. "You traumatized me." Then she read on:

Our time in Laos had the positive effect and produced the outcome we'd hoped. The learning curve has been steep, but I am so happy to report they've embraced the methods we taught them. The funding has ended and I'm writing this before I board a plane home.

Being on the same continent with Fredrick was too close for comfort. Harlow forced her focus back to the screen.

I hate that I don't know where you are, or if this e-mail will even reach you. Just in case, I've sent a hard copy to your post office box. I also left a message with your father's secretary, but I've heard no response, which leads me to believe you didn't go home to the Windy City.

I know you're not the type to hold a grudge, but I ask for your understanding anyway. It's taken me some time to come to grips with being oblivious to your need for self-mutilation—

Harlow slapped the computer lid shut. She shot to her feet and paced in the small space as her thoughts pinged all over the place.

Self-mutilation? I did that one fucking time to get away from you!

She couldn't wrap her head around what she was reading, even though she should have expected as much. Fredrick was placing the blame on her. He didn't ask for forgiveness. Fuck, he may as well have asked why she made him so mad that he had to smack her around.

Breathe in. Let it out. You are in control. The power is yours.

But did she have the control to delete the rest of his message without reading it?

No.

Harlow poured herself a glass of Fireball, threw a few ice cubes in and sat down. She lifted her laptop lid and found where she'd left off.

. . . was a cry for help and I didn't have the proper mind-set to help you. I knew nothing about that addiction, but I've managed to read quite a bit on it and feel I'd be in a better position to help you now.

"Help me?" God. She could just imagine it. He'd know exactly how to cut her and then he could blame it on her addiction. Her denials would be just that—difficult to believe.

I've missed you, H-bomb. The weeks leading up to your departure were a blur for me due to concerns about funding, and I'm sorry I didn't give you the attention you deserved. I worried you blamed me for your need to cut yourself to get my attention. So after you left, I was ready to pack up and race to your side to support you. And then you, my angel, proved your dedication to the cause, your generous heart and your forgiving nature.

"What?" The next sentence turned her stomach.

By asking your father to provide the funds we required to stay on-site for another year and a half to continue the good work we started.

No way. Her father had not given Fredrick money! Why would he do that? Moreover, why wouldn't he tell her?

Goddammit. She picked up her phone to call him.

She set it down.

She picked up her drink.

Then walked over and dumped it in the sink.

She needed to have the conversation with her father face-to-face. And she'd have plenty of time to figure out what to say to him on the long drive back to Wyoming.

Chapter Twenty-four

*L*ater that night after the rodeo, Riss said, "What's goin' on with you and Hugh?"

"Difference of opinion," Harlow said to her, watching Hugh lead animals into the semi.

"You had a fight."

"Actually, no. I don't know what we had, which is why it's not easy to slap a label on. And no, I don't want to talk about it."

"Oughta be a fun ride home."

"He'll sleep." Or feign sleep, which was fine by her.

"I probably won't get a chance to say this later, but I had a great time getting to know you."

Harlow rested her head on Riss's shoulder. "Same here. I hate the thought this is a work thing and we won't see each other again."

"Me too."

But Harlow had been through this many times, saying good-bye to coworkers. It didn't seem to matter how close they'd gotten; when they weren't in the same work environment, they lost that common thread.

"How long you stayin' in Muddy Gap?"

"It depends."

"On if you and Hugh patch things up?"

She watched him moving among the livestock, absolutely in his element. "No."

"Does he know?"

She shook her head. "It's become obvious to me the last couple days that our fundamental differences will always be an issue. It's best to chalk it up to a summer fling and move on." It made her stomach twist to even say that.

"That makes me sad."

"Why?"

"You clearly care for each other beyond just hot sexy times. If that doesn't factor in, then I've lost all hope that I'll ever find a guy who looks at me the way Hugh looks at you." Riss shrugged her shoulder and Harlow lifted her head. "Looks like I'm up next for loading."

"Looks like. Drive safe."

"I will. You too." Riss hugged her. And the hug lasted a beat too long when she whispered, "He looks at you like you're everything, Harlow. Can't that be a beginning instead of an ending?" Then she walked off.

The horse trailer was the last to load. Ike left his semi idling while he waited for Hugh, which just made Harlow feel even more incompetent.

She situated herself in the cab. Adjusting the seat. Making sure her water and snacks were within reach. She found a hard rock station on her phone that should keep her awake. She draped her earbuds around her neck and fiddled with the mirrors. When Hugh still hadn't finished loading, she plugged the address for the Split Rock into the GPS and watched as it showed route options. There were two.

Finally Hugh climbed into the cab.

"We ready?"

"Yeah."

"Which route?"

He leaned closer to the dashboard to read the GPS. She had to curl her hand into a fist to keep from running it down his back and shoulders. He was close enough she got a whiff of his cologne and the musky scent of his sweat. She wanted to nestle her face in the curve where his neck met his shoulder and go back to the way things were two days ago.

Hugh sat up and pulled his phone out. "Ike? Remind me which way you told Riss we're goin' back. Uh-huh. Yep. Later." He poked the route guidance. "This one."

"Thanks."

"No problem."

She felt his eyes on her and she looked at him. "Anything else?"

"Nope. Let's hit it."

Hugh didn't scrutinize her driving or watch her to see if she did something wrong. He just let her drive. After fifteen minutes or so, he settled the seat back and pulled his hat over his eyes. "You need anything, wake me."

"Will do." Harlow popped in her earbuds and cranked up the music.

❧

She woke him only when they needed to stop for gas.

He filled the tanks and she used the restroom.

Then they were back on the road with him in the driver's seat. The silence between them was nearly suffocating.

Harlow positioned the vents so cool air flowed over her and she faked sleep until real sleepiness took over.

The *bump bump* of wheels leaving pavement jarred her awake. She immediately blocked the early morning sun to see where they were, which turned out to be the gravel road that led to the back pastures at the Split Rock. She saw Riss had already backed up her semi to the bull pasture. Renner, Tobin and Flint were unloading bulls.

She unbuckled and started gathering her things. Hugh's hand on her arm caught her attention and she realized she still had her earbuds in. "What?"

"What happened to us?"

"You really want to talk about this *now*, after we've been in the truck for ten hours straight?"

"We should've been talkin' about it during that time," he said coolly.

"Well, we didn't and I'm not in the mood now."

Renner jogged over. Hugh rolled down the window. They had a cryptic conversation and she'd reached her limit.

She paused with her hand on the door handle. "I've got a key to the horse trailer that I'll return later today. I need to get my stuff out before you drive to Renner and Tierney's place."

Hugh unbuckled his seat belt. "I'll help you."

"Don't need it. Since I had so much free time the last three days, I'm all packed up."

"Harlow—"

"See you around, Hugh." She bailed out. After unlocking the horse trailer, she hauled out her cooler, which she'd have to return for later, since it was too heavy to drag uphill to her trailer. She hefted her duffel bag over her shoulder.

Then she hoofed it up the hill and stopped to catch her breath, looking around. She waited for that "I'm home" rush of relief to fill her. But it didn't, because this was just another temporary landing spot.

⌁

After pacing and packing and second-guessing her second guesses, Harlow headed to the lodge.

She knocked on her father's door and wasn't surprised to see Karen answer it so early in the morning. But she was shocked to see Tierney there, sitting across the desk from their father.

Tierney smiled. "Hey. I didn't think we'd see you for hours yet."

"Because I'm a lazy ass who sleeps her life away? Because the kind of volunteer work I do, there are no schedules and no responsibilities? We just stand around a fire, holding hands, singing 'Kumbaya'?"

Silence.

"Um, no, I thought I wouldn't see you because you just pulled in at seven a.m. after a ten-hour drive. Hugh said you drove most of the way and were exhausted." Then Tierney leaned back in her chair, her expression cool. "What's with the accusing attitude?"

Harlow looked between her sister and her father. "Please don't deny you've both been condescending about the path I chose to take with my life. It's not constant, but it happens often enough that, yes, I'm sensitive to what you might think is an innocuous comment. Everything from your"—she pointed at Tierney—"smart remarks about me not having a head for numbers or business practices, to your"—she pointed at her father—"snide remarks about me getting a real job, attending a real college and being more like my sister. It's gotten old over the years. I don't have the energy to ignore it anymore."

More silence.

Then Tierney stood and hugged her. Hard. "I'm sorry. So sorry, sis. I love you. Even if what I said wasn't intentionally hurtful, it still was, and I'm sorry. If it happens again, don't let it slide, okay? Call me out on it."

"Okay."

Then Tierney grabbed her by the face. "But if I hear you knocking yourself before you think I'll do it first, I'll call you on that too. And I've always been happy you chose your own path. I'm proud of all the good you've done. So don't ever assume I discount it."

She nodded.

"Now that I'm slowly getting over pregnancy brain, it's time we had a real, adult conversation that's not about my kids, or my husband, or my way of life here in Wyoming, or Dad's health issues and subsequent personality change."

He yelled, "Hey, now."

Tierney and Harlow exchanged a quick grin. Then Tenacious Tierney returned. "You're a great listener, Harlow, but that means I talk too damn much. So be prepared to spill your secrets to me, because I'll be relentless in doing my part to be a better sister to you." She hugged Harlow. "Because you've been a great one to me."

Overcome with emotion, Harlow bit her tongue against blurting out every ugly detail about her last assignment, and the unresolved issues with Hugh. Her tears fell. "Thank you."

Then Tierney stepped back and wiped her eyes. "So what's going on? You arrived with a purpose."

"This won't make much sense to you and I promise I'll explain it later," Harlow said to Tierney before she faced her father. "Fredrick sent me an e-mail. He's back in the States. Please tell me he was delusional and full of shit when he told me you funded his organization for another year after I got out."

He tapped his fingers on his desk. He looked more robust, more like he was back to his old self, more like the shrewd businessman he was. "I didn't fund his cause for a year." He paused. "I funded it for a year and a half."

"Why?"

"Simply because it would keep him away from you for that long. I would've paid triple that, Harlow, to protect you from him. To allow you to heal from the damage you sustained from him in Laos. It wasn't a power play; it was a preventative measure." He gave her a long look. "I'd do it again, because you're standing in front of me and you look . . . whole. You broke, but, sweetheart, you put yourself back together stronger than ever. And like your sister said, don't discount what that means to me. What *you* mean to me. I don't understand why you do what you do. I've tried—and likely failed—to be supportive. But that is in the past."

But he had been supportive and proactive in the way he knew how: throw money at the problem. She had to admit this time he'd done the right thing. Who knew where she'd be emotionally if Fredrick had come back to the U.S. the month after she'd left him? Her father had prevented that from happening.

He slowly stood. "Do I get a hug?"

Harlow stepped into his arms. It was strange how the scent of his cologne could both soothe her and make her nervous. She hoped that nervous feeling would finally go away.

Her dad patted her back and returned to his chair. "Now, you did seem to have a purposeful look when you stormed in."

"Before your heart attack I was offered a yearlong teaching position at Bleeker College, in LA. It's a small school, but they have incredible outreach programs as well as offering in-depth seminars for people in all professions who need a sabbatical but have issues that keep them from taking one. I was lucky enough to end up in one of those seminars at the first of the year. It really opened my eyes to some of the problems that are shoved under the rug in service organizations. My experiences—good and bad— are extensive enough to qualify me to teach."

"Harlow! That is fantastic! I can't believe you didn't tell us before now." Tierney winced. "Is that out of line?"

She laughed. "No. Saying 'You don't have a bachelor's; are you sure this is an accredited college?' would be out of line."

"Noted. But now that you mention it, I do remember you saying something about a sabbatical. I'm happy that it's giving you a different focus."

"That will be a learning experience for you too, Harlow. Congratulations." She smiled at her dad. "Thanks."

"Dad has news too," Tierney prompted.

"I've decided not to retire."

Not exactly news, Harlow thought.

"Between Karen's and Tierney's observations about my rash decision a few weeks ago and being here pretty much going stir-crazy, I reconsidered. I *can* retire at age sixty-five, but that doesn't mean I *have* to. With my ticker fixed"—he knocked on the desk—"and a few lifestyle changes, I have several good working years left ahead of me. Who knows? Maybe I'll convince Tierney to return to Chicago and take over PFG."

Tierney rolled her eyes.

"And with that decision, I'll be staying with your sister and her family for a few days before I return home to Chicago."

"That will be great for both of you. But the last thing I wanted to mention is I'm leaving today."

"What? Why? You just got back!"

"I know. I need to get my spinster schoolmarm vibe on before I meet with my students." Harlow loved how that sounded.

"Will you come over and say good-bye to the kids?"

Harlow shook her head. "Isabelle is dealing with enough. Rhett is oblivious. So let's say our good-byes now."

This time there were surprisingly few tears.

Until Tierney whispered, "What about Hugh?"

"Can we talk about that another time? It's too hard right now."

"Of course."

As she walked through the main part of the lodge and prepared to leave, for the second time in her life she wasn't sure if she'd ever return.

Chapter Twenty-five

*H*arlow wasn't answering her cell phone.

Normally that wouldn't bother him because she wasn't tied to the damn thing like so many people. But given how it'd been between them the last day they'd spent together and the awkward way they'd parted this morning, he worried she was dodging him.

When Hugh realized she was probably visiting with her dad after being gone for two weeks, he decided to head up to the lodge. He pushed back from his desk and stood.

"Where you goin'?" Tobin asked.

"Up to the lodge. See if I can't track down my missing woman."

Tobin pushed back his chair and stood. "I'll tag along. I could use an excuse to stretch my legs."

Company wasn't what Hugh had been angling for, but there wasn't much he could say to dissuade Tobin.

Halfway up the hill, Tobin said, "I need to talk to you. And I wanted to do it away from the barn."

Didn't sound good. "What's up?"

"I gave Renner my notice this morning."

Hugh stopped in the middle of the path and looked at Tobin. "Why? What is goin' on? Something with your family?"

"No." He propped his hands on his hips. "Look, I don't know how to say this without coming off as a total whiny fuckin' pussy, so I'll just say it straight out. I'm lonely. And this will sound weird as fuck, but since you've been seeing Harlow, and then when you were on the road, it hit me. This loneliness ain't gonna get any better for me if I continue to live here. In fact, it'll just get worse, so I gotta get out."

"Jesus, Tobin. I don't know what to say."

"I didn't tell you this to make you feel guilty. We're friends and colleagues. I've spent more time with you in the last four years than with anyone. So I thought if anyone would understand, it's you."

"I do. But have you told anyone else besides Renner?"

Tobin blushed. "Garnet. Last week she jammed up her garbage disposal and called me over to her place to fix it. We got to talkin' about 'honey-do' lists and marriage, which shifted into her usual off-the-wall topics, and I mentioned I was thinking about moving."

"Think that was wise?"

"I don't know if it registered with her. She said it was time. Then she patted me on the cheek and said she'd thank me by fixing it. But I'm sure she meant to thank me for fixing her garbage disposal."

"You never know with her." Hugh clapped him on the back. "It's never easy making a change. But sometimes you just gotta do it."

"I won't leave Renner shorthanded, but I won't put conditions on it either. He may kick my ass out tonight."

"Unlikely. But if he does?"

"I'll be fine for a while."

"Let me know if you need anything."

"Thanks."

They continued up the hill.

Hugh half expected Tobin to ask him about his future with Harlow, but he didn't. Which was a good thing, because he wouldn't know how to respond.

Instead of entering through the side door, they rounded the building for the main entrance.

The first thing he heard in the foyer was a smack of wood against wood and then a warning. "Stay back. This is between me and her."

"Maybelle, this is ridiculous!"

Hugh and Tobin looked at each other and crossed into the main great room of the lodge only to stop in the doorway with their mouths hanging open.

Vivien and Miz Maybelle were facing off, each brandishing a wooden sword. More accurately, Maybelle waved hers at Vivien as Vivien retreated. The other Mud Lilies were gathered around—Tilda and Pearl seemed to be in charge of crowd control. In case a crowd happened by—the only other people in the room were employees Lela, Yvette, Dodie and Flint.

When Hugh and Tobin stepped forward, Tilda blocked them with her arms out. "Sorry, boys. There'll be no interference. This has been a long time coming and we need to let it play out."

"Let what play out, Tilda?"

Maybelle swished her sword in the air, looking like she'd been watching a marathon of *Pirates of the Caribbean* again. "Fight back, damn you."

"Maybelle. Be reasonable."

"Reasonable? We'll settle this the old-fashioned way."

"Right. You've gone beyond reasonable to ridiculous." Vivien shook her sword. "These are wooden practice swords. We can't even hurt each other with them."

"Wanna bet?" Lightning fast, Miz Maybelle moved in and whacked Vivien on the upper arm.

Vivien gasped, "I cannot believe you just did that!"

"Believe me now?" Maybelle raised her sword straight out in front of her, her left leg behind, as if preparing to attack. She appeared to know what she was doing, even if she didn't look the part of a swashbuckler, wearing a floral-printed housedress and orthopedic shoes.

"That's it." Vivien tossed off her fire-engine red suit jacket and assumed a similar attack position. "I'll warn you, Maybelle. My kids studied martial arts, so I'm familiar with swordplay."

"I heard that you're getting a lot of play in with his *meat* sword," Maybelle said with a sneer.

"Meat sword? That's crude, even for you."

Maybelle sliced her sword through the air à la Errol Flynn. "Vivien, I've been taking fencing classes. So en garde."

"Jesus. Seriously?" Hugh hissed.

"Don't." Tobin set his hand on Hugh's arm. "This I gotta see."

Wood cracked audibly as they started smacking swords and circling each other.

"I'm so mad at you, Viv!" Maybelle shouted. "How could you?"

"I didn't know! I thought you two were just friends."

Whack. Crack. "Did *he* tell you we were just friends?" Maybelle demanded with another *whack* and *crack* as Vivien parried. "Or did you just assume that because you're younger and thinner, he wouldn't be attracted to a more substantial old broad like me?"

Attracted? What the hell . . . ? Shit. Now Hugh understood what this was about.

"I never assumed anything, Maybelle." Vivien dropped her sword to ward off a strike at her knee. Her eyes narrowed. "Low blow, lady. You know I had knee surgery last year."

"Didn't seem to stop you from getting on your knees for him, did it?" Maybelle swung hard and Vivien ducked.

"At least I can still get on my knees!"

This was seriously going downhill fast.

"I really liked him!" Maybelle huffed.

"So did I!"

"And you stole him!" Maybelle was swinging with less finesse and more angry enthusiasm.

But Vivien had gotten angrier. "I did not! I can't steal what you never had."

Then time seemed to slow as Garnet—where the hell had she come from?—raced in between Vivien and Maybelle. She raised her arm toward the ceiling and fired the pistol in her hand. A sharp crack echoed.

Lela, Yvette and Dodie screamed before they hit the floor.

Smoke eddied around Garnet as she glared at Vivien and Maybelle. "What is wrong with you two? Our motto has always been 'Lilies Before Willies'! And you're fighting over a dadgum man?"

Bernice tore in, red faced and wheezing. She snatched the pistol out of Garnet's hand. "Next time I'm cuffing you to the dashboard."

Janie and Harper ran in to see what all the commotion was about. A few guests peered out of their rooms on the second floor.

Flint squinted at the ceiling, looking for a bullet hole. Tobin and Hugh stood there in shock and total disbelief.

Vivien looked at Maybelle and said, "Garnet is right. Lilies Before Willies." Then she threw her sword on the ground.

Maybelle looked as if she might take one last shot at Vivien before she laid down her weapon, but she tossed the sword aside and said, "Lilies Before Willies."

Then Tilda and Pearl joined their crew.

They probably would've chanted "Lilies Before Willies" as a group, but Janie Lawson barreled across the floor. "Garnet Evans, how *dare* you come in here and fire a gun! I oughta call the sheriff on you."

Immediately the Mud Lilies locked arms, facing outward, keeping Garnet protected in the middle. "Gonna have to go through us first, Janie," Bernice warned.

"All of us," Tilda added.

Janie was pissed as hell. "Then I will have *all* of you arrested! Goddammit. Someone could've gotten hurt!"

"Ah, Janie—"

"Shut up!" She glared at Bernice.

"But she's only trying to tell you—"

"You can shut the hell up too, Tilda!" Janie snapped. "We have guests here." She shook her finger at Garnet. "You put them in serious danger with this stunt!"

"Well, technically I didn't, because—"

"Omigod! Stop talking! There isn't an excuse in the world—"

Pearl had broken rank long enough to let out an ear-piercing whistle, which was actually louder than the gunshot. "As I can see your firearm knowledge is sadly lacking, I'll inform you that Garnet fired a *starter pistol*. There are no bullets and no danger. The noise you heard was from a cap."

Janie stood her ground "That doesn't change the fact—"

Harper grabbed ahold of Janie's arm and whispered in her ear.

A mulish expression settled on Janie's face, but she nodded.

Then Harper plastered on a big smile and waved at the guests up on the balcony, and turned to offer the same encouraging wave to the guests lurking in the entryway. "Thank you, everyone, for being our surprise test audience for the melodrama *Pistols and Petticoats*, which we'll be debuting as weekend entertainment next year at the Split Rock! So we definitely hope you make your reservations now."

Tobin masked his laugh with a hacking cough and Hugh lowered his hat to hide the grin on his face. Harper was fast on her feet; he'd give her that.

"It needs a little work," a female guest up on the balcony suggested. "The resolution of the conflict wasn't really clear."

"Yeah," a man on the other side chimed in, "and the issues should be explained in more detail at the beginning."

Several guests nodded.

"Everyone got an opinion on everything, don't they?" Tobin muttered.

Pearl clapped her hands. "Okay, everyone. Show is over."

"But wait," a boy of about ten shouted down. "Who was the villain?"

Silence.

Hugh expected one of the ladies to say Gene Pratt's name, or at least claim the villainy happened offstage. So his stomach dropped when the Mud Lilies all focused on him.

Shit. Would it make him a pussy if he made a break for it?

Tobin laughed. "I knew this was gonna come back and bite you in the ass."

Fuck.

The women started toward him, spread out in a line.

Maybelle spoke first. "This is your fault, Hugh."

"What?"

"You begged us to do the favor for you," Vivien pointed out.

"And I told you it was a bad idea from the start," Bernice tossed out.

"Now wait just a damn minute." Why the fuck were his balls sweating? "I didn't—"

"Think it through?" Garnet demanded. "Now this 'discharging a fire-arm in public' incident, coupled with me spending a night in the clink last week, means my family is gonna make good on their promise to put me in assisted living so someone can keep an eye on me." Garnet burst into tears.

And Hugh was forgotten.

The Mud Lilies gathered around her, and Tobin stood outside the circle.

He knew Tobin would fill him in later, so he backed up—slowly as to not draw their attention—and practically tiptoed away to look for Gene Pratt.

But he didn't have to go far.

Gene, and his sidekick Karen, lurked in the hallway.

"Enjoy the show?" Hugh demanded. "I see you stayed in the chickenshit seats."

"In the interest of full disclosure," Karen said, "*I* kept Gene from going out there. He survived a quadruple bypass. I wasn't sure he'd survive them."

Hugh looked at Gene. "But you are gonna fix this, right?"

Gene sighed. "If you mean by skipping town? The answer is yes. I'll be spending my last three days in Wyoming staying with Tierney so she can keep an eye on me while Karen has her adventure."

"I didn't get to do all the touristy stuff while I was here, so I'll be back," Karen said.

"Wait. Why can't Harlow keep an eye on you?"

"Because she's leaving."

All the breath left his body. He managed a hoarse "What?"

"Harlow has a teaching job in California. Guess she's had it since before my heart attack. Classes start in two weeks."

"Did you know about it?"

Gene shook his head. "She didn't tell anyone."

"What else happened?"

"What do you mean?"

"Harlow is running. So did Tierney say something that had Harlow doubting her self-worth? Or maybe you did. Tell me," he ordered.

"I will." Gene pushed away from the wall and rested both hands on his cane. "But not here."

Hugh followed Gene into his room, hating that things had gone to hell so fast. He was impatient to hear whatever Gene had to confess so he could go to Harlow.

Karen got Gene settled in his chair and left them alone.

"Sit," Gene said to Hugh as he loomed over him.

"No thanks. Tell me what happened."

"Evidently Harlow received an e-mail from that Fredrick fellow she had the . . . problems with in Laos. He told her that I'd funded his organization the past year and a half."

"Did you?"

"Yes."

"Why the hell would you do that?"

"You have to look at this from my perspective. My youngest daughter got herself into a bad situation. I pulled her out of it. I also knew, since Harlow wasn't pressing charges, that Fredrick would believe he'd done nothing wrong and maybe contact Harlow or even come after her when he returned to the States."

"How did you know that?" Hugh demanded. "Because Harlow didn't mention that you'd gone to Laos personally to rescue her."

"While Harlow was in the hospital in Laos, I talked to her friend Erika." He paused. "At length."

Hugh saw the anguish in Gene's eyes and realized the father knew more of what his daughter had gone through than Harlow had told him.

"I wanted to see that pompous prick burn, but I couldn't risk having anything traced back to me, so I decided to fund his work for eighteen months and keep him away from Harlow while she healed."

"You should've had him killed," Hugh said.

"Yes, well. Hindsight and all that. But I truly worried that if my daughter found out, I'd be dead to her too."

"Yeah. She does take issue with violence." When Hugh felt Gene glaring at him, he backtracked. "I'd never raise a hand to her. But some dumb fuckers pulled a dirty trick on her and I called them on it."

"More like you called them out?"

"Yep. I got knocked around some. She and I ain't been talkin' much since."

"I suggest you talk to her now while you still have the chance."

Two knocks sounded on the door. Hugh opened it, expecting Karen, not all six of the Mud Lilies to file in and spread out in front of Gene Pratt like a defensive line.

"To what do I owe the pleasure of all you ladies' lovely company today?" Gene said smoothly.

"Cut the crap, Casanova," Pearl said. "We're here on official business."

"By all means . . . continue."

Tilda spoke next. "As shareholders in the Split Rock, it is within our purview to overrule management decisions. We are not a rehab facility and we were not consulted on granting you an extended stay."

"So we are invoking our right to refuse service."

Gene looked at Pearl. "Meaning what?"

"Meaning that you are outta here, you two-timing Romeo," Miz Maybelle snapped.

"Pack your bags and leave this facility. Immediately," Vivien said.

"You're kicking me out?"

"You bet your bad toupee we're kicking you out, you lying lothario," Garnet said hotly.

"I don't wear a toupee," Gene said evenly. "This is my real hair."

"Whatever, Slick. You are done here."

Somehow Hugh managed to keep a straight face, but, damn, did he like to see these gals all fired up and indignant. He'd never tell them that Gene had decided to leave before they'd given him an ultimatum. They needed this moment of power. This incident would fuel the gossip mill—no doubt the facts would get wildly embellished in the retelling—and reinforce the local hype that the Mud Lilies were not to be messed with.

"There's no room for negotiation?" Gene asked.

"None," Bernice practically spit. "Pack your crap and get out. You have two hours."

"And we'll be back to make sure you follow through," Pearl promised him.

"I understand," Gene said somberly. "At the risk of having weapons

LORELEI JAMES   314

pointed at me, can I just say meeting you ladies has been . . . there really aren't words to describe it."

"You're darn tootin'," Garnet said, which made no sense.

"We'll be gone within the hour," Karen said from the doorway, pointedly holding the door open.

The ladies filed past Gene. Although he didn't flinch when Bernice cracked her knuckles and Pearl flashed her piece, it gave Hugh a feeling of satisfaction to see the back of Gene's shirt soaked from nervous sweat.

The man had gotten off easier than he deserved, but he'd allowed the ladies to save face too. Now Hugh had other concerns to set right. He booked it to Harlow's trailer.

⌇

The SUV was still parked in front. His anxiety level went from ten to eight.

He knocked on the door twice before he opened it and said, "Harlow?"

"In here."

All the lights were off in the living room. She sat in the middle of the couch, her white dress drawing him to her like a beacon.

Hugh dropped to his knees in front of her. She looked as lost as the night he'd seen her in Denver. "You okay?"

She shook her head. "I'm leaving."

"I heard. From your dad." He forced himself to stay calm. "Why didn't I hear it from you?"

"Because I was afraid."

"Afraid of what? Darlin', you're the bravest woman I've ever met."

She closed her eyes, but her tears fell anyway. "Afraid you'd convince me to stay."

He framed her face in his hands and wiped her tears. "Of course I'd try and convince you to stay. I love you."

"I know. I love you too. Which is why this is so hard."

"Can you look at me, please?"

She opened her eyes. "I didn't plan on this. Falling for you."

"My sparkling personality and cowboy charm finally won you over, huh?"

"Absolutely."

"Tell me what's goin' on and why you look so damn sad after I told you I love you."

"Because I've always known I'd return to California."

He lowered his hands and reached for hers.

"Bleeker College offered me a teaching position the week before my dad had his heart attack. The staff has gotten to know me since I've been involved in an intensive seminar there for the past six months."

Hugh said, "Harlow, that's great," even as his heart began to crack.

"I thought so too. I've never had anything permanent like this. Never thought my education was enough, but the years I've spent in the field qualifies me to teach about modern-day humanitarian organizations. But being here with you . . ." She laughed softly. "Before we had sex again, I told myself I'd keep it only about sex between us. We'd have a hot fling, get each other out of our systems, move on from the past, and when it was time, I'd move on. Literally.

"But from the moment I told you about Fredrick, I felt the link between us tighten. I tried to discount it and attribute it to lust, but I realized that was unfair. That's why I asked for neither of us to label it. And spending two weeks with you on the road just cemented my feelings. I knew it was different than the friendships I made on a trip where we spent hours and days together. I seriously considered telling the Bleeker admin I had family issues to deal with and I'd return at the start of the second semester. I'd stay here, continue to take care of my dad, help Tierney out and figure out where this was going with us."

Another chunk of his heart splintered. "Did you get dizzy with all that back-and-forth?"

"Yes. Then a couple of things happened." Her hands tightened on his. "Fredrick sent me an e-mail the morning after you got into that fight."

Fuck. He hated that he'd misread her signals and had too much fucking pride to ask what was going on with her. "So you weren't pissed off about me fighting?"

Harlow's eyes widened. "No, not at all." She paused. "That's why you were back to being such a broody guy? Because you thought I was mad about you fighting?"

"Yep. And I was sulking because I wasn't sorry for goin' after them guys, so I wasn't gonna offer up a bogus apology."

She smiled. "I didn't expect one. Anyway, the e-mail was a piece of fiction. At first it pissed me off. Then I got a little scared he might try and track me down—and that fear of him pissed me off too."

Right then, Hugh decided to get Fredrick's full name and contact information from Gene Pratt. Even if he and Harlow couldn't find a way to work things out, he'd warn the guy off.

"Like you said, highs and lows, going round and round. But I finally came to the decision that I had to keep the teaching position. During the seminars, I learned I wasn't the only volunteer who's gotten into a situation with a leader like Fredrick. And it's important I use my experience as a warning to others that it can happen to them. Especially in a closed-in environment."

"You said the e-mail was the first thing. What was the second?"

"I wasn't happy when I found out my dad had funded Fredrick's organization, but I understand why he did it—to keep Fredrick out of the country and away from me. I also realized that my father wouldn't give up a career opportunity to sit by my bedside for weeks on end. Don't get me wrong—I love him. The fortunate result of his heart attack is we did spend time together and got to know each other in a different light. But my dad was hiding here. Now he's going back to Chicago. Sitting in a room at the Split Rock, with his family close by, as well as his assistant, as well as entertaining ladies, has reminded him he's not ready to retire."

Hugh kissed her knuckles. "I've never met anyone who is so tuned in and so dead-on with assessments of people and situations, doll. It's humbling and scary as fuck."

She pulled on his hands. "Get off your knees and come up here and hold me."

One last time hung in the air between them.

He settled her on his lap, wrapping his arms around her, kissing the top of her head. "What happens now? I love you. I wanna be with you."

"I want that too. But I don't see it happening."

"Ever?" he said with gut-wrenching fear.

"I don't know. And it sucks that when I've finally found the real deal"—her voice broke—"I can't have it."

"Wrong. You have me, Harlow. You have all of me."

"You're rooted here. I'm rooted there for the next year. And, I have to be totally honest, even when it's killing me"—her voice broke again—"but you deserve to know."

Hugh's arms tightened and he kissed her temple. "Just say it."

"I like to visit here, but I couldn't live here. Not permanently. Not the way you and Tierney do. I have gypsy feet. The need to be part of something larger in the world, to contribute even a small amount . . . that makes me happy. And it defines me. I can't give that up without losing part of myself."

"Harlow. I love you just the way you are. I'd never ask you to change for me."

"And I'd never ask the same of you. I'm not telling you this to denigrate your life choice, Hugh. I'm just saying it is *your* choice. And it'll never be mine."

She cried silently for a while.

Finally when the hopelessness wasn't sucking at his soul, he managed to ask, "When are you leavin'?"

"Tomorrow morning," she said.

Hugh knew she was lying. He knew she believed it'd be easier if they didn't say good-bye officially.

Fuck that. Nothing would make this easy. But it wasn't good-bye. He couldn't—*wouldn't*—accept that.

"Well, I'm hopin' you spend your last night with me. And I promise it won't be a repeat of three years ago."

She buried her face in his neck.

He tipped her head back and kissed her. Not with grand sweeping passion or sadness, but like he was stoking the embers of the fire they'd lose themselves in later tonight.

Her tears were a dead giveaway that she considered this a farewell lover's kiss.

He touched her hair, her face, her arm, and followed the curve of her hip down her thigh and then back up, stopping to lightly smack her ass. "It sucks, because I'd like to spend every moment with you, but I've gotta talk to Renner about some stuff."

"I understand." Harlow placed one last lingering kiss on his lips before she stood.

Hugh put his hat back on and let his knuckles graze her cheek. "I love you, Harlow."

"I love you too."

"I'll see you later."

"Later."

Chapter Twenty-six

$\mathscr{H}$arlow wasn't leaving at the crack of dawn tomorrow morning.

She was leaving now.

As much as she wanted to spend the night with him, it would kill her to hear Hugh repeat the sweet words of love he'd murmured as she'd cried in his arms. No, she just couldn't bear it, knowing this was the end.

She always traveled light. It hadn't taken long to pack her belongings. No hugging her family this time or tearful good-byes to her friends.

Gravel crunched beneath her tires as she headed for the main road. But she hit the brakes when she saw him sitting alone on the top of the fence next to the road.

Harlow remained frozen in shock, watching him jump down off the fence and erase the distance between them with that long-legged stride. Fifty feet. Twenty feet. Ten feet. Then his hands were on the hood of her car and his body was a human barricade.

He lifted his head, his face still shadowed beneath the brim of his cowboy hat. He dipped his chin toward her car door in a silent sign for her to get out.

So she did.

Hugh was anything but still, or quiet, or stoic. He hooked his arm around her waist and pulled her body flush against his. "I watched you leave last time and didn't do a goddamned thing to stop you. Not this time."

"How did you know I was going today?"

"Because you are a shitty liar."

She let out a nervous laugh.

"Two things I need to know," he said, his face intent. "Do you trust me?"

"Yes."

"Really trust me to find a way to make this work for us? Whatever it takes?"

The fierceness on his face and the love warming his eyes turned her knees into tofu and made her soul sing. "Yes. Whatever it takes."

"Good." He kissed her. Once. Twice. Three times.

"What's the second thing?"

"Text me whenever you stop, so I know you're safe and awake. It's a long haul to California."

"I will."

"You'll hear from me soon." He stepped back.

Harlow stared at him, this man who loved her enough to let her go.

Another soft kiss. Not with heat and passion, but as a solemn promise.

She climbed back in her car.

He closed the door only after seeing her buckle up.

She drove away, watching him in her rearview mirror, standing in a cloud of orange dust in the middle of the road.

He remained so still he could've been a bronze statue. Beautiful. Solid. Determined.

Before she made the final turn, she checked her mirror again.

Yep. Hugh was still there.

Maybe the end she'd feared for them would turn out to be a whole new beginning.

Chapter Twenty-seven

*H*ugh called Ike before he headed to the barn to talk to Renner.

His nerves were oddly calm, considering he was about to upend his entire life.

Renner was in the office, but not at his desk. He leaned in the doorframe leading into the arena. A bottle of Jack Daniel's dangled in his right hand.

No doubt it'd been a shitty day for Renner with Tobin giving notice. Hugh hated he was about to add more to it.

"I imagine Tobin told you," Renner said, taking a swig from the bottle, but not turning around. "Or maybe you've known for a while."

"No. He just told me today."

"Were you surprised?"

"Yes." He paused. "And no."

"Well, I didn't have a fuckin' clue he was so miserable."

"It's not the work or working for you, Ren. You know that. Tobin deserves a chance at finding the same kinda life that you have with Tierney." *The same kind of life I want with Harlow.*

"And he ain't gonna find that here. The woman or the place to call his own."

"Not likely."

"Fuck."

"How much you been drinking?"

He shrugged. "Some." Then he turned. "While you're here, let's go over some of the immediate changes in the daily schedule. You'll have to pick up Tobin's morning feed and cattle check so you're completely up to speed when he goes."

"No, thanks."

"What?"

"I said no, thanks."

"Please tell me this is some kinda sick joke, Hugh."

"It's not. I'm not takin' on more of the chores associated with the Jackson Cattle Company."

Renner's laugh held a bitter edge. "You hitting me up for a raise? Now?"

"Nope. But we need to talk."

"About?"

"Have a seat and I'll get started."

Renner kicked out the chair across from Hugh's desk and plopped down. He set the whiskey on the desk between them.

Hugh slid a copy of the spreadsheet across the desk.

"What's this?"

"Itemized breakdown of expenses and income for the two-week road trip."

"I don't need to see this right fuckin' now, Hugh."

"Yes, you do."

"Bullshit. I'm the boss. If I don't wanna look at it, I don't have to." He pointed at Hugh. "And if I tell you to pick up the goddamn slack while I'm tryin' to find a replacement for Tobin, you'll do that too."

Hugh ignored his outburst. "On that spreadsheet you'll see that our profit is right around ten percent."

"And your point?"

"My question. What is your profit margin for cattle?"

"Slightly higher. And what does that have to do with—"

"Everything. Just pointing out that the profit from the stock contracting business allowed you to invest in the cattle business. When was the last year you sunk the profits from the stock contracting back into that business and didn't funnel it into something else?"

A dark glint entered Renner's eyes. "Last time I looked, Jackson was the name listed on both the stock contracting business and the cattle company, not Pritchett."

"Exactly. You hired me to oversee Jackson Stock Contracting, not Jackson Cattle Company. And over the last two years you seem to have forgotten that. I end up doing daily ranch-type chores same as Abe and Kyle do. That is not what I signed on for, Ren. Being a rancher is not why I moved to Wyoming. That is your dream, not mine. And again, you've forgotten that."

"What the fuck, Hugh? Are you telling me I need to give you clearly defined job requirements?"

Hugh stared at him. "Be a wise choice for whoever you hire to replace Tobin, so he knows exactly what's expected of him."

"I'll take that under advisement," he said coolly. "Anything else?"

His gut tightened. "Yeah. Are you phasing out the stock contracting side?"

Renner stared at him. "Where's this comin' from?"

"Answer the fucking question. It's simple enough. Yes. Or no."

"Yes."

"Why? I've shown you the profit. You've got top-notch livestock. You spent years building the business. It was your obsession when I met you. And when you've finally made it to the top tier of contractors in the country, you're throwing in the towel? That doesn't make sense. On any level."

"I suppose it doesn't." Renner grabbed the Jack and took a big swig.

"Can you tell me where your head is at?"

"Good fuckin' question." He sighed and tipped his head back to stare at the ceiling. "I used to be the planning and scheming guy. I envisioned big things. Took over a stock contracting business and tripled it in size within five years. Invested in good stock, lived my life making contacts in all areas of the ag world. I knew at that point my life was about work. When I thought of happiness, besides making big piles of money, I remembered when I visited my grandparents here. So I became obsessed with buying land, building a resort and trying to re-create that happiness."

"And it worked. You met Tierney."

Renner grinned at the ceiling. "Lucky bastard that I am, even after I got the girl, I had grander ideas. A genetics program for the stock contracting business and experimenting with different breeds for the cattle company. Buying enough cattle so I didn't look like a fuckin' hobby rancher around here, among my friends who are the real deal."

That wasn't an angle Hugh had considered. Renner's need to keep up with his ranching buddies Abe and Hank Lawson, Bran Turner and Kyle Gilchrist.

"Meantime, the resort was doin' well, mostly booked year-round, and Janie's done such a bang-up job as GM that she don't really need me around. Tierney's financial consulting business took off and the woman made us a shit ton of money. So for the first time in my life I didn't have to hustle, plan and scheme. For the first time in my life I didn't have to work twelve or fourteen hours a day. I wanted to be home with my beautiful wife and I could be.

"That pull just got stronger after Isabelle came. Now with Rhett, there are some days when I don't wanna leave the house. I'll never get this time back. I don't want to live with the same goddamn regrets that I see in Gene Pratt. So that's what I've been stewing about since Tobin gave notice. He probably thinks I don't give a damn about any of this anymore. I've always passed the shit jobs off on him and he's gladly done them with a smile on his face. I haven't used him to his full potential. Figured he'd always be around. I see that's a damn fool attitude." Renner quit staring at the ceiling and met Hugh's eyes. "And then there's you."

Hugh waited.

"Give it to me straight."

"What?"

"All of it."

He exhaled. "You know I quit working at the Ashland Stockyards as soon as you offered me full-time employment. I never aspired to bein' a landowner or running my own herd. I love everything about stock contracting. The travel, the people, the discovery of new rank stock. I've missed it. After I moved here, I figured I could deal with five months' worth of ranching stuff if the other seven months was contracting. Last two years it's not even been a two-months-to-ten-months ratio."

"I know you ain't been happy with the cutbacks. And it makes me a total prick for saying this, but it's an all-or-nothin' thing. If I can't run the contracting business the way I've done in the past, then I don't wanna do it at all. Let it die and I'll always have the memory of what it—and what I—used to be." Renner snorted. "And that sounds stupid as fuckin' shit when I say it out loud."

Hugh laughed. "Maybe a little."

"So go on, tell me what I oughta do."

"Do what your dad's friend did. Sell it to someone you trust. Keep a small portion, like he did, and walk away. Be an adviser. Be proud of what you built and go on to do something else, because I have a feelin' that's why you're so damn restless lately."

Renner didn't say anything.

So did he wait for Renner to come to the conclusion on his own? Or did he offer his own plan?

"I see them wheels churning, so share with the class," Renner drawled.

Hugh leaned forward. "Sell Jackson Stock Contracting to me. The stock, the trailers, all the past and present contracts."

"You alone?"

"No. Me'n Ike. He's getting out of the cattle brokering business. He knows his stuff, he's great on the road and we get along well."

"Ike? Not who I was expecting you to say."

Hugh frowned. "Who were you expecting? Tobin?"

"No. Harlow."

Just hearing her name gave him a pang of sadness. "Really?"

Renner shrugged. "Stranger things have happened. What's the deal with you and her anyway?"

"I love her. She loves me. I'm figuring out how to make it work for us long term."

Renner's eyebrow winged up. "Don't you mean long-distance?"

"No. I'll be moving to LA."

Silence.

Then Renner chuckled. "Good one."

"Renner. I'm serious. We haven't worked out the particulars, but I'm sure we can."

"Why are you . . . ?" He shook his head. "LA. Really?"

"It's where she is."

"Just like that?"

"Yep. I love her," he emphasized. "I go where she is."

"Man. Do you know what—"

"Renner," Tierney said from the doorway, "stop."

He turned around in his chair. "How long you been standing there listening in?"

Tierney sauntered forward. "Long enough. I've been looking for you." She looked at Hugh. "Harlow deserves a man who will follow her to the ends of the earth." She smiled. "Literally."

"That's me. Now and wherever she decides to roam. I hope she'll wanna roam with me during rodeo season."

"She will. It's about compromise. Making it work on your terms. Both you and Harlow are good at that in your jobs." Tierney moved in behind her husband, setting her hands on his shoulders. "We were lucky in that we both wanted to stay here. But we would've made sacrifices to be together if we'd had to. We'll still do that."

Renner closed his eyes, as if bracing himself.

Tierney said, "Renner will be happy to sell the stock contracting business to you and Ike. I'll come up with a fair market price and we can negotiate from there."

Hugh didn't bother to hide his shock. "Sounds good." He paused. "But . . ."

"But it's Renner's business and shouldn't he make the decision?" Tierney squeezed her husband's shoulders. "*Someone* has been keeping secrets from his wife, so I had no idea that he struggled with being pulled so many different directions."

"Darlin', you were dealin' with enough of your own stuff without havin' to worry about mine," Renner said softly.

"And that is where you're wrong, Mr. Jackson. We're in this together, for the long haul, remember? So for the good of our family and my husband's sanity, I'm doing what he couldn't: making a decision."

Renner kissed the hand on his shoulder.

"Thank you. Neither of you will regret this," Hugh said.

Tierney took off Renner's hat and set it on the desk. "Now I need to have a private conversation with my husband, so you might wanna leave."

"Baby, where are the kids?"

"Home. Dad and Karen are there. I thought I'd take advantage of our rare alone time." Then Tierney threw a leg over and parked herself on Renner's lap. "Close and lock the door behind you on your way out."

No need to tell him twice. He pushed back and stood. "I'll just . . . uh, yeah."

They didn't notice him leave.

But Hugh easily put them out of his mind and he started a mental checklist of all the things he needed to do.

Chapter Twenty-eight

One week later . . .

*H*arlow hadn't heard from Hugh in five days.

She'd texted him at every stop on her way to California.

After she'd crawled into her bed at her apartment, she let him know she'd made it back.

He'd texted: *Good. Get some rest.*

That'd been it.

When she'd tried grilling Tierney for Hugh's whereabouts, her sister had been incredibly vague and demanded Harlow tell her everything that'd happened in Laos.

So she had.

Tierney's tears weren't surprising, but not once had Harlow felt her sister's pity, just her support. And her sister was making good on her promise to be a better listener. She hadn't known how much she'd needed that.

Today Harlow had finalized the paperwork for her teaching position. She marveled at her office—tiny as it was. She paced the length of her small classroom, imagining herself lecturing in the space, even testing out the acoustics. She never would've imagined this would be one of the most exciting adventures she'd undertake.

She just wished she could share it with Hugh. She missed him in a way she'd never missed anyone. She longed to hear his deep laughter. To feel his arms around her. To fall asleep to the steady beat of his heart as they cuddled beneath the covers. She wanted to tell him everything that had happened to her since they'd parted ways in Wyoming. She wanted to hear every detail of how he'd spent his days at the Split Rock. She wanted to know if he'd meant what he'd said.

Do you trust me? Really trust me to find a way to make this work for us? Whatever it takes?

Harlow had told him yes. So she told herself repeatedly to be patient. She reminded herself that Hugh defined "methodical." He wouldn't share his plans until they were rock solid. That was just the kind of man he was.

She exited the freeway and zipped down the palm-tree-lined streets, her mind running in a million different directions as she pulled into the parking lot of her apartment complex.

After she exited her car and locked it, out of the corner of her eye she saw a flash of white. She turned to see Hugh striding toward her. Her Hugh. His booted feet ate up the blacktop as he headed toward her with a big grin on his face—an obvious beacon of happiness even beneath the shadowed brim of his hat.

Harlow shrieked and ran toward him, throwing herself at him.

Then she was in his arms, his mouth on hers, and nothing else existed but this moment, this man, who was now here with her.

Hugh kissed her with his usual hunger, but also with such a sense of relief. Then he tore his mouth free from hers much quicker than she liked. He laughed softly against her cheek when she tried to reconnect their lips.

"Hold on, hippie-girl. Let's take this someplace more private." He placed a possessive kiss on the side of her neck and squeezed her ass before he stepped back and took her hand.

Harlow was still too stunned to move as she looked into his handsome face. "I can't believe you're here."

"Why? I told you I'd do whatever it takes to make this work between us. Didn't you believe me?"

"I did. And I didn't."

His expression softened. He curled his hand around the side of her face. "Harlow. I love you. That ain't something that's ever gonna go away. Not when we've been apart for one week or one year. What do I have to do to prove it to you?"

"You being here is all the proof I need."

"Good. Give me a sec and I'll grab my bags."

Harlow watched him jog back toward his pickup. She wasn't so busy staring at his fine Wrangler ass that she didn't notice the boxes in the bed of his truck when he dropped the tailgate.

Boxes?

Her heart hammered. Her hopes soared. She hustled toward him.

Hugh slammed the tailgate shut and seemed surprised when he turned around to find her right there. "What is it?"

"What's in the boxes?"

He shrugged. "Dishes and other odds and ends. You mentioned you didn't have much household stuff, so I brought what I have to get us by."

"Wait." She planted her hands on his chest. "You're not just here to visit me?"

"Nope."

When she gaped at him, he framed her face in his big hands. "No half measures when it comes to you. Or us. Ever."

"Hugh," she breathed his name like a benediction.

"Tell me you want me here."

"I want you here more than anything in the world."

"Let's start there." He kissed her with sweet heat. "I'll explain it all, I promise. I just don't wanna do it in the damn parking lot."

"Okay." She retreated and pointed to the boxes. "But you ain't in Wyoming anymore. You leave that stuff out in the open like that, it won't be there when you come back."

"Fine. You drag my suitcase and I'll get these."

He loaded his boxes onto a handcart.

Of course he had a handcart. He'd come prepared.

Meanwhile nothing could've prepared her for this: Hugh moving in or at least planning on an extended stay.

He followed her into her apartment building. An awkward silence fell between them in the elevator. A silence that continued as she led him down the hallway to her place, the last apartment on the third floor.

Harlow unlocked her door and stood off to the side as Hugh wheeled in the boxes.

As soon as the door shut, he had her pressed against it, kissing her like crazy, stopping only to drag his mouth down her neck and mutter, "Missed you so fucking much, Harlow. I thought I'd never get here."

"Ah. About that. How come I didn't know you were coming?"

Hugh pulled back. Frowned. "I left a message on your voice mail."

She shook her head. "My phone has been by my side twenty-four/seven since I left Wyoming. I've been waiting to hear from you. No word at all since your last text."

"Well, I used some pretty raunchy words in the voice mail." He blushed. "I wonder who in the hell got the message about all the dirty things I planned to do to you as soon as I reached LA."

"No idea." Harlow twined her arms around his neck. "Maybe you should show me what you were planning."

"With pleasure. Take me to our bedroom," he murmured in the low-pitched husky tone that sent chills down to her core.

Harlow ducked under his arm and clasped his hand. Her one-bedroom efficiency was big enough for her, but add Hugh to the mix? It wasn't going to work for long. Especially when he saw . . .

"A single bed," he said with a laugh. "Well, darlin', that's gonna be cozy." Then he sat on the edge of the bed and pulled her between his legs before he rolled them back onto the mattress. He grinned. "I could get used to you sleepin' on top of me like this."

"My apartment is small. Barely big enough for one, let alone two."

"We did fine in the horse trailer. A smaller space just means we're gonna be closer to each other all the time and that suits me fine."

While she could've basked forever in the way Hugh just kept staring at her, love shining in his eyes and that sexy half smile on his lips, she needed answers. "So you're moving to California."

"Yep."

"Because of me."

"Yep."

She stared into those warm brown eyes. Almost immediately her eyes welled up.

"Harlow. What's wrong?"

"Nothing. Everything is right. But it's like a dream. I've never had this, a man who's loved me enough to move halfway across the country to be with me. I don't want to screw it up." *What if I'm not worth it?*

"You are worth everything to me, doll."

She hadn't meant to say that last part out loud. Maybe she hadn't. Maybe the man was just that good at reading her.

"C'mere." Hugh circled his arm around her shoulder, bringing her head down to rest on his chest. "We'll figure it out together as we go. 'Cause this is all new to me too."

"So you just . . . quit working for Renner?"

He chuckled. "Nope. Bought him out except for ten percent. The other ninety percent of Jackson Stock Contracting is split into a partnership between me'n Ike."

Harlow lifted her head and looked at him. "Seriously?"

"Yep. I'm doin' the business stuff, 'cause that can be done for the most part anywhere. Ike is doin' the day-to-day stuff in Wyoming. The rodeo stock has always been kept in separate pastures from Renner's cow and calf pairs operation, so basically we're renting the land from Renner, keeping the animals there until we get dates on next year's schedule. Since I won't be around to help with that part, Ike has hired Riss as our first official employee."

"Riss? Really?"

"Yeah. They came to some kind of truce. I didn't ask the details and they've promised to keep their personal issues out of the business side. Which is a huge load off my mind, since I can factor in her hauling capabilities when I'm bidding on rodeo contracts. Ike and I divided the list of previous rodeo venues. And I'll be exploring other options in this part of the country, since the bottom half of California is in the southwest circuit." He smiled at her look of confusion. "What? You thought I'd be the freeloading boyfriend? Sitting in this apartment all day playing video games? Or I'd be out learning to surf?"

She put her hand over his mouth. "Never crossed my mind."

He kissed her fingers and she moved her hand to let him continue speaking. "I'll be plenty busy getting this business back on track. It'll entail some travel for me, but I'll always come back to you just as soon as I can."

"Or I can come with you," she offered.

"I'm hoping that when school is out in the spring, you'll be able to hit the road with me for at least part of rodeo season."

"So I'm a decent hired hand?"

"You learned from the best. Got ya trained the way I want you." His eyes narrowed. "But no more topless steer ridin'."

"Deal." Harlow paused. "And after the summer ends?"

"Who knows? We've got time to plan. Maybe they'll want you to teach some more. Maybe you'll wanna do something else." He kissed her nose. "I'll get a passport so I can tag along as your hand and learn about these causes that mean so much to you."

Her eyes were getting misty again. "You'd do that?"

"Yep."

No long-winded explanations. Just his word. And that was more than enough for her. "You've got a big heart and a bit of a gypsy soul yourself, cowboy. I love that about you. I love you."

"You own me, Harlow. Heart and soul."

She nestled her head into the spot against his neck that was made for her and thanked the universe for bringing this man into her life.

Continue reading for a preview of

What You Need,

the first book in Lorelei James's
brand-new contemporary romance series.
Available from Signet wherever books are sold in January!

————

The Lund name is synonymous with wealth and power in Minneapolis–St. Paul. But the four Lund siblings will each discover true love takes a course of its own. . . .

As the CFO of Lund Industries, Brady Lund is the poster child for responsibility. But eighty-hour workweeks leave him little time for a life. His brothers stage an intervention and drag him to a seedy nightclub . . . where he sees *her*: the buttoned-up blonde from the office who's starred in his fantasies for months.

Lennox Greene is a woman with a rebellious past, which she conceals beneath her conservative clothes. She knows flirting with her boss during working hours is a bad idea. So when Brady shows up at her favorite dive bar and catches her cutting loose, she throws caution aside and dares him to do the same.

After sparks fly, Brady finds that keeping his hands off Lennox during office hours is harder than expected. Though she makes him feel alive for the first time in years, a part of him wonders if she's just using him to get ahead. And Lennox must figure out whether Brady wants her for the accomplished woman she is—or the bad girl she was.

Prologue

BRADY

The first time I saw her I nearly walked into a wall.

Not the behavior expected from the CFO of a multibillion-dollar corporation.

And not the behavior I wanted the willowy blonde with the killer legs to witness. I'd suffered through too many years of being the gangly, bumbling, tongue-tied twerp to even approach her. Even now, when supposedly I was one of the most eligible bachelors in the Twin Cities, I erred on the side of acting aloof.

So as far as she knew, I hadn't taken notice of her at all.

But I had. Had I *ever*.

We'd crossed paths maybe . . . half a dozen times since I'd first set eyes on her in the lobby of Lund Industries.

Ten months later I still didn't know her name.

I didn't even know which department she worked in.

It was information I could've easily accessed, given my last name was on the letterhead of the company that employed her. But in my mind, that might be misconstrued as borderline stalking behavior. I wasn't opposed to using my position to take shortcuts, but with her, somehow that seemed like cheating.

But I did know a couple of things about her.

She was brusque, especially around upper-level management.

She had a husky laugh, which she shared only with her coworkers.

A laugh I'd heard thirty seconds ago.

So the mystery blonde worked on this floor, in my department.

Interesting.

Before I headed toward her cubicle, I made damn sure I knew where all the walls were because nothing was going to trip me up this time.

Chapter One

LENNOX

"*W*hat's *he* doing in our department?"

I glanced up from my computer, knowing even before I saw the suit at the end of the hallway who garnered the reverent tone from my coworker Sydney. I had the same reverence for the man; however, I did a much better job at masking it.

"Oh hell, here he comes. How do I look?" she whispered.

"You know the only thing that matters to him is if you look busy."

Sydney smoothed her hair. "Lennox, lighten up. And ignore me while I busily and silently compose sonnets to that man's everything, because he is the total package."

I laughed—longer than I usually did. "Go for it, Syd. I'll just be over here, you know, doing my *job* while you're waxing poetic about him." I returned my focus to spellchecking my notes from this morning's meeting. I knew I had a misspelled or misused a word but I couldn't find the damn thing.

"Wait. He's stopping to talk to Penny," Sydney informed me.

I felt a slight sneer form on my lips. Of *course* he's stopping to talk to Perky Penny—she hadn't earned that nickname from her disposition. Even I couldn't keep my eyes off her pert parts—which she kept properly covered in deference to the dress code at Lund Industries. But I knew, given the chance, she'd proudly display them like she worked at Hooters.

Wouldn't you?

Nope. Been there; done that.

Sydney muttered and I ignored her, hell-bent on finding the mistake. I leaned closer to the computer monitor as if that would help. Ah. *There it is.* I highlighted the word in question. Had he meant to say "disperse"? Or "disburse"? And was there enough difference in the definitions to warrant a call for clarification?

Without checking the dictionary app on my computer, I said, "Sydney. You were an English major. What's the difference between 'disperse' and 'disburse'?"

"'Disburse' means to pay out money. 'Disperse' means to go in different directions," a deep male voice answered.

I lifted my gaze to see none other than Brady Lund himself, the CFO of Lund Industries, looming over my desk.

Outwardly I maintained my cool even when I felt my neck heating beneath the lace blouse I wore. I picked up a pen and ignored the urge to give the man a once-over because I already knew what I'd find: Mr. Freakin' Perfect. Brady Lund was always impeccably dressed, showcasing his long, lean body in an insanely expensive suit. He was always immaculately coiffed—his angular face was smoothly shaven; his thick, dark hair was artfully tousled, giving the appearance of boyish charm.

As if a shark could be charming.

My coworkers and I had speculated endlessly about whether the CFO plucked his dark eyebrows to give his piercing blue eyes a more visceral punch. And if he practiced raising his left eyebrow so mockingly. For that reason alone, I avoided meeting his gaze.

Okay, that was not the only reason. I didn't make eye contact because the man defined hot, smart, and sexy.

But he also defined smug—half the time. I wanted to ask if he job-shared with an evil twin, but I doubted he'd laugh since he had no sense of humor, from what I'd heard.

Aware that he awaited my response, I said, "Thank you for the clarification, Mr. Lund."

"I shouldn't have to clarify that since you've worked here for what? Ten months? Financial terms should be familiar to you by now."

He was chastising me? First thing? My mouth opened before my brain screamed *Stop.* "I've been employed here for almost a year, actually. And, sir, I'll remind you that just because the office temps department is located on the sixth floor—one of the five floors that are the providence of the financial department—we floaters don't specifically work *only* for the finance department at Lund Industries. We also float between human resources, marketing, development and acquisitions, as well as legal."

"Explain what you mean by 'floaters.'"

"You had absolutely no idea that our small department exists, let alone what we do, did you?" I said tartly.

I heard Sydney suck in a sharp breath next to me. "What she means is that since as CFO you have an executive assistant and don't normally personally utilize the services of the office temps—also known as floaters—you wouldn't personally be aware of the breadth of our responsibilities," Sydney inserted diplomatically. "Our department is supervised by personnel."

"Indeed. Then please, enlighten me on which department you're transcribing that document from?"

"Marketing."

"Mind if I take a look?" Then he sidestepped my desk and sidled in behind me.

My body went rigid as he literally looked over my shoulder. I wasn't as disturbed by the thought he might see something I had done wrong, as I was by his close proximity. His very close proximity, since I could feel the heat of his body and was treated to a whiff of his subtle cologne.

He put his hand over mine on the mouse and murmured, "Pardon," as he completely invaded my space. I didn't move because it'd be my luck to shift my arm and elbow the CFO in the groin.

Three clicks and two huffed breaths later, he retreated. "I apologize. I understand your confusion. Marcus in marketing misused the word. It should be 'disburse.' Nice catch."

"That's my job."

"Since it's a formal request, Marcus will have to correct it before you can pass it on to legal. If you'll give me the original paperwork, I'd be happy to drop it off in Marcus's office is on my way to my meeting."

"Thank you, sir, for the offer. But company protocol requires me to deliver the paperwork directly to Marcus—Mr. Benito."

His shoes were so silent, I didn't hear him move. One second he was behind me; the next he stood in front of me. "A real stickler for the rules, aren't you?"

"Yes, sir." I finally met his gaze. "With all due respect, how do I know this isn't some sort of performance review pretest?"

His lack of a smile indicated he wasn't amused.

But I didn't back down; I needed this job. It was the first job I'd ever had where I wasn't slinging drinks or scrubbing toilets. Besides, the CFO of all people should be aware of the rules.

"Bravo, Miss Greene. Sorry. That's an assumption on my part. Or is it Mrs. Greene?"

"No, sir, Miz Greene is fine. But I prefer to be called Lennox."

Then Mr. Freakishly Perfect bestowed the mother lode of smiles: his lush lips curved up, his dimples popped out and the lines by his eyes crinkled. "Well, Lennox, please see that Marcus—Mr. Benito—is aware of his error before day's end because I *will* follow up on this."

"Yes, sir."

He nodded and started down the hallway.

I clenched my teeth to keep my jaw from dropping. Not just from the weird interlude, but because the man looked as good from the back as he did from the front.

"Holy shit," Sydney breathed after she was sure he'd gone. "What was that?"

"No idea."

"Lennox. He knows your name."

"Of course he knows my name. It's right here on my desk." Working as a floater meant my nameplate went everywhere with me, but on the days I was at my desk I usually didn't bother putting it out.

Aren't you glad you bothered today?

"Come on. He was fishing for information on whether you were single."

I groaned, hating that Sydney wouldn't let this go. "So now he knows."

"Maybe he'll ask you out," she said with a drawn-out sigh.

"Maybe you should put some of that creative thinking into your report," I retorted, and got back to work.